Death, Lies and Otto

The Eleventh Otto Fischer Novel

Jim McDermott

Copyright 2022
All Rights Reserved

Abbreviations and acronyms used in the text

DVL - *Deutschen Versuchsanstalt FüR Luftfahrt*: central establishment for German aeronautcal research, based at Berlin-Adlershof airfield

OKH – *Oberkommando des Heeres*: High Command of the German Army of the Third Reich, headquartered at Maybach, site 1. Though it was nominally subordinated to **OKW**, Hitler appointed himself Head of OKH from early 1942 until two days before his suicide, when he placed it once more under the authority of **OKW**

OKW – *Oberkommando der Wehrmacht*: High Command of the Combined Armed Forces (Heer, Luftwaffe, Kriegsmarine) of the Third Reich, headquartered at Maybach, site 2

RSHA – *Reichssicherheitshauptamt*: the Reich's Security Main Office, SS-controlled umbrella organization comprising **SD** and **SiPo**

SD – *Sicherheitsdienst*: SS Intelligence Service

SiPo – *Sicherheitspolizei*: domestic police umbrella organization comprising *Geheime Staatspolizei* (Gestapo) and *Kriminalpolizei* (Criminal Investigations)

WASt - *Wehrmachtauskunftstelle für Kriegerverluste und Kriegsgefangene* (later, *Deutsche Dienstelle*): Wehrmacht organization responsible for keeping all military personnel records, liaising with hostile powers (via the International Red Cross) re: prisoners of war, and informing the domestic civilian population of dead, missing and captured servicemen

1

'I suppose that hurts still, Hauptmann?'

Hardly at all, thanks to the fistful of Pethidin I swallowed an hour ago.

'Not as much as it ...'

'Forgive me! That wasn't an intelligent question.'

His cheeks burning, Oberstleutnant Krohne distracted himself - for the third time since the interview commenced - by shifting a small pile of papers on his desk. When the redeployment had satisfied his military instincts he cleared his throat and met Otto Fischer's eye once more. It didn't seem to require an effort, which the other party found gratifying.

'Have you been told anything about the work we do here?'

'Only that you coordinate and polish the field units' reports.'

'We do, yes. We're also a liaison and training office, though the training part seems to have died in its crib. As for liaising, we formerly reported directly through the Luftwaffe chain of command here at the Air Ministry, but recently we've been required to clear all material with RSHA and the Propaganda Ministry also.'

Fischer nodded, giving Krohne the serious-but-unconcerned face that acknowledged unpleasant realities. The *Kriegsberichter der Luftwaffe* - the War Reporters' Unit – was a relic of a very brief age in which Germany's air aces had dominated the skies of Europe. Military briefings being thin gruel for public consumption, the regime had encouraged an element of creativity to embellish tales of heroism against formidable odds (and parse the strafing of columns of retreating enemy soldiers and civilians as something more glorious than it was). All *Luftflottes* had military journalists attached to their establishments, their reports filed with the Air Ministry on Wilhelmstrasse, tweaked and then published in *Der Adler* or *Signal,* and occasionally broadcast to ease the nation's anxieties about having declared war upon half of God's Creation

But the war had turned, and the Regime's grip on the flow of information from battlefield to home-front had tightened accordingly. Storming victories could be allowed a degree of not-quite-literary latitude, but debacles demanded far more careful (or artful) reinterpretation. As the gap widened between what was known and what the German people needed to know, reportage had evolved into something else – a monstrous breaking and reconstitution of events to portray reverses as advances, insane side-steps as brilliant anticipations and fumblings as dexterity. It was a credit to Oberstleutnant Krohne's department in meeting this noble challenge that neither Goebbels or RSHA had yet entirely removed Luftwaffe's ability to put out its own situation reports.

Fischer no longer tried to follow the news, but his experience of the winter war in front of Moscow had taught him the difference between military consolidation and frantic retreat. His personal backward odyssey had ended on the afternoon of 14 January 1942, when considerable parts of two burning aircraft came to rest on his artillery emplacement. After that, he couldn't speak to any detail of the campaign's progress, but a year later the central Eastern Front remained considerably west of its former extremity, and in the meantime the Stalingrad debacle had excised an entire German Army - an episode which even the most creative, hopeful journalism couldn't gild. He fondly recalled the profession's occasional attempts at verity, yet much like the Panzer III it had become outmoded, and war-production had ceased. Nevertheless, here he was, in an office at the heart of Operation Inexactitude, offering himself as a recruit to the cause.

So far, there had been nothing relentless about the interview. Oberstleutnant Krohne seemed a decent type, though out of place. The tough, war-weary look that an eye-patch usually bestowed didn't quite convince in his case, and he seemed to occupy his perfectly-tailored uniform rather than wear it. He had introduced himself as a former newspaper editor and weekend flyer who had volunteered for the Air Reserve during the peace. His combat record had begun and ended in Poland, where a stray anti-aircraft round, ascending to three thousand feet, had entered his Stuka's cockpit and missed everything but an eye socket, to which he waved apologetically.

'I'm afraid I wasn't much of a return on the Führer's investment. The other eye's not very good – I'd wear a monocle if it didn't make me look so damned Prussian. As I could no longer fly I was brought to Wilhelmstrasse and given the job of building this department. You'll find that everyone here has a good excuse not to be at the Front. We have amputees, a broken neck that won't heal properly and several punctured abdomens, and if we had nurses too it would be wonderful. The point is, if you came to work with us you'd get no second glances.'

For Fischer, there could be no stronger attraction. Coming to terms with one's mutilations was a difficult process, not assisted by their all-too-visible effect upon others. A few hours each day in which he didn't need to care what his appearance was doing to nearby stomachs would feel like rest-leave. Carefully, he cleared his throat.

'Do you have any questions regarding my previous work?'

Krohne glanced down at his papers. 'You were a *kriminalkommissar*, in Stettin, for a number of years?'

'I entered the Criminal Investigations Department directly from Police College, in 1931. I resigned a few years later, and volunteered for the Fallschirmjäger.'

'1931?'

It wasn't a question - more Krohne's way of reassuring himself that he wasn't about to hire someone with strong, modern convictions.

'Yes.'

'And then you resigned? That doesn't happen much, I'd imagine.'

'Things changed. I didn't'

Things *changed* from the moment the National Socialists took power and invented the concepts of preventive custody (arresting people before they'd thought to commit crimes) and protective custody (arresting people without putting Gestapo to the inconvenience of stating a charge). The Oberstleutnant smiled, taking the dodged point precisely.

'Would you like a drink? I have some quite disgusting Romanian Brandy.'

Apparently, Fischer had met the Air Ministry's stringent requirements for the post. He nodded by way of accepting both.

'Here's your copy of a training manual that I drew up - it's quite useless, other than to put between your glass and the table.'

He took a single sip and then Krohne's advice. It *was* disgusting, and when the Pethidin wore off his damaged throat tissue would remind him of his error. He'd already conducted rigorous tests upon strong spirits to determine whether getting so drunk that the pain went away was worth its triumphant return with a hangover and puking. The results had made abstinence seem almost attractive.

The silence between them dragged slightly, and Krohne, pleased that *Kriegsberichter der Luftwaffe*'s establishment had fattened slightly, leaned forward and gave his new recruit's nearest shoulder a comradely punch. Fischer froze, the blood draining from that side of his face that could offer such subtle signs of distress. The apology, though heartfelt, had no anaesthetic effect whatsoever. Eventually his breathing slowed, and he put Krohne out of his misery.

'Can you tell me more about the work?'

'Yes, of course. But come and meet the others.'

2

The main office (or 'Den') was three doors down the corridor, staffed by half a dozen invalids of varying degrees of incapacity. Krohne gathered them around and introduced Fischer, who shook hands with his shrivelled one, tried and failed to memorize the names – Reincke, Weber, Lehmann, Weiss, Holleman, Schell – and was shown to a small desk, formerly the territory of *poor Ahle*.

'You'll be working here. Each morning we receive the previous day's field reports; I sift the material for what can go directly to *Signal*'s editorial staff and bring the rest to this office. We talk about what we have and what it requires before release, and then it's apportioned among you. I expect your first drafts to be on my desk by noon.'

'And then?'

'Then I return them, and tell you all to try harder.'

'Are we allowed to discuss our stories with each other, and ask for ideas?'

One of Fischer's new colleagues, a large, ugly man with an artificial leg - Holleman, it might have been – snorted. Krohne frowned but didn't turn.

'I don't encourage it, but it happens. As long as you don't take *all* suggestions to heart. Now, as to our current work. You'll appreciate that the past few weeks have been … difficult for us. There's little we can say positively about Army Group South at the moment, so Goebbels has told us to leave it entirely alone. However, things may be improving in the north. We've had initial intelligence that the operation to smooth out the Rzhev Salient is going well, and if it succeeds it'll release a large number of divisions for deployment elsewhere. For the moment we're hinting at good news to come, but I expect we'll be getting the nod soon, and then it'll be a rush of data and a lot of work to turn it around.'

Another snort interrupted this heartening news. 'It's still a fucking retreat.'

'Freddie, try not to say what you think, will you? We're equally confident that the Donets fighting is turning our way after a difficult start, but as I say it's too early for us to report anything. You'll have noticed something, perhaps?'

'You've mentioned nothing about Luftwaffe.'

'And yet we *are* Luftwaffe. Our heroic efforts to defend and supply the Stalingrad forces failed, as you and everyone else knows. We destroyed thousands of Soviet aircraft and brought almost thirty thousand men out of the pocket, but in doing so we lost a third of our entire strength on the Eastern Front. Naturally, efforts to replace the machines are proceeding frantically, but the death or capture of hundreds of skilled pilots can't be made good quickly. The Reichsmarschall has ordered us to play down the day-to-day story of what Luftwaffe are doing to support our ground forces until the service can make a substantive effort once more.'

The big fellow interrupted once more, but quietly. 'It's like tanks. We don't talk about tanks at the moment.'

Fischer turned to him. 'Why not?'

'Because when *Barbarossa* started we went in with more than three thousand of them. What's the score today, Karl?'

Krohne shrugged. 'Just under five hundred, as of last week. And the best we have can't stop a T34 unless it catches it from behind and blows up the engine. We all know about the new models being developed, but until they go into the fight ...'

'Right. So, may I ask …?'

'What *do* we put out at the moment?' Krohne turned to his men, who shouted the answer in almost perfect unison.

'The personal story!'

'Heartening anecdotes of courage and self-sacrifice – the man who carries a comrade to safety, the gunner who destroys a Soviet emplacement with his last salvo of 20mm ammunition, the maintenance man who turns around an ME 109 in the time it takes his pilot to have a crap and a cup of coffee - believe me, there are plenty of tales to tell, and we hardly need tweak them. We could exist on the individual heroisms indefinitely, if it wasn't for the implication.'

'Implication?'

'When one has crowed about smashing victories, an absence of crowing is noticed.'

Fischer nodded. Truth aside, the very language of war had change. For months now, news bulletins had been referring to *consolidations*, *redeployments* and *fighting in the direction of* rather than *towards*. Even Goebbels, the Prince of Gloats, was speaking less of victory and more of what the German people might expect at the hands of the supposedly smashed Red Army, should things go from Bad to Fairly Catastrophic.

He glanced around at the men he would be working with. They called their boss Karl, not Oberstleutnant, and their casual irreverence surprised him. It was a long time since he had heard thoughts expressed with such little apparent care for the ears that might catch them. He was a stranger here, and it was hardly beyond possibility that he was a Party man who would be happy to repeat every loose comment he heard. Hell, he wouldn't even need to pick up a 'phone to betray them. Prinz-Albrecht-Strasse was literally around the corner from the Air Ministry - a short stroll, a word in the ear of RSHA's new Director, Ernst Kaltenbrunner, and he would return to an office emptied of all but the bloodstains. Could they be indifferent to that prospect?

'You'll appreciate that things area little informal here.' Krohne put his hand on the shoulder of a young man whose face had been altered almost as drastically as Fischer's, albeit by something other than fire. 'Young Detmar insisted on being very *military* when he first came to us, but that didn't survive his baptism.'

'Baptism?'

'Most of us have been through it, so I suppose we must call it a tradition. There's a place nearby ...'

'A *holy* place.'

'As Salomon says, a holy place. Your new comrades will take you there and explain how things work while you try to stay on your feet. After that, you'll either fit in or request an early transfer.'

'Transfer? To where?'

Krohne shrugged. 'I don't know. No-one ever has – requested one, I mean. The *explanation* appears to have done the job so far.'

'I assume that alcohol is involved?'

'Yes, but only tremendous quantities, so don't worry.'

'Karl's teasing.' This was the big, older man again. 'It doesn't take much of the *Silver Birch*'s vintage reserve to loosen the uniform. And the explanation's just a list of the many worse occupations a German might find for himself in 1943. If you want to make a contribution still, there isn't a better option. Or would you rather go to WASt?'

The opportunity to inform elderly parents of their sons' death or mutilation in battle had been offered to Fischer already, and hadn't been difficult to refuse. It was necessary work, but he doubted that he had the stomach to bear the cold processing of lives in that manner. And God alone knew what damage he'd do if he was required to turn up at their front doors with the news.

'No, I wouldn't.'

'Well, then.' The lumpy face beamed. 'Welcome to the Lie Division!'

Krohne winced. 'Freddie, I've told you about that. But yes, welcome, Otto - I may call you Otto?'

'Of course. When should I start?'

'Tomorrow?

'May I have a day's grace? I'm new to Berlin, and I need to find accommodation.'

'Aren't you in barracks?'

'Until two days ago I was at Reinickendorf Lazarett, under observation. Then I received my transfer notice, to the barracks at Adlershof.'

'Adlershof? That's a research and testing facility. What the hell would you do there?'

'I don't know. Neither does anyone else, I suppose. When I reported to the the Deputy Commandant he blanched and told me I could have a private accommodation permit. He had two addresses in Alt-Moabit where rooms are available.'

Krohne's pained expression told Fischer that he'd read the situation accurately. No commander of active-service men wanted such a graphic reminder of their own, possible futures walking past them every day. He shrugged.

'Well, that would be perfect – you'd have a short, pleasant commute across Tiergarten. Go and see the rooms, make your choice and report to the Air Ministry's personnel office the day after tomorrow – which we'll mark down as a travel day, not leave. In the meantime, I'll organize your posting papers.'

'Thank you, Herr Oberstleutnant.'

'Karl, please.'

Fischer nodded, picked up his cap and waved it towards his new desk. 'May I ask - why *poor* Ahle?'

'He died.'

The room was populated by men who had almost died, and who bore the obvious marks of their misfortune. That one of them had completed the journey hardly seemed sufficient reason for the epithet. Krohne noticed the question in his new recruit's eyes and pulled a face.

'He died very badly.'

3

That afternoon, Fischer went looking for a home. The first address he dismissed quickly, though not so decisively as had allied bombs. It was now a small reservoir, fed from a fractured water-main that a small *gastarbeiter* squad was attempting to locate and seal. He offered a cigarette to their foreman and asked directions to Jonas-Strasse. The man tossed his head.

'Next street, General. Just the other side of the Markthalle.'

In less than four minutes he stood on the stoop of Jonas-Strasse 17, a red brick house supported on one side by large wooden struts. He knocked, stepped back, and when an old lady opened the door glanced at the piece of paper given to him at Adlershof.

'Frau Traugott?'

She shuffled forward and peered with forensic intensity at the visible damage. 'You've come for the room?'

'I'd like to see it, yes.'

'Well, it's two. There's a separate sitting area, if you don't mind?'

'That would be very pleasant. May I …?'

He sneezed, violently, and a moment later found the cause of it. A large black cat was rubbing itself against his ankle.

'This is Chancellor Bismarck. He doesn't scratch or bite.'

He doesn't need to. For a moment, Fischer wanted to excuse himself and flee, but the prospect of a suite of rooms so close to the Air Ministry exercised a powerful counter-pull. It would mean one more type of medication, but it could hardly hurt, and if he was careful to keep his door closed the ordeal might only last the span of each day's negotiation of hallway and stairs.

She frowned. 'Don't you like cats?'

'Very much. I have a mild allergy, though.'

There was nothing mild about it, but he didn't want to deter her with the prospect of epic snottery.

'Well, if it's mild. I have *three* cats.'

Hell. 'How lovely. May I see the rooms, please?

Trying to quench his spluttering he followed her to the second floor and was shown into a neat, clean sitting-room. Two chairs, a small table, a carpet and fireplace, a wash-basin in the corner – he couldn't have hoped for more, or better. She looked meaningfully at the connecting doorway to the side of the chimney-breast.

'It's a *single* bed.'

He smiled and gestured at his face. 'I won't be entertaining. What's the rent, please?'

'It doesn't matter. Whatever you can afford.'

For a moment he was startled by this, but the expression on her face hinted at something other than indifference. Embarrassed, she cleared her throat.

'You're Luftwaffe?'

'Yes. Based at the Air-Ministry.'

'Ah. Well, it you could help with food …?'

Of course. What use was money, when there was nothing to spend it on? But an extra ration book – particularly an Armed Services item, bringing access to foodstuffs that civilians no longer saw, much less ate – would compensate amply for a disfigured, constantly sneezing tenant. He assured her that not only was he a light eater but might occasionally get the opportunity to bring home scraps from the Ministry's canteen. After that, he doubted that she would have allowed him to refuse the rooms. Anxiously, she pointed to the carpet.

'I have two other guests, widowed sisters. They have rooms below, but they're very quiet. They shouldn't disturb you.'

'I'm sure they won't. May I move in tomorrow evening? I'll be bringing only the single bag.'

'That would be perfect.' She paused and bit her lip. 'I'll try to keep Marlene, Sigi and Chancellor Bismarck out of your rooms. But cats, you know …?'

'That's very kind. I hope my sneezing doesn't disturb the ladies below.'

The face she pulled suggested that the sisters could go hang themselves, or at least find alternative accommodation, if it became a problem.

'Come downstairs. We'll toast your arrival.'

They did so with a sweet liqueur whose taste he couldn't identify but was every bit as bad as the Oberstleutnant's brandy. He sipped it from a cloudy, chipped glass, offered a few necessary compliments on her sitting-room (it was decorated in a style popular during the Third Silesian War) and watched her struggle inwardly with something. He knew about the cats already, so a stream of other tenant-repelling possibilities occurred and were dismissed in turn. The street wasn't a major thoroughfare, had no u-bahn directly beneath or s-bahn adjacent, so noise was hardly likely to be a problem (in any case, bombing raids had quite removed the average Berliner's objections to more habitual disturbances). He knew already that she was a widow, so a drunken husband wasn't likely to disrupt his evenings. If she had children they must be approaching middle-age and probably elsewhere (there were no signs of more than single occupation of the ground floor), and he considered a jealous boyfriend to be outside the bounds of possibility. Unless she played the flügelhorn very badly or had a habit of bathing in the hallway he couldn't ...

'I'm ... epileptic.' She waved a hand as if to scatter the words. 'I hope that doesn't alter your decision. It comes rarely, but when it does it's the *grand mal.* My doctor used to prescribe Luminal, which helped a little. It's not to be found these days, though.'

Fischer had no opinion on epilepsy, but the wretched, hopeful cast to her face required that he embellish his indifference.

'I had an uncle who suffered. I'm quite used to it, so please don't worry.'

Both his parents had been only children, but the lie calmed her and she smiled for the first time since their brief acquaintance began. It made her hard-worn face almost pretty, and he realised he'd gone too far when she turned to the liqueur bottle to refresh his hardly-touched glass. Hastily, he excused himself with something about the necessity of returning to base. Being a man of obviously considerable military importance (the face and gloved right hand helped with this, if nothing else), he was escorted to the door with as much ceremony as an elderly widow in slippers and torn stockings could manage.

Returning to base took a while, because Luftwaffe's Berlin-Adlershof Station was on the south-east edge of the city. He had been posted there for less than forty-eight hours, yet he wasn't sorry to be departing. The larger site had been occupied by the *Deutschen Versuchsanstalt FüR Luftfahrt*'s principal aerodynamic-testing facility since 1912, and its northern perimeter hosted production works for Henschel and Focke-Wulf. The British were perfectly aware of the station's value and had devoted much (if often mis-aimed) effort to flattening it over the past year, making Adlershof as fraught a posting as many operational airfields – hence the Deputy Commandant's acute sensitivity to Fischer's impact upon local morale.

He reported to the personnel office, presented the letter permitting him to live off-barracks and offered his new address. Oberstleutnant Krohne's posting papers had arrived already, so the orderly had no more to do than counter-stamp them and make a new entry in Fischer's *soldbuch* (doubtless to ensure that he wasn't misplaced). The entire process was ridiculously convenient, and when the *soldbuch* was returned to him the orderly - an elderly *unteroffizier* with thick glasses and pleasant manner - wished him good luck. It was his slightly doubtful tone that made Fischer pause.

'Do I need it?'

'No more than anyone else, I suppose. But central Berlin's gets attention these days, doesn't it?

'It does, though Allied bombers need to pass through two flak rings to reach it. This site … ' he glanced around, though no damage was visible from the office window, '… has only the one to hold them off. As far as I know, the Air Ministry hasn't been touched to date.'

The orderly pursed his lips. 'Still, it's not a lucky place, is it?'

Fischer didn't believe in luck, good or bad, but a wise man listens when bad news is being offered *gratis* (even if it comes too late to be useful).

'It's not?'

The question seemed to surprise the other man, who had applied himself to his duty rosters. He looked up.

'You can ask that, after what happened to poor Ahle?'

4

Fischer's first morning in his new job brought an immediate immersion in the art of twisting truths. He had only just settled himself at his new desk, made sure that his three pencils were usefully sharp and swapped good mornings with his new colleagues when Oberstleutnant Krohne entered the room with a sheaf of papers.

'The Mga operation' he said, no no-one in particular.

'Never heard of it.'

'Yes, you have, Freddie. We mentioned it a week ago.'

'I mustn't have been listening.'

The Broken Neck, Salomon Weiss (whose blond hair and allegedly un-cut cock belied the name), poked up a finger.

'The Ivans started something there, to wipe out our salient. It's on the Northern Front?'

'Near Leningrad. Well, it's a victory, of sorts.'

Everyone in the room except Krohne and Fischer cheered sourly. Holleman (who had already flagged himself as the departmental comedian) glanced around and laughed.

'What, the Ivans forgot to bring their rifles?'

'They met stubborn resistance. From the Spaniards.'

'What sort of stubborn?'

Krohne pulled a face. 'The worst sort. There's hardly a Blue Division any more. They took seventy-five percent casualties, but with support from the Latvian and Flemish Legions they managed to halt the offensive.'

Detmar Reincke coughed politely. 'Were *any* Germans involved in this triumph?'

'Yes, *SS Polizei*.'

'And we can use the story, despite the casualties?'

'The Propaganda Ministry says so. It demonstrates the pan-European resistance to Communism, apparently. It isn't going to be substantial, so I won't pass it around. Who wants a stab at it?'

A near-perfect silence answered Krohne. He pulled another face. 'Come on, you lazy ...'

Fischer cleared his throat. 'May I try?'

No seasoned soldier volunteered for anything, ever, so this must have been a symptom of first day nerves. The Oberstleutnant waved his papers and looked meaningfully at the rest of his men, doing the new man no favours.

'That's the spirit! Now, you'll be trying to give a hint of how desperate it all was, but don't go too far – the object is to reinforce a sense of the *Volksgemeinschaft* without buggering morale. So, for example, when you write about the Ivans, you can say that they pressed *remorselessly*, but not *relentlessly*. You see?

'One infers that they're merciless, the other unstoppable.'

'Exactly. When you mention our boys - or the poor Spanish bastards, in this case – think of ways to emphasise their heroic resolve without making it seem like suicidal fatalism. It's good to celebrate self-sacrifice in the individual story, because we all love a hero who takes one to save his mates. But suggesting that entire units are throwing themselves under tank-tracks sends the wrong message about how bad the situation is, yes?'

'Got it. What do I say about Luftwaffe?'

Frowning, Krohne consulted his papers. 'There isn't much. A fighter-bomber attack on Soviet positions around Kolpino on the first afternoon relieved the pressure on the defenders, but it won't do.'

'Why not?'

'Because it's the only mention of us being there at all. And it happened several hours after the offensive began, which means that we had to struggle to put something together. The Reichsmarschall won't want his arse kicked around the Chancellery again, so leave it alone.'

For the next hour, Fischer worked on his first piece of literature. The initial draft was more or less as blandly factual as the field-report, if in a slightly different style. That went into the bin. For his second attempt he tried to put himself in Goebbels' tiny shoes, but embarrassment killed the creative flow and that version joined the other. He stared at a third, unsullied piece of paper for a while until a polite cough made him turn. Freddie Holleman was looming over his desk.

'Adjectives.'

'I'm sorry?'

'The special sauce is adjectives. If our men resisted an attack, they did it *valiantly*, or *unstintingly*. A counter-attack that failed was pushed *rigorously*. One that succeeded was executed *brilliantly*. Retreats aren't called that, naturally, but one that's carried off without too many casualties will have been done *adeptly*.'

He turned and waved towards a small bookcase at the other side of the main room. 'There's a notebook on the second shelf. Whenever we come across an adjective our thick heads haven't found for themselves we put it in there. We put it in there *conscientiously*.'

He smirked at his weak joke, making the face even less lovely. 'This is easy. Just remember that we're writing things better than they are, but not so much that people think that everything's sweet in the world. Because if it is, why are all the front lines getting nearer?'

The last was so close to firing-squad talk that Fischer couldn't think of a reply that wouldn't put him in front of one also. He smiled, just, and changed the subject by tapping his new desk.

'How did Ahle die?'

Holleman frowned. 'Why do you ask?'

'His name was mentioned by someone at Adlershof. It seemed a strange coincidence.'

'Not really. Ahle was a draughtsman back in civilian life, so he worked in the technical office there, for a while. Then he came to us.'

'Oh. I thought perhaps he'd found fame because the manner of his death was so terrible.'

'He didn't, but it was. He was found in two parts, on and off an S-bahn line.'

'He killed himself?'

'That's what they say.'

No, he damn well didn't could hardly have been more emphatic. Fischer waited. Holleman glanced around, satisfied himself that no-one was interested in their conversation and sat down.

'Bruno Ahle came back from France with a kilo of metal in his guts. They managed to get some of it out, but a lot remained where it was. He couldn't stand straight, much less lift himself over a two-metre wire fence. And where he was found, the fences on both sides of the track were intact for a long way, either way. But that's not the biggest turd in the pie.'

'What is?'

'I used to be police - did you know that? I still have a *Kripo* mate, an older guy who didn't get to retire at his time. He saw the at-scene photographs when they were sent to Alexanderplatz. He said it looked to be as clean a decapitation as if Ahle had been guillotined, and ...'

'A train wheel wouldn't do that.'

'Not even spinning at maximum speed. The neck would be wholly gone, crushed. And if the train was moving more slowly – which it had to be, through Rummelsburg - there'd be dragging, lots of dragging. I've helped to scrape up a few railway suicides in my time. It isn't something you do before eating lunch.'

'No.'

On unofficial punishment duty during his time at the Police Praesidium at Stettin, Fischer had attended such a case at the dockside marshalling yards. The body had been mangled horribly; the head they found only half an hour later, and it resembled something that a trainee butcher would have apologized for. Nothing about that particular form of self-murder was clean.

'Perhaps it *was* a guillotine, then?'

'Shh.' Holleman glanced around once more. No-one in the Reich had access to a guillotine except the judicial system, which used the device profligately. It had been a lazy thought, and Fischer let it go. There were any number of ways that a man could find his way to the blade – only the previous week, three near-children had been separated from their heads for the crime of principle - but even National Socialism went to the trouble of holding a trial beforehand.

'Anyway, he won't be reclaiming his desk.' Holleman stood painfully. 'Your baptism's today, by the way. Two o'clock alright?'

Oh God. Fischer smothered the wince. He wanted to be on good terms with his new colleagues, but he also needed a functioning liver. Scorching to the right lung aside, his major organs had been entirely missed by the wall of flames that had otherwise attempted to obliterate him, and he was sufficiently grateful to care about their wellbeing. Could he demand to stay on the beer, or was home-distilled poison obligatory?

At least he'd have time to line his stomach first in the Ministry canteen. Whatever the great chefs thought of German cuisine it was usefully heavy, particularly in late winter. A careful choice, even of rationed portions, might sandbag his defences sufficiently to save him the embarrassment of being the first to fall down. Even so, it was hardly an ideal end to a first day's work.

Holleman had been right about adjectives, though. Within an hour he had written something that sounded better than the fight-to-a-standstill he was describing, and when he took it to Krohne he was pleasantly surprised to find that his new boss was pleasantly surprised also.

'Excellent, Otto! My spirits are raised and yet I'm not incredulous. Nor have you been too creative.'

'You don't want creativity?'

'It's a movable concept. Throw in a pleasing anecdote about one of our boys rescuing a *babushka* from her burning hovel and I won't alter a word. Ascribe a local victory to the Archangel Michael leading our panzers by the light of his burning sword and I'll make you write it all out again.'

'I'm not likely to do that.'

'Freddie Holleman did, two months ago.'

'Why?'

'He was bored, allegedly. I hear they're taking you to the *Silver Birch* today?'

'There's no way that I can refuse?'

'Of course you can, but it would cause bad feeling. Ahle got away with it because he didn't have much of a stomach remaining, and Reincke quite brilliantly conceived a sudden, violent bout of diarrhea - which means that you can't, obviously. No, you'd better get it over with. Don't come back to the Ministry afterwards, though. It wouldn't look good to the wrong eyes.'

Later, Fischer ate heartily in the canteen. Later still, he ingested too many rounds of what tasted like tractor fuel in a cramped, seedy establishment that, against all reason, began to feel warmer and more welcoming as each filthy song blended into the next. Shortly after that he lost all of his lunch and half the alcohol over bins in an alley way. It was probably this evacuation that spared him the worst effects of what had put several of his colleagues face down on the *Silver Birch*'s wooden floor. Even so, he had little recollection of his lonely walk back to Alt Moabit – or, until he found grass on his boots the following morning – any idea which route he'd taken.

When he woke – or rather, regained consciousness - the boots were stood neatly in the corner of his sitting room and his tunic was hanging on a chair next to them. He could only imagine that Frau Traugott had somehow managed to manoeuvre him up the stairs and into bed, for which he was both grateful and profoundly ashamed. On only his second night here he had offered her more than ample reason to kick him out.

She didn't, though. Her face seemed a little set (their short acquaintance didn't allow him to decide whether it was an habitual morning cast), but she said nothing about the previous evening and served him fried potato on rye bread for breakfast. A half-memory made him go upstairs and check his tunic pocket, and he returned to the table with a waxed paper package containing slices of *blutwurst* he'd extracted from the Ministry canteen the previous day. Her delight extinguished his fears of homelessness, though he was obliged to endure an interminable monologue on ways to cook and serve the bounty.

His expected hangover had failed to report for duty, his throat hurt less than he deserved and only the gaps in his recollection of conversations in the *Silver Birch* marred an otherwise fine morning. Some of the latter would have been about the job - its doubtless advantages, small inconveniences and why any man would be a damn fool not to want to sit out the war in such a sweet posting. He didn't mind losing those passages, but another had made a start on his peace of mind. Freddie Holleman had said something that had made him forget his growing dizziness and stand almost to attention – and had waited until the chorus of an obscene version of *Sieg Heil Viktoria* was banging out at full volume before saying it. There wasn't a single word that Fischer could recall now, but, like scratches on rough masonry, a faint imprint tugged at memory. He could almost swear that it had been more about a suicide that wasn't.

The thing had stayed with him, worming into his head, since the previous morning. Neither a policeman with more than a week's experience nor a coroner on his very first day would have concluded that Bruno Ahle died *in situ*, yet the determination had been made quickly and apparently without challenge. It would have taken some weight to make that happen, and Fischer didn't want to begin to think about who, why or how, because it wasn't his business. It was so *far* from being his business that he resented having been told anything about it. True, he had asked the question, but why had the answer been so ready, and obliging? Anyone who cared about his arse would have said very little – *what's it to you*, or a shrug, would have told him everything that was needed. Was Holleman being stupid, or leading him towards a precipice? The man was a stranger, and it was equally likely that he had survived his loud, loose mouth for so long through sheer luck or because he was the sort who encouraged others to wander into verbal minefields and then put through a call to Gestapo. There was a thriving fashion in betrayal, one that had only become healthier as the prospect of a thousand year Reich shrank to nothing. A wise man would trust no-one he didn't know as well as himself.

He sipped his acorn coffee and resolved to begin again at his new workplace. He had been a policeman, content with it until the job and culture turned to shit. As a fighting soldier, trust had never been an issue. Ever-present danger required and ensured that a man rely absolutely upon his comrades, as they did upon him. This new career, though, sat at the heart of an organism that polluted by proximity - that ruled by finding an enemy everywhere and then crushing it. His Knight's Cross was no shield against a wrong word, a pointed finger, a false friend. He needed very much to keep his own counsel, even if it gained him – yet again – a reputation for being a cold, distant bastard.

5

KriminalKommissar Hubert Kranzusch lit a cigarette, inhaled deeply and blew the smoke towards the ceiling of the tiny two-man office. His partner, a non-smoker, looked up from the other side of their shared desk and shook his head.

'They'll kill you.'

Kranzusch pulled a face at the pipes that traversed the ceiling on their way from and to somewhere else.

'I don't care.'

'More importantly, they'll kill *me*.'

'To which prospect I'm equally indifferent.'

The two men were of the same rank, but Kranzusch had longer tenure in this over-heated coffin, so Gerd Branssler made no further objection. He liked more than disliked Hubert (which was as much as one could hope for), and enjoyed the faint glow of reflected glory that came with partnering a man who had helped to bring in the monster Ogorzow (though Kranzusch's footballer's legs, thuggish face and gorilla-gait belied his claim that he'd been one of the 'Transvestite Squad' who'd walked the streets as *faux* female bait during that investigation). The man could tell a story, take a ribbing and didn't go for a piss when it was his turn to buy a round, and if help was needed on a case he would volunteer advice readily and not take credit afterwards. On the debit side of the ledger was his chain-smoking, a weakness for forcing out spectacularly foul farts whenever Branssler unwrapped his lunch and the methodical manner with which he excavated nostril-matter with a forefinger as he read departmental circulars. The man was a more of a pig than not, but even pigs didn't entirely lack endearing qualities.

Hubert Kranzusch was bored early today. It was not yet 10 am, and the ceiling pipes weren't usually scrutinized until the early afternoon, when food lay heavily on the stomach, elusive phrases kept reports from being completed and nothing interesting loomed on the duty calendar. Recently, much of the department's time had been devoted to the Black Market (the only non-armaments growth-industry in wartime Germany), though this was by no means a fraught struggle against armed gangs and desperate odds. Their typical cases involved housewives, *blockhilfers* and warehousemen, coalesced into small, fearful syndicates who bartered modest quantities of allegedly unavailable foodstuffs. Neither Branssler nor Kranzusch tried too hard to run down these felons. It was hardly real police work, and given that the Regime's hierarchy continued to ensure that their favourite restaurants (of which *Horscher's* was only the most notorious) had a steady supply of 'impossible' goods, it hardly seemed like real crime either.

Most other 'crime' failed the evidence test, being framed upon the word of semi-professional denouncers. A confetti-storm of letters arrived at Alexanderplatz each day, alleging blackouts not being rigorously observed, amateur prostitution (another way of bumping rations), defeatism, petrol theft, and, occasionally, an idiot son who had been missed somehow by Aktion 4 and its successors. None of it could be ignored, and none of it could make a proper policeman feel as though he were earning his wages.

Kranzusch yawned, put the cigarette in his mouth and clamped it to one side with his lips. He picked up a piece of paper and read its contents aloud.

'To the responsible Authorities. My neighbour, Frau Margret Kettler of Uthmannstrasse 42, Neukölln, has access to black market food. She and her two children have been getting fatter for three months now.'

Branssler snorted. 'We're *all* getting fatter. It's what happens when you eat nothing but potatoes and macaroni.'

''I confronted her and she told me that I was an old sow. My husband died at Verdun, she shouldn't have said that. I hope you will be investigating this'. Bless me ...' Kranzusch waved the paper, '... there's no signature.'

'Whoever could have guessed? The good patriot Anonymous, still at it.'

'Fuck!' The paper went back on to its pile, the cigarette into the ashtray and Kranzusch's eyes returned to the ceiling pipes.

'I want a *murder*, Gerd. It's not too much to ask, is it, that someone who cares about police morale puts himself to the trouble of cacking an old lady? One that's complained about a neighbour, perhaps?'

'You *had* a murder last week. And one three weeks before that.'

'Yeah, but they don't count. Both times, it was ausländers doing what ausländers do. They're always easy to pin.'

'They're always easy to pin because we pin everything on them.'

Kranzusch frowned. He didn't like to be accused of framing innocent parties, but it was a fact that any foreigner, particularly a *gastarbeiter* (or, better still, a *fremdarbeiter*), was burdened by a presumption of guilt of some crime or other. When a swift result was required, Criminal Investigations often didn't break into a sweat before arresting someone whom Berliners would regard as an obvious fit.

'Well, these two did it. The first one hadn't got around to wiping the blood off the knife, and the second confessed to offing his mate even before we laid a finger on him.'

'I know, I was just pulling your nose. You can't expect a murder every day, Bert, not when most of those who'd fit the profile are currently doing it to the Ivans, or British.'

'I wish *I* was out there, fighting with our lads, instead of chasing civilians for no good reason.'

'You do?' Like Branssler, Kranzusch was too old to serve in uniform. They had seen plenty of their younger colleagues go off to war, and a fair few retirees had returned to Alexanderplatz to fill the gaps they left. Until today, he had shown no obvious appetite for active service.

'Do I hell. I'm just *bored*.'

'So am I, but there are worse things to be. We have a nice warm office ...'

'Too warm.'

'... a decent salary and pension to come, and the Allies haven't bothered themselves too much with Berlin ...'

'Yet.'

'Boredom isn't much of a price to pay for all that, is what I mean.'

'But in the old days ...'

'Which are gone. And they weren't, anyway.'

'Weren't what?'

'The old days – not like you remember them. In the last years of Weimar we hardly got sleep, some weeks.'

'Yeah, but then the Protective Custody Order came in.'

'And we were busier than ever, but only for the month it took to round up all the old offenders. After that, they set us to chasing for chasing's sake.' Branssler nodded at the papers in front of his partner. 'That's the job as it is, these days – green- or black-badging anyone we think *might* be a problem, and waving them off to the camps. No point being bored with any of it.'

Kranzusch sighed. 'I know. But another Railway Murderer would be nice. That was only a couple of years back. There must be another Berliner who fancies killing a lot of people.'

'Only in the Chancellery.'

'Eh?'

'Nothing, just clearing my throat. Why don't you make a start on getting your arrest reports up to date?'

'Oh, fuck off!'

Kranzusch was legendarily allergic to any form of paper that wasn't a pay-slip. It was the only (but persistent) black mark against his record, a failing that drove their boss, *Kriminalrat*

Vielhaber, up one wall and halfway down another. Modern Germany had been built on paperwork, but National Socialism had gone further, creating a surveillance State in which every citizen's every twitch was recorded somewhere. Until the forms were filled, stamped and filed, *something* remained intolerably nothing. Kranzusch didn't seem to mind nothingness.

'Anyway, we nearly had another Orgorzow recently, didn't we?'

Branssler sighed and looked up from his own report. 'No, we didn't. It was proximity, that's all. And it was a suicide, remember?'

He said the last pointedly, and his partner sniffed. The body had been found on railway lines only half a kilometre from the same Zobtenerstrasse signal box in which Paul Orgorzow had planned several of his murders. There was a massive convergence of tracks there, the point where two networks met and crossed, so it was equally attractive for a would-be suicide or a murderer, throwing a body from a passing train, who preferred not to be discovered. In Bruno Ahle's case, however, the latter possibility had been ruled out within just forty-eight hours of the body's discovery, before the incident file had acquired contents other than the scene photographs and the duty *orpos*' brief report. Even more strangely, as the curtain descended upon the infant case - one that sat squarely within Amt V's responsibility – all further questions pertaining to it were directed to Amt IV - Gestapo. This was generally taken to mean that there should and would be no further questions.

Naturally, almost every man in Criminal Investigations *had* further questions, though no-one gave voice to them. Branssler himself had thought far too much about it, particularly after he discovered that the deceased, a wounded Luftwaffe veteran, worked in the same office as one of his oldest friends. He knew that he should have kept his mouth as firmly closed as the file that carried Ahle to oblivion, yet he had stifled his common-sense, arranged a meeting with Freddie Holleman in a bar where neither of them were known and then blurted everything he knew about the case. Freddie had been police once, which if anything made the error of judgement worse. He had asked his own questions – pertinent, perceptive questions – and Branssler knew that the answers would keep his mind in a place that someone at Alexanderplatz or Prinz-Albrecht-Strasse had taken care to sweep clean. He trusted Holleman, but not so much as to put his own neck within reach of the guillotine …

He almost winced, wishing the word hadn't come to mind. How many other implements could remove a head so neatly, so precisely, as Herr Ahle's? A man with a sword would need to be adept, and as strong as an ox. A surgeon could do it, probably, but almost certainly he'd need assistance, and two medically-trained psychopaths struck him as an improbable perversion. No doubt there was a deal of industrial machinery that could manage the job, but Ahle had worked at a desk and wasn't known to have frequented factory sites in his off-duty hours. Still, it was a possibility …

Stop thinking, you cock. A dozen times over the past weeks Branssler had reminded himself that he had a wife and daughters, any or all of whom would break something heavy over his head if they knew where his mind was wandering. It was too late – years too late – to mistake this job for a vocation, or care about how or why things were done. He clocked in, tried (and often failed) to get through days without doing anything that shamed him too sorely and took the adequate reward. He had a decent home, five thousand per year and no enemies, and if things got too bad in Berlin he could send his family to stay with relatives far enough from Allied targets to pass the war in safety. It was a lot to be thankful for, and definitely not worth risking to satisfy himself on the matter of how a severed head had become so.

Kranzusch was watching him, and it probably wasn't the beauty of the vista that was holding his attention. They had risked just the one conversation about Ahle - a brief, almost whispered exchange that had been nothing to do with the manner of the man's death and everything to do with what or who he was. Luftwaffe, yes, injured severely during the 1940 campaign in France and since occupied in a half-recovery and a succession of desk jobs. So, why were Gestapo's hands on this? Had Ahle been a communist? A saboteur? Religious activist, Homo, Gypsy, Freemason or Weimar liberal? The trouble was that 'anti-social' covered such a vast field of sins that Amt IV could take an interest in almost any deviation from the cowed norm. But *why* would they, in Ahle's case? The man was dead, after all, and even Gestapo had no Afterlife Department.

It was at this point that their hushed discussion had paused, both *kripos* having arrived simultaneously at the cliff's edge. Officially, Gestapo and Criminal Investigations were joined at the hip, but those *kripos* who hadn't thrown themselves enthusiastically into the business of making war on their own people kept more than a corridor's distance from their political colleagues. This was sensed and resented, and when Gestapo could use their jurisdictional weight they tended not to tiptoe, or apologize, or give much warning - what they did, almost invariably, was to stress loudly why it was that Criminal Investigations weren't qualified to deal with a snatched case. It salted the wound, and Gestapo were fond of salting. In Ahle's case, though, they had moved swiftly and silently, thrown the business into a hole and filled it in. Neither Kranzusch or Branssler had since voiced his feelings about that, but one man's expression mirrored the other's thoughts every time someone made mention of the *railway suicide*.

Today, though, Kranzusch's expression said a little more. His wilful nature could be teased by boredom, and having no attachments (he was a widower, with a son who had gone travelling years earlier and never returned) he lacked the circumspection that a family encouraged. Branssler's gut lurched slightly as it occurred to him that he shared a room with a man who might be about to attract fire.

'Gerd, I'm thinking ...'

'Don't.'

'It wouldn't hurt to have a quick word with ... ' Kranzusch glanced down at a piece of paper next to his elbow; ' ... *Unterwachtmeister* Petersen. He was the first on the scene. At Rummelsberg, I mean.'

'Why did you make a note of his name, Bert?'

The shrug said nothing, but Branssler's gut took another turn. Neither man had been in any way involved in the still-born investigation. It had been assigned to *Unterkommissar* Stoltz, one of their formerly-retired colleagues, whose delight in having it snatched away almost immediately had not been disguised. The manner of its going had raised hairs on necks, but even had the hint not been sufficiently heavy, why would any sane man now point himself towards trouble?

Branssler stood, opened the office door, checked the corridor both ways and returned. There was a faint smile on Kranzusch's face (as if he knew what was coming), and the other man sorely wanted to punch it off. He resisted, mainly because it would require more than knuckles to correct the illusion that a safe job in a largely safe city, far from where vast armies were doing their best to expunge each other, was in any way a guarantee that tomorrows would continue to arrive.

'Bert, if you're *bored*, buy a book. Or learn to crochet. Console yourself that there are places your nose shouldn't go if it wants to stay on that fucking ugly dial. Believe me, I'll smack it right off if you do or say anything that pushes *me* towards trouble.'

'Alright, Gerd, alright.'

Kranzusch spoke mildly, his eyebrows high, but Branssler's gut remained tight. He knew how easily his partner's preoccupations followed his mood, and how little it would take to bring them back to a dangerous place. There was no law that said a man who was very good at one thing (as Kranzusch was) couldn't be a damn fool in almost every other respect. In fact, it was often the way that confidence in one's aptitude expanded beyond reason and prudence (Germany was on its present path precisely because of that quality in their leader), and if fear for the self couldn't rein in such imbecility it was hardly likely that the health of friends and colleagues would do it.

Fists and reason wouldn't work, and Branssler could hardly put distance between himself and a man who sat less than two metres away. The only other option was to knock on *Kriminaldirektor* Rauh's door and request a transfer, but he'd be asked the reason for it and could only offer the truth, which was unthinkable. He wished fervently to be elsewhere, to have retired early, to have a reputation as an unthinking Party man, to entirely undo his conversation with Freddie Holleman – most of all, he wished that whoever put Bruno Ahle on the rail-tracks had tried a little harder to make it look like a suicide.

6

Major Nimtz was a rare specimen – a Wehrmacht medic in whom humanity was not strictly rationed. Fischer had seen him often at the experimental burns unit at Potsdam, asking questions of the skin-men who had been attempting to transform a charcoaled semi-corpse into something resembling the man it had been. The process had been anything but linear. Early efforts to graft skin had failed utterly, leaving wounds that added greatly to Fischer's underlying agonies. Like his colleagues, Nimtz had been as fascinated by the failures as the eventual partial successes, and regarded the patient with much the same delight as a child would, waking on Christmas Day to a new tin army. Unusually, however, he had always tried to raise the victim's crushed morale by not lying about the process - by explaining how their science was as yet a crude but hopeful thing, and that Fischer's pain was a symptom of continuing tissue-life, if much corrupted.

When the diagnosis began slowly to improve, the Major made a point of pausing on his rounds and asking how Fischer *felt*, rather than consult upon how the treatment progressed. The answers were almost always bleak, but Nimtz, if he was discouraged by them, never let the smile slip from his face. The patient, swathed in bandages, pain and protocols, had drawn a little balm from these fleeting visits, and he was genuinely pleased today that Nimtz presided over his official release into the world of unmutilated creatures.

'You're taking painkillers still?'

'I try not to when I don't have to be in company.'

'Good. They can become habitual.'

Fischer had noticed that doctors avoided speaking of *addiction*. After the Regime's about-face on Pervitin, Germans were no longer permitted to acknowledge anything symptomatic of moral weakness (much less indulge it), which was why doctors had become very fond of prescribing *pull yourself together*, or *you must bear with it*, however horrific the prospect before them. In contrast, Major Nimtz deferred to pain and its ravages, at least to the point of not voicing any opinions he might hold.

He looked up and beamed too brightly. 'You've been posted, yes?'

'To the *Kriegsberichter der Luftwaffe*. I'll be working at the Ministry.'

'Excellent! You know that the building's blessed, I expect?'

'I didn't. In what way?'

'The British have missed it every time so far. It's had a few windows blown in, but the poor old Prussian Parliament building next door's been hammered. I'm surprised they didn't mention that.'

'Perhaps they didn't want to break their luck?'

'Possibly not. Well, you'll be at the heart of things. If you run into the Reichsmarschall, please let him know that Potsdam needs more morphine, would you?'

'I'll poke him with a stick, I promise.'

That earned a polite smile. For a few moments, Nimtz shuffled his papers distractedly. Fischer braced himself for something hearty and hopeful, but was pleasantly disappointed.

'Hauptmann, what you've endured here has been the easy part, in some ways. You've been in our hands, and Science has done what it's able to do. I'm sure that it's been agonizing, but each improvement has been measurable and sometimes apparent, possibly even to you.'

The Major took a deep breath. 'What comes next may well be … disappointing. You'll be aware already how some people react to your visible wounds, but I'm sure *that* ordeal will ease in time. What may be more difficult is how you regard yourself. I understand that you have no immediate family?'

'I'm divorced, without children. There's a brother-in-law – my sister is deceased – and a nephew. We're not close.'

'That can be good or bad. Many badly-wounded men find the pain they put upon their families hard to bear. Others take great comfort from the support they receive. The universal hardship lies in coming to terms with the fact that future improvements in one's condition will be finite.'

'I don't expect ever to be beautiful.'

'I'm not talking about mere vanity. We're beginning to understand that the mind often doesn't recover in the same manner, or even to the same degree, as the body. As yet, we don't know *why* that is, but I expect you'll have days in which your injuries weigh much more savagely than others. At such times it would be beneficial to speak of it a little – perhaps to a close friend?'

I have no friends.

'Yes, I'll do that.'

'Well, then ...' Nimtz stood, and Fischer took the hint; '… you must continue to apply glycerin to your wounds, twice each day after bathing the damaged areas. And try to use Pethidin only when the pain is unbearable.'

'Of course.'

'Well, I wish you luck, Fischer … Oh.'

'Yes?'

'Just a moment. You're going back to the Ministry now, I expect?'

'I am.'

'The s-bahn's a mess at the moment, you'll have noticed on the way here. Let me see ...'

Nimtz picked up his telephone receiver and dialled a single number.

'Colonel Deisler, please. Hello Hansi, it's Peter. What time is your briefing today? Ah. Listen, would you give one of my former patients a lift? He works at Wilhelmstrasse 97 these days. Wonderful. Yes, I'll tell him.'

The receiver returned to its cradle. 'The Colonel is presenting his monthly report to *Inspektion 14* at 3pm. He says he'll see you down at the parking garage in twenty minutes. Don't make him wait, will you?'

So it happened that Fischer's official release from the care of his doctors was marked with some style. He had never ridden in a Mercedes before, nor kept a Colonel's company (they hardly spoke; 'Hansi' excused himself as they settled into their seats and devoted himself to the report he was to make), and the novelty enhanced the smooth, comfortable passage through the delightful Königswald. In fact, the only complaint he might have made was that the journey was all too swift. Less than thirty minutes after departing Werder the car purred to a halt in front of the Air Ministry's main entrance, at which Fischer was dismissed with a faint smile and a nod. Emerging from the car he came to attention and salute correctly, which earned a wave of the hand that held the pen.

Upstairs, his colleagues were staring with varying degrees of bewilderment at their assignments. Holleman's mouth moved as he read, while Salomon Weiss held his paper aloft, at arm's-length, as if it were primed to explode. Detmar Reincke snorted quietly as Fischer passed his desk.

'What is it?'

'Army Group Centre, situation report on the Rzhev Salient, from two days ago. We've been given the job of making it smell sweet.'

'Doesn't it?'

'They're calling it a preliminary partisan-clearance, to allow our lads to be able to concentrate entirely on what's in front of them as they pull back – sorry, I meant straighten the line.'

'Well, that's sensible.'

'Yeah, it would be, if there *were* any partisans. The operation's complete, and they've sent us the results. We won't be publishing much of the detail.'

'Why not?'

Without comment, Reincke passed a sheet of paper to Fischer. It was a list of casualties and captured weaponry. Almost three thousand Russians had been killed – all of them *partisans* who had been planning to attack rear-echelon Wehrmacht units. Except that they had been spectacularly ill-equipped for the job. The bounty included fewer than three hundred rifles, forty pistols, sixty machine guns, a handful of mortars and anti-tank weapons and sixteen small artillery pieces that almost entirely lacked shells. In other words, General Model's 9th Army had mostly been executing unarmed civilians.

'Yes, I see.'

'Model's a hard bastard. They say that even the Führer gets nervous when they're face-to-face.'

'So, what will we make of this?'

Reincke shrugged. 'Hard to say. Karl gave it to every one of us – it's what he does when the heroic story's well-hidden.'

Holleman cleared his throat loudly and addressed the entire room. 'What about: 'Units of the 9th Army have been engaged in manoeuvres to neutralize partisan forces that have been launching cowardly assaults on German support groups and local civilians alike. The area around Rzhev has now been cleared at high cost to the enemy, though many were able to use their knowledge of the terrain to flee eastwards and shelter with the Soviet main forces. Local officials have thanked our men for intervening to preserve innocent lives.''

'That's good, Freddie!'

Holleman smiled modestly. 'Always flip atrocities on their head – you can't hide them forever, but they're difficult to point a finger at.'

'I don't think we can run anything on this.'

Oberstleutnant Krohne had entered the main office while they were talking. His own copy of the briefing was in his hand, and he pulled a face at it.

'However we tell it, there's precious little to shine. And of course, Luftwaffe weren't involved in any way, so it shouldn't really be our job to do the shining.'

'But you gave it to us, Karl.'

'I know, Detmar. OKW's Press Office at Zossen pushed it my way to see if we could make something of it, which is flattering.' He looked up. 'We have a good reputation, apparently.'

'For taking shit and making it smell of strawberries?'

'Just that, Freddie. *This* shit might have a grenade hidden in it, though.'

'How?'

'OKW want something to put out, but I've just heard from a friend in the Propaganda Ministry that we might be stabbing ourselves if we do. He told me that Model and the Führer have been talking about making the salient less of a potential threat to our forces when they withdraw and the Ivans move into it.'

'What, dig it up and take it with them?'

'In a way. Model want to pull out cleanly, and he's worked out that the Soviets' biggest weakness still is supplying their forces as they advance. So, he's been given permission to *hinder* that process.'

'Something that the Geneva Convention might have an opinion on?'

'He's going to flatten all the towns in the Salient, poison the wells and deport the largest concentrations of its male population.'

'To where?'

Krohne shrugged. 'To ditches, probably. Or if they're really unlucky, to work-camps in the occupied territories. He intends to leave nothing that the Red Army can use to replenish its losses. In the meantime, he's preparing deep defensive works for the 6th to enter at the conclusion of its back-step.'

For a few moments, no-one spoke. Every Army Group Commander on the Eastern Front would be desperate not to have another Stalingrad attached to his reputation. The Wehrmacht no less than SS had gone East with explicit instructions not to regard the enemy in the same manner as they might more 'civilized' foes, and now, facing increasingly overwhelming numbers, even once-honourable men were setting aside the inconveniences of conscience.

Holleman had been frowning at his desk. He cleared his throat and raised a finger.

'So, if we draw too much attention to this bandit-clearing business, we ...'

'Might well be flagging our intentions and culpability in the larger, subsequent matter.'

'Ah. Whereas if we say nothing now, our very-publicly expressed disgust at the summary executions of suspected collaborators by advancing Soviet troops ...?'

Krohne nodded and held out his free hand. 'I'll have your copies back, please.'

Gratefully, the Liars returned them. Holleman looked around.

'Early lunch, lads?'

'Stay where you are, Freddie. I haven't yet seen your piece on the magnificent work done by Luftwaffe's ground staff in forward airfields. And the rest of you - I'll find something on Rommel's headlong retreat for you to turn around. This is war, not a rest-cure.'

Krohne's final comment was taken up by almost everyone in the room before it was half-out. He rolled his eyes and withdrew to his office. The Liars returned to their desks, and a low, desultory buzz replaced the earlier silence of failed inspiration. Detmar Reincke pulled a copy of the *Berliner Morgenpost* from his desk drawer and turned to the back pages, his handless right arm twitching occasionally as it attempted to make a contribution to the manoeuvres. Udo Lehmann (severe groin wound) and Klaus Weber (head trauma-induced fits) played football across their shared desk with a crumpled piece of paper. Salomon Weiss, perched on Freddie Holleman's territory, listened as something was whispered in his ear and giggled at the undoubtedly foul punchline. No-one appeared keen to resume the task of restoring morale among their readership, so Fischer sat at his own desk, removed his notebook from a pocket and re-read the exercise regime that Major Nimtz had drawn up to restore some use to his damaged shoulder, arm and hand.

Predictably, it consisted of a series of gentle stretching movements, to be replaced gradually by more vigorous exertion as near-useless muscle and sinew began to earn their keep once more. The kindly Nimtz had given him the address of a recently shuttered gymnasium in Mitte that might supply a few exercise-weights at little cost (the owner having died in North Africa, his widow was anxious to secure what she could from a never-profitable business before its metalwork was stolen by the Munitions Ministry), and provided a watchword – *persistence* - that the convalescent was directed to repeat to himself several times each day. Fischer couldn't help but think that the Major was allowing optimism too much rein.

There was also a dietary sheet – which, under the present national circumstances, represented a triumph of positive thinking. Fortunately, it recommended that meat play only a minor role for the foreseeable future, making a virtue of dire necessity. However, it also steered the recovering patient away from starchy foods, which two words neatly summarized Germans' war-time diet. The only readily available dish that appeared to fit the guidelines precisely was cabbage or kohlrabi soup, a prospect that appealed to Fischer as much as replacing water in his diet with the *Silver Birch*'s home brewed battery acid. He re-read the sheet twice, folded it carefully and dropped it into his bin.

'Have you thought any more about what I said?'

Holleman, a large man whose innate clumsiness was enhanced considerably by his artificial leg, had somehow crossed the space between their desks without giving any hint of his approach. Fischer barely managed to remain in his chair. He breathed deeply, knowing exactly what Holleman meant without being able to recall a single detail of it. What could he say? If he admitted to having no memory of the conversation he might once more hear something detrimental to his health. If he bluffed his way through it, the lie might rattle a man who could be a friend or potential enemy. *Was* there a correct answer?

'My head's been hurting too much to think.'

'You seemed alright when you went home.'

'You mean the last time you saw me I was upright still? Believe me, it didn't last long. I puked in the alley.'

'*That's* what I skidded through!'

Holleman seemed cheerful enough, which was slightly reassuring. Entrapment was a delicate business, and usually the effort was apparent. The other man was keeping his voice low, but given the broad matter a little discretion was only prudent. And as they were hardly close acquaintances - much less friends – a slight reticence was natural.

And yet here was that conundrum again – they were hardly more than strangers, so why would Holleman push himself out on a thin branch by discussing 'poor' Ahle at all? Fischer doubted that anyone would look into his ruined face and think *now, here's a man I can trust*, or *what the hell, we're both ex-police, I'll tell him everything*. His two medals were something of a testimonial, but only to courage, and there were plenty of courageous, ardent National Socialists who would betray a wrong word or thought without hesitation. What else told the world that Otto Henry Fischer's was a willing, trustworthy ear?

'Well, did you read it?'

Read what? 'Not ... yet, no.'

Holleman sighed and held out a massive hand. 'You'd better give it back, then. And don't say anything to anyone, right?'

Several unpleasant possibilities occurred almost simultaneously. Whatever *it* was, Fischer might have dropped it as he bent over the *Silver Birch*'s bins, relieving himself of his lunch. It may have gone missing somewhere in Tiergarten as he staggered his way back to Jonas-Strasse. It was possible, even, that his bleary, drunken self had discovered a mysterious object in his pocket and decided to test his residual flinging function as he passed over one of the Garden's many water bridges. At best, he might have managed to reach his accommodation with the object intact, but that wasn't reassuring. At that very moment, Frau Traugott could be sat on his bed, memorizing its fatal contents – or, worse, passing them on to her local *blockhelfer*.

He swallowed, twice, and attempted to seem vastly more nonchalant than he felt.

'To be honest, I was so drunk last evening that I completely forgot about it. Would you give me another day, to read and then consider the thing? I'll say nothing in the meantime.'

Holleman's eyes narrowed. He glanced to either side and then at the window (for a moment, Fischer feared being grabbed and defenestrated), scratched his nose and belched. Finally, he leaned forward and whispered.

'If you do, you know they'll cack you as well as me, just to keep things tidy?'

They. Until Fischer could read whatever it was that Holleman had given him, *they* could be anyone. He wanted to excuse himself, rush back to Jonas-Strasse, find the damn thing and make a start on understanding what he had - entirely inadvertently – dropped himself into. This was just his second day in a new job, though, and while Karl Krohne seemed an amenable fellow, it wouldn't do. He nodded at Holleman.

'Not a word, to anyone.'

For the rest of the day he tried and failed to move his mind back to his work. *Don't dwell upon things you can't alter* was an admirable adage, but hard to stretch to. He wandered around his predicament instead, trying to pin the moment at which he had failed to spot the incoming shrapnel, and excused himself when several of the Liars tried to interest him in another evening's exploration of the *Silver Birch*'s pitted oak flooring.

He left the Ministry as soon as wouldn't look bad and almost jogged to Alt-Moabit, hoping to reach his rooms un-intercepted; but when he arrived at Jonas-Strasse 17 he found Frau Traugott sitting on a stool on her stoop, skirt drawn up to give the neighbourhood the benefit of her green bloomers, peeling potatoes. Obviously, a *good evening* wouldn't do. She asked about his day, complained about the fine weather (too dry and warm for the time of the year, apparently), and thanked him once more for the blutwurst, which brought an apology for not having raided the Ministry canteen one more that lunchtime.

She shrugged philosophically. 'It's alright. I make as good a potato soup as any could be. Even the sisters enjoy it. I tidied your room, by the way.'

He excused himself and cleared two flights of stairs in a matter of moments. His few possessions hardly required tidying, but somehow Frau Traugott had managed to rearrange everything that wasn't in one of his pockets. At least her efforts had saved him the trouble of parsing his drunken mind's logic. Whatever hiding place he had found for the object, it had been unearthed and placed in the middle of his small sitting-room table, keeping company with a small vase of daffodils.

It was a small notebook with a metal clasp, the sort of item carried by any stationer's or bookshop in the days before most non-newspaper pulp was requisitioned for the war effort. Usually, the owner would have entered his or her name in the space provided in the frontispiece, but Herr Ahle had made at least a cursory effort to be discreet. The pages that followed were filled by a small, carefully-printed script that gave away little of the author's idiosyncratic hand and was extremely easy to read.

An hour later, Fischer regretted that blessing intensely.

7

Two gentlemen, senior officers in RSHA Amt V, met on the south side of Unter den Linden, in front of the Komische Oper. They sat down on a bench a few metres from where a street vendor was hoping to interest passers-by in his roasted chestnuts. Both glanced at him casually, and then at the broader near-field for any familiar faces. Their names were Bernauer and Messenfer, though they referred to each other as Herr Schwarz and Herr Blond, an affectation that, despite its longevity, still amused them (Schwarz's eyes apart, he might have been mistaken for an albino, while Blond was almost as swarthy as a Mediterranean fisherman). Today, they dispensed with the usual pleasantries, being upon business that neither man felt comfortable with.

Having satisfied himself (to a degree) that the chestnut vendor was neither Gestapo nor Inland SD, Blond turned to his friend.

'Why have we been doing this?'

'Because we were instructed to.'

'By whom?'

'Ah.' Schwarz scratched his nose, a familiar nervous reaction. 'The order came from the Gruppenführer himself, of course. But as to who wanted it …'

Slowly, Blond nodded. 'But what business is it of ours – I mean, other than in the obvious, procedural context?'

'Damned if I know. It's … perverse.'

'Which brings me back to *why*?'

'Obviously there's something we don't know.'

'There's a hell of a lot we don't know. Doesn't that make you nervous?'

'Extremely. I almost made an appointment to see the Gruppenführer, to ask outright what it is we're doing.'

'I'm glad you didn't.'

'It was a momentary urge. Then it occurred that he would have offered the details already if we were meant to have them.'

'Why the hell is *he* bothering with this?'

Schwarz sighed. 'A favour? A quid pro quo? He's being leaned on?'

'Who has the balls to lean on *him*?'

'Precisely what I was wondering. Which is why we don't need to know what this is about, only why we're involved.'

Blond watched a young mother with two children negotiating a price with the vendor.

'I would have thought it's late in the year to be selling roast chestnuts.'

'It's food, and not rationed. Of course, we could just accept that the thing's done now and forget about it.'

'The sensible course, definitely. But it would be nice to know that none of it can return to embarrass us.'

'Give that we lost almost a quarter of a million men at Stalingrad recently, I doubt that this thing could register on laboratory scales, much less raise ghosts.'

'It shouldn't, unless it's something that impacts upon the real war.'

To very senior men, the *real* war was not waged with aircraft, tanks and submarines, but with whispered insinuations, frantic searches for tiny barbs and the seizing of momentary ascendancies. Its battleground extended hardly a kilometre in every direction from where they sat, yet the implications of its outcome for every German could hardly have been more profound.

'I wouldn't have thought so. The man wasn't anyone, was he?'

Blond looked curiously at his friend. 'If he wasn't *anyone*, why did it happen the way it did, and why are we trying to find its edges?'

'Forgive me, I wasn't thinking. It's almost one o'clock; shall we go back?'

They stood and smiled at the young mother and her handsome children. Though both men belonged to Criminal Investigations, their rank (both men were SS-Standartenführers) was such that they pointed themselves not to the east and Alexanderplatz but westward, towards Prinz-Albrecht-Strasse, where most of the Reich's intelligence, security and police organizations' hierarchies had desks.

They walked in silence for a while, each man looking for signs of bomb damage with the professional interest that most Berliners had developed since the start of the war. For much of the past year, RAF Home Command's efforts had been devoted to the submarine threat in the Atlantic, and Berlin had been bothered by them only nine times during 1942. True, the leadership had been mortally embarrassed on 30 January 1943, the tenth anniversary of the Party's seizure of power, when two Mosquito raids disrupted important speeches by Göring and Goebbels, but the physical damage they did was hardly greater than what their namesakes might have accomplished. As yet, the British did not have the aircraft necessary to reach the city with significant ordnance, or to stay over it for more than a few minutes, so the visible damage was slight. That done to citizens' nerves was harder to assess, but the longer the pause lasted the greater the hurt to morale would be, once the raids recommenced.

Schwarz and Blond cared for the popular mood precisely to the extent that the Führer did, as his anxieties could often wound indiscriminately. Criminality was their concern, and though they had for some time been able to plead manpower shortages whenever small spikes in urban crime occurred, the Einsatzgruppen had now been disbanded and their many police personnel returned to Germany, so excuses were no longer accepted. In the past three months there had been two large-scale, very-publicly conducted operations against black marketeers, hooliganism (a wonderfully vague offence) and ausländers (because why not?), so Amt V was being seen to be doing its job, even if it had to manufacture crime before it could stamp on it.

This *thing*, though, was a troubling reminder of how ripples within the Reich's many and conflicting jurisdictions could drop a steaming pile into the laps of even the most adept box-tickers. If the party ultimately responsible for it couldn't be known, how was it possible to gauge the exposure? Neither Schwartz nor Blond had been privy to whatever discussion had brought about this accommodation, but the acquiescence – or rather, head-turning – of both men had been necessary for it to happen. They were, therefore, accomplices to something. But *what*?

'Have you spoken to the Gruppenführer recently? I mean, on any other matter?'

Schwarz said it casually, but Blond didn't mistake it for idle conversation. They had asked the same of each other every few days for several months now, a collaboration as careful as that of surgeons over an operating table. What the Gruppenführer might have said to either man would doubtless have interested the other, but that wasn't the purpose of the query - it was rather the condition of the man himself that exercised their minds.

'He had a meeting with Gestapo Müller last Friday, and briefed me afterwards.'

'That must have been pleasant for him. Did they discuss opera, or was it the availability of champagne?'

Blond smiled thinly. Müller's reaction to either subject would probably be akin to that of a pig invited to express an opinion on a frock. The man was a brute – an efficient, tireless brute whose preoccupations had narrowed in recent months to a matter about which Schwarz and Blond knew far more than they would have wished, given a choice.

'It was the *Business*, of course, as it almost always is these days.'

Schwarz grimaced. 'Not the best way to get the Gruppenführer's head back to where it belongs.'

'No. I'm afraid his eastern experiences have marked him out as someone to be consulted, but ...'

'I wonder if anyone else has noticed – Müller, perhaps?'

Blond thought about that for a moment. 'I doubt it. To see the change one would have needed to know the man prior to 1941, and while Heydrich was alive Müller was too busy fetching balls for his master. As heads of their respective Amts they met formally, of course, but I can't think they were at all intimate. Face it – who would willingly seek Müller's company, much less his friendship?'

'Who else, then?'

'Well, *we've* noticed.'

'Yes, but we're more or less a bottleneck these days, aren't we? You've taken on V/C as well as A, I'm running B *and* Wi, so there's only Bredermann at Forensics, and if he ever raises his head to look around I'd be amazed. In effect, you and I are the Gruppenführer's only link to those who might otherwise be best placed to notice.'

Schwarz paused and pulled a face. 'And it isn't as if he's twitching - not yet, at least.'

'I don't suppose we could persuade him to take some leave? If we made a joint approach?'

'We'd need to apply instruments of torture. A man who's forever looking over his shoulder isn't going to give anyone a reason to gossip.'

'No. But what, then?'

'Nature will take its course, I expect. A lot of our men who came back from … *that* are showing similar signs of strain.'

'Not all of them report directly to Ernst Kaltenbrunner twice each month.'

'No, they don't.'

'And you know what *he'd* do with the slightest hint of human weakness.'

They had come to the corner of Behrenstrasse and Mauerstrasse. Schwarz stopped and put a hand on Blond's arm.

'You go on. I'll wait a few minutes and follow.'

'Paranoia?'

'Why not? The order came to us, and we acted on it. Whoever pushed the Gruppenführer into issuing it may well know that. I wouldn't want them to think that we were keeping it mind what was done, much less discussing it.'

'We might simply have been walking – taking the air. It's a pleasant morning.'

'We weren't raised to this rank to take our ease on a working day. And together? It will look exactly like what it is. Forget about *why* this thing happened. The men who had the juice to push it almost certainly work on or just off Wilhelmstrasse, and we need to cross it to return to our offices. What sort of view do you want to give them?'

'Not this one, for sure.'

8

When Fischer had finished reading, he closed the notebook and put it in his inner tunic pocket. About a third of the way through it he had started jotting down memoranda in his own notebook, and now he ripped two pages from it and tore them into tiny pieces.

Idiot.

The thing was a diary of sorts, which was an offence under the Military Code. Herr Ahle must have been a brave, foolish or careless man, and Fischer was none of those for very good reasons. To record dates, places and movements of resources during a campaign – however incidentally - was as good as to invite the sort of incident that had almost given General McClellan a victory at Antietam. Wantonly letting the enemy know what you were doing was never a good idea.

There were enough veiled references to indicate that Ahle had at least tried to be discreet, but even Fischer (whose unit had not served in *Case Red*) needed only a few minutes' careful reading to pin the formation in which the man had served. The early entries describe several fraught missions over England, in which Ahle's Battle Wing suffered heavy losses during night raids. He had been a pilot, but there were several references to his crew and one mention of losing his side-gunner to a Hurricane attack, which meant that his aircraft was a Heinkel HE111, not a Junkers JU-88. The betraying item of information was a brief note of the loss, on 14 August 1940, of the Battle Wing's commander. Though he was unnamed in the diary, Fischer recalled both the stir that the news had caused at the time, and the name – *Oberst* Alois Stoeckl – which told him that Ahle's flight had been part of *Kampfgeschwader* 55.

The fighting entries ended in early September 1940, at which time Ahle had been wounded in action. The pause lasted for almost a year, before a few brief notations recommenced, mostly to do with his painful, protracted recovery. Then, in late-1941, Ahle was transferred to southwest Berlin, Adlershof airfield.

At this point in the sparse narrative, Fischer had paused and returned to earlier entries that preceded even the Battle for England. His attention had been taken and held by a brief note, made a few days after KG55 had been involved in Operation *Paula*, the Luftwaffe's attempt to finish off the French Air Force in the Paris area. Ahle's squadron was moved up to Reims, and the assault was launched on 3 June 1940. Its results – initially overstated drastically – were disappointing, but that hardly mattered, given the ongoing collapse of French resistance on the ground. Rather than make another attempt, many units were transferred immediately to the Calais area and Belgium, to concentrate for the decisive air campaign against the British mainland. KG55 – or at least part of it - lingered at Reims for a further three days, however. Fischer knew this after reading an entry made on 7 June:

The squadron moves out tomorrow. I'm glad, because the M. has been behaving very badly.

It was a curious thing, curiously put. What constituted very bad behaviour in field operations? Had 'M' been strafing enemy pilots as they parachuted from their stricken aircraft? Pointing his guns at fleeing civilians? Pissing out of the cockpit hatch during landings?

And then Fischer noticed *the*. A title or designation, then. The most obvious reference was to the squadron leader, who almost invariably held the rank of Major (unless a hauptmann was in temporary command following the wounding or death of his immediate superior). It might refer to a mechanic, of course, but then Ahle would probably have written *my M*, or *Schmidt's M*. In any case, how did mechanics *behave very badly*?

If it *was* the Major, he would be a pilot, and Heinkel HE111 pilots didn't operate guns, so his bad behaviour was something else. Cheating at cards? Not paying his Mess bill? Flying while inebriated? Referring to their beloved Führer as an Arse? All of it *bad*, but not really capable of being cured or tempered by leaving the vicinity of Reims.

Eventually, Fischer realised that it was Ahle's choice of words that had brought him back to the entry. *Behaving very badly* was an almost prissy way of skirting detail, and it made him wish that he'd known the man. He might have been a pious type, the sort who helped out at his local church before the war, but there weren't many delicate temperaments that could weather more than a few weeks of life in uniform. Profanity and casual obscenities were as much a part of communication between soldiers as the transmission of orders, and any hint of finer feeling was sniffed out, pounced upon and beaten from the offender before God, His angels or the barracks sergeant could intervene. It just wasn't the phrasing that one would expect from a man who had served since the outbreak of hostilities - and, soon afterwards, helped to cook the East End of London.

It's not my business.

He kept repeating it to himself, but what had killed the cat was also hard for a former *kripo* to overcome by the application of mere common sense. Having danced around the meaning of a single phrase for almost half an hour he flicked forward in the notebook, to Ahle's return to the war effort at the DVL facility, Adlershof.

There were a few brief references to his relevant but long-unused experience, his anxiety that he might be found out and returned to active service (as if a man who could no longer climb into a fuselage might be of use at the Front) and a predictable resentment of men who didn't try to be sufficiently accommodating of his injuries. Nevertheless, he appeared to have got on top of his new responsibilities quickly, and was assigned to the main draughting office. On his first day there the establishment was graced by a visit from the Luftwaffe's Head of Procurement and Supply, the famous, dashing air-ace, Ernst Udet. The great man was introduced to Ahle and shook his hand, a pregnant moment marked by an annotation in the margin: *Clearly intoxicated!* Barely two weeks later, another entry recorded Udet's death in a test flight without further comment, though a cross placed next to his name suggested the diarist was feeling a degree of remorse about his earlier entry.

He hadn't been so foolish as to set down any details of his work at Adlershof. A few names were mentioned more than once, but the comments were judgmental rather than technical. He seemed to have formed grudges easily and then let them stew, though it hardly needed a psychologist's intuition to sense that most of them were directed against men of greater rank, expertise and standing. A rejection from one of the female secretaries was pored over, buried, exhumed and re-suffered, the commentary alternating between an impressively inventive analysis of her sluttishness and his own inadequacies. Fischer couldn't help but think that the man had needed a friend to apply a few brisk slaps, but clearly, Herr Ahle didn't mix easily with human company.

Then, the tone of the entries changed abruptly. They became terse to the point of redundancy, as if being made only for habit's sake. It might have been a period in which nothing of note occurred or of exceptional busyness at Adlershof, but

Fischer suspected that it was something else. A lonely, introspective man who gave voice to his emotions on a page didn't suddenly cease to have them, nor find an iron self-control. Had he been disciplined for the secretary episode? Was his work unsatisfactory? Either might have been too shameful to be rehearsed in the diary, or have inclined him to be more careful with his pen. But then a further entry offered another possibility.

I saw him again today. What is he doing here? 'Who' is he these days? I don't believe he recognized me. I'm thinner now, and stooped, but he's just the same – a handsome, confident bastard. A few of the secretarial staff gave him the up-and-down as he passed through the pool. If only they knew! I must find out who he is.

This was dated 12 January 1942 – just two days before a certain Hauptmann Fischer burned in a forest, far to the east. It was also written upon the very last sheet of paper in the notebook. There was no further entry on its other side.

Frau Traugott unlovely voice wafted upstairs, calling him down to supper. It was her fifth attempt, and it had acquired a keening edge by now. He was far enough into the life of Bruno Ahle to find the prospect of potato soup less than irresistible, but having come to an unavoidable pause there was nothing to be gained by fasting. He tucked the notebook into his inner tunic pocket and buttoned it.

His landlady hadn't lied about being able to make the best of very poor ingredients; even so, he resisted the temptation to ask how the soup had been raised beyond its expected limits. Unusually, his neighbours the Schultz sisters – in fact, they were identical twins - had joined them. They nodded silently as he was introduced, sat down, and, without a word, set themselves to the task of emptying their plates. For several moments Frau Traugott regarded them balefully, then commenced a monologue, ostensibly directed at her newest tenant, that required very little input to sustain. The price of knitting wool, gangs of ausländer muggers haunting Moabit's darkened streets that the authorities couldn't or didn't want to stop, the growing fashion in part-time wantonness among younger wives whose husbands were serving heroically at the Front and what-was-the-world-coming-to when prying *blockhelfers* made a fuss about respectable widows allegedly buying minuscule quantities of horsemeat on the black market – all of it paraded into Fischer's left ear without his offering more than a grunt whenever it threatened to slow. She had made a start on falling attendances at Sunday Service when the sisters (having tried and failed to remove the faint pattern from their bowls), stood and left the room without thanks or a goodnight.

That made Frau Traugott pause. Her eyes narrowed. 'They haven't paid rent now for four months.'

Surprised, Fischer looked up from his soup. 'Why don't you give them notice?'

She shrugged and sighed, pushing her own bowl away. 'It wouldn't be decent. Their husbands died on the same day in 1917, did I say? At Third Flanders. It must have been fate, and I don't want to add to something like that. They're no trouble, apart from the money.'

Fischer suspected that her hard-worn exterior sheltered a real Christian's heart. He offered no further comment, and it took only a further consignment of new air for her to launch into how pensions were hardly ever paid on their due-date any more. He nodded sympathetically, but his head was too far in Herr Ahle's business still – or rather, how that business might come around to bite his own tender parts.

Freddie Holleman wanted the diary returned, and the wisest thing would be to give it to him without making any comment upon its contents. He had never known Ahle, hardly knew Holleman but knew very well where a man might go if he crossed any one of the many people who might want this thing to be forgotten. Having already received an over-generous portion of ill-fortune he was under no illusions as to how well or long his luck might hold. The choice was easy enough.

But he couldn't forget what he had read, and having half a story was worse than none or all of it. Bruno Ahle had been a frightened man, though about *what* wasn't clear. According to Holleman he had transferred from Adlershof to the Lie Division in February 1942 - an unusual sidestep, given his aptitude for technical draughtsmanship. Had he asked for it? Had the handsome gentleman with the secretarial following been the catalyst? And what, if anything, had any of it to do with his subsequent decapitation and relocation to an s-bahn line?

He sensed already that he was going to discuss the thing with Holleman, despite every sensible reason not to. The diary's content had convinced him that there was no trap being laid by the other man – it was both too subtle and too dangerous a matter for any amateur Judas to touch when there were so many other, simpler hooks upon which to hang a denunciation. Unless he was an accomplice to Ahle's death there was a great likelihood that the denouncer would go the same way as the denounced, and probably into the same ditch. Still, it left the question of why he had approached Fischer, a stranger, with such a dangerous document.

He finished his soup, thanked Frau Traugott, had his offer to wash the dishes declined and decided to re-read the diary before sleeping. When it was done, he was more firm in his intention to discuss the matter with Holleman. They could hardly begin to address the mystery, but getting a thing out into the air often reduced its weight, and if they could then wash their hands of it the easier he would feel.

He fell asleep quickly, his mind soothed by the decision. Afterwards, he could recall no dreams, but at some point during the night the phantom that Major Nimtz had named the black cloak fell upon him, and when he awoke he couldn't get out of bed, much less dispose of a dangerous business.

9

Gerd Branssler ate his lunch with relish, though the bread roll was stale and its 'cheese' payload had been deployed from a tube. At least the cucumber that garnished it was fresh, having been plucked only that morning from the Branssler glasshouse (a tiny but indispensable construction beneath the south-facing kitchen window), and was bringing an unlikely hint of summer fields to Alexanderplatz.

The relish was supplied by an absence of Hubert Kranzusch - or rather, his arse and its noisome emissions. Usually, Branssler could get his food down only by closing his palate as a swimmer might, which blocked the farts but also the taste of what he was eating. Today, his partner was elsewhere, their tiny office felt a little more spacious and the (mostly) unpolluted air gave his appetite a rare edge.

The vacuum flask beside him contained real coffee, almost the last of a small stock of the Turkish variety that he and Kranzusch had uncovered during a raid on a blackmarketeer's home and partly re-allocated for their own use. Branssler's share lived in the same glasshouse, carefully wrapped in wax paper in a tray beneath the cucumbers, and given that one of his beautiful wife Greta's many virtues was an intense dislike of coffee, he had the treasure to himself.

He was savouring the last of that day's ration when a timid knock on the door had him scrambling to hide the evidence. A young man in an *OrPo*-green uniform and thick glasses entered, cap in hand, and cleared his throat nervously.

'Kriminalkommissar Kranzusch?'

Half-choking, Branssler gave himself a moment to clear his own throat while he shook his head.

'I'm the pretty one, Branssler. What do you want?'

'Nothing, sir. It's the Kriminalkommissar what sent for me.'

'Have you found his pearl earring, then?'

'I'm sorry?'

'Never mind. He's not around at the moment. In fact, I haven't seen him this morning. Who shall I say called?'

'*Unterwachtmeister* Petersen, from Nöldnerstrasse Station. He didn't say what it was about.'

The name rang a tiny, ugly bell, and the location confirmed it. Petersen had attended the discovery of Ahle's corpse, and Branssler couldn't say a word about it because it was already a non-corpse. No doubt Petersen had been very firmly apprised of the same fact, so what the fucking fuck Kranzusch thought he could accomplish by dragging the lad to Alexanderplatz was beyond imagining. He scowled at the innocent party.

'It's alright. I know what this is about, and you're no longer needed. I'll speak to the Kriminalkommissar.'

And by speaking, I mean I'm going to wedge my foot deeply into his fart-hatch.

For a moment, *Unterwachtmeister* Petersen looked as if he might argue the point, but then some small sentient spark told him that this was probably work that he hadn't wanted being taken from him. He nodded, fumbled with his tunic's breast-pocket button and removed a slip of paper.

'Will you countersign my summons slip, sir?'

Shit. The paper was evidence that the lad *had* been summoned from Nöldnerstrasse to Alexanderplatz, and that was a trail upon which Branssler wanted to leave not the slightest mark. He could think of no legitimate reason to refuse, however. He took the chit, made his signature as much of a scrawl as possible (as if that might deter a sensitive nose) and handed it back. It must have been nerves, or idiocy, that made him open his mouth and keep a dying conversation going instead of merely tossing his head at the door.

'What's keeping your station busy these days?'

Petersen shrugged, forgetting himself. 'The usual. Hooliganism, defeatist talk, petty theft, burglaries and busy street corners. I imagine it's the same everywhere.'

'Yeah, sounds familiar.' Branssler paused, inviting the boy to fill the silence, but he said nothing more. His face was open, unconcerned, so however the railway thing had been closed down at his station it had caused no obvious palpitations. *Ordnungspolizei* expected to have serious crimes taken from them at the earliest opportunity, and hell, this one had been fairly whipped away. Perhaps it hadn't been necessary to do more than give him the usual frown and careless talk speech to ensure his silence.

And Hubert Kranzusch had been thinking of uncorking the bottle. How stupid was the man?

Petersen was hovering still, and Branssler couldn't tell whether he was waiting to be dismissed or expecting more. He was about to wave him out of the office when the lad coughed.

'We also had that … suicide. On the S-bahn. We've had a few of those, over the past two years, but it's women, usually. We found the body.'

Branssler could feel his face warming. He nodded abruptly.

'Yes, we heard about that. But as you say, it happens … '

The word registered finally, and before he could stop himself his policeman's mouth betrayed him.

'We?'

'Me and Joachim - *Anwärter* Joachim Gaertner.' Petersen pulled a face. 'It was teamwork. I stumbled over the head, Joachim found the body.'

'Bad luck. It couldn't have been pleasant for either of you.'

'I doubt it bothers Joachim any more.'

'Why?'

'He died a week ago. He was hit by a car, they think. No other clues, so far.'

When Petersen had gone, Branssler took the deepest breath he could manage and held it for a few moments. At least now he had the means of stopping his partner in his tracks. It was perfectly possible that the unfortunate *Anwärter* Gaertner had been the victim of bad driving, but *kripos* were a suspicious breed who tended not to believe in random acts of fate. That *something* was wrong with the business was beyond doubt, so anything that reinforced the wrongness was circled with a red pen. Even Kranzusch would take heed, unless he had a mind to go the same way as Gaertner.

Branssler went out into the Pen, where a dozen unterkommissars were sharing space, stale cigarette smoke, and, at that moment, pornographic images confiscated from an arrested pimp. A couple of them noticed the interruption and grinned like schoolboys.

'Look at the size of these, Gerd.'

'Magnificent, Udo. Has anyone seem Bert this morning?'

'He came in about two hours ago, and went straight to the *OuK*'s office.'

'Are you sure?'

'Yeah. The *Kriminalrat* told me to pass on the message if I saw him, so I did.'

It might have been another formal boot up Kranzusch's arse for not doing his paperwork (though it shouldn't need the exalted foot of an *Oberregierungerat-und-Kriminaldirektor* to apply it), but Branssler's present state of mind wouldn't allow that possibility. He went back to his room, picked up an arrest report and stared at it for almost half-an-hour without taking in a single word. If this was as bad as he feared, there was a very sensitive trip-wire and Hubert Kranzusch had blundered into it. Whoever Bruno Ahle had been, and whatever he'd done, someone wanted his death to be forgotten, so the question was – how tidy would they make things? Kranzusch had flagged himself by summoning Petersen to Alexanderplatz, and on a usual working day the man sat a mere two metres from his partner. Was that proximity going to be fatal?

The tiny office suddenly felt far more claustrophobic than cosy. He glanced at the arrest report he was holding. A suspected arsonist had been detained at Güntzelstrasse station, and a Criminal Investigations officer was requested to conduct a preliminary interview. Normally, he would have handed the job to one of the unter-bulls in the Pen, but he had a sudden, strong need for fresh air and clear thinking. He stood, turned to grab his coat and almost leapt into the air when the office door crashed open behind him.

Huubert Kranzusch blocked his escape route. He was grinning – an idiot, smug grin that a man in his predicament had no right or reason to wear.

'Who's the rising man, then?'

'Eh?'

"Go on – ask me.'

'Who, then?'

'Hubert Waldemar Kranzusch, is who!'

'What's happened?'

'Elevation, mate. One or more of the idiots upstairs have realised that I'm too precious to be wasted on shit-shovelling. As of today, I'm assigned to *V-WI*, Breslau, with the rank of *Kriminalrat*, acting.'

'I didn't know that Breslau had an economic affairs Amt.'

What Branssler had meant to say was that he hadn't suspected their superiors of *that* degree of blind idiocy, but apparently he had misdiagnosed them. Kranzusch knew as much about corruption and crimes against the economy as he did about basket-weaving, and had an equal interest in both.

'It's being set up at the moment. The *OuK* said they needed an energetic type to make sure that it bolted rather than staggered out of the traps.'

Again, Kranzusch's idea of heavy lifting was to excavate both his nostrils before the morning's first coffee-break, so Breslau's fledgling *WI* department was likely to remain in 'the traps' indefinitely. Branssler, dumbfounded, managed at least to find the right form of words.

'Congratulations, Bert. No-one deserves it more.'

'No, they don't.' The grin, unbearable already, was enhanced by an unconvincing attempt at pleased surprise. 'The *OuK*'s even organized my train ticket! I'm leaving tomorrow evening.'

'Tomorrow? That's ...'

'Just enough time to hand over to my replacement. You're getting a new partner. His name's Dieter Thomas.' Kranzusch sniggered.

'What?'

'You'll need to watch your mouth, Gerd. His uncle's in Amt IV. He must have some pull, because young Dieter's a strapping young lad who'd grace any front-line regiment, and yet doesn't.'

Branssler groaned. A Gestapo nephew was the last thing that any sane man would want as an item of furniture. No doubt the little bastard knew nothing about real police work and less about the difference between right and wrong, which meant that as a working partner he would be as much use as a gate in a bowling alley, and doubtless as obstructive. Worse (and this was what was giving the loose-mouthed Kranzusch the tickles) every word that Branssler uttered would have to be vetted as it passed his tonsils if he wasn't to get a helping of what he'd been dishing out to suspects for years.

Kranzusch looked around their tiny office and smacked his lips. 'What this place needs is a little more ideological *soundness*.'

He was close to losing teeth at that moment, but then the door opened once more and a very muscular young man squeezed himself into the paltry free space. Nervously, he nodded at both men.

'*Kriminalkommissar* Branssler?'

Kranzusch pointed a finger at the other resident and smirked. 'You'll be Thomas, I expect. I'll leave you two sweethearts to get to know each other. Gerd, if anyone asks about my paperwork, tell them ...'

'Yeah, I know. '

10

Frau Traugott opened her front door to a man in uniform. Though not an expert on war and its dress codes, the eagle on both cap and tunic suggested that he was Luftwaffe, which steadied her heart a little. As far as she knew, Luftwaffe didn't have an SS branch.

The gentleman wore a dashing eye-patch and a handsome smile, both of which stirred vestigial girlish urges. He even saluted her, a slightly loose, debonair wave of the hand that couldn't have been to regulation but certainly worked on her. She returned the smile (fearing that it might seem more of a simper).

After the salute, a little bow. 'Good afternoon, Frau …?'

'Traugott.' She squeaked a little.

'I'd like to see Hauptmann Fischer, if I may?'

'He's not in trouble?'

'Trouble? Of course not. I understand that he's a little … poorly?'

'He's …' She was going to say *unsettled*, but that could mean anything from preoccupied to drooling, and she wasn't sure how far between those states his present condition stood. All she knew for certain was that mental fragility didn't get too much official sympathy these days, and any uniform – dashing or otherwise – was a symptom of officialdom.

'… not at his best.'

'Oh, dear.' The officer frowned, and though Frau Traugott was no more an expert on frowns than military attire, it seemed to convey more concern than irritation, or impatience.

'I'm his commanding officer, Oberstleutnant Krohne, from the Ministry. They gave me the message that he wouldn't be coming in today. Was that you …?'

She nodded. 'There's a number in the directory. For the Luftwaffe. Was it the right one?'

Krohne suppressed a smile. The Air Ministry was fully sensitive to its own grandeur, and he could only imagine the outrage at its telephone exchange when an old lady called to explain that Herr Otto Fischer wouldn't be coming out to play today. Fortunately, when his name was located to the KdL (known to the building's other staff as the Cripples' Newsroom) tempers had cooled. The message had been passed on to Krohne without comment, though quite brusquely.

'Yes, it came straight to me.'

'You'd better come in, then.'

She showed him up to the top floor, gestured at a door and withdrew. He knocked once and entered. The truant, braces unslung and shirt sleeves rolled to the elbow, was sitting at a small table by the window, staring at his hands. In an ashtray, three half-smoked cigarettes had been stubbed out, and a bottle of Slivovitz sat unopened beside it. That at least gave Krohne hope that he was seeing a treatable case of something very familiar.

'Shall we have a drink, Otto?'

'Mm? Oh, hello, Karl. Here ...' Fischer slid the bottle towards his boss; '... have some, if you like. It's too much for my throat.'

'I won't, then. To be honest, I think that stuff's as bad as the *Silver Birch*'s extra reserve piss.'

Fischer half-smiled. 'It's poison, isn't it? I don't know what I was thinking.'

'You probably weren't. Did you have a bad night?'

'How did you know?'

'It's usually night when it happens. The darkness amplifies everything.'

'It does, doesn't it?'

'May I guess what it was?'

'If you like.'

'As long as you were in care, getting treatment and seeing small improvements it was alright – bad, but bearable, because it was a process with a start and a finish. Now, you're back in the Normal, only nothing *is* normal, is it? You've reached the all-the-rest-of-your-life part, and you can't see how it's going to work out.'

Fischer nodded slowly. 'Is that how it was for you?'

'Christ, no! I just lost an eye. In another age it might have been a duelling injury, and they don't come any more fashionable than that. No, it's what I've seen sometimes since we first staffed the Lie Division.'

'I thought you didn't like that name.'

'Only because it's too near the mark. The thing is, there's probably also a name for what you're ...'

'A doctor at Potsdam called it the Black Cloak. If you'll forgive the pun, it fits.'

'It sounds right. Some people experience it, others don't. Salomon Weiss was very bad for a while. He thought he wasn't fit for anything, any more – didn't even want his parents to know about the injury, but of course he couldn't keep it quiet indefinitely. Bruno Ahle dealt with it - if *dealt* is the right word – by retreating into his personal trench and very rarely allowing his head to show. Freddie Holleman, on the other hand ...'

'He was alright?'

'He was in a dark mood one day, and my diagnosis was bad. When I mentioned his injury in a sympathetic way he stared at me for a moment and said *it's a fucking leg, Karl - nothing to cry about.*'

'I envy him.'

'I wouldn't. It's probably a lack of imagination, not fortitude.'

'Still, if it helps ...'

Krohne smiled. 'He's not really as thick-headed as he pretends to be, but it's a damned good act.'

'Do you trust him?'

'Trust? In what way? With my wallet, never – at least, not in a bar. But next to me in a fight, without doubt. Why do you ask?'

'Because I want to keep you talking about something other than me.'

Krohne smiled. 'I'm sorry. Am I prying?'

'It's the whole psychoanalytical thing. Looking too deeply into a swamp ... I don't know. What will it tell us, other than it's dark, muddy and smells bad?'

'Well, the Party agrees with you on that. Ironic, really, given the many excellent test subjects Herr Freud might have found among them.'

Fischer looked sharply at his visitor. There it was again - an almost suicidal indifference to offering offering an opinion that could put a man under the blade. Was there something in the Air Ministry's water that removed discretion? Or did a badly-burned face give a man an iconoclastic air he didn't warrant? Holleman, Reincke and now Krohne had said things that should never have met air, much less be offered to a stranger. He was beginning to wonder if Adlershof might be a safer posting after all, notwithstanding its inadequate defences. At least there the bombs would come only from the one direction.

'You're thinking I should watch my mouth?'

Krohne wore an open, guileless expression, as if they were discussing the etiquette of belching before or after Holy Communion.

'I am, yes. You don't know me.'

'True, but I've never met a man returned from the Front after taking a kicking who's managed to hold on to his … *enthusiasm*. And I've never met anyone who's taken as much of a kicking as you.'

'Hardly a robust measure of who might or might not turn you in.'

'And yet I'm breathing still. Not only that, but I'm sometimes sent to Prinz-Albrecht-Strasse to brief Kaltenbrunner, who they say can sniff out bad thinking like a pig finds a truffle.'

'You're a man of two faces, perhaps?'

'At least that many. How could I have been a newspaperman, otherwise?'

Fischer had the impression that Krohne's nonchalance was well-practised, and that he could throw out a *Heil!* with as much fervour as anyone who had to deal with Kaltenbrunner. It was an interesting theory, though. Offhand, he couldn't think of a single poor bastard in his ward at Potsdam who'd had a good word to say about anyone in a brown uniform (or black, for that matter).   Men who don't suffer the consequences of a decision (or an *enthusiasm)* have little cause for regret; but suffer them long and painfully enough and it takes a rare stupidity not to wish that one's feet had taken a different path.

It came to him suddenly that Krohne's amateur therapy – if that's what it was – might be having an effect. When he'd woken that morning he couldn't pull the sheet from his face, much less get out of bed. What would have been the point – to wash as usual, apply glycerin to mutations that would never subside and pretend that he was moving towards a semblance of life as it had been before 14 January 1942? A weight of hopelessness pressed him into his mattress, a comfortable, warm place to be, and urged him not to bother getting up, dressing or conveying himself to a desk from which he would spend several hours telling lies to the German people.

Now, he felt ridiculous, because what had been a mood had become a performance (albeit with an audience of just one), and Otto Henry Fischer was a laughable tragedian. That Krohne had managed to pin even a part of his misery made the thing almost cliched, and the sufferer likewise. He stood and stretched, making his boss wince as a bone in his back cracked.

'I'll be in this afternoon, if that's alright?'

'Take the whole day if you need.'

'No, your cure seems to have worked. I am no longer a burden to the Reich, unless they need me to do press-ups.'

Krohne grinned and picked up his cap. 'That's the way! And if you relapse I'll send Freddie Holleman in my place next time.'

'A threat that works better than morphine, believe me.'

'Strangely, he seemed a little twitchy this morning, when we got the message that you weren't well. Do you owe him money already?'

For the first time since he awoke, Fischer recalled the diary in his tunic pocket. It was something to be twitchy about, certainly, but the black cloak had flattened his sense of perspective. For several hours the enemy had been the threat of future days, not an unquantifiable mess gifted to him by Freddie Holleman (for God knew what reason). It was almost a relief to feel the familiar gut-punch of anxiety once more.

'Tell him I haven't forgotten the little matter we discussed, and that I'll speak to him later. And thank you, Karl. It was thoughtful of you to make the effort.'

'We surplus-to-establishment gentlemen have to stand together. Besides, it's been a pleasant morning away from the Ministry.'

'I doubt it. Were you told that this was part of the job, when you set up the Lie Division?'

Krohne snorted. 'I don't believe the Reichsmarschall gives much of a damn for the welfare of those of his men who can't fight. His own war is going too badly, I think.'

It was no secret that Göring was losing the battle of Wilhelmstrasse to Himmler. He had made too many promises to the Führer and failed to meet them, and at each failure the bland little clerk had been waiting to pounce upon another sliver of his once-wide empire. Lately, it hadn't been a fair competition, given that Göring's enemies fought back in the skies above Europe, whereas the Reichsführer wasn't held accountable for the field operations of his Waffen SS. He was measured only by the success of operations against the Reich's domestic foes, who were proving very amenable. They obeyed clearance orders, packed their own suitcases and queued at the railway stations, and even Hitler could hardly fault the pace at which German streets were being cleared of their presence.

Stalingrad had probably removed the last memory of the Führer's affection for the Reichsmarschall, whose visits to the Air Ministry were increasingly devoted to rattling the cages of his subordinates in turn and demanding more of what wasn't possible. It was hardy a wonder that he had little time for other men's agonies.

Fischer shrugged. 'As are all our wars. But of course, I wouldn't dream of saying so.'

11

A summons to Obergruppenführer Kaltenbrunner's office was never sugar-icing on anyone's day, but Herr Blond wasn't worried by it. The Director of RSHA often bypassed his Amt heads to speak to their immediate subordinates on operational matters, and some of Blond's responsibilities – particularly surveillance – were of personal interest to him. In fact, his obsession with stamping out homosexuality in German society came close to raising suspicions, and every raid that netted some well-known (non-Party) figure with unconventional sexual tastes was guaranteed to goad the man into some new scheme to eradicate the ailment. His latest suggestion – not as yet taken up by the Chancellery – was to implement a statutory castration programme for all convicted offenders, so Christ alone knew how he would better that one.

No celebrity homos having been dragged recently from a crowded bed, Blond was mildly curious as to what matter might be so urgent as to call him upstairs. He told his secretary to free the morning (Kaltenbrunner rarely spoke briefly about anything, including the weather), checked his appearance in the washroom mirror and took the stairs two at a time.

He was waved into the Obergruppenführer's office. Kaltenbrunner was standing by his bookcase, making even his large office look smaller than it was. He had a fearsome appearance, not softened by the scars that disfigured his left cheek, so the book in his hand seemed as appropriate as lemon torte in a wolf's mouth. He looked up with an entirely unconvincing air of distraction.

'Standartenführer Messenfer. Thank you for coming.'

Blond never used his SS rank (he still thought of himself as a Reichskriminaldirektor, which in any case sounded more impressive), but he knew better than to say something about it. His heels clicked together smartly, and he offered a shoulder-spraining salute.

'Heil Hitler!'

It was absurdly formal, but, like other Austrians in senior roles, Kaltenbrunner insisted that the proper forms were observed.

'Please sit.'

Blond settled himself into an armchair. The cigarette box was offered but he declined. The rumour was that, lately, the Obergruppenführer had been affecting his patron Himmler's distaste for the habit, so abstinence was almost certainly going to become the fashion at Prinz-Albrecht-Strasse.

Kaltenbrunner sat behind his desk and offered his guest a pleasant smile (it seemed a trespasser on that face).

'How long have you been with the police, Standartenführer?'

It was a rhetorical question. RSHA had detailed files on all its personnel, and particularly thick ones on those who had clambered to the top of the pole. Nevertheless, Blond played the game, and even made a pretence of consulting his memory.

'It must be, oh, twenty-four years now. Yes, I came back from the war in 1919 and went straight into Criminal Investigations, here in Berlin. In fact, the year before the Gruppenführer himself joined.'

'So he was the new boy! Ha!'

Unsurprisingly, Kaltenbrunner's attempt at jocularity was even more forced than the smile, but Blond affected to find the feeble thrust hilarious. He slapped his thigh and laughed.

'Yes! He was assigned to my group for a short time, and I helped show him how things worked.'

'Like the coffee pot!'

Jesus. 'Indeed. A *kripo* needs fuelling, Herr Obergruppenführer.'

'Yes, well. You've enjoyed the challenges, obviously.' Kaltenbrunner glanced done at his notes. 'And you've never been seconded to other departments within RSHA?'

'We haven't *been* within RSHA for fully four years yet. Before that, the best and most advantageous experience was to be found exactly where I was.'

'I suppose that's true. I ask because we've been looking at manning recently ...'

Here it comes.

'... that is, since special operations in the East were terminated and personnel returned to the Reich. It seems that Amt V is somewhat overstaffed at present.'

'Not at the top, surely? I've had responsibility for two departments for the past few months, and Standartenführer Bernauer has the same.'

'Yes that's a temporary difficulty. In fact, we're thinking of moving several senior Amt IV men to Amt V, and we'd like to have you go the other way. A year's experience over there will be invaluable for your future prospects. You're all *Sicherheitspolizei* now, after all.'

Blond really didn't want to go to Gestapo – not even for a week, much less a month. He had no reservations about their work or methods, but having Heinrich Müller as his immediate superior was a prospect to be relished as much as a difficult tooth extraction. The man regarded a day with his feet up as an unthinkable abomination, and he expected his subordinates to feel the same way. He was also unreadable, having a 'personality' that made Himmler's seem almost a model of openness. Friendless, disliked by most senior men in the Party (he had joined late and very reluctantly), utterly secretive and not in the habit of explaining his orders beyond the minimum required to have them executed efficiently, Müller would be a grinding taskmaster.

But this was RSHA, and career paths weren't laid out at a man's convenience. Blond managed a smile, and did his best to sound pleased.

'It's an honour to serve as best I can, Herr Obergruppenführer. Will I retain my present rank?'

'For the moment, yes. But be diligent, and who can say what will come next?'

'May I ask to which Amy IV department I'm to be assigned?'

'It hasn't been decided finally, but you have a good deal of experience in surveillance, and I wouldn't want that to be wasted.'

The work of *all* Gestapo departments (with the exception of C - Administrative and Party Matters) was built upon surveillance, so Blond was no wiser for that. At least he'd be useful, which meant that this probably wasn't a demotion by another name. It could hardly be regarded as good news, but there were many worse reasons to be summoned to Kaltenbrunner's presence than to be offered a side-step, however strangely timed.

'When shall I transfer?'

'With immediate effect.'

'But my present workload ...'

'Will be effectively assigned, you needn't worry about that. I'd like you to speak to Gruppenführer Müller today – he's in the building now, in fact, interviewing ... ' Kaltenbrunner paused, made a poor show of thinking through something, and then smiled.

'I shouldn't really say this yet, but you'll be pleased to know that you'll not be feeling like *the new boy* when you start. Standartenführer Bernauer has already accepted a transfer to Amt IV, so you old friends will be going across together. I hope you won't be giving poor Müller a hard time!'

Blond felt the ground move beneath him. Suddenly, it all made the very worst sort of sense. He and 'Schwarz' had given themselves headaches wondering who might have wanted the body on the tracks to be buried – in every way - as a suicide. That still wasn't clear, but the second, most important part of the question was halfway to its answer. If the Director of RSHA himself was manoeuvring them both out Criminal Investigations at short – at *no* – notice, then they needn't concern themselves further with how dangerous this might be. Blond no longer cared why an insignificant Luftwaffe veteran had died badly and then been carefully misplaced, only that his own name be dragged as far from the business as possible. If it took a transfer to Gestapo to do that, he hardly cared if they put him in charge of Yellow Star relocations, or the card index.

12

Fischer kept his word, put in an afternoon's shift at the Air Ministry and didn't disgraced himself. During those hours he and Holleman exchanged looks several times, but they had no opportunity to speak. Just before the office closed at 7pm he went to the bookcase to replace the adjectives folder, and on his way put a box-file on the other man's desk. It was empty, other than for a small, deadly notebook. The relief on Holleman's face was almost comically obvious, but the other Liars were too busy tidying away the day's work to notice.

'Are the others going to the *Silver Birch*?'

For once, the name didn't light up Holleman's face. He nodded wistfully.

'Yeah.'

'Is there anywhere else we can ...'

'Nowhere I'd care to be overheard.'

'We'll speak tomorrow then.'

Fischer feared another night's close examination of an invisible ceiling, but he slept well and dreamlessly. He was wakened early by Frau Traugott, who brought him coffee (it was her excuse to check his mental condition before he had a chance to upset the sisters below). Reassured, she retreated to allow him to wash, dress, refuse another fried potato breakfast and leave the house early.

Like all bureaucratic hubs, the Air Ministry largely kept to office hours (the not-infrequent senior panic-briefings aside), and Fischer entered an almost empty reception hall at 7.20am. One of the guards on the main doors (a fallen-arched First War veteran who had been pointed out to him as the building's - and possibly the city's - premier supplier of black market prophylactics) nodded morosely as he arrived but declined to come to attention. For a moment he was tempted to put the rhetorical boot up the man's fundament, but a recollection of Krohne's kindness the previous day made him think of stones, cast. He softened his reaction to a frown and a nod.

Holleman was in the Liars' den already, smoking his way through the *Morgenpost*. Two steaming mugs sat on his desk, and he pushed one towards Fischer as he entered.

'I saw you coming through the gates. What did you think of it?'

'The notebook? My first thought was that it shouldn't exist.'

'No, it's not what you'd expect. I suppose he didn't get enough excitement dodging English wing-cannons. Why else would a man take a risk like that?'

'He was an idiot?'

Holleman smiled. 'Or a literary type, keen to capture historic events before his memory failed. Which is as much as to say an idiot.'

'You didn't know him well?'

'No-one here did. He was a lot more discrete in life than on paper. We tried to get him out of his shell a few times, but he didn't play, and jokes either went over his head or he had no sense of humour. He definitely had no conversation beyond his work.'

'No family?'

'Widowed, I think. No children – at least, none he mentioned. When he came back to Berlin he lived in barracks at Adlershof and then Tempelhof.'

Fischer stared down into his mug of … something, though certainly not coffee. 'If you didn't really know him, why are you bothering with this?'

The big man sighed and scratched his head. 'I've been wondering that. When my *kripo* mate told me the details I got the old tingle, but it's been years since I was police. It's not my business. It isn't *anyone's* business - that's been made clear enough. But ...'

'But?'

'It isn't right. The poor bastard was harmless – I mean, he couldn't raise his cap without needing to brace himself. He'd done his time, got his wounds and made it home, and that's all that should be expected of a man. But some swine decided to cack him, and not for rage's sake. It was fucking cold, and planned.'

'You can't be sure of that. A machine might have ...'

'A machine might have. But a machine didn't carry him to the s-bahn and arrange the body. And no machine then frightened the police into pretending they'd found a suicide. It was an execution, and if Ahle had done something to deserve it there should have been a trial first and a few lines in the papers about it.'

Holleman's rough logic was sound, but it didn't address the real issue. Fischer raised both his hands, palms upward.

'What can be done? I mean, what can *we* do, other than talk ourselves into trouble? We're not police any more, and even if we were, I don't recall that investigations were ever conducted on a voluntary basis.'

'I know, but ...'

'And if we *were* daft enough to push our faces into this, where would we start looking, and what would we be looking for? Can we demand to see witness files? Knock on doors and ask questions? Interrogate your *kripo* mate's bosses about why they decided to pretend that a train's wheels took off poor Ahle's head?'

Christ, I'm doing it now. I'm calling him poor Ahle.

Holleman squinted at the wall for a moment. 'I don't know, I don't know, no, no and no. I just want ...'

'What do you want?'

'To just *talk* about it.'

Fischer blew out his cheeks and looked around. At 7.45am the den was empty still, and no better opportunity was likely to present itself (particularly not later, at the *Silver Birch*, where intelligent thought and quiet voices weren't likely to survive a first round of Special Brew).

'Alright. What do *you* think?'

'He was scared of something.'

'I don't know if we can say that. He was *surprised* about the presence of someone at Adlershof, and perhaps anxious. He didn't like the man, certainly, but he seems to have disliked quite a few people. And the diary ends before we get a better sense of where it was going.'

'Was *he* the same one whose behaviour Ahle complaned about in France, in 1940?'

'The one he called *the M*? I wondered about that.'

'I thought M must mean major, his squadron leader.'

'My first thought, too. I don't suppose Ahle ever mentioned him?'

'No. But his squadron was KG55/1, and I checked its complement in June 1940.'

'You did *what*?'

'Don't worry, I didn't even need to open my mouth. You can wander in and out of Personnel Records – no-one ever asks what you're doing up there.'

'Up there?'

Holleman jabbed a finger towards the den's ceiling. 'Next floor.'

'Jesus.'

'Anyway, during Operation *Paula* his squadron leader was Major Hans Korte.'

'The name's vaguely familiar.'

'He was promoted to Group Commodore two months later, after Alois Stoeckl got shot down over England.'

'I don't suppose there's anything in the records to suggest that Korte was known to behave badly?'

'No, but as he's now the General commanding 13th Flieger-Division, I doubt that he's the one who offended Ahle.'

'Good soldiers can be bad men.'

Offended, Holleman shook his head. 'Not in Luftwaffe. SS or Heer, possibly.'

It *was* doubtful that a man of poor character would have risen as far and as fast as Korte. Luftwaffe retained an absurdly inflated sense of its knightly ethos, and frowned upon those who stained it. The sins of a fighter pilot with a good kill record would be tolerated for utility's sake, but men promoted to Group level and then the General Staff needed to know how to behave among the porcelain. Again, Fischer wished Ahle hadn't been so delicate about what, to his mind, had constituted bad behaviour.

A scraping of chair legs made both men turn. Detmar Reincke was attempting to manoeuvre a full cup of something steaming on to his desk while making space for his arse in the seat. Given that one of his arms had been amputated at the elbow this was necessarily more complicated than it might have been for lesser men, and his desk was already half-covered in spilled liquid.

Holleman tsked. 'Put the cup down, you cock! *Then* move the chair.'

He turned back to Fischer, and when he spoke again it was almost a whisper. 'Do you know what I think?'

'That we've exhausted this conversation?'

'That people who keep diaries don't decide not to, any more.'

'Samuel Pepys did.'

'Who?'

'Never mind. You think there's another volume somewhere?'

'The final entry was on the last page of the notebook, and Ahle didn't die for several months after that date. Could he have made another entry the next day, in a nice new notebook?'

'Where is it?'

Holleman shrugged, and sat back. 'I found this one while I was clearing out his desk. Perhaps he kept it here because he didn't trust anyone not to search his barracks box. What if the other one was in his tunic pocket?'

'Then it's beyond our reach. In fact, it's almost certainly burned.'

'Yeah – *if* the diary's why he was executed.'

'If it isn't, we're even further from any clue as to what happened.'

'I know, it's frustrating. Hush, here's Karl with the day's crap.'

Their leader was at the door of the den, beckoning his troops with a sheath of papers. Though his uniform was neat he had the pained, distracted look of someone who had spent the previous night in a tank ditch, or hedge, and there was a trace of what might have been blood on his shirt collar. Holleman sniggered quietly.

Fischer glanced at him. 'What?'

'He's been banging his hairdresser.'

'Eh?'

'Karl's a man who loves women.'

'I thought he was married.'

'A correct thought, but the vows didn't stick. Every few weeks the pressure in his balls hits the red line and he has to spin the valve. His latest relief is a young thing who works in a salon. He pays part of her rent, apparently.'

'And his wife doesn't mind?'

'If she knew he wouldn't need to worry about his balls – they'd be in the dustbin. I can only think that he must miss the danger of flying.'

Though Fischer had known Krohne for less than a week, the man's kindness had left a mark and he felt obliged to put a case for the defence.

'Perhaps he just had a rough night?'

Holleman laughed loudly. 'Oh, he had that, alright. I refer you to the lipstick mark. No doubt there's one that matches on his other collar.'

Having nothing more to offer on that subject, Fischer went to his desk. From Krohne, Holleman received a situation report on the Luftwaffe's deployment of the new Messerschmidt 323s to resupply the Afrika Corps and was told to make a national celebration from it. He had only just put his pen in his mouth and given the paper a preliminary frown when a shadow crossed his desk. The new man had returned, and he looked worried.

'What's wrong?'

'My desk drawer – Ahle's, I should say. The lock's been forced.'

'Fuck.'

'So it's settled one question.'

'Which one?'

'The one about whether there's another, subsequent diary. If there isn't, they wouldn't have known to come looking for the earlier one, would they?'

13

In the offices of *Deutsche Versuchsanstalt für Luftfahrt*, at the south-eastern perimeter of Adlershof airfield, a man in a well-cut suit was leafing through a technical report (a large part of which, if pressed, he might have quoted from memory). He had been involved in the process it described since its inception, some four years earlier. Being an aerodynamicist, he had spent much time here and at the Reich's other major wind-tunnel facilities, slowly perfecting the necessary innovations to accommodate the project's ground-breaking technology. That phase was now over (or would have been, if a certain gentleman could make up his mind as to what, precisely, he wanted the finished machine to *do*), but whenever he was called to Berlin he used this office to transact project business. Familiarity had made it a comfortable place to work, despite the site's ever-present danger of being done unto as he and his colleagues planned to do to the Allies.

The intercom on his desk buzzed, and he pressed the receiver.

'The gentleman from Völkenrode is here, Herr Direktor.'

'Please send him in.'

The man who entered carried a bottle of French champagne, and as he held it out his face wore a familiar *goodness, how did this come to be in my hand?* cast that always made his host laugh. They were old friends, long-associated with almost every major research project intended to make objects fly higher, faster and with ever-more deadly intent.

'Hansi, you old thief! Have you raided the Reichsmarschall's personal Mess?'

'Alaric's fabled treasure? If only I had the map. No, this has been sitting in my office at Völkenrode for months now. I always hope for an occasion to open it and I'm always disappointed. I know that you aerodynamics fellows have more frequent occasion to pop the champers.'

'I was going to ask about your engines.'

'Don't, Ludwig - it would be the same answer as always. The Juno is more reliable, the BMW more promising, but problems with the fuel-feed system, vibration issues and quality of available alloys are what keeps us awake at night. The successful test flights raised us all, of course, and we expected to make rapid progress after that. But you know how it is with resources these days – everyone has priorities, and Willy Messerschmidt concentrates on what he can build and put into the air in significant numbers, not his difficult births. The delay's been disappointing for all of us, but it's still new science.'

'Have you heard anything from the Chancellery lately? You have more contacts there than I.'

Hansi's face darkened. 'Also as before. I have no opinion of course, but were a hypothetical case to be made, I would say that a ground-attack bomber would be a ridiculous waste of our efforts. Even if it did the job brilliantly we'll never produce enough of them to make a difference against the Red tide. In any case – and it's not a small issue - I suspect that we'll be unable to design external bomb racks that won't tear off during dives that approach 650kph. A pure fighter, on the other hand, would not only do much to re-secure air-supremacy in the east but break up the mass bomber formations that the western Allies are almost certainly going to send over, sooner or later. It's frustrating, not to be able to have the argument heard.'

Ludwig had been nodding gently as his friend spoke. 'The problem is, Göring is the only man who could put the argument effectively, and he's not listened to these days.'

'I know. It's damned ironic that his fall from grace came just as we finally managed to raise his enthusiasm for the project.'

'Well, circumstances may help us as we overcome the technical problems. You know that the test flights so far suggest that the aircraft has the potential to be highly manoeuvrable – far more so than the FW-190 and BF-109. That quality will be wasted if it's overloaded with ordnance.'

'I'm sure that the Führer will want both versions to go ahead, but you know how it is. If he insists that the *schnellbomber* takes priority, tooling and production issues will ensure that we never make more than a handful of the *schwalbe* that the Luftwaffe really needs. And when, inevitably, those noble few fail to make a strategic impact, he'll turn to us and say *see - I was right all along.*'

Ludwig said nothing to that. They were dangerous words, if prescient. They had all learned to be stoical, and having given the matter a little air there was no point in working it further. Besides, it wasn't why he'd asked Hansi to fly in from Brunswick.

He cleared his throat. 'I was wondering if there'd been any further ... *embarrassments* in the Wind Tunnels Maintenance Department?'

There were wind tunnels aplenty at Völkenrode, but no department devoted solely to their maintenance. Hansi got the point immediately, however. He shook his head.

'None. It was made clear that if an incident occurred on site there would be only one suspect, and he would face the full rigour of a legal investigation. Naturally, he isn't permitted to visit Braunschweig unaccompanied. He doesn't seem to mind the restrictions, and may even be relieved that the choice has been removed. He *did* ask for a period of home leave recently. It was refused.'

'Good. Has his work suffered?'

No, it's exemplary. He's provided many of the weight-shifting calculations that will allow us to put more MK 108 cannons in the nose section, should we get the pure fighter that we want. *And* he's doing the same for the proposed anti-tank variant.'

'Anti-tank. Dear God!'

'I know. It won't happen. I mention it merely to stress his importance to the project. There aren't many of our colleagues who can think sideways, as he often does.'

'As long as he's kept … well, safe.'

'I spoke recently to an old friend. He's a head trauma specialist at Heidelberg, but in his university days he had an interest in aberrant psychology.'

'A courageous man.'

'One could think of such things, back then. These days he's more prudent, obviously. In the most general terms I spoke of the problem and its potential persistence. He said that it isn't uncommon for certain conditions to be worsened or alleviated by external stimulae.'

'What, drugs?'

'I think he meant conditions or circumstances, not treatment. We all know that war can have an extreme effect upon men's minds. Perhaps its absence – or rather, its removal to a safe distance – lessens the effect.'

'*If* it was war that caused it, rather than something in the womb.'

'Yes, but as I say, he seems not to be as much … *moved* by the old urges as he was.'

Ludwig rubbed his cheek. 'Well, I leave it to you to ensure that he continues to behave. I've done everything I can at Prinz-Albrecht-Strasse. To be honest, I didn't think they'd be so obliging, or prompt.'

'It was fortunate that we have a friend there.'

'Not so much a friend, more an enemy of an enemy.'

Hansi smiled. 'He can console himself that he did the right thing – or the least wrong thing.'

'You know the man, at least by reputation. I doubt that he's ever consciously applied himself to what's *right*.'

They both laughed. Ludwig rose from his desk, went to a cabinet and removed two glasses. His first instinct had been to save the champagne for a special occasion, but the present one would have to do. It wasn't as though the project had been burdened by happy news in recent months - and in any case, offering his friend a glass of something delightful was infinitely preferable to telling him about the unfortunate complication.

14

Karl Krohne returned from an appointment at Prinz-Albrecht-Strasse with a faint smile on his face. This was sufficiently unusual for the Liars to start a book on what it might mean. The shortest odds were offered on a quick detour to around-the-corner Friedrichstadt for a restorative poke with his hairdresser; the longest on Freddie Holleman's suggestion that America had abandoned the British after their reverses in Tunisia and sued for peace. Everyone risked three marks on the outcome (including Fischer, whose career with the *Kriegsberichter der Luftwaffe* was as yet too unsteady on its feet to carry a miserable sod's reputation), and Salomon Weiss pocketed his winnings an hour later when the likeliest cause – a small German success on some front, somewhere, was announced to them.

'And for once, we can play up Luftwaffe's major contribution to the victory.'

'We were there, were we?'

'We were there in *force*, Freddie. Manstein himself made a point of praising Luftflotte 4's efforts. They flew more than a thousand sorties a day for almost four weeks, keeping our ground casualties down and the Ivans' up.'

'And the result …?'

'We've re-taken Kharkov and Belgorod!'

'Is there anything in either city still standing by now?'

Krohne frowned at his briefing paper. 'It doesn't say. It doesn't matter. What we produce will be going to both *Signal* and *Der Adler*, and I'm told that Goebbels may incorporate our Luftwaffe comments into his broadcast tomorrow evening, so *I can't be arsed* is not our motto for today, right? All of you will get a copy of this, and the one whose version I like the most will get a very small bottle of real french perfume for the wife or loved one.'

The Liars each took their copy and read it through. Kharkov and Belgorod had been cleared of their Soviet defenders two weeks earlier, so this was hardly news to them. Word had been withheld from the German people, however, until Army Group South could be certain that Zhukov hadn't organized another double pincer movement that might re-re-capture this most fought-over ground. A little crowing was now in order, though having lost five cities in February to retake only two in April, it was hardly likely that von Manstein would be getting a rosette just yet.

Fischer read his copy and was straining his empty mind for something inspiring when a giggle made him turn. Holleman had requisitioned a towel from somewhere and was wearing it on his head like a prizefighter as he slumped over his desk, staring down at his briefing paper. The other Liars were grinning, waiting for a version that almost certainly wasn't going to be broadcast to a hopeful nation. Eventually, he groaned, lifted his head and spoke in a deep microphone voice.

'The knights of the air, careless of danger, threw themselves upon the Soviet masses, death swathing through their degenerate ranks. A bloody dawn had broken over Kharkov, while the mincing *florenzers* of II SS Panzer Corps were still climbing into their French knickers.'

'Ha! Wonderful!'

Every Liar's head (including that of their Xenophon) turned to the door. Incredibly, it was partially blocked by the body of Generalfeldmarschall Erhard Milch, Inspector-General (and, since Udet's death, Master-General) of the Luftwaffe. Behind him, an ashen-faced Krohne glared furiously into the den but otherwise seemed paralysed.

Milch must have been at the Ministry for a high-level meeting because he was carrying his feldmarschall's baton, an object useless for everything except prompting people to jump quickly in the right direction. No doubt Göring was here too, though as usual his contribution would be less than that of the men who brought the coffee and cake (it was commonly understood that, at an executive level, the Reichsmarschall's job was to wear ridiculous uniforms and be shouted at by the Führer, while Milch did everything else).

He had never before visited the War Reporters' Unit, so it could only be their rare good news that had brought him here today. He turned, beaming at each astonished face in turn, and Fischer only just managed to close his mouth before the Imperial gaze alighted upon him and lingered for a moment to take in the damage. Finding the right man for morale purposes, Milch strode across the room and took Fischer's hand before it could be raised to salute formally.

'Good job, good job.'

That was it, The Great Man moved on, and ridiculously, Fischer felt hugely flattered. Not every other right hand was grasped (Reincke's couldn't be, as he had misplaced it somewhere over Serbia), but Milch had a comradely punch, slap or pinch of the cheek for everyone – everyone except Holleman, who was awarded the Stabbed Finger.

'I love it! You mustn't use it, though. I have good relations with SS, but they have no sense of humour whatsoever.'

Holleman clicked together his heels (or rather, his only heel against a metal joint), threw out his arm and bellowed.

'Jawohl, Herr Generalfeldmarschall!'

Smiling, Milch retreated towards the door, but was intercepted *en route* by two Liars. Holleman watched them with disgust.

Fischer came across and whispered to him from the side of his mouth. 'Don't pretend you're not impressed.'

'A bit, I suppose. But look at Lehmann and Schell, begging for his signature. If it was attached to a chit for a month's leave it would be useful, but they just want a keepsake!'

'He's Big. It's understandable.'

'As if it makes up for losing several metres of colon, or fits.'

'Milch didn't start the war.'

'No, but he's doing well from it.'

'He *did* fight to have the ME110 withdrawn from service, remember?'

'Yeah, there is that. Fucking death-trap.'

When Krohne had finished thanking the Presence for his visit and seen him safely to the lift he returned to the den. If strong feelings could have harmed, Holleman would have resembled placental matter by now, but one of the qualities to be expected in an oberstleutnant was coolness in crises. Still, he glared at the blackest of his sheep and shook his head.

'You utter cock!'

'Karl, he loved it! He said so.'

'He also said he got on well with SS. That's an understatement. Milch is the best friend they have in Luftwaffe. He's negotiating with them to have their camp workers put into aircraft production. The thing's being arranged by Gestapo Müller, with whom he's said to be on first-name terms.'

Müller has a first name?'

'Oh, shut up!'

'Sorry, Karl. What was he doing here anyway? We're hardly the Front Line.'

Krohne shook his head once more. He seemed as stunned as everyone else in the room.

'I don't know. He just appeared in my office, no warning, and said he'd like to meet our wounded heroes.'

Reincke snorted. 'If he wants *wounds* he could find them on any floor in this building. He'll be here at the Ministry for a meeting, and we're three storeys from the Great Hall. That's a real detour, isn't it?'

Holleman looked meaningfully at Fischer and whispered. 'Do you think ...'

' ... that the Luftwaffe's second-in-command, the man in charge of aircraft procurement, development, production and support, went out of his way to find out who's inherited Ahle's desk, and now he's marked me as being in possession of an earlier diary? No, I don't. He singled me out because I'm the most pitiable spectacle and therefore a convenient prop to demonstrate how deeply he cares about the common man.'

'Göring would never do that. You're too ugly.'

'That just makes him less of a hypocrite.'

Holleman stuck a finger in an ear and twisted it. 'I suppose so. We've had less curious starts to a shift.'

The other Liars were drifting back slowly to their desks, and Krohne, having reassembled some of his scattered wits, nudged them.

'Come on, you burdens on the Reich – we've a story to write. I want cold, righteous heroism, a dangerous but beatable enemy, a plausible comrade-saving-another-comrade anecdote or two, no visions of St Michael's flaming sword over Kharkov and *definitely* no French knickers. And I want a first draft from *all* of you (Holleman took delivery of another pointed stare) in two hours. The Generalfeldmarschall's visit was your morning break, so pick up your pencils and get on with it.'

Down in the Great Hall, Erhard Milch wagged a finger at his *aide de camp*, who came as quickly as he could excuse himself and dignity permitted. Both men glanced casually to either side as he approached.

'Wolfram, there's a hauptmann with half a face, a new man in the War Reporters'Unit. I've just met him. He sits where our little issue used to sit. He may be an issue himself.'

Wolfram frowned at the magnificent marble floor. 'What's your feeling, Herr Generalfeldmarschall?'

'I don't have one, yet. Put resources on to him. I want to know if he knew the other one.'

'Ahle?'

'Was that his name? Put some surveillance on him – his home, acquaintances, history, and if ...'

'if?'

'Never mind. Forget what I've just said. This man is an ally, obviously.'

Wolfram frowned, trying to see what was *obvious*, but said nothing. When the Generalfeldmarschall's head began to move it went in directions that he often couldn't follow. It was better just to await instructions, and then jump energetically.

'Listen carefully, and make what I ask your only concern. I'll let Speer know what you're doing, but otherwise this is not to be discussed. God knows, we don't need another fucking disaster.'

15

Frau Hilde Bensen was not one to make decisions lightly. In fact, she preferred not to be confronted by them at all, unless they were of the mundane, daily variety regarding food, clothing or whether to risk bringing on a rainstorm by hanging out laundry under thick clouds. As a mother of three girls, she had been party to many life-determining choices, but her husband (God rest his soul), being blessed with the gift of almost always being right about anything upon which he had an opinion, had relieved her of much of the weight that bowed a parent's shoulders. He was no longer here to carry that burden, but the girls were grown now and married themselves, and if Frau Bensen was called upon rather too often for baby-sitting duties, the choices they demanded were no more onerous than they had been the first time around.

Lately, though, she had been troubled greatly, and about more than the obvious thing. Poor Bruno's death had moved her further than she might ever have expected, a fact that tweaked her guilt considerably. The gruesome manner of it, the fact that she – his only surviving sibling – hadn't been able to attend his faraway funeral, and their long (if largely involuntary) estrangement colluded to make *this* decision ever harder, if that were possible.

It was the occasion of his death that made it necessary, of course. She couldn't think why he had placed the thing with her, knowing perfectly well that prevarication came as easily to her as breathing did to others. He had sent no instructions, no suggestions, only that she should keep the thing in a safe place until …

Until he asked for its return. But now he never would, so what was she supposed to do? Keep it in the memento chest beneath the bed until her own death made the matter moot? Destroy it? Take it to the authorities? If it stayed with her she would fret forever, as if a wood-troll with a poking stick had taken up residence. If she tore it up or burned it she would bear the guilt for the remainder of her life – a brother's last request to her, dishonoured because she preferred a life without knots in the weave. Which left only the dutiful option.

And that terrified her, because she didn't know what it was that she would be handing to them. She had opened it, just once, despite his urging (underlined three times in his letter) that she shouldn't. In the event, she had understood almost nothing about it. Row after row of numbers, sections headed by some sort of code, totals carried to pages that summarized a lot of nonsense with equally nonsensical brevity - all that she'd recognized was the arithmetic, the subtraction of sets of numbers from other sets of numbers to give a final net figure, though whether it referred to angels, beans or wishes she couldn't begin to guess. She very much hoped that it wasn't money, because that many of them couldn't possibly be an insignificant matter.

And even if it wasn't to do with money, why would Bruno have gone to the trouble of asking his sister to keep it safely hidden, if what it contained was an innocent matter? She was a patriotic German, but not stupid. She was aware that, war aside, circumstances had changed and that many things that didn't used to be against one or more laws now might be. If she took this thing to the police, what would they think? Worse, what would the people to whom the police handed them think? That Hilde Bensen was an entirely innocent party, merely doing the correct thing as she saw it? Was it likely that they'd congratulate her and then give her a lift home? As inexperienced in the ways of crime as she was, it didn't seem at all likely.

They couldn't hurt Bruno now. Nor could they question him, and that frustration might make them less willing to believe that she knew nothing of what he'd been doing. He had no other family, and she was fairly certain that he had no more close friends or colleagues now than when he was younger (he could always form a grudge more easily than a bond), so who else would they assume might know something?

She needed advice, but who to trust? Close friends – and there were three women, all widows like her, whom she counted as such - weren't ideal. One, Petra, was a devout National Socialist, and so, rather than offer an opinion, she would march Hilde straight to the nearest police station and demand that she tell them everything, trusting in the Führer's infinite wisdom and bounty to keep her from the interrogation room. The second, Gisela, had a heart condition that wasn't likely to be eased by weighing matters of life and possible death. The third, Susanne, was a treasure in every way, but as slow as a steam tram and as likely to offer useful advice as the device itself.

Seeing the world in a very traditional way, Hilde would have preferred to put the case to a man, one of known character and qualities; but her world had emptied of men, whether from bereavement or conscription, and what remained was not the best of the crop. The local *blockhelfer*, Herr Schever, would scurry straight to his *blockwart* with anything she might tell him, and then Gestapo would be knocking on her door before she could boil a kettle. Pastor Greven, a discreet, kindly man, would have been a safer choice of confidant, but it was common knowledge around the town that he was soothing the spiritual torments of the *Kirchenkampf* with heroic quantities of alcohol, and Hilde wasn't sure that telling her secret to a man who was drunk for most of every day would keep it that way.

Eventually, and only for want of any feasible alternative, she thought for longer than was sensible about Adel Buckwalter. Had her mind been entirely composed she would have concluded that putting one's trust in a man who had no good word to say about (or to) another living soul was absurd. But it wasn't, so she didn't. She thought instead about how the German language needed a stronger word than *verschlossen* to describe what he was. Graves gave up more secrets, dark caves showed more of their nature and runes cast by blind men held greater insights than Adel chose to offer to his once-fellow man. He was as tight with his mouth as a money-lender with his charity, and just about as content to be so.

He hadn't always been this way. Hilde recalled him as a pleasant young man, as fond of company as anyone else, but then his wife had run away with his beloved elder brother (which, as her late husband used to say, was as much shit as could happen to a man). After that, he hadn't become reclusive so much as hermetic (though without the spiritual complications). Sightings were made during his occasional foraging expeditions to the food market, but contact of any sort had proved beyond the wit of any of his former friends. Over the past twelve years, Hilde, trying her Christian best, had managed to get a single *um* out of the man, and that from a very recent and opportunistic street-interception to inform him of her brother's death. In a nation riven by the busy betrayals of amateur spies, sneaks and double-dealers, Adel Buckwalter was a rock of indifference.

Speaking to him might be no more useful than addressing her kitchen wall, but it could hardly be dangerous. Before walking away from his old life he had been a foreman at the Krupp Germaniawerft yard at Kiel, so he was a man with some experience of the world (or at least not as innocent as a calf). If she could prise as much as an opinion from him, the inconvenience – his hermit's cave was a small farm, five kilometres out of town – would be nothing.

An hour later, having dressed, washed the breakfast dishes and fed Satchmo (inherited from her youngest granddaughter, who hadn't found the moral strength to deal with hamster dung), she paused at her back door, half-in and out of her coat. In the larder was a cake, made from the last of her good flour, the last of her sugar and the last glazed cherries anywhere in the world (she suspected). It was to have been a prize in the local Winter Fund lottery, but pride and cupidity had weakened her resolve at the moment of parting. Did Adel even like cake? In such thin times the gesture would be enough, she hoped.

There was a bus route that would take her within a kilometre of the farm. It was tempting, but she decided to save the fare for the return journey. Her legs were good still, money was tight, it wasn't raining, and only her fear of what the sight of a cake tin, filled with the requisite product, would do to otherwise law-abiding folk gave her pause. She found her husband's old rucksack, shoved the tin inside and put one strap over her shoulder, pleased that its weight was easier to bear this way.

It was almost an adventure – or at least the first two kilometres felt that way. By the time she reached the farm two hours later the novelty had withered and died, but the effort left a virtuous afterglow that a smearing of pig manure on her shoes couldn't quite extinguish. When she reached the yard door she raised her fist to knock. It opened suddenly, leaving her offering a strange, threatening salute to the man who stepped out.

'What is it?'

An unexpected visitor can often brighten a day, but Hilde didn't think she was doing that. Adel Buckwalter gave her an impressive scowl - it occupied most of his face the way a dog did a hearth, comfortable with its situation and not inclined to move. The rest of him provided no greater reassurance. His (grubby) shirt had neither collar nor buttons to secure one, the sleeves were rolled sloppily up thin arms and his braces dangled to each side of his waist, as if he were about to shave or undress. She told herself that this had been a very bad idea, cleared her throat and tried to smile.

'Hello, Adel. It's me, Hilde Bensen - Hilde Spiegelmann that was. We went to school together, do you remember?'

'No.'

'Frau Schuller was our teacher in first class.'

'Her name was Schiller.'

It wasn't, but Hilde had no intention of fertilizing the scowl.

'Was it? My memory isn't good. May I have a word with you? It won't take long.'

'We have no business with each other.'

'No, but I'd like to tell you something, and ask what you think about it.'

Buckwalter looked dumbfounded. 'Think?'

'I mean, I'd like your advice. Look, I've brought a cake.'

The prospect of cake didn't seem to lessen his perplexity, but he took half a step back. It allowed an unpleasant odour of too little domestic hygiene to escape and reach her nostrils. She couldn't help but sniff slightly, and he noticed.

'My dogs. It's a farm, there's no point washing them.'

'I like dogs. May I come in, Abel?'

'You're not …?'

'Not what?'

'It's not about money, is it?'

'Of course not. Really, I just need an opinion. But it's confidential.'

He snorted and opened his door wide. Something behind him growled and he answered with the same, which sent the offender scurrying away. When he turned back to Hilde the scowl was gone, but what had replaced it was no more welcoming. She could have been mistaken, but it looked very much like a reaction to something either obscene or mad.

'Confidential? Who would *I* tell?'

'Call me Freddie.'

Fischer didn't want to call Holleman anything but Holleman (if that, even). He was already much too far into the other man's confidence – a man who, on short acquaintance, seemed incapable of discretion. On the other hand, it was better to have a wandering mouth as a friend rather than enemy, so he made the effort.

'I'm Otto.'

'Yeah, I know. Otto Henry Fischer. Why not Heinrich?'

'We were Huguenots, way back. It's a family tradition.'

'It should be Henri then, surely?'

'*Too* French, after Jena. After Waterloo my ancestors settled on Henry. Anglicisms were very fashionable then.'

'Not now, though.'

'I promised my mother that my sons would be Heinrichs. It didn't happen, though.'

'You're not married?'

'Divorced. You?'

'Wife and two boys. Twins.'

'Inconvenient.'

'You have no idea. They're almost at the difficult age.'

It was lunch time, the first sitting, at the Air Ministry. At noon precisely the younger Liars, having robust appetites, had flung themselves down the stairwell as quickly as their injuries permitted, leaving 'Uncle Fred' and the new elderly gentleman to cover for them. According to Holleman, Krohne had sneaked out at the same time to find a different kind of oral sustenance, so the two men had most of their corridor to themselves.

So far, they had avoided *the* subject. Fischer didn't think for a moment that Generalfeldmarschall Milch had picked him out for any darker reason than his wounds, but the spectacularly surprising encounter had unnerved him, reminding him that he was a lowly hauptmann, pushing his rearranged face into places it shouldn't ever go. What Holleman thought of it he couldn't say, and he wasn't going to ask. With luck, he'd feel the same – that he'd wantonly raised his head above a parapet and got away with a centre-parting. Poor Ahle could rest in unfortunate peace, as an undecipherable cautionary tale to anyone who cared to recall him.

Fischer was beginning to feel uncharitably good about this, when Holleman spoiled his morning.

'I spoke to my *kripo* mate again last night. He says that his partner wanted to sniff a bit more around our Ahle business. He called in the anwärter who found the body, to have a chat about it. By the time the lad arrived at Alexanderplatz the other *kripo* had been transferred – no warning, no interview, just off you go. A promotion, apparently, but the timing's strange.'

'Christ. Are you getting the pointed message yet?'

Holleman frowned and studied his fingernails.

'Yeah. Except that we haven't done anything stupid, like that *kripo* did. No-one knows that we're interested in what happened to Ahle.'

'Well, don't you think that someone – the *wrong* someone – might get to know, if we carry on? At some point we'd need to ask questions, wouldn't we? The moment that happened, who could say who'd find out?'

'Um.'

'Bury Ahle's diary - in a sewer, or similar. He has no family who'll want it - or want to know how and why he died, for that matter. And before you tell me that *you* want to know, think of your wife and twins, and how much more difficult their *difficult* age could get.'

'You're right, obviously. I'm sorry, Otto, I shouldn't have dropped this on you. It's just that when Karl said he was interviewing an ex-*kripo* for Ahle's job I thought it had to be Fate.'

'Fate would have brought you someone who'd enjoyed police work.'

'You didn't?'

'For a very short while. While we were chasing bad people, not sweeping over their stains.'

Holleman nodded. 'It was easier for an *OrPo* like me, breaking up fights or grabbing the ankles of someone halfway through a shop window. No moral issues there.'

'Except whether to pocket what was already missing from the shop.'

'Yeah, there was that.'

'For us it was whether or not to ignore the crime or pin it on a non-Party member, and preferably a Jew, and then … Hell!'

'What is it?'

'I seem to have misplaced discretion and found my mouth.'

Holleman beamed. 'See? We're comrades already.'

Fischer stifled a groan. Working with a group of invalids had seemed a comfortable option – as much a laying-down of arms as was possible in the midst of universal war. He hadn't suspected that honourable wounds could fool a man into thinking he was somehow protected, or invisible, or excused the necessary muscular practise that kept lips firmly together. Or was it that, if one twisted unpleasant truths into palatable nonsense often enough, all realities became plastic? Holleman seemed to swerve between insouciance and brief moments of sensible terror about what he was doing. Perhaps all he needed was to be reminded – often - when and where he was.

Fischer tapped the desk. 'If they – whoever *they* are – get any hint that we're pissing in their soup, Karl will be recalling us to our replacements as poor Holleman and poor Fischer.'

'I know.'

'If we're lucky our bodies will be found, eventually. If not, your family's going to wonder which crop you're fertilizing.'

'I *know*.'

'Then let's stop, now. Forget Ahle. Forget that you used to be police. If the injustice of it gives you a rash, think of all the other, greater ones being visited upon most of Europe at the moment.'

'But ...'

'Think about it - there are no *buts*. The very best thing to come out of this is that we live, you get to feel a little pleased with yourself and Bruno Ahle remains in two ugly parts. He's already buried and forgotten by everyone except his few colleagues. The more probable outcome is no less pointless but far, far messier.'

Even Holleman seemed moved by the logic of that. He pursed his lips, breathed heavily through his nose and then nodded. Slowly, he undid his tunic jacket and removed a familiar item from his inside breast pocket. Fischer stared at it, horrified.

'You're carrying it around with you?'

'I didn't dare leave it here, after what happened to your desk. And even I'm not so stupid as to hide it in my house.'

'But you must do, at night.'

'Nah. Every evening I put it a hole under a hedge, three streets down.'

Fischer closed his eyes. 'Christ on the Cross.'

'It's alright. I wrap in a piece of tarpaulin first.'

'So, twice each day you go through this pantomime, presumably for the benefit of whoever's been put on to you by Ahle's killers?'

Holleman blanched slightly. 'You don't think that's likely?'

'I have no way of knowing. Do you?'

'I'd be dead by now.'

'Well then, don't press your luck.'

'Right.' Holleman picked up his waste basket, tipped its contents into a neighbour and began to tear pages from the diary.

'You can't burn it here – the alarm will sound before it's half-gone. Take it down to the furnace and throw it in.'

'What if someone sees me?'

'What if they do? They aren't going to dive in after it, are they?'

'If they ask?'

'It was a book of filthy photos. You found it under your son's bed.'

'Who'd believe I'd throw away something like that?'

'A *mind your own business*, then.'

'Yeah. That'll do.'

Holleman was gone for twenty minutes. Towards the end of that time the younger Liars shuffled back into the den, finishing off conversations about football, family or new secretaries in the building. Karl Krohne was immediately behind them, slightly flushed, as if he had hurried from an assignation (or perhaps the assignation itself was to blame). He almost collided with his rowdiest subordinate in the doorway.

'All quiet, Freddie?'

'Apart from the Führer wanting to have some grammar put in a speech.'

'Good.'

Holleman came straight across to Fischer's desk, grinning all the way.

'Done.'

'It was the sensible thing.'

'I know. You won't guess who I saw downstairs.'

'Dolly Haas?'

'A clue - he was fat and wore an ice-cream vendor's uniform.'

'The Reichsmarschall?'

'Call Me Meyer himself! Jesus, the man's got a mouth on him. He was telling someone where he'd be for the next two days, and that someone was stood at the other side of the Reception Hall.'

'Where will he be?'

'The Wolf's Lair. To see the Man.'

'He probably wants everyone to know that he's still getting invitations.'

'Ha! That'll be it. I'm beginning to wonder if you're our lucky charm, Otto. Milch the day before yesterday, Göring today - who's next?'

'If I had a vote it *would* be Dolly Haas.'

'She's take American citizenship.'

'Lilli Palmer, then.'

'Gone, too. And Jewish. So, not much chance of Lilli.'

'Are there *any* German actresses still?'

Holleman shrugged. 'Hollywood's where the money is. And Clark Gable, of course. Anyway, who'd want to film stuff that's been scripted in the Chancellery?'

Detmar Reinke was the last of the early diners to return from lunch. He saw Krohne closing upon the others with a sheath of papers and made straight for Fischer's desk.

'I've just seen something surprising.'

Holleman nodded. 'Yeah, we know. Göring's blessed us with a visit.'

'Has he? That wasn't it. There's a Feldgendarmerie unit downstairs, gorgeous in their gorgets. Someone's in trouble.'

'They were here to guard Fat Hermann, I expect. He was leaving when I saw him.'

'No, they're on their way upstairs. And they posted men at reception to catch any runners. Like I said, someone's for it. Have you been writing your stuff with a British accent, Freddie?'

The smirk on Holleman's face fell off as a commotion at the Den's door made Fischer and Reincke turn. Six men in Feldgendarmerie insignia were fanning out into the room, machine pistols pointed at the floor. One of them noticed an oberstleutnant's uniform and saluted, just.

'What do you want?' Krohne managed an authoritative squeak that seemed not to cow the man, who scanned the room and pointed at Fischer.

'Him.'

'Why?'

One-handed, and without taking his eyes from the half-face, the Feldgendarme opened his tunic breast pocket, extracted a folded piece of paper and held it out towards the enquiry.

'Better not to ask, Herr Oberstleutnant.'

17

In the Arminius Markthalle, Frau Traugott examined the available comestibles with pursed lips, hoping to give an impression of critical indifference. This was because she had noticed that Frau Speigl was in the hall also, and Frau Traugott would have been as content to show her bare posterior on Turmstrasse as any hint of longing for, or inability to buy, the non-rationed goods on offer.

Frauen Traugott and Speigl were currently at war, though the *casus belli* was lost to both of them. It was an undeclared conflict, its sole means of prosecution their respective mouths, with which aspersions, slights, damningly faint praises and pitying slurs-dressed-as-concerns were deployed with sufficient delicacy to be mistaken for sisterly banter until the blood began to seep.

The most recent engagement had been an unequivocal tactical victory for the Speigl camp. The lady had several familiars, and so held an advantage over Frau Traugott (most of whose friends had succumbed to winter ailments during the past few years). A rumour that her epilepsy was excited or even caused by excessive consumption of cherry schnapps had seemed to come from nowhere yet spread efficiently through their part of Alt-Moabit. The first that the victim knew of it was when the local *blockhelfer*, Amon Dunst, knocked on her door and launched straight into a stern lecture on the moral humiliation of addiction.

He had departed with a flea in his ear, but the damage had been done. Since then, Frau Traugott had been obliged to join the district's Temperance Society, endure evenings of self-righteous bleatings on the horrors of drink and - in order to be seen to be clean - wear out her shoes distributing its pamphlets in streets where she was known. As yet, she had not conceived an adequate revenge for this torment, but she intended it to be condign.

Her hand was hovering over a peach that she almost certainly couldn't afford when her radar pinged. She pretended not to notice.

'Oh, they're French. I much prefer a Proskauer.'

No doubt Frau Speigl could as readily tell the difference between peach varieties as she could the feathers on angels' wings, but Frau Traugott had no intention of skirmishing. She fixed her once-friend with a cold eye.

'We have to set aside preferences, in times like these.'

'Still, it's a shame that some Frenchman gets our money, instead of an honest Silesian.'

'I doubt very much that he was *paid* for his produce.'

Frau Seigl sniffed, but left it alone. Contemptuously, she examined the rest of the stock – some stunted, home-grown tomatoes and tiger marrows – and then took out her purse, picked up the very same peach that Frau Traugott had fondled and handed it to the stall-owner.

'This one, please.'

It was a cheap triumph, but her opponent took the thrust badly. She hadn't particularly *wanted* the peach - it was rather the strength of her own reaction that soured her mood. She never came off best when she was angry. All the cutting retorts occurred to her several minutes too late (if at all), while Frau Speigl had a hateful ability to wield the knife spontaneously. With an effort, she calmed herself and picked up one of the marrows. It was cheaper than a peach, and more useful.

'Soup.'

Frau Speigl smiled. 'Ah, lovely. If you need onions, I have too many at the moment. They'll go bad before I can use them.'

Kindness was of course the most brutal instrument in the torturer's rack, but Frau Traugott, seeing an opening, felt a marvelous serenity come upon her.

'Thank you, I have some. You could make an onion soup, perhaps, for your lodger … oh, forgive me!'

A month earlier, Frau Speigl's paying guest (a signalman at the Westhafen junction) had moved out, making no secret of his dissatisfaction with his landlady's cooking. Not wishing to waste or squander a windfall, Frau Traugott had hoarded the matter until now, and the other woman's purpling face amply rewarded her self-control. Without another word, the enemy turned and marched off towards a used furniture stall, leaving the field to her adversary.

It wasn't a great victory, but it brightened the overcast afternoon tremendously. Frau Traugott paid for her marrow (and the onions she needed), and counted what change remained in her purse. It was irresponsible, but she hadn't sat in a café with a cup of coffee in front of her for almost three years. There was one on the corner of Thusnelda Allee, and the local word was that their product tasted less foul than its ingredients warranted. She had earned a little indulgence, and God knew when the opportunity for another would come along.

The café offered old-time uniforms and courtesy at no extra charge. She was led to a small table near the kitchen door, from which a blast of wonderfully warm, pastry-laden air emerged and surrounded her every few seconds. By the time the waitress came to take her order she had determined to eke out her only coffee for as long as it took to put a spring thaw into her bones, but when it was poured the young girl whispered that mothers of Germany got a second cup free of charge. A minute later, a small bun (garnished by a tiny dollop of lingonberry preserve) arrived to keep the cup company, and Frau Traugott's idea of Paradise had been largely realised.

All her adult life, doctors had been urging her to aid digestion by eating more slowly, so they would have been delighted by the protracted death of the bun. It was a taste of peace-time, savoured to the last calorie, and several people arrived, drank a coffee and left between her first and last bites. She filled the minutes between with a forensic survey of her fellow customers, assigning to them vices, virtues, good deeds, misdemeanors or crimes based upon her cursory impressions (one man, catching her eye and smiling pleasantly, ascended from probable philanderer to upstanding citizen in a moment). The young waitress was among the pantheon of saints already of course, and a second complementary coffee, served with a conspiratorial wink, merely shifted her upward a step. In all, it was one of the most pleasant hours Frau Traugott could recall, and had not one tiny ripple marred its sublime surface she would have called it perfect.

The upstanding citizen's smile had stirred something so fleeting that it was only after he had gone that she noticed it – or rather, him. He was neither handsome nor objectionable, in every way a median of the species; but Berliners were famously reticent and didn't make a habit of smiling at strangers, even when their eyes met across a café. Yet this was the second time it had happened today, and because she had returned the first with a nod and averted her eyes swiftly (turning to make a pretence of locking her front door again), she couldn't quite say that both smiles hadn't belonged to the same man.

She would tell Hauptmann Fischer when he got home that evening, and ask his advice. He would probably say it was nothing, a coincidence. Mentioning it would ease her mind, though, and knowing that a hero of the Reich was aware of the man would surely remove any possible threat. A civilian wouldn't dare to cross someone who wore the Knight's Cross, or even his landlady.

As it happened, she didn't tell Hauptmann Fischer, because he didn't come home that evening or the next.

18

Being the only two men in the department old enough to shave daily, Oberstleutnant Karl Krohne and Leutnant Friedrich Holleman appointed themselves the Temporary Emergency Committee of the *Kriegsberichter der Luftwaffe*. A third, who would have qualified also, was the sole reason for the committee's establishment and the only item on its informal agenda.

The Committee had convened in Krohne's office after that morning's work (a second attempt to paint the Tunisian retreat as a tactical regrouping) had been distributed among the other Liars. Holleman raised the first point of order.

'Who the fuck can we even speak to about this?'

Nervously, Krohne glanced at the warrant in his hand. 'I don't know.'

'Who signed it?'

'Generalmajor Ano Aach.'

'Don't know him.'

'Me neither, but it's a Luftwaffe stamp.'

'What branch is he?'

'It doesn't say.'

'Have you looked in the field directory?'

'Yes. He's not in there.'

'Shit. Where's Otto been taken?'

'It doesn't say.'

'The charge?'

'It doesn't say.'

'Fuck your mother!'

Krohne rubbed his only eye with the back of his free hand. 'It hardly matters. They wouldn't necessarily take him to a stated destination, and the cause is always 'protective custody', isn't it? At least by saying nothing they're being honestly arrogant.'

'Yes, but who are *they*?'

'Christ knows, Freddie. At least it was the Feldgendarmerie who took him, and not Geheime Feldpolizei.'

'Is that any better? They both recruit thugs.'

' I wonder what the hell he did?'

'What do you mean, *did*?'

'We hardly know the man. What if he's passing on stuff to the Ivans?'

Holleman snorted. 'They didn't capture him, so how could they turn him?'

'He might be a lifelong Red, put where he can do the most harm.'

'In the Lie Division? Well, that'll bring the Reich to its fucking knees.''

'Yes, alright. What if he has contacts on the Quartermaster-General's staff? They might be selling stolen goods on the black market - parachute silk, or something.'

Holleman sniffed and thought about it for a few moments. 'It's … possible. But do you get the impression he's that sort? I mean, talking to him, I …'

'You … ?'

'He makes me feel rough-edged. He's got *manners*. He came over to my desk to ask for an opinion yesterday, and he actually excused himself. This is Luftwaffe, for God's sake, not the Humboldt Library. I just can't see some criminal sort being that agreeable.'

'A good false-dealer would make you think that.'

'I know. But you get a smell for it in the Police. Otto isn't trying hard to seem straight - he just *is*.'

Krohne sighed. 'Well, whatever he has or hasn't done, I have to put in a report, and it's probably going to go to the people who lifted him. What do I say?'

'That we're a man short once more, and can we have him back, please?'

'Be serious.'

'Talk to your boss. Ask him what you should do.'

'D'you think the Oberst would lift a finger? He runs the support establishment for most of Berlin's flak-ring, and he regards it as his only job. As far as he's concerned, being given the Lie Division was a bad joke on someone's part, and when he finds out who it was ...'

It was a measure of Krohne's discomfort that he forgot himself and used his department's unflattering pseudonym. He had a professional journalist's pride in being able to move the public mind, however reprehensibly, and took it very badly that his men took their job less than seriously. He paused and breathed deeply.

'Anyway, he'd rather pilot a Yak than do or say anything that got him noticed for the wrong reasons. British bombs allowing, he intends to survive this war by being invisible. And he is. He doesn't speak to me if he can avoid it, and he's *never* spoken to you lot. You don't know his name, do you?'

Holleman squinted at the window. 'It's ... Becke.'

'It's Böck. And once he gets my report, he'll push it straight into a drawer. If Fischer was taken by the Feldgendarmerie, no further questions will be asked by him.'

'But we can't do nothing.'

'We can't not do nothing. Where do you think your rank entitles you to go, prod and question, Freddie?'

'That's not the point ...'

'No. The point is that you wear a uniform, yet you get to see your family most days. How many soldiers can say that?'

'Not many.'

'No. I'm one of them also, and I'm not going to do anything to risk that luxury. We don't know Fischer - he seems a nice fellow, but he might not be an acquaintance we can survive. What if the Feldgendarmerie have just cut out an infection that might have taken everyone in this corridor?'

Holleman blew out his cheeks and gave the window more attention. 'It doesn't seem … right.'

'What does, any more? Remind yourself that he's been a comrade for five days now, for which service he's earned a cheerful *good morning* and a round of drinks at the Silver Birch, not our taking a bullet on his behalf.'

'What if it's not about Otto? What if it's about Ahle?'

'How could it be?' Krohne's eyes narrowed. 'What have you been doing, Freddie?'

'Me? Why would I have done something?'

'Hm. I don't see how it could be. And if it somehow *is*, I'd be even less inclined to stir things that shouldn't be stirred. We've been told that Ahle killed himself, and that's that. It is, isn't it?'

'Of course it is.'

'Good. Whatever Fischer's done, it's beyond my power to alter. All I can do is try to ensure that this department isn't smeared by his shit. If I'm questioned I'll say that he settled in quietly, mostly kept his own company and did nothing I could criticize. It's all true, and we're all blameless.'

'Ye… s.'

'Oh, Christ. What is it??'

'Otto may be a mistake. It may have been ...'

'Who?'

'Me.'

'*What?*'

'I told him that Ahle didn't kill himself.'

'But ... Ahle *did* kill himself.'

'He didn't, and I'll tell you why.'

It took a while. Krohne had an admirably foul vocabulary, and he deployed most of it during his enlightenment. When it was all out, he sat back and held his head in both hands, looking to the ceiling (or beyond) for guidance.

'So, you decided that a smothered-in-the-cradle police investigation into what was probably an execution is something that a couple of buggered-up veterans could take on as - what, a hobby?'

'Well ...'

'While hiding possibly deadly evidence in your desk drawer instead of burning it?'

'I *have* burned it. Otto made me do it.'

'And now he's in the hands of people who have the elbows to stop police going after murderers. Who may *be* the murderers, in fact. Do you know what I'm wondering about Fischer?'

'Where he is?'

'How well he can take pain. What if he does the sensible thing and points a finger directly at you before they start hitting him? I know *I* would, you daft bastard!'

Holleman squirmed. 'It just didn't seem right, poor Ahle not getting a decent investigation. Otto's ex-police, so I thought he'd agree. He didn't, though.'

'That's because he uses his head for more than cap-warming. Not that it's done him much good.'

'No. I feel bad about this.'

'I expect you'll feel worse when he turns up cacked.'

'Oh, fuck!'

Krohne regarded his most difficult subordinate for a few moments. Though a former newspaper editor he wasn't entirely without compassion, but Holleman's outraged sense of justice had threatened the entire department – a place intended (by Krohne at least) as a haven for broken men, not a convenient location from which to show one's arse-cheeks to the Reich. However amenable he found the company of Otto Fischer, and however foul the man's luck, the *Kriegsberichter der Luftwaffe*'s Emergency Committee could offer no help with his present predicament.

As the sole mover of that predicament, Holleman looked to be running through the full spectrum of remorse - which meant, probably, that he'd behave for a few days at least. Perhaps, if his desk was moved to face that of poor Ahle (and, latterly, poor Fischer) his circumspection might stretch into the following week. A small mercy, to set against that which his new comrade certainly wouldn't be receiving.

'Go on, Freddie, back to the Den. Give that briefing from Tunisia a workout. It'll distract you.'

'I can't think of work with what's happening to Otto!'

'Not thinking hasn't ever stopped you before, has it?'

19

Hilde Bensen stood outside her local police station, the *thing* clutched to her chest, hoping to press her sprinting heart into submission. She had been there for almost fifteen minutes, and it wasn't working so far. In fact, mere anxiety had become something more during that time, and her head had begun to spin. Probably, she was making a bad, dangerous decision, but even now it seemed her least worst hope.

Adel Buckwalter's firm advice to her (being other than what she wanted to hear) hadn't helped at all. He had asked five questions, all of them pertinent, and then offered the obvious answer. But it wouldn't do.

'Your brother's dead?'

'Yes.'

'He left no instructions?'

'No.'

'You opened the package?'

'Yes.'

'Do you think what's in it might be dangerous?'

'I can't see how it couldn't be.'

'Does anyone else know you have it?'

'He wouldn't have told anyone.'

'Burn it, then.'

But burning it would be the same as washing her hands of her brother's memory, of her last duty to him (and God knew, she had hardly been a dutiful sister). So she thanked Adel for his time, asked him how he was doing (he had replied with a shrug), and then came home.

She had made up her mind before she reached her front door - to stand or fall upon trust, and whether she made a good enough job of resealing the envelope with gum. It was a rare commodity these days (trust, not gum), as all kinds of new rules and proscriptions had made clear to the German people, so she knew that she would need to be very convincing in her professions of naivety and unworldliness. She couldn't know what purpose Bruno had in mind when he embarked upon his plan (if it was sufficiently thought-through to even *be* a plan), nor what he might have wanted her to do had he anticipated his self-murder; yet as hard and as long as she thought about it, no innocent possibility came to mind. Anything secretive or carefully hidden from view had to be against *some* law that the Reich had conceived, which is why Hilde was now standing in the street in front of the police station, failing to be calm at the prospect of her imminent arrest.

Eventually, her feet found the courage her head lacked and they carried her forward, through the double doors and to the reception hall counter. Sensing a presence spoiling the otherwise empty vista before him, the duty wachtmeister looked up from his schedule and gave Hilde a look that was neither welcoming nor discouraging - rather, it conveyed the cold, resolute impartiality of National Socialist justice (he had practised it in his wardrobe mirror until it sat as comfortably on his face as did his eyebrows), and immediately the last of her courage vanished. Before he could ask her business, she began to babble.

'I'm sorry to trouble you, but I don't know what I should do with this. It's from my brother, he asked me to keep it for him, but he didn't say why. He's dead now, put his head on a railway line. In Berlin. We hadn't spoken for some years, so I was surprised when I received his note. I didn't keep it, I'm sorry.'

She held out the large envelope to the wachtmeister, hoping that the trembling wasn't noticeable. He took it from her, examined the front and then carefully wrote down her name and address. At that moment she might have fainted, but a small, sensible voice told her that it was perfectly obvious that he would do this as a matter of routine. It kept her on her feet, just.

Having made his note he turned his attention back to the envelope. Frowning, he tapped it.

'Did you notice the frank?'

'Frank? No, my eyesight isn't very good.'

It wasn't, but really, she hadn't even noticed the sender's mark other than as a smudge on a problem, and it had been the problem itself that seized every bit of her attention. She peered more closely now, and as she did so he rotated the envelope slowly so that she could scan the circular writing.

'It's Reichsluf …. something.'

'Reichsluftfahrtministerium. The Air Ministry, in Wilhelmstrasse.'

'Is that bad?'

'It just *is*. Did your brother work there?'

'He was a pilot, in bombers. But then he was injured.'

'When?'

'About two years ago. He sent me a letter a while ago, saying that he was better but not recovered.'

'But you say that he killed himself?'

'I was notified by the Luftwaffe. About six weeks ago.'

Despite her anxiety, the recollection brought tears. It had been a terrible shock, the more so because they hadn't reconciled. She would never have believed him capable of it, as miserable as he could be sometimes. They were from a staunch Catholic family, and suicide was a mortal sin, never to be forgiven. He must have been in a terrible state, to have done it.

Notwithstanding his practised demeanour, the wachtmeister was not a callous man. He lifted the latch and came from behind the counter, taking her arm gently and leading her to the hard bench that sat against the wall.

'Would you like some coffee?'

'No, thank you. Am I in trouble?'

'For what?'

'For not bringing the envelope immediately. I was upset, you see …?'

'Of course you were. Did you open it to see what was inside?'

'Oh, no. It wasn't my business. I just put it in a drawer. That's why I forgot about it.'

Being upset already, the lie didn't betray her. He patted her hand.

'You've done the right thing, so I can't see any harm in it. We'll make sure that it goes straight back to the Ministry. It's possible that someone there may want to know more, though.'

'Would I have to go to Berlin?'

'I doubt it. There's a war on, and plenty for the Ministry people to be occupied with. It may be that they'll be content with my report.'

When she had gone, the wachtmeister went back to his counter and lifted the package. There was some weight to it, almost like a book without covers, and he had absolutely no intention of satisfying his curiosity as to what it might be. The woman's brother shouldn't have used official stationery, so at least a minor offence had been committed, even if the man actually worked at the Ministry. The contents themselves might make it a major offence of course, but that was for some senior Luftwaffe fellows to decide, not a lowly *OrPo* desk sergeant. Rules, broken, could spread like spilled treacle, and stain hands.

He made sure that his report was as thorough as anything relating to a mysterious, unseen object could be, and then he walked it upstairs to his haupwachtmeister. As he had expected, his boss was delighted that he hadn't succumbed to momentary idiocy and opened the envelope. He agreed that it should be returned to Wilhelmstrasse as soon and as securely as possible, and that no effort should be spared to indicate how correct the precinct's handling of this matter had been. And just to ensure that no stray splash of ordure returned from Berlin, the hauptwachtmeister made a point of telephoning his Oberst der Polizei (who happened also to be his cousin), a very political man and close friend of their deputy Gauleiter, to apprise him of the business.

For once, he didn't have to endure the pomposity with which senior Party men compensated for their lack of breeding. His cousin's advice was unequivocal, and pleasingly concise.

'Oh hell, Franz, get rid of the thing. Don't open it, don't discuss it with anyone and above all don't ever mention it again, even in passing. And send it from the General Post Office, not through the internal. Whatever the headless man was doing, we don't want to know, do we?'

'I'm not going to ask again.'

Fischer regarded the large, hard-featured man who sat at the other side of the narrow table. A long scar, silvered by age, ran from his right-side temple to the jaw-line - a noble, almost flattering wound (unlike Fischer's crop of mutilations) that officers in the old Prussian army would have paid decent money to have inflicted. His eyes – which so far had offered no hint of emotion – sat too close together, giving him what fashion magazines almost certainly didn't dare refer to as the Heydrich Look, while the mouth performed its usual functions without moving a centimetre more than was necessary. His name (he had offered it readily enough) was Wilhelm, and every syllable of his body language was an inadvertent health warning.

'I said no.'

'Alright, then.' Wilhelm reached across the table and wrapped a fist around the last square of *donauwelle*, lifting and cramming it unbitten into the economical mouth. He chewed briefly, swallowed, made a face and repeated his criticism.

'Aargh. Too sweet.'

'And yet it's your fourth.'

'Why would anyone use too much of something so … *unavailable*?'

'You said it was baked by the deputy commandant's sister?'

'Yeah.'

'Perhaps those with access to sugar like to flaunt their privilege?'

'Mm. Could be.' Wilhelm licked his fingers, placed both hands together on the table and examined his knuckles, all of which looked to be exercised regularly. Whether he regretted not having the opportunity to bounce them off his present guest was hard to say. When Fischer first arrived at his new accommodation he had been shoved roughly into the cell, but since then violence had been expected – as something that, in such a place, was easier to inflict than not – rather than threatened.

Having always been a model soldier, Fischer couldn't say whether those who staffed military prisons brought more or less brutality to their job than their Weimar predecessors. He doubted that they were trained by pacifists, or under orders to gently coax the bad out of their charges, yet although Wilhelm seemed very much of a type he had been as pleasant as anyone that anyone marched into Spandau might have hoped to confront. Things might change, of course, but rigorous interrogations didn't usually commence with an offer of cigarettes and a decent meal.

Wilhelm looked up from his knuckles. 'How was the onion soup?'

'Actually, delicious.'

'Another one of hers, apparently.'

'Is it her habit to cook for the prisoners?'

The big man laughed. 'I wouldn't think so. But you were put down for special treatment.'

'Which means something so much less enjoyable, usually.'

'Yeah, it's a one-off, for sure. Still, what the man wants he gets, no questions.'

'Which man?'

'Ah.' Wilhelm wagged a forefinger. 'We were told to do no damage, for the moment. Nothing was said about telling you stuff.'

'Am I allowed to ask how long I'll be here?'

'Of course you are.'

As his gaoler appeared to be enjoying the banter, Fischer didn't feed him the line. It was unnerving to be taken and held without any formal process, but if someone had intended to cast him into a pit they wouldn't be bothering to feed him fine soup and too-sweet cake, much less provide almost-amenable company. There was a purpose, a reason, and if he had to wait for it to take three buses to arrive, that was fine. Almost a year's residence in a burns-ward had taught him the value of patience.

Still, he pondered the cause. It *had* to be something about Bruno Ahle, unless he was being punished for importuning the nurses at Potsdam (which he hadn't, he reminded himself). Yet apart from reading through Ahle's diary – twice – he couldn't see what his offence might be. And if it *was* that, who had betrayed him? Not Holleman, who was standing much further out from the shit's shore-line than he. It could only be Frau Traugott, then. She had found the thing while tidying his rooms, and gone straight to her blockhelfer. He wouldn't have thought she was the type to do that, but what *was* the type, these days? Everyone was cowed, everyone peered constantly over one shoulder, hoping that the breeze they felt on the back of their neck was on its way to someone else.

If it had been her ... but the more he thought about it, the less likely it seemed. What was written in the diary, to make a civilian that think it was poison? For that matter, what would *anyone* think, who didn't know about Ahle's suspicious death? It contained not much more than a few gripes, moans and petty observations about people the man didn't like. When Frau Traugott found it, she *must* have assumed it belonged to Fischer, and if she had betrayed him he would presently be charged under the Military Code for keeping a journal, not held incommunicado, awaiting ...

What? What utility was there, in holding him at Spandau? It had been a military prison originally, and then a place where protective custody 'criminals' could be held until the new special camps were built. By 1937 they had all been cleared out, and he wasn't sure how the place had been used since. One question pressed particularly unpleasantly, given the circumstances of Ahle's death. Did it have a guillotine?

Even under the present Regime's busy hand, not all major prisons were places of execution also. As far as he knew, most death sentences passed in Berlin were carried out at Plötzensee and Moabit, but he was not (nor wanted to be) an expert on judicial executions. Perhaps every establishment was supplied with one - as with slop buckets - as a matter of course. Perhaps Ahle had been a one-off, a special job, who had christened an otherwise unemployed device ...

No. Spandau was in the west, and Ahle's several parts had been discovered in Rummelsberg. Even people who regarded themselves as untouchable wouldn't have wanted to invite attention by transporting their gruesome cargo all the way across central Berlin. If it had been a guillotine that did the job, Moabit's would have been far more convenient.

Wilhelm was watching him, as carefully as a physician might an acute cardiac case. It was quite flattering, or worrying. Fischer had arrived in the company of three feldgendarmerie, and it was they who had performed the initial shoving duties that had introduced him to his cell at considerable velocity. Since then, he had seen only one other person than his new companion, a sour-faced guard who had relieved Wilhelm for a few hours the previous night. No words were exchanged during that time - in fact, the man had hardly looked at his prisoner, and when he did it was with no more interest than he might have examined one of the bricks in the cell wall. At dawn, Wilhelm had returned with a breakfast of (good) bread rolls and (better) coffee, dismissing his colleague with a toss of the head.

Thinking back upon that moment, Fischer wasn't sure if they *were* colleagues. They were both Luftwaffe but wore different insignia, and that toss of the head had been more abrupt than one comrade might have offered another. Had they argued, or did one of them not belong here?

'Stop thinking.'

'Was it obvious?'

'You were frowning. I *think* you were frowning. It's hard to tell, with that face.'

'Alright, I'll stop. What did you do in the Peace, Wilhelm?'

'Butcher.'

'Has that been useful in your present work?'

The other man sniggered. 'Not often. It helped in Greece. We had a comrade who'd worked from farm to farm before the war, trapping rabbits. He could almost tease them out of the ground, and when he did, I skinned and cleaned them. We ate fucking well, in Greece.'

'I was in Crete.'

Fallschirmjäger?'

'Yes.'

'I hear you had an interesting time.'

'The experience offered valuable military insights.'

'Like how you shouldn't drop onto intact machine-gun units that have a clear view of your looming arses?'

'That, and don't go in with just the one water canteen.'

Wilhelm waved vaguely towards his face. 'Was it where you …?'

'No. That was on the Eastern Front, with an artillery unit. I was seconded to them, after Crete.'

'Good fortune's got you on a golden chain.'

'Yes, I feel blessed.'

The big man removed a pack of cigarettes from his pocket and offered it. 'You're sure?'

'My lungs don't like it. They probably never did, but now they make a point of saying so.'

'Ha! You're alright, mate.'

Wilhelm lit his own cigarette and blew the smoke at the ceiling. The mild compliment was probably as close to effusive as any prisoner had the right to expect, so this particular one relaxed slightly. Interrogators everywhere had certain conventions, and one of them was to not get too friendly with people they were about to beat, or put in the frame, or drag outside to a guillotine. Fischer had no doubt that Wilhelm could snap a man's neck and plough into a hearty lunch before the body had stopped twitching, but even he would need to have his mind in the right place beforehand. This didn't feel at all like what he had feared.

'What d'you think's for lunch?'

Fischer looked up. 'Eh?'

'Lunch. I was just wondering. Pork would be nice.'

The German penal system provided for two meals, early morning and evening (neither sufficiently varied or of a standard to make the recipient *wonder* what was coming). Lunch was definitely not to be expected, other than as a tormenting odour wafted from the guards' Mess. It occurred suddenly that Wilhelm's large, brutal physique had been utilized less for any imminent unpleasantness than as the means by which he had fought off competition for a sweet job.

'We could ask for the menu. And a couple of beers while we make our choice?'

Wilhelm closed his eyes and smiled. 'Wouldn't that be wonderful? I have to say, killing you is going to be like cutting my own throat.'

21

Outside the meeting room, one man stayed another with a hand and waited while the others hurried away. The gesture may have been noticed (in their world, alliances were feared, imagined, alleged and endless pored over), but the business was too absurd, too pressing to wait for a more discreet moment. When the staircase below them had cleared the captive audience began the conversation.

'That was … surprising.'

The other man shook his head. 'Was it? He has a habit of saying one thing and meaning another. His only loyalty is to whoever he needs the most at any moment, and at this moment it's Sauckel.'

'But Sauckel isn't providing what he's been promising.'

'What does that matter? The Führer appointed him, so he's a *fait accompli*. And no-one else can supply what's needed to the Four Year Plan. Therefore, as our illustrious Coward presides over the same, Sauckel is his favourite boy for now.'

'*Coward* is a little strong, surely?'

'Permit me to say, my dear Speer, that my experience of the man's moods and methods is considerably greater than yours. Whatever he was in the old days has been entirely excised by power, luxury, disappointment and cocaine.'

'It's true, is it? About drugs?'

'It is. I suspect that Sauckel knows also, and has been dropping gentle hints to keep our man not only obliged to him but fearful of the consequences should he cease to be.'

Reichsminister Speer rubbed his forehead. Like his colleague, he had been astounded by the course the meeting had taken. They had arrived with considerable evidence of failures and had it swept away as if it were a trifle not to be considered. They had been told to expect support, and instead the carpet had been whipped from beneath their feet by the very man who had promised to back them up. Yet their just complaint went to the very heart of what might prevent a cataclysmic defeat for Germany, or – should it be ignored – help greatly to bring on that disaster.

'No-one backed us. Not one of them'

Generalfeldmarschall Milch snorted. 'Did you notice that when he all but called me a liar, Bormann half-smiled? Keitel's useless - he won't ever offer a word unless he's first pointed towards it, and Himmler isn't going to say anything because he doesn't want SS to end up with the responsibility if Sauckel's removed. I'm beginning to see why Goebbels didn't attend.'

'You think he knew it was going to be an ambush?'

'Why wouldn't he be here, otherwise? Have you ever known him miss a meeting where all his enemies are present?'

'No. My God, this is terrible. I could hardly believe what Göring said to you.'

'You were meant to take some of it for yourself, Speer, believe me. He just doesn't dare accuse you directly, not when you're in such good odour with the Führer.'

'I'm not – at least, not as much as I was.'

'You should have remained an architect, then.'

'I wasn't offered the choice. Forgive me, Milch, but given what was said today I have to tell you something. It's rather embarrassing.'

'Well, you've caught me at a good moment. I'll hardly notice a little more embarrassment.'

'Göring had a quiet word with me a few days ago. He told me that I should be careful - that you were unreliable, and when your interests were at stake you'd trample over your friends. He said he was telling me this because I seemed to enjoy working with you.'

Milch laughed sourly. 'He said the same to me about you, word for word almost.'

'So his promises …?'

'Aren't worth a sparrow's fart. It's just you and me, Speer – everyone else is more interested in winning the battle of the Führer's ear than the war itself.'

'And yet we need them.'

'We do. We must make our case so strongly that all manoeuvres against us will come to be seen as sabotage.'

'And to do that we need more evidence.'

'We *had* more evidence.'

'I know. You suggested that you might …'

'I did, yesterday. At best, it gives us a few more days.'

Speer nodded. In the year since succeeding Fritz Todt as Minister for Armaments and Munitions, he had often wished fervently that the man's aircraft (upon which Speer, too, should have been a passenger that night) had managed to stay aloft until it reached a runway, and never more than now. Half the battle was the job itself, but its intrinsic difficulties were hugely amplified by knives flung from behind. Rational minds would accept that production of the means of waging war should have absolute priority over everything other than feeding the nation, yet National Socialism had somehow raised to high office a collection of men for whom the exercise of power for its own sake transcended love of country and even the physics of consequence. He genuinely wanted to ask these people what the purpose of obstructionism was when it served only the existential enemy, but the question would have confounded them. To them, personal interest and that of Germany were synonymous, however much common sense said otherwise.

Fritz Sauckel was a fine example, both of the breed and its impact upon the war effort. A quite fanatical Party man of no discernible talents, he had been appointed Head of Labour Assignment in preference to Speer's choice - the far more capable Karl Hanke - because Martin Bormann, the Führer's Machiavelli, felt that putting distance between Speer and Hitler was vastly more important than giving German industry the manpower it needed desperately. Since that little victory, Sauckel's efforts had been devoted almost entirely to concealing his own failures, rather than correcting them. Until today, Speer and Milch had assumed that Göring's hatred of Bormann was a trustworthy asset in their struggle to put right what was wrong with manpower supply. They had forgotten that the Reichsmarschall was every bit as prone as the rest of them to salting and then devouring his own tail.

Speer trusted Milch at least, because the man had no-one else that *he* could trust. They were two souls in a life-boat needing four hands to row, thrown together because they shared a curious belief that Germany could no longer afford or absorb amateurism, much less half-wittedness excused by a low Party membership number. If anything, Milch had the harder job. Speer had taken on his role reluctantly, but the Führer's personal friendship had been a powerful thicket-clearing tool; his colleague was not only Inspector-General of the Luftwaffe and (since the hapless Udet's suicide) Generalluftzegmeister in charge of production of aircraft and munitions, but discharged these onerous duties in the face of constant obstruction, obfuscations and - as had just been demonstrated graphically – betrayal by his immediate superior, Reichsmarschall Göring.

Speer and Milch, with Paul Körner, State Secretary of the Four Year Plan (and therefore another of Göring's immediate subordinates), had been charged with the coordination of all armaments production. One of their primary responsibilities was to allocate manpower resources between war production, other industries and agriculture, which brought them up against a whole clench of vested self-interests, most prominently those of Fritz Sauckel.

The Führer (unlike his more modern-minded enemies) refused to countenance the wholesale conscription of the nation's womanhood for factory work. Given that the Armed Forces were a voracious consumer of their sons, husbands, brothers and sweethearts, the vast gap had to be filled by forced, foreign labour. It was, to Speer at least, a regrettable necessity, but Milch didn't have any such qualms. He saw it as an entirely logical resource, and, through his many SS connections, had already organized the ad hoc transfer of many camp inmates to aircraft production sites. But then had come Sauckel's appointment as forced labour Supremo.

A Gauleiter, he was already hindered by bombastic self-belief in his own abilities. Now, charged with doing something that was measurably useful, he not only fell short but regarded it as part of his official function to disguise his failings. He was a numbers man, first and last, and given a target he strove to meet it - on the single ground of quantity.

An armaments manufacturer might require a thousand men. A form was filled, signed and dispatched to Sauckel's office. He authorized the transfer of that number from the camps and duly put a line entry in his schedules. Of course, the factory managers, receiving former farmhands, accountants, professors and tobacconists instead of the men with technical experience they had requested, promptly sent back a large proportion of their allocation. To Sauckel this was not a recordable event, and if anyone said that it was or should be, he first denied everything, and then, if a complaint was pressed, sought the help and protection of those within Government who believed that to criticise the work of good Party members was to criticise the Party itself.

Without the right manpower, Speer and Milch couldn't meet their production targets. Sauckel's allies saw a double opportunity here – to protect their own and hurt the real enemy, and as their man was yet another of the Führer's appointees, he was as untouchable as Speer himself. Predictably, the struggle had ground to an unproductive (in every sense) stalemate. Today's meeting had been intended – at least, by Speer and Milch - to unjam the mechanism, and Göring had promised to help. Like idiots, they had believed him.

Milch was pondering the view through the tall staircase window. This building had been constructed to house the Chancellery secretariat, so that business could proceed as usual during the Führer's increasingly protracted stays at

Berchtesgaten. For those obliged to attend it was a pleasant break from Berlin, but today the magnificent setting only added to the sense of unreality. The Americans and British were building fleets of new aircraft that could easily reach Germany's major cities and linger long enough to do their work properly. On the other flank, the Soviets were assembling armies sufficiently large and well-equipped to render irrelevant both their chaotic field-command structure and Stalin's habit of interfering with military operations. Meanwhile, production of a revolutionary new fighter aircraft was waiting upon their Leader's vacillations about what, exactly, he wanted it to be, and their new medium, T34-killing tank had so many teething issues they were thinking of code-naming it *Blondi*. And yet here they were, two of the three men responsible for equipping Germany to survive the deluge, obliged to arm-wrestle for the most basic means to do it, to fail and then (Speer checked his watch) to endure an interminable afternoon tea, replete with chocolate fancies, during which the Führer's old cronies would doubtless attempt to entertain him with sentimental reminiscences about the Struggle's early days. By comparison, Nero's violin-sawing might have stood as an example of rigorous governance.

...it gives us a few days. Speer tried to smile.'I have to say, I quite like your plan. It has a certain elegance.'

Milch snorted. 'It has a certain desperation, but what else are we to do? We *must* get the data.'

'If all else fails, we could ask the industrialists to repeat the exercise.'

'That would require a couple of months, at least. By then, how far might things have slipped?'

'We do it your way, then. But you're certain they think they know their man?'

'I've done everything except paint 'It's me' on his forehead. If they don't get the hint, they're bigger fools than even I believed.'

'Who is he?'

'No-one - really, no-one. His name...'

'No, don't tell me. I feel bad enough about this already. If you give me a name I'll put a face to it, and then how will I sleep?'

Milch laughed, genuinely amused for the first time that day.

'Believe me, Speer, if you put the correct face to this man, you might never sleep again.'

Were his colleagues, friends and loved ones to list the qualities that made Friedrich Melancthon Holleman the man that he was, thoughtfulness would probably not rank highly on the aggregated result. As a policeman he had been an effective (if not exemplary) street-pounder, and if his record as a fighter pilot was modest it was only because he had missed the Polish campaign through illness and then took an unlucky burst of 20mm ammunition from a pair of Hurricanes before he could make a mark on his squadron's tally sheet in Belgium. Following a long convalescence from that latter mishap, his work with the *Kriegsberichter der Luftwaffe* had been as assiduous as was necessary to mould hard truths into hopeful dissemblance. All these careers had required attention to detail and a willingness not to give comfort to the enemy. None of them demanded an aptitude for deep contemplation.

Lately, though, this workaday mind had been pondering more than family, country, breasts, bare-faced lies and whatever the *Silver Birch* was serving for lack of beer. For the moment at least, Otto Fischer had moved up the crowded field to take a nose's lead. Though he was very much a stranger still, Holleman was beginning to like the man – certainly, as much as was needed to regret having cast him into a sty's-worth of excrement. Whether that counted as fondness he couldn't say, but he was pestered by increasingly circular examinations of why, how and how quickly he had managed to turn idle speculation into a possible death sentence. His wife Kristin had noticed that he was preoccupied (her antenna outperformed any *seetakt* receiver), and was giving him the sort of glances that suggested an interrogation was brewing. No lie or deflection ever got past her, so in addition to kicking himself he was searching for a way to explain it all that didn't make him seem as much of a cock as he actually was.

He was perfectly aware that he could be impetuous, but Fischer's cautionary words had been so obviously don't-suck-a-pistol-while-your-finger's-on-the-trigger that he could hardly believe he hadn't managed to summon at least some of them himself. What possible good could have come of it? At best, a stray ray of brilliance might have illuminated the circumstances of Ahle's death, but what might he have done with that revelation, other than award himself a pat on the back? Mentioning any of it would by like cutting his own throat, and probably that of his audience also - which made him think of Fischer once more, because he *had* mentioned it. In effect, in attempting to find justice for poor Ahle he had made another Ahle.

And Karl Krohne had been right, too - nothing could be done about any of it. The heavies had Fischer safe (if that was the word) from God's own intervention, which meant that Holleman's fate was entirely out of his own hands. At some point, Fischer might reasonably say stop hitting me, it was that bastard Freddie Holleman's doing – he's the one you should be practising on. Who could blame him? And then not only would Kirstin be widowed and lose a war pension, but the boys would gain a new father of sorts - the Hitler Jugend. And all because of …

He was an idiot – in fact, the worst sort of idiot, because he'd known exactly what the consequences might be and risked them anyway, and all for the memory and reputation of a man who wouldn't have cracked a smile if he'd won a day at the races and a night beneath Brigitte Helm. Whatever was coming, he deserved it.

'Freddie?'

'Yes, my darling?'

'Set the table, would you? The soup's ready.'

The boys played for their school football team and would be late, which meant that the *pater familias* would get at least a helping and a half of his favourite dish, split pea soup. Like any domestic goddess, Kristin Holleman had heeded her wise grandmother and carried her family through thin times by always having a sack of the delectable legumes tucked at the back of her larder. They kept forever, defied the hungriest rodents or weevils and needed only water and an onion to be transformed from gravel to gut-clogging ambrosia. Even the inevitable absence of that delightful garnish, ham hock, could take only the thinnest edge from his anticipation, and as he laid the place settings he almost forgot the matter of poor Ahle and its blast radius.

He ate heartily, but noticed the lingering looks from his chief love and only inquisitor. Usually, nothing more was needed to force a confession, and if the cause of his present dolor had carried fewer seeds of disaster he might have got it off his chest between mouthfuls. He needed more time to think this one out, though, so before she could sharpen the ordeal with a question he threw in one of his own.

'Don't you want that?'

She looked down at the soup she had been toying with.

'Yes.'

'Pity.'

'It's bland.'

'A little more salt, perhaps, but it's nearly perfect. What do you think about us tarting up the lake house?'

Surprised (and distracted), she looked up. 'The lake house?'

'It's been mouldering since my stepfather died. I thought we might put it right. It would be a nice place to take the boys, wouldn't it? In summer?'

'But ... how? We couldn't afford the materials. We couldn't *find* the materials. And who would do it anyway?'

'Me.'

'With your tin leg? How would you get up a ladder, even?'

Several cutting retorts came to mind, but Holleman smothered them. Her attention had been dragged away from what was ailing him, which was the entire point of the conversation. The lake house *had* been on his mind for a while now, but only as a fond dream for when All of This Shit was over. She was right - about the cost, the materials, his likely comic turn on a ladder - but why couldn't they plan prudently, take things steadily and not get too ambitious (or too frustrated when new, unforeseen jobs sprouted like dandelions on a lawn, as they would, for sure)? It would be a project, and even the word pleased him. He'd never before had a *project*.

'Anyway, you're not handy. Look at what you did to the chimney, even with two legs.'

'That chimney couldn't be saved – it was rotten all the way through, which I only discovered once I got up there. And what have legs to do with renovations? All they're for is steadying.' He gave her his wounded dignity face. 'And I'm re-learning my balance.'

She shrugged. 'Alright, if you want to. But you'd better ask the Führer for some time off work. And a van to move stuff, if he has one spare.'

'Don't be sarcastic. It's a plan, that's all. But the longer we leave it, the more my inheritance ...' he searched for the word ' ... depreciates.'

'It'll be expensive.'

'And once it's done we'll have free holidays forever. In the Spreewald.'

He could sense her resistance crumbling. Being a country girl at heart, she loved the Spreewald. They had done much of their courting there (his step-father had been too drunk to notice, most of the time), had their first, best, most illicit fuck in the old boat-shed and eaten countless ices with their feet dangling in placid, deep water. They were beyond most of that now, but for parents of healthy, noisy, tireless twelve-year-olds there weren't many places better suited to snatch a little peace and quiet. Of course it was impractical, but what else offered a faint, sweet hope of things that war had ripped entirely from life?

She lifted her spoon, lowered it and looked up. 'We might move there, eventually.'

Astonished, he momentarily forgot both Ahle and Otto Fischer. He had been born, raised, put to work and decayed to middle-age within the bounds of this city, and its soot thickened his blood as it did that of the rats that infested the crypts of the Berliner Dom. But just five words, spilling unexpectedly from his wife's mouth, excised every sentimental stay upon his hopes for something better than *now*. A magical vision of rural

Freddie, knee-deep in rich Lusatian earth (well, watching his employees in the same), opened the gate and invited in a swarm of possibilities. Once the house and boat-shed were repaired they could buy some punts and rent them out to tourists, perhaps build a small tea-hut for refreshments, and allow their takings to carry them through the close seasons. His lungs, blood-pressure and temper would improve, and in time he might stand for local office, making his little mark in a new world and earning the love and respect of real, soil-bound folk. Hell, he might even learn Lower Sorbian, and pretend not to understand the tiresome fucking Germans who swarmed into the forest and spoiled things with their stink and city ways …

'Freddie?'

'What, my love?'

'You were off, somewhere else.'

'Was I? Sorry. Look, I'll speak to Karl Krohne, and get a few days' leave and go down to the house. I'll just look at it, get some feel for what needs doing, and then we can have a proper talk about time and costs when I get back.'

'Will that be alright? Leave, I mean?'

'Yeah. Karl's good to his cripples that way, probably because he's always taking time off himself to poke one of his tarts.'

Kristin shook her head. 'His poor wife. Do you think she knows?'

'I hope not, for his testicles' sake.'

Is that why you want a few days away from me? To see *your* tarts?'

"Sweetheart, who else shares your truly awful taste in men?'

She sniffed. 'There aren't many, I suppose. You'll 'phone me, every night?'

'I promise. I'll sleep at the house but have my supper in that little guest-house outside Raddusch, and call from there.'

They finished their soup in silence. Holleman's head could hardly pull itself out of the Spreewald, but the matter of how much longer he might be alive couldn't be stifled entirely. Perhaps it was fate, that an impulse would be taking him a safe distance from his family, should the men who killed Ahle come for him. It would be the very best part of a foul fate, if it were only he who suffered for his blind stupidity.

Be a good fellow, Otto. You've been through a lot, God knows, but don't break when they start leaning on you.

23

Frau Traugott sat at the small table in Herr Fischer's sitting-room, staring at the modest collection of personal effects that comprised her lodger's worldly estate. Perhaps *modest* overstated it, because the table (as small as it was) retained sufficient free space to host a breakfast without making the said items feel at all crowded. There were eight children's books whose fragile condition suggested that he had been the child in question (she had stacked those), an old photograph of a man and a woman (his parents, presumably), a silver pocket watch containing a lock of red hair and a silver hip flask, dented from long service but which smelled of nothing when she removed the cap. The whole suggested a life that had been passed through rather than lived, and the pity she felt for the man strengthened considerably as she surveyed it.

At least the presence of the collection killed one possibility – that he had found better accommodation and fled without paying what he owed. Not, of course, that she would have believed him capable of that, but a landlady hadto regard it as one of the potential perils of her business. To her mind, two infinitely more terrible (and more likely) alternatives remained: that he had been murdered in a dark alley by ausländers, or that the burden of his wounds had overcome his will to continue, and he was presently hanging beneath one of central Berlin's many bridges. Whichever was the case, she should contact the police – or rather, she *should have* contacted the police, and the previous day at the latest.

She had her excuse polished already – Herr Fischer was an important military man, and at times of war could be summoned away at no notice. Who was she, an elderly lady with spare rooms, to be asking or expecting to know his business? She had waited until now, three days since he left the house, because she had been hoping that some lackey might arrive with a message from the Luftwaffe, explaining - in very general terms, naturally – that he was on a vital mission and that she shouldn't worry, he was good for the rent.

Having rehearsed it (and found it irrefutably sound), her fears for herself eased considerably. Her worries about alleys and bridges remained, however. She was under no obligation or weight of loyalty to her paying guest, but a man who had no family or known friends, who was a stranger to the city itself, should surely have at least the lukewarm (though possibly posthumous) comfort of his landlady's concern.

So, feeling both reassured and somewhat virtuous, she summoned the courage to go to the local police station and report a missing person. It took a little longer than she expected, because on the way she encountered her blockhelfer, Amon Dunst, and made the mistake of explaining her errand to him. Before she had finished the story he was almost quivering with offended delight.

'A deserter, obviously. I shall inform the Feldgendarmerie.'

That Dunst was an idiot came as no revelation to anyone who had met him, and usually, Frau Traugott only pretended to accept his pronouncements as Scripture because it was easier and safer than arguing. Today, however, anxiety and emotion overcame prudence.

'You will? Tell me, Herr Dunst – do you imagine that the Air Ministry suffers many desertions?'

'The Air Ministry?'

His smirk had gone, and the contralto squeak suggested that his ersatz shock had been replaced by the real thing.

'Yes, on Wilhelmstrasse. Herr Fischer is an extremely important person, a friend of the Reichsmarschall …' (it might be true, she couldn't say, and it seemed more likely than not) '… and you accuse him of something treasonous.'

Frantically, Dunst waved a hand in her face. 'No, Frau Traugott, I assure you, it was a preliminary opinion, based upon my …'

'You said *obviously*.' She punctuated her emphasis with a stabbed finger, and had it been a blade it couldn't have done the job more pleasingly. Dunst staggered back a step, the poison splashing the wrong way for once, and had a vehicle been passing at that moment the neighbourhood might have lost an assiduous servant of the people (much to their pale regret). Before he could find a plausible defence she had presented her back to him and continued on her errand, leaving him to wonder (she hoped) what would be said to his friends at the police station.

Of course, she didn't mention him. She made her report as concise as possible and was pleased to be told that no bodies in Luftwaffe uniforms had been discovered anywhere in Berlin over the past seventy-two hours. That didn't mean that he hadn't been stripped naked before or after the event, but the officer behind the counter confirmed that none of the four corpses received at the mortuary during the same period bore old mutilations. He took her details, thanked her for her vigilance, promised to consult WASt to determine whether Hauptmann Fischer's *soldbuch* had been handed in and suggested that some quite legitimate military necessity may have detained him at the Air Ministry. As this was as much as she had tried to tell herself, she was almost convinced.

But not quite. Surely, he would have sent home some word, if only for a change of shirt? No doubt even senior officers at the Front were used to privations, but she couldn't believe that the Air Ministry permitted the odour of stale sweat to permeate its monumental spaces. And if for some reason pressure of work kept him from even the basic needs of hygiene, she was certain that his boss – now, there was a *real* gentleman – would have found a way to let her know something of the situation.

She was poring over and through her doubts when, on the corner of Waldenserstrasse and Bremerstrasse, she bumped into (or rather, failed to avoid) Frau Edith Preusker, one of her great enemy Frau Speigl's familiars. For once, however, the lady didn't take pains to freeze the air between them with her obvious contempt. She seemed upset, and almost eager to talk.

'Did you hear about the raid, Frau Traugott?'

'Raid? No, I didn't.' The sirens had sounded the previous evening, as they did most evenings. Even when the enemy didn't risk their Mosquitoes to make a petty point, the civil defence authorities ensured that both Berlin's defences and her citizens' readiness were tested. Naturally, hardly anyone took notice any more; Frau Traugott herself had bothered to go to her nearest shelter only twice in the past year when the wailing summoned her, despite the threat of fines (rarely imposed) for willful deafness.

'Sankti Paulus - a single bomb struck its wall on the Oldenburgerstrasse side. They say the Stations of the Cross have been smashed. Are you coming to see?'

Frau Traugott sniffed. In her opinion, too many Dominicans were enthusiastic Nazis. The previous January, she had attended a Pontifical Mass at Sankti Paulus and had been scandalized to see swastika flags flying among the Order's white-and-yellows. If God had sent a British aeroplane to punish them for their worldliness it was hardly surprising.

Still, a church was a church, and she felt guilty for having slept through it. To view the damage required only a five-minute detour, and if she didn't go no doubt Frau Preusker would spread the word that she was an atheist – or, worse, a Protestant. Reluctantly, she nodded and followed the other woman.

Sankti Paulus' west front (perversely, it faced north) was on Waldenserstrasse, but a crowd was assembling around the corner, near the bomb damage. A few familiar faces peered intently into the rubble, as if they might divine from it the nature of the guilty ordnance, its nominal yield and Arthur Harris's plans for the rest of the neighbourhood. A group of children were attempting to purloin shattered pieces of the orange-red brickwork for souvenirs, but a battle-wing of blockhelfers, sensing in their bones that this sort of behaviour must be against some rule, somewhere, had formed a cordon which was hindering the firefighters' efforts to rewind their hoses. An argument was playing out between these two branches of the civil state, to the crowd's growing enjoyment.

The damage didn't seem to be too severe, and Frau Traugott decided that a few more minutes' vigil would be enough to mark her card as a dutiful citizen. She gave an impression of listening to Frau Preusker's almost seamless commentary upon the RAF, the flak ring's inadequacies and the curious absence of fighter cover, but her attention remained on Herr Fischer's disappearance and its implications. Consequently, she didn't notice the stranger's arrival until he spoke, almost in her ear.

'It's a terrible thing.'

She didn't bother to look up at this expected observation. 'They should be able to repair it. The Dominicans can afford some new bricks, I'm sure.'

'I meant war. It takes the good as well as the bad.'

This was a sufficiently dangerous sentiment to make her turn, and surprise became something more
when she recognized him. It was the man who had been following her – or at least (and she was *almost* certain of this) who had appeared outside her front door and then later that day in the café. He gave her another smile, a slightly sadder one this time, and a little bow (the way gentlemen used to before the First War, though he couldn't be that old). She returned it, but kept her smiles to herself.

He gestured at the bomb damage. 'I supposed I should be pleased, they being the enemy. But God's House has many rooms as they say, and I hate to see any of them defiled like this.'

'Enemy?'

'The Catholics, but especially the Dominicans. I'm a pastor. I have a congregation in north Wedding.'

'Oh.' Frau Traugott's fears of being viciously assaulted receded considerably, but she felt she had to make at least a small stand for the religion she was born into.

'*I'm* a Catholic.'

He seemed pained. 'Forgive me, it was a poor joke. But at least the injury to the church seems minor.'

'Yes.' She gave the shattered brickwork a professional glance. 'They didn't want them here, did you know?'

'The Dominicans? I understand there were riots, at the time.'

'In 1869. They called it the Moabiter Klostersturm, afterwards. A mob tried to get in, but the police stopped them and two people died. My father brought me to see it the day after. It was a different building then, of course, but the damage looked a lot worse than this.'

'Well, there are bad people on all sides, as well as the good. May I apologize, on their behalf?'

He was teasing her, but in a pleasant way (it was made more pleasant by Frau Preusker's obvious resentment at being entirely excluded from the conversation), and she decided that he was probably as good a man as a pastor could be. It was definitely he who had smiled at her in the café, but now she thought more about it she really couldn't say that he'd been outside her house also. It was her old woman's raw nerve-endings that had made the connection.

They exchanged a few more meaningless comments, until Frau Preusker tired of being ignored and walked away. Without giving the matter the consideration it deserved - in fact, almost entirely impulsively – Frau Traugott decided that if a churchman (of any denomination) couldn't be trusted with a problem then the world was a poorer place than even she imagined it to be. That settled, she didn't waste further time searching for a form of words that would make the best sense of it, but simply let it spill out.

'My lodger's disappeared.'

'I'm sorry?'

'He's a Luftwaffe officer - a hero, badly wounded at the Front. I'm worried for him. He left the house three days ago and hasn't returned.'

'Have you been to the police?'

'Yes. They said I shouldn't worry, but ...'

'But of course you're worried. You say badly wounded – is he crippled? Does he need help?'

'No, he was burned. But he gets depressed about it, I think. He may have done something.'

'Oh.' The gentleman was distressed to hear this. He put a hand to his mouth and regarded the street beneath his feet for some moments, the frown moving constantly. When he looked up he opened his mouth but paused, as if considering whether he should speak at all.

'Before my calling found me, I was a policemen - not one of *those* ...' he added, hastily. 'I still have a few friends at Alexanderplatz. Your lodger falls within the military police's jurisdiction, but in Berlin they'll need to be coordinating with their civilian colleagues. I can probably find out if they've found him, or at least ask them to let you know when ... I mean, if ...'

Embarrassed, he left the offer in the air, and Frau Traugott scolded her unchristian heart for having assumed the worst of him.

'That would be very *kind* of you, Pastor.'

'Please, I'm Johann. Now, what can I tell them about him?'

'One side of his face was burned away. They've repaired it, but not very well. He doesn't get lost in any crowd.'

'Well, that's helpful. But I was thinking more of friends and relatives that he might have contacted, or perhaps taken refuge with.'

She looked at him blankly. 'He hasn't got any friends. And he's not married. I think his parents are dead.'

'Correspondence?'

'I've cleaned his rooms twice since he went. I haven't seen a letter. But ...'

'What is it?'

'He has some books. There might be something between their pages. I haven't looked.'

'Well, shall we see?'

'Would you mind? It's only a few minutes away.'

As they walked, Pastor Johann told her more about himself. He had abandoned his congregation temporarily to look after his sister, who was not expected to live much longer yet seemed to have perked up considerably since acquiring her unpaid home help, and was taking full advantage of the situation.

'She's very particular about how she has things.' He smiled ruefully. 'I'm ashamed to say that the morning I saw you in the café I'd gone absent without leave. It was the quietest hour I've had since I came to Moabit. Ah, are we here?'

Frau Traugott led him into her home, introduced her cats (unlike Herr Fischer he found them delightful, and they fussed about him like old friends), had her offer of tea refused graciously, and then together they searched the top-floor rooms for evidence of where her missing lodger might be. There were no letters in the books, nothing other than underwear, socks and shirts in the bedside drawers and just a spare pair of Luftwaffe trousers hanging in the closet. Pastor Johann handled everything carefully, which she took to be a mark of his respect and discomfort, and he seemed happy to end his trespasses as soon as they had reassured themselves that there were no discoveries to be made.

Down in the hallway, he stooped to rub Sigi's head.

'Your gentleman travels light, doesn't he?'

'He arrived with one small bag, the one hanging behind his door. I think he was at the lazaret for a long time, before he came to me.'

'The poor man. Well ...' He straightened, took an envelope and a pen from his pocket and wrote something. 'I see you don't have a telephone. Here is my sister's number. I'll speak to my friends at Alexanderplatz and ask them to let me know if they hear anything. If not ...'

'Nothing can be done, I know. May I call you tomorrow?'

'Of course. Goodbye.'

When he had gone, Frau Traugott sat for a great while, allowing her cats to climb over her. She was quite exhausted but felt a little more hopeful, having met someone who was walking proof that decent, selfless folk could still be found in a wartime city. Naturally, the chances of her lodger being alive and safe hadn't improved by the mere fact of her having met Pastor Johann, but that *something* might be done was at least a small blessing. It almost amused her, that because she had gone to the police (who had been polite but useless) she had encountered a former policeman who was willing to put himself to some trouble for a stranger. Whether that was a coincidence, fate or happy chance she couldn't say, but being both religious *and* superstitious she couldn't help but feel that some agency was at work on Herr Fischer's behalf. And as the good Lord knew, he needed it.

On the other side of Tiergarten, Pastor Johann walked into the radar-control annexe of Flakturm Zoo, waved his badge at a Luftwaffe leutnant and asked to use a telephone. He was shown to a small office, where he waited until the young man withdrew and then dialled a direct number to an address in Prinz-Albrecht-Strasse. To the person who answered he identified himself with a name that, like Johann, had been chosen at random, and made his very brief report.

'He's a ghost, and in the air.'

'You think he has it?'

'I'm thinking why would he run, otherwise?'

'But you're not certain?'

'I couldn't be, either way. We have no choice but to assume that it's in his possession.'

'True. I'll let our friend know.'

'Tell him I have continuing access to the gentleman's home, but my feeling is he won't be coming back. The personal effects he left there are too sparse and impersonal to be convincing.'

'Nevertheless, keep your team on site. If he *does* return and he has the item, secure it and lose him.'

'You don't need him questioned?'

'We considered it, but the risks of his people finding out and coming for him before he's squeezed are too great. A nice, uncomplicated accident would make everything moot – assuming, of course, that he has the item.'

'And if he doesn't?'

'Then he's probably an innocent.'

'In which case?'

'It doesn't matter whether it looks like an accident or something else.'

24

On the fourth morning of his stay at *Pension* Spandau, Fischer reached the limits of his endurance. He hadn't tasted his breakfast, had answered Wilhelm's many (and usually glib) comments with grunts while focusing his mind on each of his fingers and toes, trying to isolate the sensation in the tips of each without touching them. The diversion didn't work, and eventually the other man noticed the perspiration on his forehead.

'What's wrong?'

'Pethidin.'

'What about it?'

'I don't have any. I last took some on Monday.'

'An addiction?'

'A necessity, unless you want to see a man climbing a wall.'

Wilhelm pulled a face. 'Hard to find, in here. I could get you some pilot's salt.'

'Pervitin? It would only help me feel the pain with a clearer head.'

'I bet they pumped you parachute boys full of it.'

'It was extremely available, yes. But I preferred to miss the highs and not suffer the lows that followed.'

'So, how bad is it?'

'I'll be shouting soon.'

'Alright. Bite your lip for an hour, if you can.'

As Wilhelm departed, his silent, miserable colleague entered, took the warm seat and invited no conversation. Consequently, the interlude felt much longer than an hour, but then, all time stretched in this place. Fischer occupied himself by counting out tranches of one hundred and telling himself after each that if he could stand what had just passed he could manage the next one also. That wasn't the case, of course, but pretending to have at least a little agency over the pain had kept him just this side of collapse during his months at Potsdam (unlike some of the men who had arrived later and departed earlier). His face hurt, but not too badly. He was more worried about the stiffness there, which came after several days of not …

Glycerin. I should have asked for glycerin also, while he was in a good mood.

The shoulder was a different matter, though – a torment of contradictory, amplifying pains, pulling at each other and making the whole the worse for it. His scorched lung and oesophagus felt as if they had ignited sometime before dawn, but this was the worst they would feel. He was fairly comfortable with *worst*. At least he couldn't be surprised unpleasantly.

He was about to ask the miserable bastard for a shoulder massage when the door opened and another toss of the head removed the potential slap. Wilhelm pulled a package from his tunic and waved at the small, hard bed.

'Take of your shirt and sit over there.'

As Fischer obeyed, the big man broke a seal and extracted a small syringe, read something on it and looked expectantly at the patient, who had half-sat before he thought to raise objections.

'What is it?'

'Morphine.'

'From where?'

'Not your business.'

'Do you know the correct dosage, because …?'

'It's a dose. He said it was a single dose. I put it all into you, then you shut up.'

'He?'

'Eva Braun's personal physician. I legged it across to the Old Chancellery.'

'It was a sensible question.'

'Yeah, well. He asked your weight and age, and whether you'd had it before. I said skinny, old and almost definitely, and he gave me this and said it's the right amount. Now, sit.'

The argument received strong support from the pain, and Fischer did as he was told. He opened his mouth to ask that the burned tissue be avoided, but before he could speak the needle had been stabbed into his good shoulder and the phial emptied. Wilhelm leaned back, examined his handiwork and sniffed.

'I have two more doses and no chance of re-supply, so make it last.'

'Glycerin.'

'Eh?'

'I forgot to ask. If you could get some glycerin also – it shouldn't be difficult, even in here.'

'Why the hell would …?'

'So my face doesn't crack and fall off.'

Wilhelm's mouth opened, but the horror of that vision killed whatever he was going to say. Fischer hadn't meant to put it quite so baldly, but he was already as detached from proprieties as he was from the pain. A warm, exquisite lethargy engulfed him, and in what seemed like the slowest motion he fall back onto his suddenly comfortable bed. Wilhelm lifted his legs and rotated the body lengthways, much to Fischer's amusement.

'Thank you, *mutti*.'

'Fuck off.'

The patient obeyed, going somewhere else entirely for a while. His mind meandered, occasionally catching a wisp but failing to hold it. During rare moments in which he managed to focus his eyes the cell seemed vast, its walls receding into grey haar. Beyond it, unseen, he heard waves gently breaking on kind shores, their coming and going a slight, soothing throb in his temples.

'This is very nice.'

'Yeah, so they tell me. Don't get used to it.'

'Hm?'

'Nothing. Go to sleep.'

Fischer wanted to obey, but the throb strengthened just enough to lose its soporific quality. Another wisp came and went but then returned, like a fly that had caught a turd's bouquet as it hurried by (the analogy made him giggle). It hovered with him for a while, companionably, and finally he recognized it.

'Wilhelm?'

'What?'

'You were a butcher, weren't you?'

'As I said.'

'Could a butcher take off a head as ...'

'As what?'

'Um. Cleanly. As cleanly as a guillotine?'

'That's what morphine does to a head, is it?'

'I'm serious. Could you do it?'

'With the sharpest, best knives in the world?'

'Yes.'

'Not a chance. You'd need to use a bone-saw to get through the spine, and it would show.'

'An ax, then?'

'I don't know. They used to top people with axes, didn't they? How messy it was I couldn't say. I doubt that any man could apply the precision *and* force that a guillotine does. But you needn't worry.'

'Worry?'

'If it comes to it, I won't be creative. A nice, clean shot to the back of the head, Soviet-style. You won't feel a thing.'

'Thank you, Wilhelm. You're a *mensch*.'

Satisfied, the wisp departed, but another took its place almost immediately. For a while, Fischer pretended not to notice and concentrated instead on the pleasing nothingness that comprised the rest of the Universe, but like a speck on spectacles it preceded him wherever he drifted. Eventually, a throat cleared itself somewhere in the distance.

'Wilhelm?'

A sigh. '*Yes?*'

'Why haven't you asked me?'

'Asked you what?'

'Whether I have it?'

'Do you have it?'

'No.'

'Right, then.'

'Don't you want to know who has it?'

'Who has it?'

'No-one.'

'Good to clear that up.'

'Wilhelm?'

A groan. 'What?'

'You don't know what *it* is, do you?'

'No. And I don't care to cure my ignorance.'

'Do you know about Ahle?'

'What's Ahle? Do you mean the river?'

'*Who's* Ahle. Poor Ahle. Poor, poor Ahle.'

'Alright, *who's* Ahle?'

'I'd better not say.'

'A bullet, or a pillow over your face. Think about it.'

Fischer tried to think about it, but poor Ahle kept getting in the way – a slightly-built, painfully stooping man with a sour personality and a lot of little grudges about life and how it hadn't come up to expectations. Of course, they had never met, so he couldn't put a face to him. But then, he no longer had a head, so it hardly mattered.

'Stop sniggering, or this is the last dose you'll get.'

'Sorry.'

Wilhelm wasn't an interrogator, then - just a guard, or executioner. Fischer was pleased about that. He was beginning to like the man, and didn't want to feel like an idiot for having fetched a thrown ball. Besides, he was beginning to suspect that a shoulder-full of opiates wasn't likely to help him fend off serious questions, even if the beating that came with them would almost certainly be painless.

No further wisps arrived, so he allowed himself to drift. A random sequence of memories – of places, events, people – took shape in the greyness and then dispersed like ink dropped into water. He recalled himself as a two-year-old, lying in his crib, almost burning up with measles, and though his mother had often related the story this was the first time he had ever seen it for himself. He was snatched from this implausible recollection and transported to his mittelschule playground on the morning that his arse had almost been kicked off by Ulbrecht Ungar, an older boy who fancied himself as both a wit and future centre-forward for Tasmania Rixdorf. Next came his wedding day (the pain of which even morphine couldn't entirely erase), then his graduation from the Police Academy, then the taste of Norwegian soil as he chewed the ground at Sola Air Station while a solitary machine-gunner pinned down his entire company, and then – inevitably – a small backward step to the night upon which a Stettin docker's boot had relocated one of his testicles to the opposite bank of the Oder (or so his nervous system alleged). At one point, part of his wandering mind wondered why the rest of it wasn't finding more pleasant moments from past-Otto – perhaps his first fuck, or the time (the only time) he had managed to score a goal for his class football team, or at least a recollection that didn't involve pain or uniforms. Never mind, he told his mind. Poor memories were a small price to pay for the greatest comfort he had known in his adult life.

He drifted on for some unmeasurable time, not even needing to tread water to float, until an unpleasant intrusion jarred the Cosmos. He snored once, and woke. He was in a small room with single, high, barred window, lying on his side on an unyielding wall-bed, watching a man eat from a plate on his knees. The intrusion was an odour, of fried meat.

'You're back, then.' Wilhelm spoke through a mouthful of berliner buletten.

'How long?'

'Nine hours. I couldn't wait for you.'

Fischer's stomach contracted violently, and he struggled to sit up. Wilhelm waved his fork.

'If you puke before I've finished I'll stab you in the eye.'

Fischer quelled a single dry-gag (there couldn't have been anything in his stomach to lose). His head was pounding, and the rest of him felt not so much as if he'd been sleeping for hours as climbing rock-faces with a full marching-pack. In all, the sequel to morphine distracted him from the pain of his injuries almost as effectively as the event itself.

'I might marry her.'

'Urrgh. Who?'

'The deputy commandant's sister. She has an angel's touch with rations. Of course, she might be a hound.'

'You're no Viktor Staal yourself.'

Wilhelm beamed. 'I'm not, am I? Do you want to try some? I can send for more, and help you eat it.'

Fischer retched and turned to the wall. For a while the other man watched dispassionately, then sighed and put down his heavily-laden fork.

'Your first time with Herr Brown?'

'Outside of a lazaret, yes.'

'Here.' Wilhelm reached into his pocket and took out a small container. 'Have two of these. With a swimming-pool's worth of water, if you can manage it.'

'What is it? '

'Codeine phosphate.'

'More of the same?'

'It'll help with the symptoms, particularly the shits.'

'I don't have the shits.'

'You will, and then I'll have to kill you.'

Fischer sat up and took the pills. The movement brought dizziness, but he resisted the temptation to close his eyes. Wilhelm reached down between his legs and passed a mug.

'Tea. Real tea.'

It was lukewarm, but excellent, and Fischer drank it all.

'Sorry.'

'It's fine, I don't really like tea. You were talking a lot.'

'While I was …?'

'Yeah. Some deranged crap about this Ahle fellow. Was he a mate?'

'I didn't know him.'

'So why is he occupying ground in your head?'

Has the interrogation started? Fischer looked at Wilhelm, trying to find a sliver too much nonchalance, and failed. The man was bored, and irritated, and perhaps irritated *because* he was bored. He didn't want to be here, even with unusually fine cuisine to hand. He was being honest - he knew nothing about Ahle.

Even so, the correct – the sensible – response to his last question was *never mind, it doesn't matter.* At the moment, however, Fischer's usually acute reserve had loosened, for which he suspected that residual effects of morphine were responsible. In any case, did he have a choice? He was alone in this, disconnected from allies (not that Freddie Holleman was much use in that respect) and any understanding of who had removed Ahle, why they'd done it and why they now wanted the inheritor of his desk in a place from which few people ever emerged. Could a man who had been cast into that sort of pit question the motives of someone who took the trouble to peer down?

'It's not a short story.'

Wilhelm laughed. 'I don't think my diary's too crowded at the moment.'

'Well, now that you mention diaries ...'

25

In the same way that a practised driver changes gear without thinking about it, Oberstleutnant Karl Krohne checked his trouser-fly with a discreet sweep of the hand as he entered the Air Ministry. He was feeling quite wretched, as he always did immediately following an ejaculation into someone other than his wife. To date, remorse hadn't managed to make the next bout any less likely to happen, but like most adulterers he earnestly intended that it should.

His mood was lowered further by the wink he received from the guard at the entrance. This was of course an offence for which the man could and should have been severely punished, but Ernst Körner (known also as Köndom Korner or Friday Ernst) knew himself to be safe from this particular direction. Krohne was one of his best customers, and received a slight discount in recognition of the regularity with which his orders were placed.

After visiting the toilets on the third floor, shame carried him straight into his office, rather than to the Den to check on whether his men had managed to polish the field reports from Army Group South. They all knew about his lunchtime adventures; the usual reactions ranged from barely suppressed hilarity (the younger men) to a mournful shake of the head (Holleman) or tight-lipped, envious disgust (poor Ahle, now unable to further embarrass his commanding officer). To each he offered his blithely indifferent face, but he was diminished by all of them.

Lacking any delicacy regarding delicate matters, Freddie Holleman had once put him on the spot about it as they sank a third or fourth round in the *Silver Birch*.

'I've met your wife, Karl. Why would you risk something so burning hot for the sake of novelty?'

There was no rational answer, and the detail of Krohne's mumbled response had been forgotten by both men as the alcohol took hold. He had asked himself the same question, and often. It wasn't a need to be loved, or admired; it wasn't because Magda fell in any conceivable way short of what was necessary to get him off; it wasn't even a biological imperative to spread the Krohne seed, as every drop invariably shot itself straight into rubber these days. All he could think was that his sinning reflected some deep-rooted flaw that a priest would blame upon childhood masturbation and Herr Freud diagnose as a subliminal urge to bang his mother (his own, not Freud's).

At present, the condition was being both teased and fed by a young lady named Bettina, a ladies' hair-stylist possessed of considerable skills. He had been introduced to her at a Party party, and very soon afterwards she had introduced cocaine to his nose and her finger to his rectum, at which residual thoughts of honour, propriety and Magda in her wedding dress had fled. In the weeks since he had made several attempts to end their liaison, and each time she had countered with a new (to him at least) token of perversion that crushed his faint resolve. It didn't help that she was also witty, and intelligent, and had a way of flattering him that was entirely purposeful but didn't seem so. In return she had asked only one thing so far – that he help her to find some hard-to-source peroxide for her would-be blond customers. Once more, Friday Ernst's pharmacy contacts had risen to the challenge, and her gratitude had been spectacularly filthy.

It won't do, his better self kept insisting; but it did, often and energetically. In one sense he was in a wonderful, fortunate situation, but that only added to the weight of his guilt. All across Europe, his countrymen were risking and losing their lives, while he was snug in Berlin, risking nothing that couldn't be treated with yet another of Ernst's products.

If only guilt didn't help with the erections.

Just that morning he had vowed to drown his libido in an ice-bucket and try to be a good husband, but the morning itself had conspired to break his will. He was fretting about his missing new recruit still (and what Freddie Fucking Holleman's blunderings meant for all of them), but while he was working up a decent head of anxiety his boss, the usually-invisible Oberst Böck, pushed his head around the door and announced that he had *a singular honour* in mind for his favourite subordinate. Böck was obliged to present a situation report at each weekly RSHA departmental meeting, but was finding that circumstances - among which, undoubtedly, was an earnest desire not to put himself in Kaltenbrunner's presence - were making the responsibility increasingly troublesome. He was therefore handing off the job to a man whose special interest was the art of communication (a hand waved graciously in Krohne's direction at this), trusting that any shortcomings in a report on the status of flak-ring supply would be identified and tweaked superbly beforehand.

Krohne had long suspected that the astonishing leeway he had been given to run his little *königreich* would one day demand a heavy price, but this was appalling. He had stood in for Böck on two occasions to date when only purely administrative matters had been on the agenda, and even then he'd stammered out his contribution. To present something every week would leave him ridiculously exposed. He managed only the one protest, and it was stamped upon almost before it was out.

'But I don't know anything about Flak-Ring supply, Herr Oberst.'

The Oberst smiled broadly. 'You don't know anything about military operations in the East, and yet you make pure poetry from them. I have full confidence in you!'

After that, Krohne had struggled on for a few moments and then called Bettina to put her on notice of lunchtime manoeuvres. The telephone receiver had only just begun to cool in its cradle (and his ardour to warm) when Holleman pushed his head around the door and asked for a week's leave. Telling him no, brusquely, was the best part of the morning so far, though it was spoiled almost immediately when Holleman's head was replaced by that of Detmar Reincke. His mouth was open, and he pointing feebly at the jamb.

'What is it, Detmar?'

'It's ...'

Both the imminent noun and Reincke removed themselves abruptly. In their place, the now-familiar and majestic Generalfeldmarschall Milch materialized. Krohne leapt upwards, but a flap of the baton halted the full-dress salute.

'Sit, sit, sit, Krohne. I'm not here. I heard about your absent colleague – Fischer, isn't it?'

'Yes, Herr ...'

'He hasn't reported since?'

'No, Herr ...'

'Then we must do all we can. Tell your men that I'm anxious that we find him – *very* anxious, say. And anyone else in the Ministry you know. We can't have our heroes neglected, just because their injuries aren't pretty. I'll put the Feldgendarmerie on to it.'

'But … it was they who took him, Herr Generalfeldmarschall.'

Milch's eyes narrowed. 'I suspect not. No arrest report has been filed, which is extraordinary. And he's not the first of your men to go missing, is he?'

'There was one other, a suicide.' Krohne needed no time or space to reflect upon whether he should explain Freddie Holleman's theory to the Luftwaffe's second-in-command. In fact, he was coming to believe that if Bruno Ahle had been murdered then he probably deserved it.

'He couldn't handle the wounds, eh?'

'It looks like that, Herr Generalfeldmarschall.'

'Well, it happens. I knew a man ...' Milch paused, and shook his head. 'Never mind. Put out the word, Krohne, and I'll do the same. Of course, if you hear anything I want to know first. Goodbye.'

Bettina had to work hard to ease the damage of *that* morning, and it wasn't until she was in the bath that he even remembered to feel awful about it. Back at the Air Ministry, he wondered for the first time whether Milch had been serious or merely playing the Göring - showering a far-subordinate with *faux* camaraderie in the hope of appearing vaguely human. Surely he could find better places to deploy that nonsense than at the *Kriegsberichter der Luftwaffe?* There were no 'heroes' here, no opportunities for him to look good in front of the Press (as if Goebbels would allow images of the Liars to be published in anything that wasn't a medical journal), and why would he promise to move mountains – well, foothills – for the sake of a man he had met just the one time?

An offer of help, unadorned by any hint of a quid pro quo - so why did the walls of Krohne's office seemed closer than before? Because it was attention, and, like his men, he preferred not to be noticed (except by pretty women who didn't mind eye-patches, of course). Ahle's death had upset him, Freddie Holleman's idiot manoeuvres had given that upset a more fearful glaze, and now Oberst Böck and Generalfeldmarschall Milch had each grabbed an ear and dragged him out into a certain prominence. Of the two, Milch seemed the lesser threat. The man couldn't have had anything to do with Ahle's death or Fischer's disappearance, otherwise why would he have shown his face here, pretending to be concerned and demanding that the latter be advertised widely? But the other matter …

From now on, Krohne would be attending weekly meetings at Prinz-Albrecht-Strasse 8, sitting with some very powerful men – Kaltenbrunner, Müller, Neve, Schellenberg, Six, Ohlendorf – any or all of whom might be wondering why the Lie Division's dead weren't being allowed to rest in peace. If anything about Holleman's theory was correct, they would hardly be likely to hesitate to tie off another potential loose end.

The thought (and too much illicit sex at lunchtime, probably) loosened Krohne's bowels. Unreasonably, he was beginning to regret having hired Otto Fischer. Without another former policeman in the Den, Holleman would have kept his mouth closed, Ahle would be a suicide still and peace and tranquillity would reign on the third floor of the Air Ministry, even as most of the rest of the continent was being consumed by flames. It was an unworthy thought, but worth treasuring.

About an hour after Milch had departed, he forced himself out of his chair and down the corridor, interrupted yet another recounting of the night that Freddie Holleman had lost his virginity to his best friend's mother, and passed on the message. It was received in silence, met only with puzzled frowns. Eventually, Salomon Weiss raised a polite finger.

'With respect, Karl, why would a Generalfeldmarschall give a fuck?'

'I don't know, Sal. I thought it best not to ask.'

Holleman sniffed. 'He wouldn't, would he? If he's not losing sleep over half the Luftwaffe being shot out of the sky by the Ivans he's hardly ...'

'Freddie!'

For a moment it seemed as if the point might be made, but a recent attack of rationality made even Holleman think twice. He folded his arms and subsided.

Krohne looked around. 'Well, there it is. We all thought it was the Feldgendarmerie who came for Otto ...'

'It was.'

Hush, Detmar. If Milch suspects it wasn't, who are we to believe our own eyes? As I say, he wanted you all to know that he's concerned, and I've told you. The best thing now would be for you to forget it, keep your heads low and hope that Otto isn't ... you know.'

Krohne had made more inspiring speeches, but this one did its job. Everyone - even Holleman – looked to be on the worried side of subdued. With one exception, they all believed that their former colleague Bruno Ahle had taken his own life, so their anxiety was on the matter of Otto Fischer. What he might have done to have the second most powerful man in Luftwaffe scrambling to understand who had taken him (and why) was not so much a mystery as a creeping barrage. And their faces told Krohne that they feared it was creeping up upon them.

Poor Fischer. A man who had held onto life by a broken fingernail was in the ordure once more, sustained only by the hearty wishes of his new comrades that he not splash it in their direction. The Liars were all recipients of bad luck, put in a place less merciful or heroic than death, a burden even to families who loved them still. There was an iron ration of comfort to be had from a predicament shared, but the company of a modern-day Sisyphus was entirely too much comfort, and even Krohne worried about the consequences of his acquaintance. You could have great sympathy for a man, and still hope sincerely that the rope had parted before he went under.

He went back to his office and thought about calling Bettina, to ask if she was in the mood for an evening matinee. But then he recalled that his elder daughter's First Holy Communion took place the following morning, and he doubted that he'd recover his composure in time to face even a representation of Christ, should he betray his wife twice in a single day.

Having failed to discourage his new partner from following him around like a lost puppy, Gerd Branssler began to take advantage of the situation. He allowed Dieter Thomas to buy most of their coffees and lunches (and every first round in the Alexanderplatz Bulls' favourite bar, the Clock), put him onto every squalid denunciation that the *orpos* couldn't or wouldn't investigate, shamelessly pushed (unpaid) overtime shifts upon him, and, when the mood took hold, tortured the lad with anecdotes about the Old Days that endured almost as long as the events they described. To his credit, Thomas absorbed the punishment cheerfully, and whenever Branssler offered useful advice about the job he was always keen to hear it. Gradually, it occurred to the older man that, if Thomas had evaded the call-up only because of his Gestapo uncle's influence, at least he wasn't the typically over-entitled template of the species.

It was also a pleasant relief not to have to look over his shoulder continuously to check that the man who shared his office wasn't wantonly digging in quicksand. Since Kranzusch's promotion and transfer there hadn't been a single word from him, and while Branssler missed the banter he was happy to forego the damage to his nerves that a certain closed case had threatened. That he now shared an office with a young man who had gone to some lengths to avoid trouble seemed to him a near-perfect arrangement.

The work was no more satisfying than before, but boredom – however Kranzusch had despised the condition – was not the worst state a man could experience. The trick was to process it as one would the slurry in a rain-sodden farmyard – energetically, uncaringly, with a large shovel and blocked-off sinuses. As always, their superiors cared only for results, however obtained.

They cared, that is, when a man actually *had* superiors. Criminal Investigations Alexanderplatz currently resembled a pyramid whose apex had been shorn off by a passing celestial scythe. In the space of a single day they had lost both of their Gruppenführer's principal lieutenants, Messenfer and Bernauer, transferred across to Amt IV with as little apparent ceremony as empty beer bottles found a bin. Each of them, moreover, had been running two departments prior to their ejection, so in effect Amt V was now being supervised by twenty percent of its second-tier complement. The Italian Army had more, and more effective, leadership.

Perhaps it didn't matter. Now that more or less everything was either compulsory or forbidden, law-enforcement hardy required strategic-level direction. Branssler and his *kripo* colleagues had long been allowed the leeway to decide whether an anonymous accusation was warranted or merely a grudge indulged, and more serious offences were investigated as before - with diligence, indifference or near-incompetence, depending upon which oberrat was in charge of a file. The higher ranks bothered themselves with crime only when pointed comments were made about the progress of an investigation, and then only for as long as was required to put a foot up someone's fundament. A war had a way of making everything that wasn't war seem less urgent than it used to be.

So, things had settled into as much normality as an abnormal world permitted when, one mid-morning, Branssler was pretending to read a report on the black market for cigarettes in Prenzlauer Berg (it was bustling, apparently). Dieter Thomas was out, busying himself at the coffee-substitute stall on the corner of Neue-Friedrich-Strasse, the din from the Bulls' Pen next door was as muted as it was ever likely to be and even the pipes that crossed the ceiling were behaving. If a man were able to put aside ever-present realities it might have felt almost like the spring of 1939 once more. For Branssler that had been a sweet time. His retirement date had been looming, and no particularly nasty clouds had threatened (or so he and most of the rest of Europe had thought) to disturb the rhythm of unremarkable days and weeks that marched away into pleasing mistiness. Despite the occasionally gruesome nature of his work he had always been a quiet-life man, so mist was his gold.

The door barged open, propelled by Thomas' knee. He carried two steaming mugs, and, held dog-like in his mouth, a pastry bag. Hastily, Branssler cleared a space on their desk, sending the report to the floor and gently removed the bag before it became sodden.

Thomas licked his lips. 'I've just seen the Gruppenführer.'

'Coming or going?'

'Going. He was with Gestapo Panzinger, I think.'

'Ugly bastard - silly hair, kid's glasses?'

'That's him.'

'It must have been an important meeting.'

'Here? Why not at Prinz-Albrecht-Strasse, where they both live?'

'No idea, unless our canteen's better than that at number 8?'

Thomas nodded solemnly. 'We're known for our premier swill.'

'Perhaps Arthur was begging Friedrich to let him have his Standartenführers back?'

'We're a little thin at the top, aren't we? But they say 'Stapo are busier.'

'They're *always* busier. Enemies of the Reich seem to be breeding like gerbils.'

Thomas glanced nervously at his partner, as he did whenever a dangerous witticism found air between them. 'Have you noticed … ?'

'I'm a kriminalkommissar, Dieter. I notice everything.'

'.. that our Gruppenführer's been looking out of sorts lately?'

'Pale, distracted, jumps a bit when a door slams nearby?'

'Something like that, yes.'

'He's been that way for a year now, at least. Ever since ...'

'What?'

'Nothing. Never mind.'

This was a clear hint, and usually, Thomas was very good at smelling and then taking them. He hesitated though, lifting his mug to his lips and sipping without taking his eyes from Branssler. His other hand nudged the pastry bag, as if he were half-tempted but not quite hungry enough to make a decision one way or the other. Eventually, Branssler – tempted himself but presently enduring a weight-loss regime insisted upon by his wife - noticed the fidgeting, looked up and met his partner's eyes. He said nothing, waiting for silence to work its magic.

'You ... were going to say *ever since he came back*.'

'I was, Dieter. So I'm surprised that we're still talking about it.'

'I know, I know. It's just that ...'

Again, Branssler said nothing. He didn't know where this was going, and didn't want to know. There was a subject that most men in Amt V preferred to avoid for very good reasons – reasons which half of them understood very precisely and of which the other half pretended complete ignorance. It was an arrangement that suited everyone, a rare coming together of very different minds.

In June 1941, Germany had invaded the Soviet Union (even now, Branssler shivered to think of it). At first, everything had gone as well as even the Führer might have hoped. Entire Soviet Armies had been surrounded by their nimbler, better-equipped adversaries and either threw up their arms or died where they stood. As the weeks passed and German forces pressed across vast distances it seemed almost inconceivable that the Ivans could continue to fling fresh formations into the fight, but then it dawned upon OKH that they had seriously miscalculated the number of divisions that comprised the Red Army (or rather, had placed far too much trust in the figure their leader had plucked from the air). After that, resources became the matter of the moment – of every moment.

Even before it occurred that Germany's land forces weren't large enough both to fight the enemy *and* pacify the near-continental landmass they had conquered, the Chancellery had sought ways to fill the holes behind the front lines. What was needed were men who didn't balk at the measures necessary to keep a brutish population quiet – men who were highly disciplined, well-organized and entirely committed to the cause for which Germany was fighting – and one obvious, ready resource recommended itself. The Party had been both politicizing and militarizing the police forces since it took power in 1933, so when *Barbarossa* began, the praesidiums and stations had half-emptied overnight, their staffs drawn to work that paid much better than domestic police work, and involved (or was said to involve) little personal risk.

Some very senior policemen, looking to grease their paths to the top of the Party, volunteered to lead these behind-the-line formations. Amt V's own Arthur Nebe took command of the deployment group assigned to Army Group Centre, operating principally in Byelorussia. Like most of his police subordinates he returned to Germany the following year, by now promoted to SS-Gruppenführer. And again, like many of the lower-ranking police, he came back altered.

Branssler remembered some of the adjectives his colleagues had used at first. *Arthur looks thoughtful*, they'd say, or *preoccupied*, or *pensive*. Typically, his old partner Kranzusch's immediate diagnosis had been *twitchy as a dormouse in snuff*, but more or less everyone noticed something - everyone, that is, except the forty-seven men from Alexanderplatz who had gone and returned with him.

Some had learned alcoholism out East, and all but five seemed as *thoughtful* as Nebe. The exceptions were men long known to enjoy the work done in Alexanderplatz's cellars; men who had never needed to be urged to use all measures necessary to extract a confession. Even they, however, shied from the most casual enquiries about what had gone on in the East, and it wasn't long before the questions dried up. If Germans had become very good at one thing, it was knowing where to step, and when.

' … he's seemed *particularly* out of sorts lately.'

Branssler gave up trying to kill the conversation with a stare, because it wasn't working. 'Perhaps he's sensing that too many unterkommissars are pushing their ugly faces into his business.'

Thomas shrugged. 'Yeah, could be. Do you want some of this bee-sting?'

'Has it got cream in it?'

'No.'

'Almonds?'

'What, in wartime?'

'Eggs, vanilla, honey?'

Thomas licked a finger, pushed it into the bag and then his mouth.

'Um ...'

'Then it's not bee-sting, is it? It's flour and water, baked.'

'I suppose so.' Thomas looked down at the desk and sighed, but his attention was on something still. Vainly, Branssler hoped that it was the parlous state of German pastries these days.

'Did I tell you my brother-in-law's a *kripo*?'

'No, you didn't.'

'In Stuttgart. *He* went East in '41.'

'Dieter ...'

'When he came back he was like Nebe. But my sister said there've been worse times, particularly when his little girl climbs up onto his knee ...'

For a few moments, Thomas seemed to lose his thoughts, but they returned in a rush. 'The funny thing is, he came back under a cloud. She told me that he'd been arrested out there for refusing to obey orders, but then it went away.'

'Eh?' Branssler's soldiering days were a quarter of a century past, but he recalled perfectly the penalty for refusing orders. It involved several comrades, all pointing their rifles at the post that the guilty party's torso was partially concealing.

'Yeah. Just like that, apparently. His boss at Stuttgart Praesidium had a word, said that charges weren't being pressed by the Wehrmacht. Even *he* didn't know why, just told Hans he was a lucky bastard. Even his pension was safe.'

'Perhaps some act of heroism out East mitigated the bad.'

'I don't think the word mitigation appears in the military dictionary.'

'Probably not. Still, it's further evidence, isn't it?'

'Of ...?'

'Things that we shouldn't even be curious about. How long have we known each other, Dieter?'

'About three weeks, Gerd.'

'Are you getting any sense of me as a disappointed mountaineer?'

'No.'

'A stunt-rider in a fairground show, then?'

'Not that, either.'

'Good. In fact, all of that – if it was ever there – was kicked out of me during the First War, when I learned that life was dangerous enough without pissing in its mouth. You can call me a coward if you want, but it's the same sort of cowardice that makes a man step out of the way of a falling rock. Or an anecdote about your brother-in-law, or Arthur Nebe, or anyone else who went East and then came back *out of sorts*. My old partner wasn't at all like me. If he got bored he used to go looking for rocks to stand beneath, which is why my handiest phrase used to be Shut Up, Hubert.'

'Got it, Gerd.'

'Good man. Now, ...'

The telephone on the desk between them rang shrilly. Thomas snatched at it, listened and held out the receiver.

'Branssler.'

'Gerd, it's Freddie. Can we meet and talk? It's about that thing.'

Branssler made some sort of noise that signified assent, made it again when a time and place were suggested, put the receiver into its cradle, his head into his hands and groaned. Solicitously, Thomas leaned across their desk.

'What is it, Gerd?'

'Rocks. Lots of fucking rocks.'

27

When Fischer had finished the story, Wilhelm took his time. He stared at the prisoner for a while, and then at the cell wall behind him, slowly scratched the scar on his face, pursed his lips and then tutted as if some part of the narrative had failed to come up to scratch. Finally, he pushed back his stool and rocked on it, making the thing creak dangerously.

'This 'M' - did you think it might be Major?'

'Briefly. But if that were the case, surely Ahle would have written *the* M?'

'Yeah. Still, the rest of it's hardly a mystery.'

'Isn't it?'

''M's behaving very badly', he wrote – a man in a bomber squadron. What opportunities would a man have, to misbehave? Was he dropping his loads on cows? There's only one thing it could be.'

'Which is?'

Wilhelm grinned. 'What'll get a front-line man on a charge sheet every time? It isn't putting civilians against a wall and shooting them, is it? Christ, you'd probably get a medal these days, or at worst a mild talking-to about wasting ammunition. If you shame the uniform, though ...'

'Rape.'

'Mm. Not that the act itself's unacceptable, just the misplacing of a noble German cock in a racially inferior *muschi*. They don't like it in the Officer's Mess, do they?'

'But this was France.'

'So? They're Gauls, not Franks – Goebbels himself says so. And what if 'M' preferred not to use a rubber? Or had a taste for Jewish ladies? If Luftwaffe are anything like Heer they'd probably kick him out.'

'Perhaps only Ahle knew. That might be a motive to get rid of him.'

'But how would the rapist *know* that he knew? Ahel believed that his injuries had changed him – would the other man have recognized him?'

'In the diary he wrote that the women in the typing pool appreciated the view, but that *they didn't know him*. Did Ahle feel that he had to confront the threat?'

'Hm.' Wilhelm nodded. 'He might have been dumb enough. Still ...'

'Still?'

'I don't know. It's a blot on a record, for sure. But enough to make someone kill an ex-comrade and then spend a *lot* of juice to have the crime buried? And then there's *you*. You think that this is all to do with your being taken off the street?'

'I was hoping you might tell me.'

'I just follow orders, mate. To keep you here, under eyes, until ...'

'Go on.'

'Until I'm told otherwise.' Wilhelm pulled a face, quickly dropped, but Fischer noticed.

'This isn't your kind of work?'

'The first three hours were enjoyable. But I don't do this, usually.'

'You said you were going to regret killing me. Is *that* what you do?'

Offended, Wilhelm snorted. 'If I had orders to put one in your head, would I have joked about it? And stop talking about *me*, it isn't allowed.'

'Sorry. To answer your question, I can't see any other reason for me being here, other than Ahle. Until two weeks ago I was still at Potsdam, in convalescence. If I've done something to offend someone, it had to have happened before 14 January 1942.'

'That would be a big grudge. Have you fucked anyone's wife?'

'Not since I was married, and then only her.'

'But you were Fallschirmjäger. I thought you boys had to fight off the ladies?'

'Perhaps someone else got my share.'

'Well, you're probably right then - about this Ahle fellow. Why, though? You didn't know him, and even reading his diary shouldn't have got you dragged into Spandau.'

'Perhaps I'm to be kept out of someone's way. Is that the point of it?'

Wilhelm nodded slowly. 'That makes more sense. Except ...'

'Go on.'

'Well, if you've done nothing that deserves a bullet, what have you done to put anyone to the trouble of keeping you alive?'

'You're ... right. No-one would care, one way or the other.'

'It's a mystery, then.' Wilhelm frowned. 'And I'm part of it.'

'Really, you were told nothing?'

'How many times do I have to say it?'

'Alright. Why you in particular, though?'

'I don't know. I've ...'

Fischer didn't try to prompt a reply. Not being told to shut his mouth was progress of a kind, to be accepted gratefully.

' ... done a few things for people that weren't regulation. They remembered me, I suppose.'

'Because you don't ask questions?'

Wilhelm stared pointedly at him. '*I* don't, for sure.'

'Alright. I won't ask names, obviously, but do you know who wanted this done?'

For a long time the other man said nothing. He kept his eyes on Fischer, weighing the question, feeling its edges.

'The one who asked – ordered - me to do it, I know him. And I know who *wanted* it done.'

'And ...'

'And no, I didn't ask any questions. Because I don't.'

Wilhelm picked up his pack of cigarettes, extracted one and lit it, drawing a line under the conversation. Fischer, satisfied, sat back on his bed. He had been brought to Spandau in a van, escorted by four members of the Feldgendarmerie. In the courtyard they had been met by Wilhelm, who handed a piece of paper - orders – to the squad leutnant. That a man of his rank should be leading the detail was in itself unusual, but he did no more than glance at the orders, nod and hand them back. Then, led by Wilhelm, the leutnant and two of his men had escorted Fischer to (and propelled him into) the cell and then departed. Only later did it occur to him that not a single word had been said from van to slammed door, by any man present.

This was a prison. It had personnel, who, from guard to Commandant, were responsible for its inmates – to hold, feed and make their lives as miserable as the Regime directed. Yet in the five days of his own incarceration here, Fischer hadn't seen a single member of staff, only Wilhelm and his sour-faced colleague (whose sole duty was to be present when Wilhelm couldn't be). He had been fed well, better than he might have expected outside; his medical needs had been more than met, and promptly; and he was fairly certain that if he asked for reading material or a pack of cards they would be provided. His first (and only) thought was that he was being wrapped in soft wool and kept from the eyes and hands of men who might wish to harm him. But who would want that, and why?

He didn't have Ahle's diary, and his reading of it had given no clues as to why it might be important to men powerful enough to kill its author and then the murder investigation. He wasn't anybody, and therefore couldn't compromise whatever purpose they had, even if he knew something. Whoever had arranged this protective custody (for once it might not be a euphemism for something far worse) presumably stood in opposition to that purpose, for what reason he could no more imagine than the purpose itself. One party thought him dangerous, but they were wrong; the other regarded his as sufficiently valuable to be worth preserving, and by the same token they were wrong, too. He was a figment of more than one assumption, a bean on a chess board, a ten-pfennig diamond mounted in brass, and when one or more antagonist discovered just what it was that they had (or wanted), Otto Fischer would be flushed.

An English poet once wrote that ignorance was bliss. No doubt his countrymen were comfortable in that state, but not knowing who wanted you dead, who wanted you alive - or, in each case, *why* - was too much ignorance to be borne, even on broad shoulders.

Much to Karl Krohne's (albeit brief) gratification, the Air Ministry's post-room staff had been substituted by *Lufthelferinen* during the previous year to release the men for active service. The ladies (most of whom were former BDM girls, and as likely to fraternize with their male colleagues as with goats) brought a new level of efficiency to what had been a stately, old-world department. Incoming correspondence to Europe's largest office building was sorted in the first instance according to the person or principal department to which it was addressed. That marked merely for the Ministry did not, by definition, relate to urgent operational, administrative or political matters, and was assigned to a holding section to be opened, read and then directed to the relevant (or most relevant) destination. Letters from relatives of missing Luftwaffe personnel were resealed and placed in outgoing bags for the attention of WASt; complaints regarding such matters as censorship of servicemen's letters from the Front, the misdirection of food parcels addressed to sons in the field, or failures to inform families of repostings or military punishments were sent across the road to a small office of RSHA Amt IV A (*Domestic Opposition* - Panzinger's department), where Gestapo personnel would decide whether the correspondence merited further investigation, a stern rebuke or a short flight to the nearest waste bin; while the rare, ingratiating item praising the performance of flak emplacement personnel in preserving the lives of German city dwellers was directed to the Ministry of Propaganda, for use or misuse by Reichsminister Goebbels.

To whom it may concern was not regarded, therefore, as one of the more important addresses in the Air Ministry. Few items so marked were opened on the day they were received, and those that were usually sat for several more days among similar before anyone found the time to direct them onward. Very rarely, something arrived at Wilhelmstrasse 97 that defied the broadest classification, and when this happened the section leader would discuss it with one or more of her subordinates.

This morning, Ilse stood in front of Hauptführerin Hedy Bauer's desk, watching the woman examine the item. According to the receiving frank on the envelope, it had arrived at the Ministry two days ago but been opened only a few minutes earlier, Ilse having drawn that shift's difficult post duty. She had removed the thing, read a few lines on the first page before flicking briefly through the rest and deciding that it was neither within her competence or interest to attempt to allocate it to a destination. She had lifted it as high as she could manage, caught the hauptführerin's eye and been summoned to the office.

Her section leader had taken the item impatiently, wanting to get back to the sorting room to keep her eye on the known and suspected chatterers. She forgot them within a few moments, however, and her irritated frown shaded to puzzlement as she turned the pages, scanning each for some key that would make the rest intelligible. It all *looked* important, but then so did the periodic tables, and hieroglyphs, and Sanskrit. Meaning alone determined value, not the form by which it was conveyed.

After a few minutes of this, Ilse cleared her throat. 'Is it a code?'

'Parts of it are, obviously. Otherwise it would have a title, and headings. The rest is, well, calculations. Look ...'

Hauptführerin Hedy turned the thing around and pushed it towards Ilse, pointing to a section.

'The number at the foot of this page is the sum of the eight above it. What they refer to I can't say.'

'Accounts, then?'

'Possibly, but I don't see double entries, or a balance sheet. And why would accounts be coded, unless ...'

'Unless ...'

'Unless no-one's supposed to know what they refer to.'

The two ladies looked at each other. *Nobody* included them, obviously, so if this document had some sort of official status then trying to parse it might be a crime in itself.

Ilse was a simple soul, happy enough to devote hours to repetitive tasks, but she was by no means stupid.

'I'll get back to work, shall I, Frau Hauptführerin?'

'Y…es. But don't discuss this with anyone.'

'Of course not. It isn't my business ...'

Any more. She stopped herself before it was out, but the look on her section leader's face suggested that she wished very much to say the same.

When Ilse had gone, Hauptführerin Bauer examined the envelope. It was addressed to *The Ministry of Aviation, Wilhelmstrasse, Berlin*, and postmarked from Kranichfeld, Erfurt. She thought about Erfurt – a beautiful, historic place, she had been through it on a cycling tour of Thuringia before the war. But what did it hold now? There was a Luftwaffe airfield there - Flughaven Erfurt-Weimar – but as far as she knew it was a purely operational site, having no administrative, research or technical function. That apart, she wasn't aware of anything within the city that was particularly devoted to the war effort. It was a sleepy place, its only recent excitement the trouble that the National Socialists had brawled out with the local communists, but that had been settled years ago. God knew, there was no-one in Erfurt these days who would admit to being a Red.

As for Kranichfeld, she couldn't hazard a guess. There was a set of Der Neue Brockhaus on the post room reference shelf. She went out and quickly checked both the reference and Gau map. She recalled having cycled past the place on the same day that she'd 'done' Erfurt – that had been almost twenty years earlier, but the Brockhaus 1938 edition didn't show it as having put on much weight since. If some new military or scientific site associated with Luftwaffe had been established there in the intervening years she would have heard something about it.

Back in her office, she lifted the thing from the desk carefully, as if it were primed to detonate. There was no mystery as to what the object was – a Faber-Castell notebook, of a type commonly used as a diary (though not in this case). Given the wartime shortage of paper its repurposing was hardly unusual, but it added to the sense of clandestinity that was making her nerves sing.

The chorus was teased by way the package had been addressed. If this was something intended for a known recipient, where was his name? If it were something lost and innocently found, the finder dutifully returning it to the proper owner, what clue had he or she found in its pages that it should be directed to the Air Ministry, and all the way from Erfurt? The more she considered it, the harder the only logical conclusion pressed – that this was something that should never have gone where it went (wherever that was), and had been returned by someone who absolutely did not want to leave a trail. That in itself wasn't necessarily dangerous to those who handled it along the way. It was rather that no judgement could be made, one way or the other, without having any idea of what it was that was being handled.

She could take it to her own superior and lay out the facts simply. It had arrived at the Ministry and been opened as all improperly-addressed items were. Her attention had been drawn to it as procedure required, and now, lacking enough information to proceed, she was unloading the problem onto her boss to lose sleep over (she'd find a more palatable way to put it, naturally). What was wrong with any of that?

Only what the spirit of their age might make of it. Like almost every other German, Hedy understood a little about how things were and refused to dwell upon the rest. The thing was *coded* – therefore, its content was intended for very few eyes, and though she had no idea who those eyes might belong to, hers were certainly not among them. What if, for all its opacity, the secrets it held permitted no allowances for innocent, accidental examination? In the interests of protecting what someone clearly intended to be protected, she might lose her job. At worst, she might lose her freedom.

Resentfully, she stared at the thing. If she did *anything* she was commencing a process whose course she couldn't predict, much less influence. She was a good German, a good Party member, and didn't deserve to be passed this poisoned chalice. If only she had taken sick leave today, or begged a day off to visit her ever-ailing mother in Panketal …

She placed the notebook in her desk drawer and locked it. It had been sent anonymously, to someone unspecified. Who was going to come looking for it? And if they did, wouldn't her claim that, lacking any understanding of what it was, she had chosen first to make discreet enquiries be the most prudent course? It spoke to her sense of duty – of understanding that she was dealing with a sensitive item without having any idea what it was.

That sounded flimsy, even to her hopeful inner ear, but what alternative did she have? Surrendering it to her immediate boss would shine a light on her (and also implicate the other woman, whose willingness to repay a thrust was legendary). Otherwise, she might wander this vast building, asking if anyone was expecting something that she probably wasn't allowed to describe, and certainly not to show to curious eyes. For the moment, doing nothing seemed the only sensible option. Ilse would never breathe a word of it, nor even think of asking how her section leader had handled the matter, and if the person for whom it was intended didn't know of its arrival, what could he or she do?

Hauptführerin Hedy had never done – had never considered doing – something like this. It was selfish, undutiful and possibly treasonous. She might be withholding vital, war-winning intelligence from the person who could best use it. She might unwittingly be abetting a foreign agent here at the Ministry by not placing the notebook in the hands of those who could expose him. But in either case, doing the right thing wasn't necessarily prudent. It was a problem that she could discuss with no-one, and even if that wasn't the case, would her confidant (more likely, her confidante) thank her for the revelation?

29

'This was a stupid idea.'

Gerd Branssler dropped the two dumbbells simultaneously, drawing frowns from the small group of HJ lads gathered around the boxing ring. Freddie Holleman, who was pinned beneath a vertical pressing frame, his single leg lifting roughly the weight of a small pony, grunted and lowered the pad slowly to its rests. Both men's faces and chests were the colour of an angry dawn, which, with their black police sports kits and pallid arms, gave them an admirably National Socialistic air.

Holleman gasped for stale gymnasium air for a few moments and then dipped his head in partial acknowledgement.

'But it's ... oh sweet Jesus ... safe.'

'How is it safe? This is something we shouldn't be *thinking* about, much less ...'

'I meant, who'd look for us here? A couple of fat old bastards?'

Offended, Branssler patted what blocked his view. 'It's as solid as stone. I'm just heavily framed.'

Holleman eyed him dispassionately. 'That bloke they fingered for the Reichstag fire was less heavily framed than you are.'

'Fuck off.'

'Old bastards, then, if you like. I just thought that it would be safe – *safer* – if we're not seen together in the usual places.'

'Usual?'

'You know, any bar in Mitte.'

Grudgingly, Branssler took the point. 'So, who is this lucky fellow?'

'I'm not going to tell you his name. That way, it can't be punched out of you.'

'Alright. They just marched in and arrested him?'

'Yeah. One of them shoved the order at my boss. He didn't try to argue it, so I assume it was done properly.'

'Define properly.'

'Good point. The paperwork appeared to be in order, according to Karl. *Administrative custody*, it said.'

'That narrows it down to anything. Who signed the thing?

'Some Luftwaffe General I've never heard of.'

'And you don't know where ...'

'They've taken him. No.'

'It's probably Tegel, or Spandau. If he's really unlucky they've swept him off to Fort Zinna.'

'All the way to Torgau? Why do that?'

'Because there plenty of other Wehrmacht prisoners there - if they need to lose someone, administratively.'

'Again, why?'

Branssler looked curiously at his friend. 'If the same people who took Ahle are behind this, they're going to cack him, make it look like another suicide and smother any chance of an investigation. The first is easy, the rest takes time. They'll want him somewhere snug in the meantime.'

'They didn't take time with Ahle. He was found less than a day after he disappeared.'

'That was different. Then, there was no history behind their methods. This time, people will be suspicious, so they'll need to be more subtle. *If* it's what you think it is.'

'I can't see what else it could be.'

'How well do you know this fellow?'

'Not at all. He seems decent, though, and it isn't as if he's had much opportunity to make enemies recently.'

'Another of the walking wounded.?'

'Yeah. You should see his ...'

'What?'

'Never mind. It would be as good as naming him.'

'Don't say any more, then. But *why*, Freddie?'

'Why what?'

'Why am I here, working on this hernia?'

Holleman squirmed slightly, and pretended that his stump was the cause of it. He rubbed it for a while, turned to check on the HJ boys (they were avidly watching one of their mates pummel another lad), and made half a move towards a ten-kilogram plate, to add it to his already-impressive stack. He was stayed by Branssler's heavy eyebrows, however, which economically conveyed a hint of *take your time, I've got all night*.

'Feldgendarmerie talk to Bulls, don't they?'

'If they absolutely need to. If a deserter's gone to ground in Berlin, or they want to go where a military warrant can't take them. It's not an everyday thing, though.'

'No, but you must know a couple of them by name?'

'I know one, but we haven't spoke for months now. I can't even say if he's in this Wehrkreis any more.'

'Could you find out? He might just know ...'

'Freddie, stop it. There's no way I could frame the question without putting myself, my family and pension rights in the firing line. What possible interest could I have in finding a Luftwaffe man who's been lifted at the direct order of a Luftwaffe General? They'd nail me to a door.'

'Yeah ...'

'This Ahle, he's poison. Did you know that one of the *orpos* who found him was dead a week later? And my partner, he got bored and decided to ask his mate a few questions. He was transferred, without notice, right out of Berlin. We *know* that the investigation into Ahle's death had to have been killed in its crib by someone high within Amt V, and while it may be a massive coincidence, the second- and third-ranking men in

Criminal Investigations were shunted across to Gestapo *on the same day*. This is just what I hear, and I'm absolutely trying not to hear anything. There may be a half-legion of other men transferred out or buried in ditches because of what they knew or made the effort to know about this business.'

Glumly, Holleman examined his artificial leg. Twice, his mouth opened as if he might make a case, but the right words either wouldn't come or hadn't been found. Branssler was right – the Feldgendarmerie might occasionally collaborate when necessary, but a single wrong word put across the divide between them would light up the enquirer like a flare. A *kripo* had no credible reason to ask who was or might be held in a military prison, any more than a Feldgendarme had the right to investigate prostitution in Görlitzer Park. The Reich was cursed by an overlap of policing agencies and security services, but certain lines were drawn more clearly than stripes on a badger. Military and civilian jurisdictions did not blur into each other, ever.

'Sorry, Gerd. I should have thought a bit harder before calling you. I just feel really bad about dropping … this colleague into it.'

'No more than I do for telling you what I knew about the state of Ahle's corpse. If I hadn't, you'd be sat at your desk now, happily excavating ear-wax and wondering if your new mate's gone to ground with an old girlfriend.'

'Shit. I would, too.'

'A man can know too much. Look at what happened to Giordano Bruno.'

'Who?'

'Never mind. The point is, neither of us is stupid. We know that Prinz-Albrecht-Strasse makes a big thing about criminality and getting it off the streets, so if what looks much like a murder disguised as something else has been buried quietly, there's a fucking good reason for it. And by reason, I mean something we absolutely don't need to go looking for, find and then pull its tail.'

'He's dead, isn't he?'

Branssler sighed and rubbed his face, transferring a quantity of chalk from his hand.

'Your mate? I don't know. Look, Freddie, I can keep an eye on prisoner transfer sheets, but that'll only work if he enters our system, and it's not likely. Obviously, I'll check the found body reports, but they can only give us the bad news. I know a few AMT IV men across the corridor, but again, I can't think what I could ask that wouldn't have them inviting me in for a long, tense conversation.'

'Oh Christ, Gerd, don't go talking to 'Stapo. I'm wearing enough remorse already.'

'I won't. My partner got transferred for being curious, but persistence will make someone peevish, so I might be re-assigned to a sewer pipe. Nothing can be done, so you need to be strong about this, Freddie.'

'I know. And thanks for not calling me a cock.'

'Believe me, I'm thinking it. Shall we find a beer somewhere?'

Holleman brightened a little. 'Do you *know* somewhere?'

'There's a bar close by, in Magazinstrasse. They have a special reserve of Berliner Weisse they keep for us Bulls, so that we don't ask them where they get their cigarettes. And there's usually fresh mettwurst on the counter, if you don't mind paying black market prices.'

'Not at all.'

'Let's get a shower, then – I'm sick of this torture. And try to wash off the guilt, eh?'

30

On the sixth morning of Fischer's confinement something remarkable happened. Wilhelm's surly mate entered the cell, leaned closely to his comrade and moved his lips, which more or less confirmed that he was sentient. This was sufficiently surprising for Wilhelm's reaction not to register immediately, and it was only when he scrambled into his tunic, buttoned it and departed without saying a word that Fischer felt a twinge of alarm. When one has no means of influencing events, anything unexpected can have teeth.

He was gone for almost half an hour, during which time Surly attempted no further human intercourse other than to convey a sense of disgust in the scowl he directed at the prisoner. This was so well-practised by now that Fischer hardly noticed. He occupied himself by surveying a small selection of unpleasant possibilities, beginning with the most obvious one – that the execution order had arrived. How it might happen – a firing squad, an unfortunate road accident, a rail suicide or the elegant pillow over the face – was hardly worth fretting about, but he fretted anyway. His small consolation was that, having commenced with the worst option the others were almost comforting. It might be that Wilhelm had been summoned to other duties, and that the unpleasant but survivable prospect of Surly's constant presence loomed. A slightly uglier possibility was that rations were no longer to be prepared by the Deputy Commandant's sister, in which case a trying ordeal would be made considerably more trying when Wilhelm took it out on his prisoner. Perhaps it had been decided that the accommodation was too luxurious, and arrangements were currently in hand to furnish an even danker, darker hole – one that didn't enjoy the flood of natural light afforded by the small, high window from which he presently had no view. Perhaps …

Wilhelm's return interrupted the survey. He almost fell into the cell, grabbed a fistful of Surly's tunic and dragged him out into the corridor (curiously, the victim didn't seem to find this behaviour in any way unmilitary, though the permanently-affronted cast to his face made it difficult to judge accurately). Fischer could hear their hushed voices through the cell door. It sounded more like a conversation than an argument, and though there was clearly some urgency to it they spoke for almost ten minutes.

One pair of footsteps receded down the corridor as the cell door opened once more. Wilhelm beckoned Fischer with a toss of his head.

'Come on. No, wait.'

This terse, confusing instruction delivered, Wilhelm disappeared once more. Fischer sat down on his bed and stared at the door, trying to keep his mind emptied of what queued to fill it. A few minutes passed, during which he could hear no noises other than from the courtyard. It had been the same since he arrived, and he assumed that he was being held in an otherwise unoccupied section of the prison (*that* had brought its own anxieties). Today, the silence was slightly reassuring, hinting as it did that nothing was being organized for his benefit, one way or the other.

Wilhelm was back once more within five minutes, carrying a Heer-green uniform.

'Strip, and put this on.'

Fischer obeyed, saying nothing. It was a tunic and trousers only, so both his shirt and boots were wrong for them. This didn't seem to bother Wilhelm; he waited impatiently, half-turning to the door several times as a Luftwaffe Hauptmann transformed himself into a *schutz*. He was buttoning the tunic when Surly returned and gave his comrade a single nod.

'Right. Put this over your head.'

Wilhelm held out a hood. Fischer opened his mouth to protest, but before he could say anything Surly tsked, grabbed the thing, took out a knife and slashed a slit in it.

'If he can't see where he's going it'll take forever to get him downstairs.'

He had a high voice, much softer than Fischer had expected, but the mild reproof was enough to make Wilhelm (who was twice his size) blush.

'Oh. Yeah. Sorry.'

Strangely, the slit in the hood made Fischer feel considerably more optimistic about his very near future, and he made no objection as Surly pulled it over his head. They moved immediately, the two gaolers taking an arm each as they moved along the corridor to a narrow spiral stairwell and then descended dizzily through three storeys. The view was necessarily confined, and Fischer devoted much attention to staying on his feet. He was rushed along another, ground-floor corridor, a brief burst of noise from a guards' mess panicking him momentarily, and then they were out in the courtyard.

The air, even here, tasted fresh after several days' confinement, and he gulped as much as he could before they dragged him inside once more. When it came, though, *inside* wasn't what he'd expected. A sudden swerve by his handlers brought him up against the back of a small grey van. Surly snatched at the door handle, pulled Fischer back and then pushed forward, and with Wilhelm's more-than-ample assistance shoved him into the rear. His journey halted abruptly when his head met the metal supports of the driver's seat. He dropped, half-stunned, to the floor.

His skull doubled as an echo chamber, and he felt rather than heard the engine start. They began to move, and, rather than stop almost immediately as they reached the outer security post, accelerated smoothly. No-one shouted, no violent manoeuvres were needed to avoid men rushing to prevent this bold escape - only a ninety-degree veer as the van joined what Fischer assumed to be the other, western Wilhelmstrasse, and then they were moving freely among traffic.

How is this possible? The Reich was built upon processes, its bureaucracy an all-enveloping, smothering blanket of duplicated documentation. It was a common enough joke, that all the Allies need do to win the war was to locate and destroy Germany's paper mills, after which everything except legs would stagger to a halt. Nothing was done without a trail of authorizations to confirm a fact, so for Otto Fischer to be removed from close confinement without being lifted upon a cloud of counter-signed orders was inconceivable. Yet Wilhelm – a man of no apparent rank, without even a clear understanding of why he was enduring his present assignment - had managed it within an hour of being told … well, something. The Second Coming would hardly have been more difficult to organize.

Fischer's head cleared slowly, and he had no sense of how long they had been moving. When the ringing faded he noticed that Wilhelm and Surly were talking quietly in the front. This time it was definitely an argument, and it was the thin, higher voice that conveyed the most anger. Wilhelm was quieter, and though nothing audible penetrated to the van's rear there was a consistent, questioning inflection to each of his contributions. Either Surly was objecting strongly to being interrogated, or options were being offered and rejected.

Christ, they don't know where we're going.

The panic returned, and this time Fischer didn't fight it. He'd imagined that his place in this business was as a tiny, unwitting impediment to some unfathomable but vast purpose. Unwitting he was, certainly, but he seemed to be in good company. It was a frightening prospect to be at the mercy of merciless men, but far worse to be helpless in the hands of dolts.

Their journey ended after what seemed to Fischer' still-confused head to be several hours, though he doubted their fuel tank could have met that challenge. He felt the van pull in to the side of a road, reverse turn and then back up several metres before stopping. There was a brief scramble, a curse as a body part collided with metal, and when Surly opened the rear door there was hardly room for it to complete its swing. Another door, dark red but missing much of its paint, loomed behind him.

'Would you get out, please?'

The politeness was yet another dislocation, and Fischer almost abandoned his efforts to understand what was happening. He obeyed, waiting quietly while Surly unlocked the red door. Wilhelm pulled a holdall from the front of the van and joined them. They entered a gloomy hallway, inadequately lit by a single skylight high above their heads.

'Where are we?'

Fischer hadn't meant to say anything, but dizziness and pain (his injured shoulder had absorbed every bump and lurch of the trek from Spandau) undid his resolve. It hardly mattered; both Wilhelm and Surly ignored him and went their separate ways, feeling their way cautiously into rooms on either side of the hall. The prisoner waited for several moments and, finding himself momentarily gifted a sliver of initiative, pulled off his hood.

Until that moment he hadn't noticed the smell. It was age, and damp, and lack of human occupation, seasoned with more than a *soupçon* of rodent shit – a perfect place to make a corpse and keep it safe from discovery.

'I'll get the stove going. We can have tea, at least.'

For a big man, Wilhelm didn't make too much noise. He had found a kettle, a prize that didn't seem to have raised his mood. A plan – Fischer *hoped* that it was a plan - had gone wrong somehow, but there was more than frustration or disappointment in the man's face, and when Surly emerged from the door at the far end of the hallway and caught Wilhelm's eye the misery filled the space between them. Whatever it was, they were going through it together.

'May I ask where we are?'

Fischer expected to be ignored again, but the question made Wilhelm half-turn in the doorway that framed him. His hand reached out and touched – almost stroked - the jamb.

'It's safe, you shouldn't worry. I doubt that anyone's been here since …'

'Since 12 May, 1942.'

A silence dragged, and Fischer looked from one man to the other. This was personal, obviously, and if he could have tip-toed back from the moment he would have done so. He didn't need them having any further reason to consider him a problem.

Wilhelm caught the glance and deflated slightly. 'Which was the date upon which the Jew Noam Fassbinder, having successfully rid himself of his entire fortune to get his wife and three children out of Germany, put a gun in his mouth in ...' he half-turned and pointed to the last doorway on the left of the hallway; ' ... the study over there.'

'You knew him?'

'He was our uncle.'

'Our?'

Wilhelm nodded towards Surly. 'This is my brother, Rainer.'

'You're Jewish?'

'*Mischlings*, as they say. Our mother was Christian, and when father died she made sure that the old *Geltundsjude* paperwork disappeared and four gentile grandparents found their way onto the new.

'That must have cost money.'

'It did, though it was largely wasted. Registrars still had the originals, naturally.'

'*Had*? How ...?'

'A favour, from a very powerful friend.'

Surly – Rainer – scowled. 'It was no *favour*. And he's no friend.'

'Well, a useful acquaintance then. There was a price, of course.'

'You mean, what you're doing now?'

'This, and other things. But even *he* doesn't know about this place, so don't worry.'

It was a half explanation, but Fischer couldn't tie it to what he'd imagined to be a proper, respectable conspiracy. What had happened in the past few hours was all too extemporary, the recourse of a half-glimpsed moment, not any sort of plot. Why else would two men who had every reason not to advertise their bloodline bring him to this crumbling monument to it?

Wilhelm, watching his face, misread it.

'You *are* worrying. You think that we can't let you live now, not with this knowledge.'

The thought would have arrived eventually, but Fischer was shocked by how disoriented he'd become. Five days of bored suspension and then this mad flight, the revelation that his goalers were a family business – he needed time to think through the threads. So he lied.

'It occurred to me, yes.'

'Are you a squealer?'

'No. But you don't know that.'

'What do you think, Rainer?'

'Stop playing games, Willy. We have no instructions to harm him.'

'Wilhelm sighed. 'That's the problem. We have no instructions. We were told to keep you out of sight, and that's all. But this morning the Deputy Commandant told Rainer that someone had been asking questions about you.'

'At Spandau? How could they ...'

'Just procedures being followed, probably. if you're trying to find a missing serviceman and you think he has help, you check everywhere. It may have been a long shot, a ticking-off of possibilities, but we couldn't assume that. We've been trying to keep the guards away from your cell, but one quick peek through the hatch would do it - that face is too memorable. So, having no instructions, we decided to rabbit.'

'How?'

'The same way we got you in, by waving this piece of paper. It's magical.'

Wilhelm handed it to Fischer. The authority was stated briefly, starkly, and signed by a Major General.

'Ano Aach. I don't know the name.'

'No-one does. It's a pseudonym. The gentleman who scrawled it works for the one who released Rainer and me from our Hebrew roots. It was a prior telephone call from him to Spandau that cleared our way.'

'Haven't you asked for new instructions?'

'When I was given this job it was made clear that I don't ask *anything*, in case the wrong ears pick it up. I'll make a very discreet report about today, no names or places mentioned, put it at a drop and then we'll wait. Rainer, did you manage to grab rations before we ran?'

'Some. About two days' eating, if we're careful.'

'Fuck. I love my stomach.'

'You could lose a little weight.'

'Yeah, probably. Not our mate here, though. He's a thick as a ribbon.'

Fischer shrugged. 'I don't have much appetite these days.'

'Then you need force-feeding. I'll see what victuals I can pick up when I drop the report. Is there anything else we need, Rainer?'

'Could you bring my *Tractatus*? It's in my kit box.'

'Jesus! You want me to go back to barracks?'

'Why not? You're supposed to be on a special detail for … well, you know who. You could have any good reason for putting your head around the door at Reinickendorf. And a pack of cards, if you would. And a chess board, if you can find one.'

'I'll need a fucking staff car to carry it all.'

'No you won't. We don't know how long we'll be here, do we?'

Wilhelm sighed. 'Alright.'

Satisfied, Rainer held out his hand for the kettle. 'I'll brew up.'

When he had gone, Wilhelm turned to his reluctant guest. 'Philosophers, eh?'

'The brains of the family?'

'You cheeky bastard - but yes, by a long throw. He studied under Heidegger at Freiburg, I boxed semi-professionally and collected debts. And apprenticed as a butcher.'

'Isn't Heidegger a good National Socialist?'

Wilhelm grinned. 'It was a big disappointment for Rainer, when he found out. His revenge was to jump the fence and become a Wittgensteiner. But don't tell anyone.'

'I don't think your brother likes me.'

'It's not you - he just doesn't care for *special* duties. In fact, he doesn't care for the Luftwaffe, the Party or the struggle against International Communism. Given the choice, he'd find a quiet little university with a vacancy for someone who likes to think and not much else, and spend the rest of his days growing wrinkles.'

'He's picked the wrong time to be a young man.'

'Haven't we all? What's your story?'

'You want to know?'

'Not details, just the canvas.'

'School, police academy, Criminal Investigations, then I quit to join the Fallschirmjåger, then Norway, Belgium, Crete, the Eastern Front, many lazarets and now here.'

'I noticed the Knight's Cross bar. A proper hero, are we?'

'Truthfully, I have no idea why it came to me and not someone else. I've never stormed a position, never carried a wounded comrade to safety, and if I've never surrendered it's only because I've never been invited to. I think a coin must have been tossed.'

'It's strange that a man should find both extremes of luck.'

'Perhaps I shouldn't have stopped saying my prayers. Perhaps I should have started.'

'Ha! I've prayed to two Gods – well, two ideas of the same God – and it never helped me that I know of. What about you, Rainer?'

Three steaming mugs went down on to the bare floor. 'There is no God. If there was, would there be a National Socialist Germany or a Soviet Union? Would He hand such power to men who don't even believe in Him?'

Proudly, Wilhelm waved a hand at his brother. 'He's got an answer for everything.'

'Philosophers do, I expect.'

For a while, the three men sat on the floor, sipping their tea. At his first taste, Wilhelm winced.

'Deutscher?'

'No, Tonga.'

'I hate ersatz tea. It makes ersatz coffee seem almost real.'

Rainer shrugged. 'Everything's ersatz now. We should have thought to build a bigger navy and merchant marine before we invaded Poland.'

'You mean, responded to Polish provocations?'

'If you like. Tonga's made in Poland, so perhaps it's their revenge. Willy, I've been thinking ...'

His brother turned to Fischer and nodded meaningfully.

' ... about this job.'

'What about it?'

'It's not logical.'

'How isn't it?'

Rainer put down his mug and used both his hands to make the point, beginning with a forefinger in Fischer's direction.

'We're supposed to keep him safe?'

'Hidden, certainly.'

'But we assume that means safe, yes? What would be the point of hiding someone otherwise? If they wanted to harm him, surely a bullet or a blade would do the job? We'd have grabbed him, done the business and been back at Reinickendorf within a couple of hours. What would be the point of all this?'

'Alright, so hidden means safe, probably. But it might mean safe *for the moment* (Wilhelm gave Fischer a half-apologetic glance at this).'

'Mm. If it did, or does, why not just snatch him and hold him in a logical place, say ...'

'Sshh.'

'I mean, why did they take him and hand him to us, rather than keep him?'

Fischer coughed. 'Perhaps they want to make sure that no-one knows they're involved? If I was held by the Feldgendarmerie, there'd be paperwork, wouldn't there? A trail?'

Rainer nodded slowly. 'That's a good reason - the best, I think.'

Wilhelm grunted. 'What's the worst?'

'I don't know. I don't want to know.'

'Then stop thinking.'

'How do I do that?'

'Try thinking about food instead. Or tits. I always tell myself there's no use twisting things around until you can't see the head or tail of a problem.'

'You're lucky, Willy. Not thinking's a skill I don't have.'

Wilhelm seemed almost pleased by the implicit insult. He sipped once more, pulled another face and patted his way to the pocket that held the cigarettes. Several smoke rings ascended to the ceiling before he spoke again.

'Anyway, we know why he uses us, don't we? It's for stuff he doesn't want to reach daylight. So if everyone else isn't supposed to know what he's doing, why should we? It's because we don't ask questions that he uses us.'

'Yes, but there's a limit to what we *don't* need to know, if we're going to get a job done. Has he ever been so vague about what he wants? He's a very careful, precise man, whose instructions come with no flex. This – this is too I-leave-it-all-up-to-you, and it worries me.'

'Ach.' Wilhelm dropped the cigarette stub into the dregs of his mug. 'It's simple enough. We keep *this* one hidden, and if anyone comes sniffing we move again. Eventually, we'll get our orders. All we need do is wait. Is that so hard, compared to …?'

'What we've done before now?'

'Yeah, think about that.' Wilhelm looked at Fischer. 'But don't talk about it. We don't want him getting twitchy.'

31

The man Frau Traugott knew as Pastor Johann re-read the short report he had drafted. He was satisfied that the process it described was as thorough as anyone – even its intended recipient – might expect, but of course it came to no happy conclusion. It was a summary of provisional measures, of intelligent stabs into gloom, and he hoped that it might encourage a reconsideration. He had asked for and been refused more resources – an entirely predictable disappointment, given that *resources* meant men, and his principal had a morbid aversion to giving *any* matter more attention than it needed. He was almost flattered that he had been fully apprised of the situation, though that didn't lessen his frustration. The situation was to be resolved swiftly, but he had fewer than half a dozen helpers, and none of them knew as much as they needed to do their work efficiently.

He had a reputation for thinking sideways, for running down answers while other men were staring at the question still, and he wasn't always thankful for it. An impressive result generated expectations of the next one, but some tasks needed more than inspiration or luck to tie down. Graft, perseverance and enough pairs of legs to do the legwork were equally necessary, and trying to explain this to some of the highest-ranking men in the Reich was as easy as shaving a cat. Police and generals seemed to understand this perfectly, but politicians believed in the force of will, and even fate.

Every krankenhaus and lazaret in the Berlin area, every Luftwaffe convalescent unit, every flakartillerie station and barracks out as far as Schönwalde had been contacted, interrogated and ticked off. Even the military prisons had been required to supply their intake sheets for the past month. He had been told 'to leave no stone unturned' (of course he had – who in the Party's hierarchy could resist a cliché?), and he had disobeyed by ignoring just one possibility – which was of course no possibility at all. Feldgendarmerie had been used to extract the subject, so he might have started with them; but the snatch had been carefully planned and efficient, the men involved had worn no unit insignia, and he knew beyond any doubt that if he tried to go down that hole there would be teeth waiting. He was supported by very powerful people, but so too were his adversaries. This was a problem to circle, not charge head-on.

To circle, while resisting its vexations. A half-faced man had no right to be a wraith, even in a nation that bore more than its share of battlefield injuries. He should have been noticed by someone – a casual glance and shocked second look, or a mention of the same by a comrade – and that recent memory stirred when the question arrived. So far, three witnesses had offered testimony that fingered two mutilations, but neither had been Otto Henry Fischer.

Nothing in the man's record suggested that he was the type to be used in a business like this, and no piece of evidence had yet emerged to hint at how and why he might have been recruited. Yet here he was (or rather wasn't), almost certainly the instrument of the cabal whose plotting was stealing sleep along the length of Wilhelmstrasse. A history would have helped enormously, but the man seemed to have stepped out of the same shell as Botticelli's Venus. Even his link to the beheaded man couldn't be established, only guessed at.

He had a landlady, of course, but she had known him for less than two weeks. In any case, she was as close to a simpleton as wouldn't get her euthanized, and chasing her had wasted almost a full day of a brutally tight schedule. He had to admire Fischer's attention to the most mundane detail. Even a clever men could fail to anticipate the damage that prying eyes and loose mouths could inflict upon a plan, but he had chosen his ground well. He had been living anonymously (despite the face), keeping company with a blockhelfer's worst nightmare – an entirely uncurious old lady.

The man who wasn't a pastor – who was, in fact, an SS-Brigadeführer named Albrecht Suhr - signed his report. It would be read immediately, and the question would return on wings - what was to be his next step? That was easy enough to deflect. He would make the usual meaningless noises about redoubling efforts, pursuing less obvious leads and placing every half-suspected party under close scrutiny, all of which gave an impression of forward movement and reassured anxious minds. But it would be thin gauze to place on a wide wound, and he didn't anticipate that it would do the business for more than a further twenty-four hours. He was beginning to hope for those most elusive tools of the inadequate investigator – the hunch, the lucky breakthrough, the stupid, uncharacteristic error on his objective's part. Otherwise, it would be a matter of slow, painstaking effort - of the careful revisiting of all faint possibilities and unlikelihoods until, inevitably, their mouse was flushed. That wouldn't satisfy his principal, though. If the man wasn't three steps ahead of his competition (and to him, just about everyone but the Führer was such) he became cantankerous, and the sources of his disappointment very often found themselves reassigned to oblivion, or a point directly in front of advancing Soviet armour. Even a man who entirely lacked a spiritual vocation could become very thoughtful at that prospect.

Suhr was reaching for an envelope when the office door opened and Kurt, one of his overworked myrmidons, entered. Kurt was a former schoolteacher whose taste for very, very young ladies, once discovered, had been extenuated by a low Party membership number and SD connections. He had since transferred to another educational institution, Gestapo, where his idiosyncracies were less likely to be judged unforgivingly. Usually to be found kicking in the doors of suspected homosexuals and the politically ill-advised, he was occasionally co-opted by his present taskmaster for the particular skills he brought to any investigation.

Given a tree's-worth of documentation to get through, even assiduous readers could lose interest, let their minds drift or accelerate the pace at which they processed the detail, but Kurt didn't do any of that. He had a metronomic mind, its aptitude for detail squandered, usually, on correcting (and inserting grammar into) his Gestapo colleagues' reports, but in any investigation in which dozens of testimonies and denouncements had to be sifted, his name rang down the corridors. *Get me Kurt* was as good as an admission that someone had been tasked with a hellish assignment.

'What is it, Kurt?'

'You wanted all transfer papers re-examined, Herr Brigadeführer.'

'I did. It's unfortunate, but …'

'I've finished.'

'Already?'

'It took longer than I expected, because I thought I should check it against complement reports.'

'That's … clever.'

'It is if it gives up something. Otherwise, it's just more arse-ache.'

'And?'

'Medical facilities, nothing. The same with all Luftwaffe barracks in the Wehrkreis. Who went in and out tallies with opening and closing totals precisely. But prisons ...'

'Which one?'

'Spandau. Total number of prisoners reported on 17 April: 38. The same on 24 April.'

'But?'

'They had a transfer in, I think, on the 18th.'

'You've found an order?'

'No, a guard shift-report, noting the arrival and departure of a Feldgendarmie detail – without a prisoner either way, if the lack of paperwork's to be believed.'

'Why would the Feldgendarmerie go to Spandau, unless …?'

'A works day out? A pilgrimage?'

'We're told they hardly have the hours to sleep, given the army of deserters they're chasing these days.'

'And yet an entire detail – six men, led by a leutnant – delivered and collected nothing and no-one.'

'Excellent work, Kurt. The Commandant needs to be interrogated.'

'Deputy Commandant. His boss is on long-term leave - bad bowels, it's feared.'

'Right. Pulling him in will only flag our interest, so I should make the pilgrimage, too.'

'Can I come?'

'You think it's necessary?'

'You have your letter of authority. It's a big thing, but I have this ...'

Kurt removed his silver Gestapo warrant-disc from a pocket and swung it around on its chain.

'It always gives them the shits when I drop it on a table. It's the noise, see? Paper doesn't do that, even with *his* name on it.'

Suhr smiled. 'Why not, then? A drive to Spandau - it'll be a pleasant day out of the office.'

'I'll bet that's just what the leutnant of Feldgendarmerie didn't say.'

32

On a rainy morning, the two aero-engineers, Hansi and Ludwig, met once more at Adlershof Airfield, the DVL offices. This time, it had been Hansi who requested their meeting (which had been arranged at less than twenty-four hours' notice), and flown in from Völkenrode on the early post-run. Ludwig had asked for and received his usual office, and, having brought with him two fine French crystal flutes, was disappointed not to see the customary bottle of champagne cradled in Hansi's arm when he arrived. The preoccupied frown on his friend's face also told him that this was going to be purely about business, and not entirely satisfactory business at that.

'I'm sorry to have roused you, Ludwig, but it's important.'

'Of course, Hansi. It's always a pleasure to see you.'

'You may not think so this time.'

Hansi threw himself into a leather armchair, reached for his cigarettes and lit one without offering the case. At anxious moments a random movement busied his right eyelid, and it was apparent now (Ludwig had first noticed it almost two years earlier, when both of them had lost much sleep trying to manage the open-legged breech-birth that had been the Heinkel HE 177). He scratched his temple as if acknowledging the thing, took a couple of drags on his cigarette and opened his mouth twice to say something without actually moving air. Solicitously, his friend tried a gentle prompt.

'Is it the wing-rack on the bomber variant again?'

'Mm? No, we've decided not to do anything about that, as the laws of physics seem not to want to oblige us. Hopefully, the Führer will take the hint and give up on it.'

'The rack?'

'The variant. He can either have a bomber with no bombs or a laden aircraft that loses its wings during attack-dives. I don't regard that as much of a choice.'

'No. The thing's meant to be a fighter, unquestionably.'

Hansi sighed and rubbed his tired eyes. 'Yet he continues to question. I've tried to make the simple mathematical case – that Great Britain produces more aircraft than we do, that Canada produces more than Italy, and that when America's production lines are running fully they'll build far more aircraft than all the Axis nations combined. I won't even mention Soviet numbers, but the point is that we can only address the imbalance by building fighters that can out-gun, out-race and out-manoeuvre anything the Allies have. That fighter exists *now*, if we're allowed to proceed. If we build it in ten variants we lose the air war, whatever miracles Reichsminister Speer can perform on the production lines.'

'I know, Hansi, I know. It's horribly frustrating, but we have a visionary leader, and visions aren't reliable. I didn't say that, of course.'

'Of course you didn't. Anyway, the wound's an old one, and we're both used to the pain. I'm here because we have another problem.'

'Oh.' Ludwig thought about their other projects. There were issues with each, as was always the case with innovative new aircraft technologies, but he couldn't see what might be urgent news to him. And then he thought about the non-technical matter.

'Not our little embarrassment?'

'I told you that he was confined to Völkenrode, unless accompanied?'

'Yes.'

'He got out – walked through the main gate, thumbed a ride into Braunschweig and disappeared for two days. He returned voluntarily, and won't say anything about it. It *may* be a coincidence, but three local girls – two of them prostitutes - were injured during that time. It's a garrison city *and* a river port of course, so sexual assaults are a fairly regular curse, but ....'

'Christ. The local police?'

'We haven't said anything to them, and they're not asking questions – yet. It may well be that the incidents will be booked in and forgotten, but my concern is that they won't be the last.'

'They almost certainly won't be. Do you realise ...' Ludwig paused, his stomach churning violently, and he almost lost his composure. ' ... that I arranged a man's death to protect this fellow?'

'To protect the *project*, Ludwig. It was the right thing to do.'

'Was it? All the poor bastard was trying to do was to expose a fiend, and for that he died – at my hand.'

'Nonsense. You merely asked a favour of men who don't lose sleep over that sort of thing.'

'There's no moral boundary between requiring and carrying out a crime.'

'Well it's done, and it can't be undone. You asked my advice at the time and I agreed that it was necessary, so we must share the guilt of it.'

Anxiously, Ludwig glanced at his office door. 'I don't know if it *is* done. Hansi.'

'What do you mean?'

'You recall that I approached Panzinger to arrange it?'

'He seemed the logical choice, given his responsibilities within Gestapo.'

'He was, and once the situation was explained to him he seemed more than happy both to make it happen and to pass the word across the corridor to Amt V that it wasn't to be investigated.'

'A fortunate choice, then.'

'I'm not so sure. Less than a week after it was done I was called in to Prinz-Albrecht-Strasse to have a word with him. It happened to be much more than the one word.'

'A problem?'

'Enough of one to make Panzinger curse his amenable nature, as he put it. I suspect he was really cursing me. One wouldn't have thought that the death of a nonentity could have stirred anyone in *that* building, but when word of it got out – and I don't know *how* it did - Müller himself came to see Panzinger and almost punched him in the face.'

'Good God. Why?'

'It seems that others had an interest in the victim.'

'For the same reason that we …?'

'Apparently not, because for them it was extremely important that he *not* die - at least, not until he'd given them something. So we've inadvertently stamped on the toes of people who even Gestapo Müller would have preferred not to upset.'

'Who could *that* possibly be?'

'I don't intend to speculate. If I had a hole to hide in I'd be spitting soil right now, but as yet no-one's come after me for this. I can only pray that it'll be seen as an unfortunate but innocent clash of intentions. I could of course argue that if everyone at Prinz-Albrecht-Strasse attempted to be a little more collegiate instead of building high walls this might never have happened, but …'

'But you're not suicidally-minded.'

'And now your news from Braunschweig, that makes me think it was all for nothing. I tell you this, Hansi – you'll need to gauge constantly just how valuable he remains to the project, and the minute he becomes merely useful rather than irreplaceable …'

'I know. And you'll know too, the same day.'

'Good. In the meantime, can't you find some bromide for the fellow? As I recall, it was everywhere during the First War.'

'I doubt that it would work. It's intended to dampen a physical urge, not a psychological condition.'

'Then keep a closer eye on him – Christ, have him locked up at nights, if there's no alternative. And when you're sure he's no longer needed ….'

'We'll hand him to the police?'

'You're not serious? And implicate ourselves in his crimes? No, when the time comes, we'll do what we'd do for any mad dog. And my conscience won't even squeak about it.'

Hauptführerin Hedy Bauer received excellent but wholly unexpected news as she ate soup at her desk (lunching in the Air Ministry's canteen would have required that she either ignore or socialize with her subordinates, options she regarded respectively as impractical and unthinkable). Almost four months earlier, she applied to join the Female Criminal Investigations Department of RSHA Amt V but had heard nothing since – a disappointment, given that her former experience as a personnel officer in the BDM was recognized as relevant to the application. Now, suddenly, she discovered (by letter, addressed to the Ministry rather than her home) that not only was she being considered but had been accepted provisionally, subject only to an interview.

Supervising the Ministry's post-room was of course an important contribution to the war effort, but her duties rarely rose above the mundane. A career with the *SiPos* demanded a great deal (a two-year training period was compulsory, before which she couldn't progress, even to the rank of kriminalsekretarin), but female detectives were highly valued for their undercover work, being far less likely to raise suspicions among the traitors and other dregs they were required to infiltrate, observe, and, eventually, arrest. It was a calling to be proud of, and it called her strongly.

Of course, she couldn't announce the news to the post-room girls, but no doubt word would filter down to them eventually, once she was gone. It would have been pleasant to bask in the respect, the admiration they would feel for her achievement, no less than the slight frisson of fear that her new profession invoked in even the most respectable citizen, yet - she told herself - a serious, assiduous member of Amt V (and she had no doubt that she would be just that) had to regard the foregoing of such little indulgences as a necessary sacrifice. She and her colleagues-to-be were sentinels, upholders of the Party's principles and policies against the corruption that still infected much of German society. Duty was all. Mere self-satisfaction had no place in her professional life-to-come.

This and other pleasing observations carried her through the rest of her (now-lukewarm) soup and tea until precisely twelve-thirty pm, when she stepped out into the main sorting-room to check that none of the girls were returning late from their own lunches. She wandered among them for a while, helping with an occasional query about where a particular addressee lived, but her mind was wandering widely upon her SicherheitsPolizei training, and where her first posting would take her. Technically, she could be sent to any part of the Reich, but she suspected that it would be Berlin or other major city. That was fine - she had no husband or fiancee, no friends so close that saying farewell would be any sort of tug, no emotional reason to keep her physically close to her mother. In fact, she felt not a hint of the second thoughts that a new course encourages, once it becomes imminent. If she could have given an hour's notice and started her new life hundreds of kilometres away the following morning she would have leaped at the opportunity. What had been a faint hope now seemed like the hand of a kindly fate, and she was ready to be shoved by it.

It was only an an hour later that the small problem cough politely and tapped her shoulder. Locked in her desk, the mysterious note-book had largely behaved itself over the past days, though occasionally stirring an unpleasant realization that it would need to be dealt with, eventually. Unfortunately, her wonderful news meant that *eventually* had flowered into *imminently*. She couldn't leave her post with the item in her drawer still, otherwise her first week's training with the SiPos would be interrupted by an embarrassing interrogation and possible arrest (subject to whatever the damned thing might be). She had to resolve the matter, either by somehow establishing who it had been intended for and getting it to them anonymously, or …

The thought was so *wrong* that she almost shuddered. To destroy what might well be something important (or, God knew, vital) was inconceivable to dutiful Hedy, the Hedy who was about to embark upon an exemplary career as a female criminal detective. But to Hedy the post-room Hauptführerin, unwilling curator of a ticking bomb, the option of flinging the problem as far and as finally from her as possible recommended itself urgently. *How*, though?

The simplest option would be to place the thing in her bag at the end of that day's shift, leave the building and walk home, taking care to adjust her normal route so as to pass a quiet stretch of the Spree where gravity could lend a hand. Even if it managed to float (despite its waterlogged pages), anyone rescuing it would have no means of knowing what it was, who it was meant for or who had thrown it in the river. Probably, after the most cursory examination, the finder would return it to its new, damp home and put the matter from mind.

The only disadvantage to this method of disposal was that it would require a degree of courage to carry through. Occasionally, security checks were made upon personnel's effects both on entry to and exit from the Ministry, and anything that was (or appeared to be) coded would have as much chance of being waved through as a biography of Winston Churchill. The last such exercise had been little more than a week earlier, so the chances of another today were small - but wouldn't that make it more likely to be effective, should it happen?

Body searches never happened, so she might tear out a few pages at a time and carry them from the Ministry in her underwear. It would take time though, and she had no idea how many more days of her present employment remained. Besides, what if a stray page managed to escape her pants and fall to the polished floor of the reception hall? It would be as good as a neon-lit admission of espionage.

Put it in another envelope and address it to someone at Prinz-Albrecht-Strasse 8. That would have the advantage of being an honest correction to the false course she had set, but she would need to address the thing in her own hand, or take the chance of being seen to use an envelope-labeller in the outgoing post-room. That wasn't a job for a section leader, so there was a good chance that she would be remembered when RSHA (her new employers, she reminded herself) noticed the Air Ministry frank and came looking for the source of their unexpected gift.

Burning it, dissolving it in acid or flinging it from her high window all received a moment's more consideration than they deserved, and she had to force herself to be calm. Whatever this notebook was or represented, it had entered the Ministry anonymously and unnoticed - surely, it wasn't beyond her native wit to send it on the same way? Was it even too late to be open about the thing, risk that its contents could harm by association and claim that it had arrived in that morning's post?

Stupid girl. She had considered all but the obvious, bureaucratic option. The notebook was meant for someone – she just didn't know who. What would an indolent, time-serving cog in this great machine do with such a conundrum, if not palm it off? All she needed was an excuse to be in another department – it didn't matter which, only that she be covered should she be seen.

A large quartermaster's requisition schedule for non-operational supplies, submitted by Luftflotte 3, had arrived that morning. It was marked *Most Urgent* (as they always were), and the usual procedure was to have it walked up to the fifth floor. Hedy placed it in a large envelope, removed the smaller, poisonous one from her drawer and carried them out into the sorting-room. She caught the eye of Petra (one of her less energetic subordinates) and smiled.

'I'm delivering something by hand. If anyone asks for me, I should be about twenty minutes.'

Puzzled by this unexpected confidence, Petra nodded and returned to her pile of correspondence. Hedy, almost certain that the message would be forgotten by the time she reached the corridor, glanced around casually and satisfied herself that no-one else was looking in her direction. A similarly nonchalant survey, conducted every few seconds on her trek from ground-floor (north) to fifth-floor (east), registered only unawareness, indifference or the occasional distracted half-acknowledgment from those she passed. Her uniform made her almost invisible, of course, being that of the Wehrmachthelferin (whose valuable auxiliary contributions were hardly recognized), and by the time she arrived at Maintenance and Supply (Field) her nerves had settled slightly.

The main office was quietly busy, its staff pushing the paper that put fuel into aircraft, bullets into wing-guns and bread into ground-crew bellies. As far as she could tell, no-one looked up as she passed through their desks and knocked quietly on the office door of their supervisor, Oberst Hann.

Expecting no reply, she walked into the office and closed the door. She knew already that General von Seidel, Quartermaster-General of the Luftwaffe, was in the building, so Hann and other senior members of the Maintenance and

Supply Group would be in a meeting room somewhere, hanging on his every rant. The large envelope containing Luftflotte 3's begging letter went onto the desk, and from habit she moved its bottom edge so that it sat precisely parallel to the desk's. From the other envelope she removed the notebook, turned, and quickly slid it into the bookcase among volumes of roughly the same height. It was done it a moment, and if her anxious mind hadn't memorized every detail of its outer surface she wouldn't have noticed it among its neighbours. She was certain that to Hann it would be entirely invisible.

In the outer office once more, she stopped at the desk of a good-looking, one-armed Hauptmann and gave him a slight, terse nod.

'I've brought a major requisition order for the Oberst's attention. I assume he's in the building?'

The Hauptmann pulled a face. 'He's being told what's wrong with Maintenance and Supply at the moment, so I assume we'll all get it when he returns. Did you put it on his desk?'

'Yes.'

'I'll mention it, then. Do I need to give him your name?'

'Not unless he's single and on the market.'

The Hauptmann laughed, making his pretty face even prettier.

'Bad luck. I've met his wife, so I assume he wishes he was a bachelor still.'

A great weight having lifted, Hedy returned to her office, offering a smile to everyone she passed on the way. She had letters of acceptance and resignation to write, and a wonderful future with Criminal Investigations to anticipate. Other than in the ever-present burden of war, she couldn't think of a single part of her life that wasn't now offering a promise of better, and even war brought its own, peculiar opportunities. She had heard that volunteering for service in the new territories more or less guaranteed accelerated promotion within the police, so she only hoped that the Soviets didn't surrender before she could complete her training, make a mark in her new job and then put herself forward for special duties in the East (whatever they might be).

If one, tiny thing could have put more glister on the day, it came just minutes after she completed her letter of resignation (and the formality of a transfer request). One of the girls, Lotta, came into her office without knocking on the door. Hedy was about to order her out and to make a proper entrance when she saw the tears and paused.

'Oh, Hedy – I mean, Frau Hauptführerin. It's too terrible! Ilse Hansen's been summoned to the Oberhauptführerin's office and told that she's dismissed – from the post-room *and* the BDM!'

'Why?'

'She's pregnant! And she doesn't even have a fiancee. Her doctor wrote to the Ministry – it came this morning.'

There was one unforgivable sin that a BDM girl could commit, and it was nothing to do with spying for the enemy. Great emphasis was put upon her duty to breed – preferably at the same rate that a sow dropped piglets - but not until the ring was on her finger. Promiscuity in a female offended decency, attacked the moral foundations of the State and put racial purity at the mercy of a flipped coin. No doubt Ilse had been frantically trying to persuade her suitor to take the knee since her doctor's appointment, but her fate had been sealed the moment he decided not to use a rubber. BDM girls didn't sleep around, unless they wanted all doors slammed in their faces.

Ilse was the only other person who knew that the notebook had reached the Ministry. Hedy hadn't been too worried that she might speak about it, but her going made even that faint threat vanish entirely. If, by some chance, Oberst Hann examined his bookcase and found its unexpected tenant, he could be as curious or suspicious as he liked, and nothing could come of it, ever.

It was difficult for Hedy not to appear delighted. She frowned deeply to kill the grin, and shook her head in disgust.

'I wouldn't have thought it of Ilse. It's a shame, but her reputation is gone.'

'Can't you do something …?'

Hedy looked severely at Lotta. 'It's our duty to uphold standards, not sidestep them. She made her choice, and it was a bad one. Is there anything else?'

Lotta's face said a lot, but her mouth remained closed as she backed out of the office. Hedy had no doubt that her reputation as a hard bitch would be enhanced considerably as word spread around the post-room, but she cared nothing for that. She would be gone in a matter of days, and if she was recalled as someone without human feelings it was all to her advantage. Criminal Investigations doubtless comprised a range of talents, but compassion was almost certainly not one of them.

34

After deciding that he needed a plan, Fischer gave the matter almost a full minute's consideration before applying a metaphorical boot to his rear.

How could he plan anything when his gaolers had no schedule, no fixed routines or inclination to provide him with a detailed map of where he was, exactly? Almost certainly, his new prison was within the greater Berlin area, but lacking either a compass, a homing pigeon's sense of *heimat* or the price of a taxi ride, bus fare or telephone call, his escape from the House of Dead Uncle Noam was likely to carry him from one state of helplessness to another. Waiting was a tiresome habit, but he needed something more than he had at present.

The first hopeful shimmer in this stasis came the morning after his arrival, when Wilhelm departed for Reinickendorf barracks with his brother's list of requirements. He said that he'd return within three hours, but Fischer, like every other serving member of the Wehrmacht, knew that a man passing through a barracks couldn't avoid being noticed by someone wanting to give someone else a bad day. Even if he produced and waved his magic authority, questions might be asked and the dragging of feet extend his absence.

There remained the problem of Rainer. Fischer had the impression that he was not an instinctive soldier, but he made up for that by persevering doggedly at a task. In Spandau, he had been told to watch the prisoner during Wilhelm's rest periods, and had done so literally, losing sight of his charge only for as long as it took him to blink. It was an impressive achievement for an obviously intelligent man, to so apply himself to a task that a ticket-puncher would find tedious.

Wilhelm had given no instructions before leaving, but Rainer's eyes were fixed firmly upon some part of the Fischer firmament for almost an hour thereafter. Attempts at conversation were smothered with a single syllable, a request for a toilet-break was merely ignored (though by way of discouragement, Rainer's hand twitched slightly towards the handle of the P08 that lay on the table next to him), and when the prisoner stood the other man did the same, as if they were two vaudeville comedians performing the venerable non-existent-mirror routine. No wire in a live warhead ever received more careful attention; no heavily-backed horse ever ran with more fervent attention paid to its every move.

Becoming heartily sick of this, Fischer stood once more and held out a hand to stay his shadow.

'I need to shit, and it will come far more easily if it doesn't have an audience.'

Rainer had the grace to blush. 'Alright. You can try to force the window, but the drop would break your legs.'

'I'm not going to try anything except to lose some weight. You're keeping me safe, aren't you?'

'That's what Wilhelm says.'

'Well, then. In any case, where would I go, even if my legs didn't break? I don't know where I am.'

Rainer scowled, but the logic was sound to his philosopher's ear. 'I ... suppose that's right.'

'The front door's locked?'

'It is.'

'And all downstairs windows are barred?'

'As you can see.'

'So if you glance away occasionally, I'll probably still be here when you glance back.'

'Don't try to be amusing. I have no sense of humour.'

'Alright. Can we agree that I have no reason to try to get away from you?'

Rainer said nothing but didn't follow the prisoner to the toilet, which seemed to indicate agreement. When Fischer returned he had taken off his boots and tunic, pulled his feet up on to the armchair and was reading a small, battered book.

'I assume that isn't Karl Marx?'

'Kierkegaard.'

'And which part of the navel did he explore?'

Rainer stared coldly at Fischer. 'He considered a great number of matters, but the inward nature of man, and how he comes to understand both himself and God, were his great interests.'

'And was he right?'

'Define *right*.'

'Sorry. I meant, do you agree with him?'

'No. There is no God.'

'He wasted his time, then?'

Rainer sighed and looked to the ceiling for strength, or sympathy. 'Of course he didn't. An underlying assumption needn't be correct for what flows from it to be of use.'

'Like gunpowder ?

'What?'

'Weren't the Chinese looking for the secret of immortality when they invented it? I hear that gunpowder's *very* useful.' Fischer frowned. 'But not for extending life.'

'Are you trying to irritate me?'

'Yes, but you mustn't mind. I'm very bored.'

With a little more emphasis than was polite, Rainer returned to Kierkegaard. For a while, Fischer examined every visible detail of the sitting room and failed to find anything that seized his attention. Eventually, tedium pressed more heavily than the prospect of pouring more Tonga into his digestive system. He stood up.

'Shall I make some tea?'

Rainer half-nodded, but perhaps a vision of kitchen knives came to him. He placed a marker in his page, closed the book, put on his boots and picked up his pistol.

'I'll do it.'

For a few moments after he disappeared down the corridor, Fischer considered the contradictions that made a man. He couldn't say with certainty that a Philosophy degree indicated a high degree of intelligence, but Rainer had studied under Heidegger, and it was doubtful that the great man would have put himself to the trouble of tutoring a dolt. On the other hand …

Fischer reached into Rainer's tunic, extracted his wallet and the key with which he had locked the front door after Wilhelm departed, and put on his own boots and tunic. As a distant kettle began to whistle he twisted the key in its lock, stepped out, relocked the door and performed a brief recce.

High, windowless walls bordered a dark alley, approximately fifty metres in length. In the space of about fifteen seconds, two vehicles passed by its entrance, suggesting a reasonably busy secondary route rather than a major thoroughfare. Fischer moved quickly, buttoning his tunic, and exited the alley.

Small shops lined each side of the road, the commercial section of a residential area, probably. He looked up. The lamp-sign told him that this was Tucholskystrasse, meaning that he was somewhere in …

Well, Berlin. To date, he had become reasonably familiar with the ground between Wilhelmstrasse and Alt-Moabit, but almost all the rest of the city was a blank chart still. The morning sun gave him a sense of where east lay, but not having a *here* from which to plot *there* (another decision he had yet to make), he may as well have escaped into darkest night.

A decision loomed. Rainer couldn't follow him (unless he risked broken legs by going through the bathroom window), but Wilhelm might return soon, and Fischer had a healthy fear of what the larger, cruder and more capable brother might do, notwithstanding his alleged duty to keep his prisoner 'safe'.

He examined the view in both directions, crossed the road and did the same again. No obvious landmarks rose above the near rooftops, and he couldn't see any road-signs that would point him in a useful direction. A young woman, pushing a large, obsolete perambulator, was closing upon him; she hadn't yet noticed the obstacle, so his face was going to be the very worst sort of surprise, and he wondered whether a smile would help or hinder an appeal for directions.

She hadn't yet looked up when a stray thought returned to him, carrying implications. Hastily, he stepped to one side, and she continued down Tucholskystrasse, likely now to remain forever ignorant of Otto Fischer. He watched her go, and began to consider how stupid he had been.

The boredom and torpor of the past few days must have dulled whatever senses remained to him. If the purpose of his abduction was to keep him *safe*, why wasn't he presently sitting in a Group Command station, a respectable distance from its forward operating fields – perhaps in Belgium, or southern Italy? There, he could have hidden from God, man and his creditors, and his mysterious abductors would have the absolute assurance that he couldn't stir a neck hair without their people knowing everything about it. Instead, he had been entrusted to the care of two men who, apparently, could call upon no resources other than themselves. They had no lines of communication, no means of defending their charge other than a single pistol and a van in which to flee pursuers, no safe recourse other than the crumbling home of a dead relative. On the other hand, they *did* have a form of authorization that could open doors and force the most reluctant party to assist them. Why had they been given that, and not the rest of what was needed to do the job?

The only possible answer came to him as he contemplated the human traffic entering and leaving a baker's premises directly across Tucholskystrasse from where he stood. He had noticed already the faded sign above the freshly-painted name of the premises' latest proprietor, that had once enticed the passer-by with a promise of berches and bagels. From the glimpses he had of departing customers' purchases, the present clientele were making do with *kommissarbrot* (a near-obligatory choice since Goebbels' historic broadcast of two years earlier, when he'd claimed that white bread had been a Jewish invention to undermine the health of the German nation). The prospect activated gripes in his stomach.

Why not? He had just flushed any possibility of escape, and filling a belly was hardly the least useful of his options. He crossed the road and took up a place at the end of a short queue to the counter. However despised *kommissarbrot* had become the smell of baking bread was unearthly, and he was happy to wait and breathe while the woman in front of him tried to pass off a counterfeit ration ticket. At his turn, he stepped forward and ordered a loaf. It was half in its newspaper when the baker noticed the hand movement towards his inner tunic pocket and shook his head.

'Keep your ration card where it is, comrade. Our brave pilots don't pay here.'

Fischer was about to correct the misconception when he realised that it was pointless, would probably be unwelcome and would occupy more of the rest of his life than was useful. He nodded, thanked the man and made space for the lady behind him.

He was back at the house within three minutes. The door was locked still, so Wilhelm hadn't yet returned. Almost as unwelcome a prospect, however, was the barrel of the PO8 pointing almost directly at his face - *almost*, because the hand that held it trembled visibly. Slowly, Fischer raised his *kommissarbrot*-bearing hand.

'Bread – fresh and free.'

'What the Holy Hell do you think you're doing?'

'Making the day less uninteresting than it was. Could you point that away from me, please? I've returned, so obviously it isn't needed.'

'When I tell Wilhelm ...'

'He'll be irritated, I expect. But I think I know why you've been told to do this. Will that make him happier?'

'Why?'

'Don't be impatient. Is there a toasting fork in the house? We could light a fire.'

Rainer didn't seem to be hungry, and he certainly wasn't talkative. He snatched the key from Fischer's hand, did the same when his wallet was produced (and made a show of inspecting its contents), and then waved Fischer into the sitting room with the gun that, very reluctantly, he had ceased to point at him.

'Why didn't you run?'

'If I'm right about why I'm here, running might be a dangerous.'

'What does that mean?'

Before Fischer could mention impatience once more, a key turned in the front door lock, and Wilhelm stepped in.

'What a fucking *heckmeck* that was!'

He was slightly flushed, and struggled with a chessboard, a book and provisions.

'What is, Wilhelm?'

'I was stopped about six hundred times – well, half a dozen at least – at the barracks. Everyone and his mother wanted to know what I was doing, where I'd been for the past few days, had I reported to the staff sergeant, where I was going with this *fucking* chessboard and why wasn't I saluting?'

'What did you say?'

'I referred them to the signature on the paper – unless it was someone of my rank, in which case I told them to press their lips to my arse. Christ, I've forgotten the bread!'

Rainer reddened considerably. 'That's alright. We have some.'

'We have? How?'

Fischer raised a finger. 'I popped out for some. There's a baker's, just...'

'What does he mean, popped out?'

Wilhelm was glaring at his brother, who glanced to Fischer for support (but then realised how counterproductive that would be) and swallowed. 'He ... escaped. But then he came back.'

'Oh, for ...'

Wilhelm dropped his various loads on the hall floor and rubbed his eyes. When he spoke again he was calm, as flat seas can be in a deep depression.

'This is military operation. I was asked for particularly, by a man who expects everything to be done at least faultlessly, and preferably better than that. Alright, his instructions weren't very extensive, but I think he assumed that at no point would we let this … *fellow* escape. '

'I *did* come back.'

'Shut up. What were you doing, Rainer? When he went for a walk, I mean?'

'I was making tea.'

'Presumably, you didn't take your key with you?'

'I took the pistol.'

'Very wise. Kettles can be bastards. But the key …?'

'It was in my tunic. I didn't think he'd ...'

'Go through its pockets? No, why would he?'

'If you're going to be sarcastic ...'

'May I say something?' Fischer spoke politely, not trusting Wilhelm's ability to maintain his composure.'

'What is it? An apology?'

'Of course not – it's my duty to escape.'

'That's from the enemy, not us.'

'Well, you've removed a valuable military resource from the Reich's use, so you're saboteurs at least. That wasn't what I want to say, though. I'm glad I managed to get outside – it cleared my head, and I think I know at least a little of what this is about. That is, why you've been asked to keep me under the tarpaulin.'

'Go on.'

It took no more than two minutes to explain the theory. Wilhelm frowned, trying hard to find the flaws in what he'd heard. His brother, being more philosophically minded, gawped.

'But ...'

'Fuck your mother!' Wilhelm shook his head. 'It makes sense. Well, more sense than anything else to do with this mess. After all the jobs we've done for the bastard ...'

'What are we going to do, Willy?'

'What we're told - what else *can* we do? Respectfully resign present duties? Ask for a transfer to another sweet billet that's several hundred kilometres from a front line?'

Rainer bristled. 'Why not? Haven't we earned it?'

'Yeah, he'd be reasonable. We might even get an honourable discharge, with long service medals and a stepped-up pension. Or he could have us welded into cockpits, pointed east and and told to dent a couple of T34s. He chose us because we don't say no, ever, to what he tells us to do. *And* because we're ...'

Fischer caught the inflection. 'Because you're what?'

'Never mind.'

Rainer snorted. 'He was going to say because we're *mischling*.'

'Why …?' Fischer stopped himself. There was no need to press the point. Something was playing out, and he was beginning to doubt that it had anything to do with what Bruno Ahle had committed to his diary. The chessboard that Wilhelm was retrieving from the floor gave him the thought – that this was more about where the pieces stood around the King and what power of movement they possessed.

He was pleased with the analogy, but needed only a moment to find its flaw – the pawns in this game had been gifted no power of movement whatsoever, and were more likely to be flattened than removed from the board. He looked up at his gaolers – or rather, the men who had suddenly discovered that their employment came with barbs. Wilhelm was returning his gaze, waiting to hear more. Rainer was staring at his brother, his expression poised somewhere between hope and helplessness. Neither man seemed to want to take up the reins, so it was left to Fischer to state the obvious.

'I suppose you know that, however this goes, we're entirely on our own?'

Wilhelm nodded slowly. 'What do we do now?'

Fischer raised the only eyebrow that still worked. 'I think it's more a case of what *can* we do now?'

35

SS-Brigadeführer Suhr told Kurt to pull into the side of the road as soon as they were out of sight of Spandau's main gate.

'What did you think of that?'

Kurt examined the steering wheel in his hands for a few moments. 'He was nervous, certainly, but that might just have been my Gestapo warrant disc. He didn't seem to become *more* nervous when he saw your authorization.'

'And yet the signature should have opened his bowels.'

'*If* he was lying. He's the deputy commandant of a military prison – in other words, nobody. Faced with that name, perhaps it was innocence that kept him from embarrassing himself?'

'Hm. You excused yourself. Presumably, you went to ask questions elsewhere?'

'The guards' room. They were happy to talk – their commandant is a hard bastard, but his deputy doesn't worry them. A few of them recalled the Feldgendarmerie squad's visit, but not the body we assume they brought with them.'

'That's disappointing.'

'But one of them mentioned that the guards have been kept out of the upper corridors of the South wing for almost a week, which is strange.'

'Why?'

Because the wing's hardly been used since the last of the administrative detainees were offed to the new camps in '37. The guards' mess is on the ground floor, and they use one of the first-floor rooms for illicit card games, but that's about it. The rest is, or should be, deserted.'

'And you think it wasn't?'

'I *know* that it wasn't. The same guard told me that he and another fellow have had sight of two uniforms – Heer – passing by the mess occasionally. The only way they can go from that corridor is out to the courtyard or upstairs.'

'Did you get a description?'

No rank or unit insignia, but they didn't move like anyone important. A big thug and a shorter, slightly-built fellow with a facial tic. The one you wouldn't introduce to your sister has a large, clean scar running from hairline to jaw, right-side.'

'It's not much.'

'No. They might have been fixing the roof, for all we know. Except ...'

Suhr waited. For all the man's acute moral failings, Kurt was an intuitive grubber of facts, half-facts and slight possibilities, and any qualification he made was likely to be worth hearing.

'I apologize, Herr Brigadeführer, this is only a feeling. The descriptions were hardly comprehensive, but they nudged something in my head.'

'You think you might recognize them?'

'No – I mean, not quite. I'm trying to recall where I heard or read something similar, but it's elusive. I need to get into Gestapo's files.'

'So these men may be prior offenders?'

'Possibly. But I'm wondering also whether they were comrades. Or competition.'

Suhr couldn't be surprised by the suggestion. Rivalries at the top of the Party had ensured that Germany's security agencies had blossomed like weeds in an unploughed field, with each trying to block the sunlight falling upon the rest. Even the great amalgamations under Heydrich and Himmler had merely brought the struggle indoors, and there remained still the military outliers – Abwehr, the separate intelligence and evaluation departments of Heer, Kreigsmarine and Luftwaffe, and Forschungsamt, the electronic listeners – who maintained high walls around their little kingdoms and looked forever over their shoulders for signs of encroachment. Overlaps of responsibility and authority were pervasive, even when organizations – Gestapo and Inland SD, for example – were supposed to be complementary arms of the same body. For the rest, dogs in a pit could be more comradely than agencies ostensibly devoted to a great, common cause.

'Speak to your colleagues, then – without explaining why, obviously. It may stir someone's memory. We don't have time to pore through the archives. In the meantime, I'll report that we're looking for possible suspects. It may ease the grip on our shoulders a little. Let's get back to Prinz-Albecht-Strasse.'

Kurt didn't start the car immediately. He half turned in his seat and cleared his throat. 'May I ask …'

'What?'

'By whom the report will be read?'

Surprised, Suhr started at his Gestapo helper. 'No. You don't need or want to know. I could wish that *I* didn't, but in my case enlightenment was unavoidable. It's someone in the Chancellery – will that do?'

Kurt's eyebrows lifted. 'Yes, definitely. I apologize for asking.'

'You're paid to be curious, Kurt. But don't let that virtue trip you up.'

They drove back to Mitte in silence, the car's front windows folded down to gather the spring air. Traffic was light in the late morning, and Kurt had little to do other than keep the bonnet badge pointing in the right direction. His lips moved intermittently, carrying a private conversation, until, negotiating the Grosser Stern, he exhaled loudly. To Suhr, it sounded more like surprise than a reaction to a crushed pedestrian.

'What is it, Kurt?'

'A light going on, Herr Brigadeführer. I think I've recalled our pair of strangers.'

'Are they a problem for us?'

'Possibly. Gestapo has old business with them. May I pull over and explain?'

'No. Continue to Prinz-Albrecht-Strasse. We'll speak there.'

The remainder of the journey took less than ten minutes. Kurt pulled up outside the dark, heavy portico framing the main entrance of RSHA Headquarters, two wheels on the kerb. A guard took a half-step towards the car to move them on, caught sight of the passenger and thought better of it. Suhr looked straight through him and turned to his driver.

'We'll speak here.'

'Right. None of this is first-hand. I heard about it because both the matter itself and Gestapo's role in it were untypical. Anyway, June 1940, France, I don't recall which sector. A hero pilot asks for compassionate leave and gets it, which is strange.'

'Why?

'Because this was in the middle of an attempt to smash what remained of the French air force as it sat on the grass.'

'Why would it matter? They were beaten by then.'

'Yes, but Luftwaffe couldn't be sure – and in any case, the Reichsmarschall wanted a little more of the glory that the infantry were scooping up with shovels.'

'Alright. Go on.'

'The hero pilot came home. A dying mother saw her son a final time and then expired promptly. He arranged the funeral and returned to his squadron, to seek further glory over British skies.'

'Laudable, I'm sure.'

'A few days later, police reports from several locations began to keep company, and a keen-eyed unterkommissar made a connection between the incidents they logged and the itinerary of a local boy temporarily home from the Front. It was a delicate business, and Gestapo got the job of following it up.'

'Why didn't Criminal Investigations continue to deal with it?'

'Because it *was* delicate, and the embarrassment in question was in uniform. Their jurisdiction was minimal.'

'Then the Fedgendarmerie …?'

'Didn't want to know about it. At the time, the honour of the Armed Forces was a heavier consideration than it is these days, and I suspect that someone very senior in Luftwaffe had a quiet word. Gestapo, however, considered this a matter that couldn't be ignored - possibly because anything that was likely to shame their former boss Göring was to be pursued relentlessly.'

Suhr smiled. 'Very likely. What was the offence?'

'Cold, extremely well-planned rape. With complications.'

'Violence?'

'In some cases, mutilations – and always with a knife. The incident reports indicate that in each case the perpetrator visited the homes of women – either single, married but with husbands in service or widows – and secured their silence with a pistol. He bound their arms and mouths, placed them carefully on the floor and removed his trousers, folding them neatly. He then put on a condom and took his pleasure with them. Afterwards – if they were lucky – he washed himself thoroughly in their bathrooms, dressed and departed, leaving them to struggle their way out of the restraints.'

'And the unlucky ones?'

'Slashed across the face, several times. No very deep wounds, but all needing stitches, and likely to be disfiguring for years to come.'

'Was it established why he cut some and let others be?'

'Formally, no. But having seen the photographs, I'm inclined to think that he objected to the prettier ones *being* pretty.'

'Christ. How many?'

'He attacked six women over the course of a month. Three were cut.'

'And he'd returned to his unit before it all came out. What then?'

'There was a pause. The rumour was that Obergruppenfhrer Müller wanted to chase it immediately, but he must have appreciated that this one had glass scattered across the floor and he needed to tread carefully. Suddenly, however, authorization came through, and from the very top. '

'Not the Reichsführer?'

'I believe it was Heydrich, which makes sense. He had a lot of Luftwaffe contacts, being a pilot himself, and it seems that he cleared a path. Three Gestapo officers were sent to Belgium – to where the suspect's squadron had relocated - to interview him.'

'Not arrest him?'

'Again, I'm not certain, but I think that an effort was made to respect Luftwaffe sensibilities. Only if a confession was forthcoming, or the suspect's story entirely lacked credibility, were they to ask that he be placed into their custody immediately. Otherwise, further investigations were to be made.'

'What happened?'

'Something unexpected. Almost as soon as the officers arrived at the air station they were offered evidence that the incidents in and around Magdeburg were by no means unprecedented. Two Luftwaffe colleagues of the suspect swore out affidavits to the effect that he had disgraced his squadron. The precise details – names, dates and so-on - weren't committed to paper, but it was said that he'd been assaulting women in France during his time there. Their squadron leader had covered it up a the time, but, being an honourable man, considered it necessary to apologize to several French families ...'

'Go on.'

' ... including a Jewish one.'

'Hell. No wonder Luftwaffe wanted the scandal smothered. This is all fascinating, but what does it have to do with our two mystery men?'

'I'm almost there. Our Gestapo team returned to Berlin and made their report. It went nowhere until the Reichsführer threw the story in Göring's face during a meeting with the Führer, at which the Reichsmarschall did the only feasible thing.'

Suhr smiled once more. 'He said that he knew nothing about it, but if anyone had been doing what was alleged then

Luftwaffe's good name had been soiled and the full weight of National Socialist justice should be brought to bear against the man. No doubt he also promised that he would personally, and enthusiastically, endorse whatever penalty the Court handed down.'

Admiringly, Kurt nodded. 'I believe that's almost word-for-word. So, an arrest order was issued and our intrepid three-man team returned to Belgium.'

'And?'

'Nothing. The man had disappeared.'

'Absconded?'

'Whisked away, rather. Rigorous enquiries were made among his squadron's personnel, but hardly anyone knew, or was willing to say, anything.'

'Hardly?'

'A member of the ground staff claimed that on the morning of the gentleman's disappearance he'd seen him accused in the company of two other men, both in Luftwaffe grey. This seems to have been the last sighting.'

'Could the witness give a ...'

'One of them was big, and scarred. The other much smaller, and he seemed to have a problem with his nerves. I recall this only because it was the very last part of the very last report made upon the incident.'

'That's it? Nothing else?'

'Only that the accused resurfaced more than a year later, openly, at a Luftwaffe research facility, and was found to be untouchable.'

'Why?'

'Because he has special technical skills that predate his active service, and was said to be irreplaceable – by Willy Messerschmitt himself, among others. Assurances were made to Gestapo that he would be supervised carefully, and that no repetition of his *behaviour* would be permitted.'

For a while, Suhr examined the back of the seat in front of him. Two broad descriptions, offered almost two years apart, and neither of them capable of being tested. It was enough to half-convince him. The two men in Belgium had been Luftwaffe, apparently, while those at Spandau wore Heer green. It was no great problem to acquire uniforms, though, and both the rapist and Otto Fischer were Luftwaffe, so it was more than possible that their good samaritans in both cases were also Luftwaffe …

'I can't keep thinking of this fellow as the rapist, Kurt. Do you have a name?'

'I need to check the files. I recall that he had a nickname, though.'

'What was it?'

'He was from Magdeburg. His comrades, clearly imaginative men, called him the Magdeburger. Apparently, he was the only citizen of that city in their squadron'

36

Eight days after she last saw her lodger, Frau Traugott pinned a small notice on the community board at the Arminius Markthalle, notifying the browser that she had a bedroom with attached sitting-room to rent. It was not a decision that she had taken easily - in fact, she passed constantly between two tortured states of guilt, the one for her base greed (though she could hardly exist without the income from her top-floor rooms), the other, much worse, for possibly bringing a terrible fate upon Hauptmann Fischer by the very act of scraping him from the roster at Jonas-Strasse 17.

If he had not gone missing without leave (and why would he, with neither family nor prospect of being sent back to a Front?), he *had* to have been murdered – by auslånders most likely, or perhaps a squad of British parachutists, dropped behind enemy lines to assassinate an important Luftwaffe officer. Or perhaps, being themselves parachutists, they had an old professional grudge against one of the enemy's?

She had gone back to the police station to ask if any progress had been made, but the dull, non-comprehending expression on the anwårter's face told her that her missing person report had already been filed under V for *vergessene*. She had telephoned the Air Ministry twice, hoping to hear that Hauptmann Fischer had reappeared (or had at least called in to reassure his comrades), but she couldn't recall the name of the nice officer who had visited Herr Fischer when he wasn't well, and no-one else there seemed to know anything or cared to say if they did. She had even gone back to her blockhelfer, Amon Dunst, and humbled herself by asking if he might put word around the district that a fine officer, a wounded hero, might be lying injured in a ditch somewhere, and, if found, could he be returned please to Jonas-Strasse 17? The triumphant gleam in Dunst's eye as his previous diagnosis of desertion was (to his mind) confirmed had almost been slapped away, but desperation had stayed her hand. He promised to mention it, and no doubt the word would go first to his blockleiter and thence to the district zellenleiter, a man in every part as odious as Dunst himself. If Herr Fischer wasn't to be recalled the length and breadth of Alt-Moabit as an absconder, God knew it wouldn't be their fault.

But what else could she have done? An elderly landlady wasn't equipped by Nature to plunge into the dark holes and sinister byways that might have taken her lodger (and be holding him, even now). She had begged assistance from the proper authorities as any conscientious citizen would, but it being done only silence remained. True, the wonderful Pastor Johann had undertaken to make enquiries among his old contacts at Alexanderplatz, but he must have failed (she hadn't heard anything since his visit and examination of Herr Fischer's effects, and no-one had picked up at the number he had given her).

She tried to sooth her conscience, telling it that she had known the man for less than two weeks and done nothing to abet his disappearance. His room had been kept clean, she had fed him as well as the available ingredients permitted, the sisters on the first floor hadn't misbehaved in the time he'd been with them, and – thank God – she hadn't frightened him off with one of her epileptic attacks in the meantime. She was blameless, so how could she feel such remorse?

And yet she did. His wounds made him pitiable, and she hadn't provided a safe home, a place where the torments that hound broken men slammed their noses against the glass outside and raged quietly. If defending his country had done that to Herr Fischer, then those who benefited from it had to do their part also. As a patriotic German, she couldn't simply dismiss him from mind, give his rooms another clean and put up an advertisement for a new lodger.

And yet she had. What to her was the tiniest of inconveniences might well be a life at its uttermost point, so her Catholic heart bore a weight of guilt. She might have unloaded some of it in the confessional, but even a crop of Hail Marys and Our Fathers seemed inadequate to this particular sin. How she felt about Herr Fischer and his going was likely to be living with her for some time to come.

Twice, in the hours following her posting of the notice, she had her coat half-on, with every intention of returning to the Markthalle and retrieving it. It took stern reminders of what sat in her larder to restore her resolve, and even then she felt bad about caring more for her stomach than another soul. When the urge arrived for the third time she surrendered, put on her coat and hat and went to see if anyone had scribbled in the space left blank for that purpose beneath the notice.

No one had – or rather, someone *might* have, but someone else had ripped off the bottom third of the notice. Shocked, Frau Traugott wondered who could have done such a thing, and then her eye caught another offer of accommodation pinned to the board. No name was given, but she recognized the address as that of Frau Speigl.

This was a marked escalation of hostilities. For a moment she considered ripping the entirety of the competition from the noticeboard, but resisted the temptation as being as base as her enemy's provocation. A few metres inside the Markthalle a man was selling old books from a trestle table. She asked him for a brief loan of the ball-pen with which he wrote out his receipts and returned to the foyer. Across the space reserved for replies to Frau Speigl's offer she printed a neat addition:

Would suit someone with an indifferent appetite, as the landlady cannot cook.

Satisfied, she took a new slip of paper and re-wrote her own advertisement. Frau Speigl would know immediately who had interfered with her notice, but of course to say anything would be to admit her own guilt. By the same token, repeating the offence would be as much as to sign a confession to it.

Much cheered by her brilliant inspiration (and the pushing-back of the moment when Herr Fischer's fate would be sealed by her cupidity), Frau Traugott returned the pen to its owner, browsed the stalls for a while and then departed without opening her purse. Her raised mood plummeted once more when, having noticed nothing as she approached her home, she found herself in the shadow of a large, dangerous-looking man who was occupying her top step. He was in uniform, a grey thing that she took to be Luftwaffe (being now almost an expert in the Reich's martial accoutrements), and for a moment she feared that he had called about the rooms. But then she chided herself – how could he possibly be here for that? Which left the even more worrying prospect of his having come with some terrible revelation about Herr Fischer. That prospect strengthened when he noticed her and removed his cap, the inevitable prelude to delivering the very worst news.

'Are you Frau Traugott?'

The voice was as rough as the rest of him. She felt her heart begin to accelerate, and when he repeated his question she saw his lips move but didn't hear the words. A long-familiar scent of ripe, fallen apples came to her (as she knew it would), and then all the world around her toppled into darkness.

'That's … impressive.'

Fischer stared at Uncle Noam's sitting-room floor, upon which, neatly displayed, lay a selection of means to kill people. Dominating the collection was a Mauser 98 with AJACK telescopic sights and a large suppressor, flanked by a pair of Erma Werke folding-stock MP40s. For the less splashily-minded assassin, an apparently brand-new Astra 900 kept company with a battered FB VIS, which did its job merely by being hard to notice. Stolen as war booty, re-designated the 'pistole 35p' and supplied to the Fallschirmjäger, the model had been Fischer's service firearm, and he felt a small stab of affection when he lifted it from the floor. As always, and ridiculously, it *felt* reliable.

Carefully, Rainer took it from him and wrapped it in a soft cloth. 'We brought them to the house over several months, with the munitions. Wilhelm thought that we might need something for when our luck turned.'

'You could plan a campaign with this lot.'

'Well, it looks like we've wandered into one. We have some money, too.'

'Money?'

'We stole it.'

'No-one minded?'

'No-one noticed. The bank was burning anyway.'

'A German bank?'

'What are we, traitors? It was in Liege.'

'So, you have a fortune in Belgian francs?'

'We only took US currency. Wilhelm said things were moving so fast it was the only currency we could hope to be legal tender for more than a few weeks to come. It's not much - about eight thousand marks, last time we checked.'

'How are you going to spend it?'

'It's for bribes, not spending.'

'And there's this.' Wilhelm came into the sitting room, dragging a Granatwerfer 36. Fischer stared at it.

'You're going to attack fortifications?'

'Nah. This is for distraction. A couple of 50mm shells dropped into unexpected company should keep heads down for a few minutes at least.'

'You're insane.'

Wilhelm considered that possibility for a moment and shook his head. 'I'm trying to cover all the possibilities. Rainer and me, we've stamped on a few toes doing other people's dirty work, and we can't expected to be protected forever. One day, we'll ...'

He paused, and blew out his cheeks. 'It's now, isn't it? That *one day*?'

'I don't know. I could be wrong about ...'

'I doubt it. If he *cared* he wouldn't have given us this fucking job.'

'He might have given it to you because you're the best he has.'

'We are, for certain stuff. But he can't know what the other side's going to send against us, can he? Putting just two men on it – two men, by the way, who know a lot that he'd rather not have known – isn't his style, usually. We're ducks on a flat pond, waiting for the reeds to twitch, and it's because he wants it that way. Rainer, what is it when no-one minds flushing you?'

'Expendable?'

'Yeah, that's us.' Wilhelm grinned at Fischer. 'Just like you, mate. Shit, isn't it?'

'It is. We should be thinking of how to make it less so.'

'I have already. It strikes me that we have one easy option.'

Fischer nodded. 'Kill me and leave the corpse here, in your uncle's house. They'll never find me, so your employer won't be too disappointed, will he? You can say that they were closing in, too many of them, and you had to make a decision. Something like that.'

'Exactly like that. And if he hadn't dropped us all in the same latrine I might have taken it. But we'd still be expendable, wouldn't we? If we came out of this breathing, what would he tell us to do next – kidnap Himmler's pet parrot?'

'Does he have one?'

'I don't know. He used to farm chickens, didn't he?'

'We could run, Wilhelm.'

'That was my second idea. We'd still need to cack this one, though - imagine trying to abscond anonymously with *that* face. And I reckon our boss would send everything he had to stop us reaching a border.'

'Why?'

'Because mouths can loosen when they're out of range.'

'Oh. Right.'

Fischer nudged one of the M40s with a foot. 'So, you need a third idea.'

'D'you have one?'

'Stock up, stay here. The war can't last forever, and we aren't going to win it, are we?'

Wilhelm grinned again. 'It isn't likely. But with our luck they'll probably make a start on Germania, and this is one of the districts marked for demolition. Or the Allies might do it for them. In any case, staying in the same place isn't clever.'

'We'd need to re-supply regularly, and faces seen often enough are remembered?'

'Yeah. Even a house that no-one knows about becomes a trap, eventually.'

'What we need is a hundred safe-houses, then.'

'That would be sweet. Any ideas?'

'No, but you do.'

Wilhelm looked to his brother. 'Hear that, Rainer? I'm smarter than I look.'

'You could hardly be dumber than you look.'

'Thank you. Tell us.'

'This is a Jewish area, isn't it? I mean *was*, of course.'

'How did you know?'

'The baker's shop across the road used to be Jewish, and businesses owned by Jews tend – tended - not to plant themselves in Gentile neighborhoods.'

'So?'

Fischer spread his arms and half-turned to sweep the room. 'How many more places are there like this one, their owners dead or gone East?'

'A lot.'

'And being Jewish yourselves – or half-Jewish – you'll know some of them quite well?'

Rainer pulled a face. 'We grew up around here.'

'And there's no housing shortage in the city, so not many of the humbler ones will have been offered to Aryan families.'

Wilhelm and his brother looked at each other. 'We couldn't do that.'

'You already have.'

'He was family, it's not the same.'

'You'd be gaining from their loss, you mean?'

'We've gained already, being *mischlings*, while a lot of people have been finding graves or slavery. It would be like pissing on their heads.'

Fischer sighed. Had they been ordered to kill him he would be full of worms by now, but to squat in empty houses was morally abhorrent, apparently.

'Alright, then. Someone wants me dead. Someone else wants me alive – for now. Your orders are to keep me out of the first party's hands, but that's it – no hint of how this is to be resolved, no alternative instructions for if or when something goes wrong and no help that you can draw upon other than what your own initiative can find.'

'That's about right.'

'Then we have one thing, at least.'

'What?'

'A little space for manoeuvre. You said that your boss would chase you to a border, but think about this. You submit a report every … what?'

'Two days.'

'A dead drop or a meeting?'

'No meetings. I'm not to risk being seen with anyone whose face might be known to … the other side.'

'Well then, if you decide to run, you can arrange things so that you have forty-eight hours' start before anyone knows about it.'

Surprised, Wilhelm thought about it. Fischer turned to Rainer. 'Enough time for you to get to Denmark - if you're not dragging that blasted Granatwerfer, of course.'

'Why Denmark?'

'Why not? To date, the Danes haven't let the occupation authorities touch their Jews, so there should be plenty of places for you to hide, for a while at least. After that, it won't be too difficult for someone with US currency to hire a boat.'

'Sweden?'

'A short paddle across the Öresund, a little more expenditure to persuade the locals to look the other way when you arrive …'

Rainer rubbed his nose. 'It's risky. How do we get to, and then across, the Danish border?'

'That's the easiest part. Forget this arsenal - you have the note in Wilhelm's pocket, that tells anyone and everyone they're not to arse-off the signatory by getting in his boys' way. You're on a mission, you tell them, and any queries should be directed to him – if they have the nerve.'

Wilhelm nodded slowly. 'You'd come with us?'

'No. You're right about my face - it would be like sending up a flare. I'd stay here for two days at least, to give you time to get away, and then leave.'

'The moment you try to get from here to somewhere else, you're dead. You can't do anything on your own, not until whatever's happening is finished, one way or the other.'

Fischer re-examined the ordnance on the floor. Wilhelm was right – he was in one piece still only because someone wanted him that way. The other party couldn't fail to find and finish him if he simply went about his business as before. He was friendless in this city - hell, in all of the Reich, for that matter – and, knowing nothing of his pursuers, could hardly make plans to avoid them. No doubt his lodgings were being watched, and probably his workplace as well …

'If you're going to run, may I have that FB? And two magazines?'

'You think that sixteen bullets are going to stop whoever's chasing you?'

'No, but nor would the rest of this collection. It's for morale purposes.'

Wilhelm shrugged. 'It's yours, then. If you bear no grudge for what we did.'

'Save my life, probably? No, I forgive you for that.'

Rainer passed the wrapped item to Fischer and turned to his brother. 'We're really going?'

'Why not? It seems that our luck's on its last legs. Do you have any loyalty to what we're running from?'

'As a half-Jew? Fuck them all.'

'Tonight, then.'

'So soon?'

'Waiting won't make it any safer. We don't know if or when things will happen, so soon is best.' Wilhelm turned to Fischer. 'There are three days' victuals here for one man ...'

'I needn't starve before I'm shot, you mean?'

'Exactly. You're clever enough – it'll give you time to think of something.'

'I have already – I think. But I won't move until you're well on your way.'

'You swear? On your Knight's Cross?'

'If you like. My mother's memory would mean more.'

'That, then.'

'You have my word.'

'Alright. Rainer, fetch the brandy.'

Remarkably, it was a large bottle of Rémy Martin (more war-booty), and Fischer, unmindful of what spirits did to his throat, savoured every drop of his four-glass ration. Within an hour (by now sprawled on the sitting-room floor) the three fugitives were the best friends that ever a man could say about any two others, and Fischer had learned both the rudiments of western philosophy and the least messy way to skin a rabbit. At one point, Rainer went upstairs and returned with an envelope, which he pushed into his new comrade's pocket.

'A few dollars, for whatever emergency's coming.'

'Thank you, Rainer. Would you like my Wounds Medal?'

'That's very kind, Otto, but I have no wounds.'

Wilhelm giggled. 'Rainer's charmed. He was shot down three times and lost a boot. Tail gunners aren't supposed to survive a downing.'

'Why?'

Rainer rubbed his face. 'The crew usually forget that there's another fellow in the back. When they're bailing, I mean.'

'Seriously?'

'No, I was being humorous. It's that enemy fighter pilots are like *florenzers* – they prefer to shoot into you from behind.'

Both brothers collapsed at the ancient, feeble punchline, and even Fischer found it much funnier than he ever had before. He tried not to smile, though, because suddenly he was interested.

'Why aren't you a tail gunner still, Rainer?'

Rainer leaned across to his brother and squeezed his arm. 'Wilhelm volunteered me for special duties, and our important friend-who's-turned-out-to-be-a-bastard arranged to have me withdrawn from active service.'

'What special duties?'

Rainer tapped the side of his nose. 'Withdrawing another man from active service.'

'You cacked him?'

'Of course not! We went to the fellow's forward airfield and literally *removed* him.'

'To where?'

'All the way home. He was valuable, we were told. Weren't we, Wilhelm?'

His brother nodded. 'Some sort of genius, apparently – vital to war production.'

'So why did it need *you* to get him, and not just a transfer order?'

'He was in trouble.'

'What kind?'

'No idea. But Gestapo were interested, and that's never good, is it?'

'Was he Jewish? Homosexual? Politically objectionable?'

Wilhelm laughed. 'He was as blond as they come, and in the short time we we knew him he cast his eye over every girl who passed by. What his politics were I can't say.'

'Do you recall his name?'

'Why?'

'Indulge me.'

Wilhelm looked to the ceiling for help. 'Jürgen … something. Rainer?'

His brother shrugged. 'It was forgettable. Like Schmidt.'

'*Was* it Schmidt?'

'I don't think so. Why?'

'The man in Ahle's diary – The M – he'd been behaving badly, remember? And Wilhelm thought it was probably rape.'

'Yeah, but ...' Wilhelm stopped, and frowned. 'That would be something Luftwaffe cared about, but Gestapo? Why would they be investigating someone at the Front for the offence?'

'Why would they be investigating *anyone* serving at the Front? A lawbreaker in uniform would be dealt with under the *Militärstrafgesetzbuch*. Unless, of course, Gestapo were serving another purpose by chasing it.'

'What could that be?'

'Supposed this Jürgen had been tried and sentenced by his superior officer, as is usual practice. Could anyone then mitigate the tariff, or even wipe it from the sheet?'

Wilhelm nodded slowly. 'Reichsmarschall Göring.'

'He's actually named in the Code as the supreme recourse for appeal. And Gestapo are no longer fond of their old boss, are they, not since they fell under SS jurisdiction? In fact, anything they might do to prevent an embarrassment to him from being quietly swept under the carpet is something that Heydrich in particular would have been keen to push.'

'So that's why the Gener ...'

'Shut up, Rainer.'

'It's alright.' Fischer leaned back against the wall. 'I've already guessed that it was Milch who ordered you to do this.'

'How?'

'He spoke to me, and less than a day later I was picked up. Generalfeldmarschalls don't fraternize with hauptmanns for no good reason, so as soon as you let slip that your boss was a powerful man, *and* Luftwaffe, *and* in a habit of helping *mischlings* lose their papers, I made the assumption. The rumour that he's half-Jewish himself has been hanging around for too long for it not to have legs.'

'You'll keep quiet about this?'

'How could I benefit by talking, and who would I tell anyway? Forget Milch, it's the other thing that matters.'

'The Jürgen fellow? He won't be your *M* – it's a coincidence, that's all.'

'That's easily decided. You picked him up in Belgium – when?'

'July 1940.'

'Ahle took his belly wound at about that time. He was serving with KG55 – with KG55/1, to be precise.'

The brothers stared at Fischer, and then each other. Their prisoner drained the last of his brandy and placed the glass carefully beside him.

'It isn't *any* sort of coincidence. In 1940, Milch gave you the job of extracting Jürgen because he was too valuable to hand over to Gestapo. Someone had poor Ahle killed because he recognised Jürgen and knew what he was. I inherited Ahle's desk and was used as a distraction – by Milch once more, who employed *you* for the job because that's what you do, it's what you're good at. But it *is* remarkable, in the literal sense of the word.'

'Why?'

'Because Jürgen was your first job for him, and I'll be the last.'

'You think this is about Jürgen still?'

'I doubt it. If Gestapo or some other unpleasant types wanted him still, *he'd* be your assignment, not me, and he'd be too precious for Milch to risk. This is something else, I think, though it's part of the same war.'

'War?'

'The one between Wehrmacht and Prinz-Albrecht-Strasse.'

He had failed to elicit a response at the first five times of asking, so Freddie Holleman put his trust in a sixth.

'It wasn't me, was it?'

One of the Schultz twins looked up and tutted.

'Don't be stupid. Anything might have brought it on.'

'Oh, thank Christ.'

Frau Traugott lay on her bed, having been carried there by Holleman on the sisters' instructions. The convulsions had ceased, the wooden clothes peg removed from her mouth (she was no longer likely to swallow her tongue), and, though deeply unconscious, she was snoring loudly. A bruise was beginning to form already on her forehead, Holleman having tried and only partially succeeded in catching her as she toppled like a tree to her stoop. His hands were trembling still, this being the most terrifying thing that had happened to him since the birth of his own twins (his plummet to Belgian earth in a fortunately non-combusting ME109 had been a strangely serene interlude by comparison), and his sweat glands were working at full throttle still. It was his first time in the presence of an epileptic fit, and every gram of his manhood had fled.

'Don't stand there blocking the view. Make some tea.'

He almost saluted, and half-turned. 'Will she drink it?'

'For us, numbskull!

'I can put the kettle on. I'm not good at tea. My wife makes it, usually.'

'You have a wife? The poor thing!'

Under the (literally) twin onslaught, Holleman's nerve broke almost entirely. He gibbered an apology and went to the kitchen, allowing their merciless audit of his inadequacies to continue without him. He managed to light the gas stove, placed the kettle on it, removed it, filled it with water and tried again. A rummage through cupboards unearthed a tin, decorated with images of dancing milkmaids, which, to his admittedly inexpert nose, contained ersatz tea. At that point, his domestic skills exhausted, he returned reluctantly to Frau Traugott's bedroom.

That was the other torment. An old lady's boudoir should have remained a mystery beyond the Holleman experience for at least three decades to come. It smelled of things not to be guessed at, and the sprawled object on the bed was a cruel reminder of what life did to life. As a pilot he had made his peace with the moment of death, but creeping physical decay was a demon to which he had yet to be steeled. His feckless father had abandoned the family and never returned; his mother died too young but mercifully, falling to a brain haemorrhage that she could hardly have felt. He had never known his grandparents, never seen how remorselessly time played with a body, and now he was confronted suddenly by atrophy *and* a horribly capricious disease, the whole framed by torn stockings and a far too explicit view of vast green knickers. He wanted to be elsewhere, as a matter of urgency.

Why had he come here? If Fischer had reappeared he would have presented himself at the Air Ministry. If he had been found injured or dead Karl Krohne would have been informed by the police or Gestapo, or at least told not to ask questions about his missing man, ever. The very last person to be informed would have been Fischer's landlady, yet Holleman had limped all the way across Tiergarten in hope of some enlightenment. Had it been a form of flagellation? If so, the pain in his knee paled against the psychological torment of bystanding this disaster.

One of the sisters (she wore a small but distinguishing red brooch, and Holleman gave her the Enemy Designation: Shrew#1) stepped back from the bed and pursed her lips. 'She should be asleep for an hour or so now. *This one* can stay and watch her.'

This One opened his mouth to protest, but no good excuse emerged. If he was badly needed at the Ministry he wouldn't have been in Jonas-Strasse 17, and he doubted that an important lunch engagement with a General would convince. For a moment he considered a simple, forceful refusal, but the sisters didn't seem the sort to be brushed off with *forceful*. They would ask *why*, and he could scrape nothing from his addled thoughts to say to that.

A question occurred, however, if only because its implications terrified him.

'You're not going to leave me alone with her, are you?'

Shrew#2 snorted. 'She isn't going to be any trouble. If she wakes she'll talk nonsense for a while, but it isn't likely. Just make sure she keeps breathing.'

The ghastly prospect of having to apply mouth-to-mouth insufflation required that he steady himself against a wardrobe. 'How do I do that?'

'Keep her on her back, of course. Don't let her turn over. And if she drools, wipe her mouth. Don't give her water until she wakes, or she might drown. We're going upstairs now.'

'Why?'

'Because we live there.'

'But … don't you want tea?'

'It's too late now, today's *Wunschkonzert* starts soon. We never miss it, do we, Heike?'

'No, dear, we don't. You - don't forget to turn off the kettle.'

Alone, Holleman hardly dared turn to check the patient in case she convulsed or rose, straight-backed from the bed, like a ghoulish apparition. Her snores were raw, ugly, as unmusical as of those of Fahnenjunker Bihl (an adenoidal flight-cadet whose night-time symphonies, broadcast from the adjacent bunk, had almost deprived Holleman of his sanity and pilot's badge). He glanced down to reassure himself that, even in her extremity, Frau Traugott wasn't quite as uncomely as Bihl, and noticed saliva trickling from her mouth to the pillow. His stomach moved slightly but he forced himself to pick up the cloth, dip it in the lukewarm, soapy water that Schultz#2 had placed on the bedside table and gently wiped the old lady's face.

Feeling that he had done all that any reasonable man could he checked his watch. Karl Krohne would be wondering where the hell he was (or perhaps he was relieved that today's briefing lacked its usual snide accompaniments), and the trek back to Wilhelmstrasse would require an hour at least, given the appeals for mercy that his stump was making. He limped to the bedroom door, checked that the hallway was clear, returned to Frau Traugott's side and poked her shoulder with a finger.

She muttered, but her eyes remained closed. Slightly encouraged, he was about to redeploy his finger when the front door bell rang. For a moment he assumed that one of the sisters would volunteer herself, but he could hear Brahms somewhere overhead, which meant that the concert had first and last call upon their attention. Cursing quietly, he went to disappoint the caller.

It was a gentleman in a grey suit of indifferent quality, not too old to serve in uniform and with no apparent wounds. He nodded at Holleman.

'It's about the rooms to rent. Are they available still?'

As far as Holleman knew, Frau Traugott's establishment was at full strength already. He must have offered his puzzled face, because the other fellow removed a piece of paper from his pocket and read it aloud.

'Bedroom with attached sitting-room for rent, second floor, would suit serving officer or professional gentleman.'

He handed it to Holleman, who glanced down at the spidery script. So the old lady had given up on Fischer. He could hardy blame her (the rent probably meant the difference between having food in the pot and semi-starvation), but it was another stone upon the man's grave, and he felt his own guilt surging. He returned the notice.

'Could you come back tomorrow, mate? I don't know anything about it, and the landlady's indisposed at the moment.'

The grey suit took the piece of paper, nodded, turned and descended the stoop without another word. Holleman closed the door and exhaled deeply. His *OrPo* days were far behind him, but a man gets a feeling for when things miss a button hole. The gentleman might have had a dozen good reasons for not being in uniform, for saying as little as would do the business, and for taking the news of his inconvenience without the slightest irritation, but it had all been dressed with a detachment that was familiar to police anywhere in Germany. Gestapo had no particular odour, but that didn't mean that a nose didn't twitch in their presence.

Holleman was confident in his judgement, but that hardly mattered. The proof of it was the indifference with which such men offered their lies, as if the power of their office precluded any need to try to convince. There was nothing unusual in someone wanting a comfortable place to rent, but finding one tended to require an address at least, and there had been none on the advertisement, only a space beneath for an applicant to leave contact details. After all, an old lady letting the world know where she lived – who knew who might come calling?

39

Two of the three men most responsible for the Reich's war production met in a room on the top floor of the New Chancellery on Voss-Strasse. The lack of peripheral furniture and a light covering of dust that dulled the wooden floor's polished finish suggested that it was used rarely. Only a large table, positioned slightly off-axis in the room's centre, disturbed the empty acoustic. Upon it, and precisely covering its entire top surface, sat a large-scale model of *Germania*, the Berlin to come.

To one of the men, the model was as familiar as his own face, and almost as loved. The other knew it well, but was surprised to find it here.

'I thought this was in the south gallery?'

'It was. It was moved in March.'

'Why? Doesn't he enjoy having visitors pore over it?'

'He *did*. But March was when he made the decision that no further work was to be done on *Germania* until victory came. After that, he wanted it out of sight, so he couldn't be reminded constantly of what's been deferred.'

The two men exchanged a meaningful look. Neither of them, straining to put a shine on things, believed any longer in victory. At best, their efforts would allow Germany to fight her enemies to a standstill - after which, hopefully, war weariness and fear of the Communist tide would persuade the western democracies to negotiate a palatable peace settlement.

'So why are *we* here?'

'Because it's the only place where our being seen together wouldn't raise suspicions in certain minds. No doubt they'd assume that you raised a detail about it and that I was flattered by the attention.' Reichsminister Speer waved a hand over the model. 'Think of an intelligent question you might have put to me, in case you're asked.'

Generalfeldmarschall Milch scanned the vista, from the great Volkshalle, down the north-south axis to the Arch of the Dead, and pulled a face. 'Why the hell did you ever imagine it might be built?'

Speer smiled sadly. 'It was a possible future, once. We couldn't conquer the world and still have modest little Berlin to welcome our client-leaders, could we? The spectacle was meant to intimidate as much as our military strength.'

'But Berlin's built on sand and marl. *That* lot would have sunk, surely?'

'My calculations say it wouldn't, not with the volume of concrete we intended to lay.'

Milch sniffed his disbelief. 'Well, you're the architect. Personally, I like Berlin as it is – slightly seedy but *gemütlich*. I mean …' his hand flicked in the direction of the inhumanly-scaled Volkshalle; '… Berliners would need to breed like mice just to fill that thing.'

'Again, practicality isn't the point. Its purpose is to instill awe, and submission.'

'Ah, well. Until final victory, then. I assume you want to know where we are with our missing item?'

'It's been on my mind, yes.'

'Then I must disappoint you. I've had the equivalent of half a fliegerdivision chasing the very many possibilities, with no luck. It seems that it's found a grave somewhere, along with the gentleman to whom we entrusted it.'

Speer sighed. 'If only it *was* with him. We could dig him up.'

'I thought about that, but given that he was examined both by the police and mortuary attendants, his little secret could hardly have been unnoticed. He must have put it a safe place – *too* safe a place – before his little accident.'

'I hear that he was beheaded. It's grotesque.'

'I doubt it was what killed him.'

'I understand that it's sufficient, usually.'

Despite the subject, Milch smiled. 'I meant that it would be an impractical method, requiring that the subject be subdued beforehand. What would be the point? It had to look accidental, or by his own hand. My own feeling is that he was poisoned.'

'Why?'

'It would be easy, quick *and* quiet. Most of all, I suspect poison because they beheaded him afterwards.'

'I don't understand.'

'They did something to ensure that not even the most assiduous coroner would bother to check for some other cause of death – in his stomach contents, for example.'

'I wonder how they did it - the beheading, I mean.'

Milch shrugged. 'A guillotine, or some piece of precision cutting equipment – there are plenty of options in the city's industrial facilities. It hardly matters.'

Speer wiped a layer of dust from the roof of an edifice that was to have occupied the site of the Kroll Opera.

'Do you think he knew what he had the care of?'

'I don't see how. He wasn't an unintelligent man, but he had no professional experience of the things we encoded.'

'So he wouldn't ...'

'Have given it up? Once can't be absolutely certain, obviously, but I doubt it. And would he have been killed after being so obliging?'

'Probably not. Do you know yet who did it?'

'No, it's the most difficult thing to understand. All the evidence suggests that our ... what, adversaries?'

'Valued colleagues?'

'... are still looking for it. That, to my mind, rules them out as suspects. So, who objected so strongly to the man?'

'Did you know him well?'

Milch, surprised, stared at Speer. 'I didn't know him at all. I asked my aide Wolfram for a recommendation, specifying only that he had to be loyal to Luftwaffe. He found this fellow - as tight as a clam, apparently, with no family or friends or prospect of making any – and as memorable as a stripped twig.

He sounded just right, so Wolfram briefed him in very general terms and took the impression that he was honoured beyond reason to be asked. I had about a dozen words with him, to the effect of *we're relying upon you, this is very important and confidential*, etc – and that was it. I never saw him again.'

'How was the item given into his keeping?'

'With the utmost discretion. Wolfram's very good at that sort of thing. You may be assured that no-one witnessed it.'

For a few moments, Speer's gaze lingered upon his biggest, never-to-be-realised commission, and then he sighed once more. 'Well, it's all spilled milk now. Without the data we can't mount a challenge, and if the timetable for Operational Order no. 6 stands, we have little or no time left to effect meaningful changes before...'

'You're *sure* that you can't go directly to the Führer with this?'

'Quite sure. Without absolute proof he would never turn upon one of his old comrades from the street days. You'll recall that he agreed wholly with him when I tried – and failed – to bring women into war production. If I speak out now he'll assume that I'm merely trying to stab the man in the back. No, we need the proof of our colleague's incompetence and failures. Anything else is insinuation.'

'And in the meantime, at this critical moment of the war, we continue to produce fewer fighters, tanks and shells than our enemies.'

Reichsminister Speer smiled, his first attempt of that day. 'You mean, our *foreign* enemies?'

The woman's hand came up to cover her open mouth, but the shock in her eyes was prominent still. In a moment she was hurrying away from the ghastly confrontation, but for Fischer the interlude dragged.

What should I do, Madam - wear a hood?

He had promised Wilhelm and Rainer three days' grace, but had managed only thirty-six hours
of self-imposed imprisonment before fleeing their dead uncle's house. He told himself that the brothers wouldn't taking more time than was absolutely necessary to get to the Danish border. If they hadn't reached it by now it was because they had been stopped, in which case his premature resurrection could give them no more trouble than they'd found already. It was clumsy, cruel logic, but the effects of good brandy had long since worn off, leaving him less concerned for their skins than for what remained of his own.

Wilhelm had given him rough directions, and he was walking south along Tucholskystrasse, which would take him across the Spree, and, eventually, to Unter den Linden, one of the few thoroughfares in Mitte with which he was familiar. His first thought had been to make the journey at night in order to offer his face to as few passers-by as possible, but he had dismissed it quickly as one of his less intelligent inspirations. Any man out late was liable to be stopped, his papers examined and a note made in a patrol's report. It wasn't likely that his name (or memorable face) wouldn't feature prominently therein, and within hours the chase would be resumed with fresh enthusiasm. In daylight he would be seen by - but to an extent lost within - crowds of civilians, few of whom would wish to recall his face, much less make a note of it. And there was also the minor point that he needed his intended terminus to be open when he reached it.

As he walked, head down and cap pulled low, he tried to let the sights, smells and sounds distract him. It should have been easy after almost ten days' confinement, but another distraction was making its weight felt already. As long as he had been a prisoner, trying both to understand why and how he might end that condition, his head had been cleared of its preoccupation with the longer tomorrow. But now that he had paroled himself a small voice was asking what the point of it might be, if all he could expect was an unending portion of what that woman had just offered him. What would be lost if he *were* to be discovered and taken by his pursuers? Wasn't he just occupying an existence that would have been better tied off on 14 January 1942?

He didn't notice the river when he crossed it, nor the occasional second-glances. It began to rain gently, and his good hand turned up his collar without bothering his mind with the details. He was back in the field hospital at Vyazma, calmly asking a doctor to push something into his veins that would take away all that tortured him. The man had refused, but only after taking time to consider it, and in the days that followed he might have done differently, if asked again. By that time, though, they had filled Fischer with enough morphine to turn OKW into a den of pacifists, and he hadn't thought - or been conscious for long enough - to repeat the request.

The months that followed had been a spectacular waste of time, energy and resources, though he didn't doubt that a few career-enhancing medical papers (listing what didn't work, mostly) had come from it. He had since wondered how many torn limbs might have been saved, what great weight of organs kept in their ripped abdomens, if less effort and highly-trained manpower had been devoted to testing unfeasible tissue replacement theories on one Otto Henry Fischer.

Some men – some *things* – are meant to find a merciful death, not be sentenced to life. In his case the proper way of things had been inverted, and what resulted could spoil the healthiest appetite at a single glance. It might not have been beyond curing, even now, but the greatest joke of all was that he had no faculty for self-murder. So, given that his broken body might endure for decades to come, the prospect of being shot in the head by people who mistook him for a dangerous man should have seemed less to be feared than waved at and invited over.

Still, an instinct to preserve the self made him crouch a little as he walked, making the target smaller, and he used every trick – reflections in shop windows, a persistently-loose shoelace and forgotten items, suddenly recalled – to reassure himself that he wasn't being followed. Finally, he came to Unter den Linden, where enough men in uniform were promenading with their ladies to give him at least an illusion of anonymity. He crossed the avenue to its south, shaded side and turned west, towards the Brandenburg Gate and Wilhelmstrasse. He couldn't know if his pursuers were monitoring his workplace, home or some point between (Tiergarten perhaps, where a man could be very conveniently taken), but it seemed to him unlikely that anyone, however powerfully connected, would try something in one of the most heavily guarded streets on Earth. If he could reach and go to ground in the vast Air Ministry among what few comrades he had, Br'er Rabbit might have found his briar patch.

He turned left, into the southern stretch of Wilhelmstrasse and a comforting concentration of reserve-battalion *GrossDeutschland* men, deployed to keep the Reich's important men from being importuned by the rabble. Almost as heavily-armed as those of their divisional comrades presently serving at the Front, they inadvertently cleared the final stretch of his flight to relative safety. He was even saluted by one of them, an oberfeldwebel at the main doors of the Foreign Office who had noticed the face and considered it worth the effort.

At the entrance to the Air Ministry he received another, sloppier salute from the prophylactic-dispensing guard, but entered the building and reached the third floor without drawing attention from anyone other than the two men who checked his pass at Reception. Immediately inside the corridor leading from the north stairwell were the closest lavatories to the Liars' Den. He half-opened the door, listened for a moment and then stepped inside. Opposite the urinal and wash basins were three cubicles, their individual doors ajar. He went to the furthest, locked himself in, checked the toilet seat and sat.

The hour that followed dragged, but Fischer felt safer than he had for more than a week now. Every few minutes he checked his watch, knowing that things couldn't be rushed but willing them on nevertheless. Eventually, at almost precisely the time he had anticipated, he heard the corridor open. There was a pause, then the hinges squeaked slightly as it closed, followed by the faint sound of a latch dropping.

Thank God.

One lunchtime, four days into his new career as a Liar, he had come to these facilities to relieve himself. The outer door had been locked, however, and he had been obliged to descend a storey at speed. Returning to the Den, he had asked no-one in particular whether their corridor's latrines were out of order. He hadn't thought the question amusing, but it had raised a snigger from most of the Liars. Predictably, Freddie Holleman had led the field with an explanation.

'It's Karl. He's just tidying up.'

'What?'

'He's been out to lunch, so to speak. And now he's making sure that everything's inspection-clean, for when he goes home tonight. He doesn't like to be disturbed while he's sluicing.'

Grinning, he swivelled in his chair and turned to the rest of his audience. 'I offered once to taste it when he'd dried off, just to make sure. He didn't seem grateful for the offer.'

Fischer had laughed as much as any of them, but he hadn't guessed then how valuable his question would prove to be. He sat quietly now in the toilet cubicle, trying to form a picture from what he was hearing. At what he estimated to be the correct moment he stood, opened the cubicle door and stepped out.

Karl Krohne had taken off his tunic and put it on a hook behind the door to the corridor. His trousers and underpants were around his ankles, his shirt and tie pulled up and tucked beneath his chin. His midriff thrust forward over a washbasin, he was applying soap to those parts that had recently been buried in foreign lands. Unsure of what protocol required of the moment, Fischer decided that a polite cough was likely to send water everywhere.

'Hello, Karl.'

'Jesus!'

41

Frau Traugott was nursing a typical post-fit headache, so the sisters' unnervingly synchronized gaze (the sort that perimeter-tower guards offer to inmates wandering too close to a wire) was less than welcome. She only kept her temper because she recognized that they were attempting to be compassionate, which was not intuitive for them.

'You're *sure* that you should be out of bed?'

'Yes, Heike, I am. There's no point or benefit in just lying around. I have shopping and cleaning to do.'

The other Schultz looked doubtfully at her sister. 'We could do that for you, if you want.'

'Thank you, Ida. But I know what I need, and some fresh air will clear my head. Really, it's best that I just carry on as usual. And thank you for looking after me while ...'

'That's alright, we knew what to do after last time. We couldn't have got you upstairs, but that man with the bad leg managed quite easily.'

Frau Traugott started. 'He was real, then? I thought I'd dreamt him.'

'No, he was real. And ugly. And useless, except for carrying.'

'I don't remember his face.'

'There's some good luck for you, then.'

'He was in uniform, wasn't he?'

'Yes. Don't ask which. It was grey.'

'Oh.' Carefully, Frau Traugott picked up her cup and sipped tea. It wasn't unusual not to recall things that happened immediately before a fit, so the vague, dream-like recollection pleased her. She had woken in the dark, but the familiarity of her post-symptoms kept her from panicking, and she had drifted off again almost immediately. Sleep being the best - the only – restorative for her ordeal, she felt better than she might have expected, her ringing head aside.

'Did he say what he wanted?'

'Wanted?'

'He must have called for a reason.'

Heike and Ida looked at each other. 'We didn't ask.'

'Perhaps he had news of Herr Fischer.'

'Or he needed directions. He seemed quite dull-witted. He didn't know how to make tea.'

To Frau Traugott that was almost a definition of dull-wittedness, but she worried still. There had been too much going on for her to think that his appearance on her doorstep wasn't in some way significant, or threatening. But would a dangerous man have gone to the trouble and pain of carrying her to her bed? She almost blushed to think of it, but without his assistance she would have passed the night on the hall floor for sure, and have much more than a fragile head to endure this morning.

The sisters were exchanging a *look*, and she recognized it instantly. Being women who kept very much to themselves they disliked saying a word more than would get a thing done, a complaint aired or a threatened conversation stifled. But the look suggested that there was more to be said, however uncomfortable the saying.

'What is it?'

'We're not quite sure.'

'About …?'

'We … had to come upstairs, and he watched you for a while.'

'You left me alone with him? In my bedroom?'

'He was dabbing your head quite correctly, so we …'

'So you went to listen to your concert? Is that it?'

The sisters squirmed slightly. 'Only for a few minutes. But then he came up and knocked on our door. He said that you'd had another caller, but that he's told him you couldn't be disturbed. It's a shame really, because the gentleman had come about the rooms.'

It took a moment for Frau Traugott to realise what was wrong with that revelation, and before she could say anything Heike Schultz, against all instinct and inclination, had volunteered further information.

'The ugly one told us to tell you that you should be careful – that the man wasn't what he seemed. And then he went away, and we came back downstairs to tend you.'

If the second man had known that the rooms were at Jonas-Strasse 17 then she must have been followed the previous day. And it stood to reason that if Ugly was warning her about the man then they couldn't be working together. That still didn't tell her why Ugly had come calling, but he was no longer her greatest concern.

'Was the second man in uniform?'

The sisters looked blankly at her. 'We didn't see him.'

'You didn't ask?'

'Why should we? We aren't interest in what men wear.'

'You don't know if he showed a badge?'

'We only know what we've told you, dear. Oh.'

'What?'

'Except that the dim one said he'd told him to come back tomorrow. Today, that is. So he might.'

'Right. Help me up, will you?'

'Here, take an arm each. Are you going out?'

'No, I'm locking the front door. We aren't at home to guests today.'

Despondently, Freddie Holleman flicked through the Book of Adjectives. It was mid-afternoon in the Liars' Den, and Karl Krohne had yet to demand that his team return their first attempts at a situation report from the Eastern Front. It wasn't like him to be this tardy, but given the difficulty of their task no-one was complaining.

How did one tweak and polish ... nothing? As far as Holleman could see, peace had fallen upon a vast arc between St Petersburg and Odesa. There were no troop movements of any note (German or Soviet), no reconnaissances-in-force, no tactical withdrawals and not even a local massacre of 'partisans' caught dragging household belongings in carts. In normal circumstances Krohne would have told them by now to down pencils and regroup at (actually, fuck off to) the *Silver Birch*, taking care not to be noticed by too many senior officers on the way out. That they were straining every inspiration was due to the fact that, despite Luftwaffe's creditable performance at Third Kharkov, Göring had suffered yet another kicking from the Führer - this time, for not having conceived and delivered a smashing blow against the Allies in Tunisia in order to relieve the backward-sprinting Afrika Korps.

The Lie Division had been charged, therefore, with knocking together something faintly feasible, that the Reichsmarschall could present as demonstrating value for his many uniforms. So far, the only idea that had met with the Den's approbation had been Holleman's 'Not One German Aircraft Shot Down for Three Days Now – Have Soviet Pilots lost the Gift of Sight?' Salomon Weiss had countered with 'Not Much Happening Anywhere – Red Army Getting Ready to Scorch the Hair off

Our Arses?', but everyone else found it too depressingly prescient to enjoy for its own sake.

The palpable fact was that, following Stalingrad, the subsequent Soviet advances and German counter-attacks, both sides were exhausted and needed to resupply and regroup. For Germany, the greatest concern was manpower losses, particularly pilots; for the Ivans (who could replace men easily), it was armour and trucks. It was obvious to almost every military mind in Berlin that the best strategy would be to put right what was lacking as quickly as possible, evacuate all forward salients, adopt strong defensive positions and await the next Soviet offensive. Unfortunately, the man who made the decisions almost certainly disagreed. To him, the only rational corrective to any parlous situation was to increase the bet and put it all one number, trusting that the Enemy's very last expectation would be more of what had preceded it. So, it was generally the view of the Liars (who, having read and either modified or inverted any number of situation reports, were at least as strategically well-informed as the General Staff) that the best, faint hope would be for the Soviets to hurriedly replenish their armies and attack prematurely before the German forces could do the same.

Which is why no news from the Front stretched all their nerves. Even Holleman, after his one, obligatory stab at levity, accepted his ration of the afternoon's pervading gloom and even tried to think of something that might be used. Eventually, having considered and dismissed aerial combat (there hadn't been any), the personal story (which needed at least the possibility of action or danger to make interesting) and the outright appeal to sentiment ('Thrice-decorated pilot mourns the death of young daughter's beloved puppy during British terror-raid; Squadron passes around the cap to buy replacement'), he turned to Detmar Reincke.

'Det, do you have the latest munitions reports?'

'Um, yeah.'

'Does it give any figures for fighter production?'

'Of course not. That's as top as a secret could be. The report just generalizes.'

'And quite right too.'

Happily, Holleman started to write on a blank sheet of paper, and in fifteen minutes had filled almost one side. He signed it with a flourish, walked it over to Reincke and returned to his seat to await praise. It came very quickly.

'Freddie, what's this crap?'

'*Crap*, young Detmar?'

Helplessly, Reincke shook his head. 'It's just ... wrong. You say that Allied bombing of our aircraft factories has been ineffective, that fighter production's up significantly, and that new models are almost ready to be combat-tested.'

'That's right, I do.'

'You can't possibly know any of that.'

'Nor can anyone else, except the people responsible and the Chancellery.'

'So it's all an outright lie, then.'

'Yeah. But who's going to complain about that? The Propaganda Ministry?'

'*Someone* will.'

'No, they won't. I've not stated any figures, so it isn't aiding the enemy. I've given the people reason to hope that everything's not all to fuck, which is our job. The worst you can say about what I've written is that it may or may not have happened – yet. We *know* that Speer's job is to increase production of all munitions, so this is just anticipating his successes. We *know* that new aircraft are being developed because Willy Messerschmitt himself said so, and when it comes to the matter of testing, is there a definition of what constitutes *almost ready*? I don't know of any.'

'But ...'

'Do you know what's wrong with what we do, Det? We're still thinking of ways to stretch the truth, rather than create it. Goebbels doesn't waste his time with what's factual, or provable – he thinks of any old shit that'll do the job and then convinces radioland that it's kosher. Why shouldn't we?'

'What if we say something and it doesn't happen, ever?'

'Hell, I don't know. Perhaps the Führer will have us apologise to the nation, him being so rigorous about not misleading folk.' Holleman leaned forward and took the paper from Reincke's hand. 'I'll bet you a pack of Junos that Karl passes this.'

'You think he will?'

'Yeah, once I've reminded him what stage this war's at. Oh, *there* he is. It must have been an epic fuck.'

Reincke turned to the door of the Den. 'Is it you or me he wants?'

'I want to say you, but ...'

Holleman pushed back his chair and clambered upright. By the time he reached his boss's office Krohne was sat at his desk, drumming on it with both sets of fingers and chewing the side of his cheek.

'Are you alright, Karl? You look pale. Well, paler.'

'Lock the door, will you, Freddie?'

'Is this another meeting of the Emergency Committee? Is there news of Otto.'

'Oh, yes, there's news.'

'Is he alright?'

'Don't worry about him. It's you and me who might be facing a firing party before the day's out.''

'Eh? What have *we* done?'

'It's what we're going to do. How often does Generalfeldmarschall Milch visit the Air Ministry?'

'Uh, not often. He's a busy man, isn't he?'

'The busiest man in a Luftwaffe uniform, they say. I just hope he's not the most peevish also.'

'Why?'

'We're going to summon him.'

'What with? Champagne? Dancing girls?'

'That's the thing. I suppose there are several ways to say more or less anything, but not this. *This* will be a fairly straightforward threat.'

Holleman gaped at Krohne. 'Have you been drinking?'

'I sincerely wish I had. Hauptmann Fischer has asked me to relay a message to the second most powerful man in Luftwaffe. He says to say that he knows what he's doing, and why, and that if he wants it to go away he'd better come and speak to him – Fischer, I mean. I just need to think of a less confusing way to put it.'

'Why am I involved if it's you who's going to say this to him?'

'Because, as this is all *your* fault, it'll be a small comfort to have you tied to the post next to me.'

43

SS-BrigadeFührer Suhr read the brief report and sat back in his chair. As always when he needed to think through a difficult matter he allowed his eyes to rest upon the book-spines in the case opposite his desk. He had arranged the volumes by size rather than subject, or author – as, famously, had the founder of an old library at Magdelene College, Cambridge, where Suhr had studied before the War. It was a cause for amusement among his present colleagues, but he took no offence. He had long found it remarkable that the mind could retain a far greater grasp of precisely what sat where when this system was utilized.

At the moment, though, his eyes rested upon his books without seeing them. He had been presented with a decision – or rather, the choice of making a decision or not. He had, he believed, what he had been looking for, but now he needed to consider whether he wanted it. Not lacking confidence in his own judgement, he might have come to his own conclusion and acted upon it. However, there were occasions upon which a man couldn't spot all the potential barbs, and this seemed to be one of them. His Gestapo helper Kurt already knew a great deal about this case, and he had felt no hesitation in calling the man and asking him to come to Prinz-Albrecht-Strasse.

Kurt was – had been – at Alexanderplatz that morning, and it took him almost an hour to palm off his work and make the trek. The delay gave Suhr time to order his thoughts. He had been given a task by a man who, in some respects, wielded greater power than anyone other than the Führer himself. Though he commanded no divisions or police agency his wishes were regarded generally as being directives of State, and met accordingly. By the same token, he took failure badly. No man had ever gone to the firing post for falling short of his expectations, but demotion and a field-posting to some hectare of interest to the Red Army often achieved the same end. With that indigestible carrot dangled before him, Suhr had no great urge to disappoint.

Had he succeeded in his task? Of course not, but that didn't matter now. He could hardly be blamed for the objective presenting itself, rather than having to be dragged from a sewer pipe. It was a timing issue, nothing more. All that might have been done had been seen to be done, and even his unforgiving taskmaster could find no fault it that.

What had happened until now wasn't the problem. He had to think about what came next, and *next* was where he might make himself vulnerable. The easiest option would be to beg his lack of authority to proceed, but knowing what all of this was about – what it was *really* about – he doubted that the plea would receive a kindly hearing. The man to whom he reported expected initiative from his instruments, being unable himself to act openly. He had accumulated his power by dancing in darkness, playing opponents against each other, placing insinuations where they would hurt without ever pointing a finger back to their source. Suhr could no more walk away from this business than a field commander could abandon a stalled operation and tell OKW to rethink their strategy.

When Kurt arrived, therefore, Suhr came straight to the point. He outlined what he saw to be the possibilities and asked the other man to consider whether there were the flaws in his logic. By doing so he risked a different sort of exposure, but as far as anyone could trust one of Müller's men not to push a knife between a handy pair of shoulder-blades, he felt reasonably comfortable presenting them in this manner.

He sent for tea while Kurt scratched his cheek and thought about the issues. An unrushed, methodical mind might find something that had been overlooked, or perhaps discounted as not having teeth, so Suhr waited as patiently as his mood allowed. Eventually, the Gestapo man looked up and nodded slowly.

'I think you're right. If there was an advantage to be had, it's gone, or at least it lies somewhere we can't see, given the information we presently have. Might your man take you further into his confidence?'

Suhr stared into his tea. 'He might, but I can hardly demand that he do so. If I put to him what I believe the situation to be, he'll either accept it or order me to proceed regardless, in which case he may feel that I need to know more.'

'And if you recommend instead that we *do* proceed, he may not see any reason to tell you more than you know already.'

'Exactly. So, given the options, I either risk disappointing him now or putting my arse in a vise subsequently.'

This sent Kurt into another meditation, though briefly. He pulled a face and shrugged.

'You're an SS-Brigadeführer. That means something, but it's not *enough*. If you go charging further into this, the opposition isn't going to flinch. You'll have become a problem, one that's likely to be dealt with quickly. And I doubt that, when it happens, your man is going to offer his protection, not if it shines a light onto what he's been doing. You'll be a casualty – to be regretted, perhaps, but not too much, or for too long. There'll always be another opportunity, another campaign to fight, and always more men to put onto the firing step.

Surprised, Suhr stared at Kurt. It was a very acute, and courageous, observation – as explicit an admission of his loyalty as anyone might hope for in their Byzantine world.

'Well, there's a report to be written. Thank you Kurt – I appreciate your help.'

'Don't forget me next time, then. It's good to get out of the office.'

When he was alone, Suhr pulled a clean sheet of paper from its press and took out his pen (no typist could be trusted to see what he was about to write). The bookcase and its neatly ascending volumes were examined briefly once more, and then he put down his thoughts without once pausing.

To: Five Five Five
From: *SS-Brigadeführer Albrecht Suhr*

Project Waldemar

You will have been informed by now that the subject was seen on Wilhelmstrasse yesterday by one of my team. He was unaccompanied. It is believed that he entered the Air Ministry, and I had two men posted there subsequently. They report that as of 11am today he had not departed the building – that is, not by the main entrance.

It seems clear to me now that we have been seeking a lockvogel - a deliberate lure. I do not believe that he had the item in his possession – or, if he did, it was surrendered to the other party before he was 'detained' by the Feldgendarmerie. The latter possibility is most unlikely, however. The whole purpose of his subsequent disappearance appears to have been to keep our attention upon him – but why?

It is my belief that the other party did not – perhaps does not still – have the item. Otherwise, why would this man have been kept in play for several days? Surely, the data would have been deployed immediately had it been available, after which no point would have been served by allowing us to continue to seek the man we suspected of keeping it out of our reach.

If the item has <u>not</u> been recovered, we have succeeded by default. Its contents cannot be used to attempt to embarrass out friends, and the other party's mere word on the matter must continue to be insufficient to convince the Führer. Further attempts on our part to locate the item would appear to be pointless; we have no clues as to where it might be (if indeed it has not been destroyed by now), and it is not unlikely that our efforts, if noticed, might lend a credibility to the other party's allegations that they do not currently enjoy.

For the same reason, I do not recommend that we continue to seek to detain and interrogate the subject. That he knows what the item is, or what its significance might be, seems unlikely. Indeed, I doubt that he has ever seen it. He is 'no-one' – probably chosen at random and flagged to us only by the fact of his arrest. To press on with our search would undoubtedly be to offer the other party (who are almost certainly monitoring him still) an opportunity to advertise our interest and, again, bolster their claims against our friends.

Let me assure you that these recommendations do not reflect any reluctance on my part to prosecute the case against the other party. I have considered the matter thoroughly, and regard the present, fortuitous situation as one that can only be compromised by seeking to press further an advantage that we already enjoy.

As always, I look forward to receiving your thoughts.

Sincerely,

Albrecht.

The last was a filthy lie, of course. Suhr, like any other sane individual, would have preferred never to have entered the man's orbit, much less continue to enjoy his attention. The potential rewards were elusive, the dangers quite distinct. Loyalty was prized only as far as it could be used, and those discarded as no longer *of* use were regarded as still-glowing cigarette stubs – to be stamped upon for prudence's sake.

It was his own fault, naturally. To be noticed had flattered him immensely, and for a while – a short while – he had imagined that great opportunities were likely to unfold before him like spring petals. Had he caught the attention of Himmler, Goebbels or even Göring that might have been the case, but this one didn't do gratitude beyond a cursory, clumsy compliment or two. It no longer mattered. Suhr had quite lost his appetite for advancement - not least because, unlike so many of his SS colleagues, he could see that only a cliff's edge awaited, and that the higher one climbed the more *abschüssig* the eventual fall would be.

His small collection of literature was a reminder that had been a cultured man once, a hoarder of knowledge for its own sake. Had circumstances been otherwise he might have been the owner of a small bookshop in a university town, and wasted his days reading what he should have been selling. Instead, he had conformed only too easily to the new German age, and he wondered sometimes if others had found the transition equally untroubling. If not, most of them concealed their angst remarkably well.

He put the note in a Chancellery envelope, addressed and marked it for the recipient's eyes only, knowing that no-one would dare to ignore the proscription. With luck (though he didn't believe in luck, good or bad), he was done with the business. He had neither succeeded nor failed, shone nor blundered, and perhaps that forgettably median result was the best he could have hoped for. When two rock faces clash furiously, anything bound too closely to either tends to suffer.

44

Generalfeldmarschall Milch came to the Air Ministry, and, though it was hardly anyone's business to notice, the pleasant demeanour he habitually offered to the lesser ranks was otherwise engaged that morning.

Consequently, salutes were regulation-smart (even from Kondom Körner), leisurely passages became suddenly brisk and efficient, and not a few courses were adjusted to take Rising Hopes out of harm's way. For all that any of this caught the attention of the man with the baton, much effort might have been spared.

Having stormed to the third floor in the company of his aide, Milch proceeded alone to the office of the Oberstleutnant commanding the *Kriegsberichter der Luftwaffe*. That individual was one of only three men in the entire building expecting this visit, for which he had prepared by smoking five cigarettes in unbroken succession and misplacing all blood higher than his chest-cavity. A half-intention to draw up a will had formed briefly a little while earlier, but his wife being a wealthy brewer's heiress this hadn't pressed as a priority.

The other man in the room, a lowly Hauptmann, seemed much calmer. His face being what it was, however, his boss couldn't be sure that what looked to be *sang-froid* wasn't merely unresponsive muscle tissue, doing what it did. Either way, it was irritating.

'Otto, try to look scared, will you?'

'Sorry, Karl. I was thinking.'

'About what?'

'What I'm going to say to him.'

Horrified, Karl Krohne had to steady himself against his desk. 'You haven't polished it yet?'

'Some of it will depend upon what he says.'

'Oh, Christ. I ...'

The door opened and Milch strode in. He glanced at both men and settled first on Krohne.

'You – out.'

'Herr Generalfeldmarschall, as his commanding officer ...'

'Go and talk to your other men. While you still have some.'

Krohne almost toppled out of his office, but had the presence of mind to drag the door closed behind him. Milch, still in his impressive overcoat, wedged himself into the fled man's chair and glared up at Fischer.

'You're alive, then.'

'Yes, Herr Generalfeld ...'

'We don't have time for that nonsense. Address me as Sir.'

'Yes, Sir. And yes, Sir, I am.'

'So you didn't have it.'

'No, Sir. But then, I think you knew that already. Otherwise, why would you kidnap me and not go to the trouble of having me searched?'

That almost raised a smile from Milch. '*I* kidnap you? You're certain of that?'

'My gaolers didn't admit to it, but it wasn't difficult to guess at. When you first met me I was sat at Ahle's desk, and you already knew Ahle, I believe. In fact, I think you placed the item you're now seeking in his care. That being the case, it wouldn't be hard to convince someone that I'd inherited its keeping.'

'Someone?'

'Whoever it is you want to keep it from.'

'So you think that I have the thing already?'

'Perhaps I phrased that badly. I meant whoever you didn't, or don't, want to find it *before you do*. If you had it – whatever *it* is – you surely would have deployed or buried it by now.'

'You led me to believe you know what it is.'

'I lied about that, but I needed you to want to speak to me. I think you'll find what I have to say worth the inconvenience.'

'What would be of use to me, if you don't know what or where it is?'

'I can tell you who killed poor Ahle, and therefore who's responsible for its disappearance.'

'Really? Fascinate me.'

'You, Sir.'

'Why …? Never mind. Go on.'

To his surprise, Fischer realised that his heart had slowed. Since dawn it had been beating out the Königgrätzer March in double time, but now he had come to the moment it had subsided to a (probably fatalistic) waltz. He gave himself a few moments to put his thoughts in an order that might best keep him alive, breathed deeply and continued.

'During the French campaign, I believe that you intervened to rescue a Luftwaffe pilot from disgrace.'

Milch frowned. 'Yes. I was given to believe that he had been embarrassing his comrades. He was too valuable to face the consequences, however.'

'He was accused of rape, possibly?'

'How did you know?'

'By eliminating the likely alternatives. It remained a guess, however, until you confirmed it. You sent two men to France, to bring him back from active service – the same men who have been keeping me out of sight recently.'

'They've been indiscreet, have they?'

'Not intentionally. They mentioned that it was their first job for you. The man, though perhaps despicable, was also – an engineer, perhaps?'

'A theorist - you needn't know the detail. He's helped tremendously with the development of new aircraft.'

'For which you're responsible.'

'In part. I didn't know *of* this man, until I was approached by someone responsible for an important project. He'd intended to have the fellow brought back to Germany in any case, but word of his transgressions accelerated the process considerably. No-one wanted that word to become a babble.'

'So he came back, joined a project, did great things - at Adlershof, perhaps?

Milch's eyes narrowed, and he regarded Fischer warily. 'There and elsewhere. A project involving the development of a new aircraft requires a great deal of inter-disciplinary collaboration.'

'I expect that it does, Sir. I mention Adlershof because one Bruno Ahle worked there for a while, in the draughting office. He'd returned wounded from France, and managed to put his former skills to use. Like your fellow, in a way.'

'I didn't know that he'd worked there. When I asked my aide to find someone suitable he was working at the Air Ministry.'

'Suitable to be trusted with an item? One that needed to be kept out of the way for a while?'

'Yes. Being of an untalkative disposition and without family or friends, he seemed to be right.'

'I wonder why your aide came to the *Kriegsberichter der Luftwaffe* in particular for his man?'

'Because it's filled with men who don't attract more than the one kind of attention.'

'You mean nobodies, Sir?'

'I wouldn't be so rude as to say that, Hauptmann. Clearly, my aide didn't cast his net too widely, but then I'd impressed upon him my sense of urgency. Perhaps if he'd looked elsewhere ...'

'He might have found someone who wasn't in the habit of getting himself killed, gruesomely?'

'At least now you can see that I could have had nothing to do with his death. In fact, it has inconvenienced me terribly.'

'And those from whom you wanted to keep the item?'

'Yes.'

'You know then that it wasn't *they* who took Ahle, interrogated him, acquired the thing and then killed him?'

'Had they done so they would have used it immediately That hasn't happened, of course.'

'So we're left with a mystery – who else wanted Ahle dead? And who had the influence or connections to have the police investigation into his death suppressed before it raised any steam?'

'It's curious.'

'As were Ahle's motives. I mean, why would a man who'd been lucky enough to come home from the war and find his ideal job suddenly give it up to become a Liar?'

'A liar?'

'It's what we call ourselves, in the KdL.'

'How very cynical of you. I don't know, to answer your question. Perhaps he wanted a new challenge.'

'Making field reports into works of fiction, when he could be helping to design aircraft? I doubt it. But he was a strange one – a timid man who nevertheless held grudges, and seemed to resent those who had achieved more than himself. Did you know that he kept a diary?'

The Generalfeldmarschal's open mouth told Fischer quite eloquently that he didn't. 'Have you …?'

'Seen it? Yes. In fact, I've read it. It covers a period in which he was serving at the Front, and so constitutes a crime by its very existence. Or rather, it did. It recently discovered the furnace in the Air Ministry's basement.'

'It shouldn't have. It wasn't your decision to make.'

'Don't be displeased, Sir. Among other things, it mentioned the bad behaviour of an unnamed man in Ahle's squadron, during a time when they were based at Reims, in support of Operation Paula.'

'My God!'

A great deal passed across the other man's face a moment, all of it tinged with horror. Fischer tried to keep relief from showing on his own. There had been a very real possibility that Ahle's presence in Squadron KG55/1 was known to Milch already, in which case he might indeed have been involved in the man's murder (and, imminently, his replacement's). His shock didn't seem to be rehearsed, though, and Fischer pressed on while it was working for him.

'So you see how he might suddenly have felt uncomfortable – perhaps unsafe – at Adlershof, if an old, unwelcome acquaintance had been revived by circumstance?'

'Ye...s.'

'And, if this other man's tendencies were known to Ahle, how we might have a found a motive for the latter's silencing?'

'I had *nothing* to do with that.'

'No, Sir. Until recently I struggled to regard it as sufficient reason to kill a man, but then I didn't have all the facts. Ahle was no-one, and this other fellow was extremely necessary to our war effort. He could have waved away any accusation – even laughed at it, I suppose. But if he *was* valuable, then someone else needed him not to be distracted by an investigation. You were asked to intervene, in 1940, to save him from exposure and bring him back to Germany. What if, three years later, a degree of panic – regarding a project that isn't perhaps proceeding as swiftly as it might – induced someone to intervene once more on his behalf, and this time more robustly?'

'To have someone murdered would be … extreme.'

'Would it? What's the purpose of the project, other than to perfect a device that will murder as many of our enemies as possible? Any rational calculation of risk would allocate a single, troublesome man his proper worth and act accordingly. I suggested that you were responsible for Ahle's death. That was unfair, of course, but had you not prevented Gestapo from moving against the misbehaving gentleman in 1940 he wouldn't have been seen at Adlershof, wouldn't have scared Ahle into applying for a job here at the Ministry, wouldn't have given the ones who made that *rational calculation of risk* any reason to arrange his murder. Perhaps you have an idea who those men were? And while you consider it, you might also ask yourself whether the fuselage works at Adlershof's perimeter uses the sort of precision-cutting tools that might take off a man's head neatly?'

Milch stared at the desk top for while, giving Fischer time to consider the thickness of the branch upon which he had just placed himself. He had presented the Generalfeldmarschall with the fact of his own, partial culpability, which might have the effect of making him either remorseful or keen to erase an exposure. A quiet word, a nod even, and a certain hauptmann would never make it back to his lodgings that evening. His new colleagues might continue to glance meaningfully at each other and the empty desk for a few days, but no-one – not even Freddie Holleman – would dare to give voice to any questions they had (other, perhaps, than to ask whether it might not be better for everyone if they just burned the damned desk). There was a single consideration, as Fischer saw it, that might make his fate of small concern, so he put the case quickly.

'As a matter of more than idle interest, has this gentleman of worth behaved since his return from France?'

Milch sighed and rubbed his forehead. 'A number of young ladies have been attacked recently in ... a city close to where he's based. The incidents took place at times when his whereabouts couldn't be accounted for.'

'He's not monitored?'

'He's supposed to be accompanied at all times, particularly if he leaves the site. Clearly, someone wasn't dong his job.'

'I suppose we shouldn't be surprised. A rapist doesn't indulge himself for the nice feeling it gives his cock, otherwise he'd try flowers, or perfume. But it begs the question of how vulnerable it makes those who've protected him – that is, should anyone with an interest in giving it air choose to do so.'

The twitch told Fischer that he'd hit home once more. In any circumstances other than these, the predilections of this creature couldn't have bitten Milch. He had headed off an investigation for all the deemed-to-be-right reasons, and who, among those few with the power to hurt him, would have done otherwise? But if it could be used in a struggle for some sort of precedence that Fischer neither understood nor cared to be enlightened about, a minor embarrassment would become a form of poison – particularly when the fate of poor Ahle was added to the scales.

'Are you a discrete man, Hauptmann?'

'As any corpse, Sir. None of this business is – or should be – my concern, which is why only your ears will ever hear any of this. I merely thought you might need to know the full extent of it. And I would remind you that, had you not decided to involve me, I would have known nothing.'

'Perhaps it's as well that I did, then.'

'I was a decoy, of course. I sat at Ahle's desk, so you invited your opponents to look in my direction. When I disappeared I confirmed their suspicions, and as long as they were trying to find me they wouldn't be looking in any of the places where the item might be?' Fischer waved a hand in front of the damaged half of his face. 'I suppose that, had they succeeded, there would have been less to regret.'

'That would have been very callous of me.'

'I can see the logic. More regrettable would have been the incidental casualties – Wilhelm and Rainier. They weren't pleased when I put the case to them. I think they felt that they'd deserved better of you.'

Milch pursed his lips. 'I *do* regret that. But their value isn't what it was.'

'You might have confided in them, and still had their loyalty. They've fled, though, to where you can't stifle their resentment, should they choose to speak of past … assignments?'

'They haven't – not quite. They were stopped just across the Danish border, by an unusually assiduous patrol who didn't take their papers and my signature at face value. Naturally, when the call came through my aide told them that the authorization was out of date, and that they should be held. I expect them back in Berlin later today, under close arrest.'

Fischer barely managed to keep his composure. He had glibly sent the brothers to their deaths, relying upon cold probabilities and giving no thought to the near-inevitability of random, foul luck. He cleared his throat and spoke before giving his words their very necessary consideration.

'Show mercy. In fact, forget that they ran at all.'

'Why would I do that?'

'Because you were content to put them in danger, and this is a way to ease a tender conscience. Because you might need their skills still, if your opponents find anything to embarrass you. Because – and we forget this - not putting someone against a wall is easier than the alternative.'

Too briefly, Milch considered the suggestion and shook his head. 'They wouldn't be reliable, not after my practising upon them.'

Fischer shrugged. 'Be puzzled. Tell them that you had no intention of their being harmed – that your trust in their ability to evade detection was why you chose them for the task.'

'They wouldn't believe me.'

'Of course they would, Sir. The absolute proof of it is in your readiness to forgive their absconding, surely?'

The Generalfeldmarschal smiled. 'You're a devious fellow, Fischer.'

'I'm beginning to think that I need to be. May I also ask if *I'm* safe?'

'From me? To continue to dangle you as bait still would be pointless, given that I'm not likely ever to find the item. As to the other thing, I trust your discretion absolutely, because speaking of any of this would be a messier option than merely putting your pistol in your mouth. I can't of course guarantee that you're safe from the other side.'

'In a way, Sir, you have already.'

'Have I?'

'You've come to the Ministry. I have no doubt that *they* know I'm here, so your arrival can mean only one thing – that we're meeting in order for me to return the item to you. What would be the point of their making a further, summary gesture *after* that event?'

Milch almost managed a smile, though the eyebrows didn't seem amused. 'So I've been dragged here to preserve your arse?'

'And to be enlightened, Sir. Knowledge is power, isn't it?'

'Usually, yes. I suppose that *not* knowing was dangerous, in this case.'

'May I then impose upon your gratitude, and ask something more?

'By all means, test my patience.'

'This much-coveted item – what is it?'

A much longer pause made Fischer regret the question. He had no *need* to know, but having been put in artillery range for the sake of the thing it seemed only fair that the mystery not remain forever so.

Milch chewed his cheek for while without once taking his eyes from the half-face in front of him. A forefinger tapped Krohne's desk, a threateningly metronomic beat that Fischer's heart gradually overtook. It stopped very suddenly, and the Generalfeldmarschal sat up in the chair.

'Do you know who I am, Fischer?'

'Everyone in Luftwaffe knows, Sir.'

'I mean, other than my Luftwaffe rank and duties?'

'You have some responsibility for munitions generally, I think.'

'I do. In fact, with Reichsminister Speer and State Secretary Körner I coordinate *all* war production. As you can imagine, we require a lot of manpower to meet our targets.'

'A vast number, surely?'

'And there's the conundrum. War requires a huge increase in industrial activity, but it also removes millions of healthy men from the workforce. Our enemies make up their shortfall in this respect by substituting female labour, but National Socialism is remarkably fearful of doing the same. The Führer believes that it would undermine family life in the absence of the father figure - and, worse, give women ideas beyond cooking and breeding. So, what are we to do?'

Fischer knew precisely what was done. Germany's conquered foes met part of their reparations in the form of manpower. Some were 'guest' workers – typically from France, the Low

Countries and Denmark - serving for fixed periods before returning to their home countries. They at least were fed and housed as humans, if at a basic level. Less fortunate were the forced labourers – *fremdarbeiter* – from those beaten nations whose bloodstock was regarded as markedly inferior to that of their hosts. For them, staying alive was more of a preoccupation than longing for their *heimats*.

'You get help, from abroad.'

'And how do we do this?'

'Via what used to be the Todt Org?'

'Todt could never supply what was needed. He had too many responsibilities and too few resources, so his organization consumed whatever manpower he could find. As you know, the *Reichsarbeitsdienst*'s successor is run by General Plenipotentiary Sauckel. Unlike Todt, he builds nothing and makes nothing; his only task is to supply labour to those who do. In principle this is an excellent reform, but ...'

'But?'

'But we – I mean Speer, Körner and myself – are finding it increasingly difficult to reconcile the numbers that Sauckel claims to have provided to German industry with what factory managers are telling us. The discrepancy is growing, and it threatens our efforts to meet production targets.'

'Can't you sit down, explain this and get him to alter things? You're on the same side, after all.'

Milch laughed. 'My dear Fischer, what an innocent you are! Sauckel is supported by men who would regard our failure as a great accomplishment, only to be partly overshadowed by the

Soviets gaining the upper hand on the battlefield as a consequence.'

'You're joking, surely?'

'I wish I were. I wish it were genuinely funny, but the cliques that surround the Führer wage their own, personal wars against each other, and sometimes the front lines are indistinct. For example, both State Secretary Körner and Sauckel are proteges of our Reichsmarschall, but Sauckel acquired other patrons when he took up the Labour portfolio, and now Göring – who's in charge of the Four Year Economic Plan, you'll recall - isn't sure where his friends end and enemies begin. Some days, I believe he suspects even Speer and I of trying to undermine him. Do *not* repeat that, of course.'

'So …?'

'The item. It is an extremely detailed report – coded, obviously – on manpower supplied by Sauckel to each of the major war industries, broken down to an individual company-level. Speer spoke in confidence to industrialists, who were happy to do the work. It took months to assemble, by the way. This was to have been our official proof of Sauckel's failure – proof that not even his allies could have diluted or brushed away. We knew, however, that they had become aware of its existence and that they were trying to acquire and discredit the data before we could present it to the Führer.'

'How did they find out about it?'

Milch pulled a face. 'The exercise involved dozens of people across the entire Reich. Clearly, our hopes that it might remain a secret from men who had their own friends in industry were misplaced.'

'If you knew that *they* knew about the calculations, why then didn't you present them to the Führer immediately, to forestall them?'

'Because he hardly leaves the Wolf's Lair or Berchtesgaten these days, and is therefore extremely difficult to isolate – particularly as the man who controls his appointments is not sympathetic to our efforts, to say the least.'

'So you placed the data in the hands of Bruno Ahle.'

Ruefully, Milch shook his head. 'The Air Ministry seemed to be the safest place for it. How would they even begin to look for it here, in the hands of a nobody from whom we could retrieve it at a moment's notice? Again, however, our assumptions were too optimistic.'

'As it seems now to be safe from *everyone*, you were at least partially right. Obviously, you had no copy made. Can't it be reconstructed?'

'That would take more months, which we don't have.'

'Rewrite it yourself, then.'

'What?'

'You know what you want it to say – the hardest part would be to make it look authentic. I'm sure your industrialists would sign whatever you put in front of them, if it helps address their manpower problem.'

'But … that would be a deception.'

It was Fischer's turn to laugh, but he managed to quash it. 'Sir, we're discussing the forced abduction of millions of foreigners who are then worked half to death – or further - in our factories, in clear contravention of the Geneva Accords. To which we're a party, of course. And your moral concern is probity?'

Milch's face coloured. 'This is a necessity of war!'

'Then what dishonour can there be in lying to your enemies, if it achieves the end? Isn't deception one of the most useful weapons of war - so useful, in fact, that we practise it on our own population also? I mean, would there be a *Kriegsberichter der Luftwaffe*, otherwise?'

'Ach, you were wasted on the end of a parachute, Fischer.'

Milch stood, shrugging to adjust the overcoat on his shoulders. 'I'm afraid it may be too late to change the Führer's mind about Sauckel. These days, he leaves most domestic policy in the hands of ...' recalling who he was speaking to, he stopped and waved a hand as if to disperse the thought. 'Never mind. We must press on as best we can. Goodbye.'

At the door, he paused and turned. 'I'm glad we spoke. And I'm sorry for the trouble I tried to send your way. I hardly need more enemies than I've made already.'

'I'm Luftwaffe, Sir, and therefore always on your side.'

'Then go in peace, back to your honourable lies.'

48

For several minutes after Milch's departure, Fischer remained in Krohne's office, waiting for its tenant's return and a strenuous debriefing. He was about to return to his desk in the Den when it occurred to him that he had in effect been on Luftwaffe's clock continuously for more than a week. He decided that this entitled him to take an hour's leave.

He paused on the steps of the main entrance and looked to either side, as if that brief recce might determine whether he was still an object of interest to very wrong people.

'Nice day, Hauptmann.'

Peering upwards from beneath his outsized *stahlhelm*, Friday Ernst examined the skies above central Berlin. His rifle was propped against his legs, allowing both hands to address the business of rolling a cigarette. Even on extremely short (and interrupted) acquaintance, Fischer had begun to wonder how the man had come to be employed and deployed (even by a parlously understaffed Luftwaffe), and why he hadn't yet been shot for innumerable violations of the Military Code. Doormen at department stores carried themselves with greater dignity – hell, ladies on their perfumery counters had a more pronounced military bearing than ...

'Körner, isn't it?'

'Ernst, please, Hauptmann.'

'Yes, it's a very nice day. Do you know of any cafés nearby?'

'New to Berlin, are we? If you want to be a tourist, try the *Eins A* in Potsdamer Platz. But the bad coffee's better in the bahnhof's waiting-room, just opposite.'

'Thank you.'

'Do you *need* anything, Hauptmann?'

Ernst didn't go so far as to tap the side of his nose, but his meaning wouldn't have escaped a nun.

'Ah, no. Not at the moment.'

'Well, Ernst Körner's your man, for protection *and* the consequences of its lacking.'

'Is that a business motto?'

Körner gave Fischer a cheerful wink, and snatched at his rifle as a grey Luftwaffe Mercedes pulled up in front of the step. From the Ministry, four high-ranking officers emerged, deep in conversation and entirely unaware of the two men beside them. After a few moments, three of them stepped back and saluted the fourth the old-fashioned way. He returned it, and as his arm dropped he noticed who stood close by and offered a curt nod. Fischer, not having the discretion which came with rank, came to attention and offered a text-book *Heil*. The damaged shoulder protested piteously, but he told it to be quiet. It wasn't every day that a Generalfeldmarschall took the trouble to notice the dirt beneath his boot.

Café Eins A's coffee was as terrible as Ernst had alleged, but the antebellum service was worth the ordeal. Fischer sat at a pavement table, watching the passing traffic, receiving glances both respectful and pitying. He found that he was bothered by neither, and this indifference pleased him. It suggested that there would be good days as well as the usual ones - that the good Colonel Nimtz had been correct. The head could be worked upon as much as damaged tissue, if not with gelatin.

An air-raid siren sounded, and no-one seemed to pay attention. Public panic at the prospect of aerial armageddon had subsided in the face of pin-prick enemy raids, but far worse was coming. A British bomber had to fly much further to reach Berlin than its German counterpart did to be over London. The push westwards to the Channel had given Luftwaffe a magnificent spread of Dutch, Belgian and French airfields from which to punish England - and, ironically, provided a strong disincentive for Milch and friends to pester for long-range bombers in any quantity. To the British and Americans such a device was a necessity, and Fischer didn't doubt that their vast resources were creating it at speed. Soon, Berliners would have a taste of what East Enders had been swallowing for several years now, and whatever Göring's vainglorious promises, Luftwaffe wouldn't be able to hold it off *and* keep the Ivans from seizing back control of their own skies. After that, the Lie Division would need to write miracles if anyone was going to believe that disaster wasn't advancing at a canter.

There – he'd managed to crush his light mood. He paid his bill, did three slow laps of Potsdamer Platz and returned to Wilhelmstrasse. Another, far more presentable guard had replaced Feldwebel Körner at the Air Ministry's entrance, and he came to attention smartly as the absconder entered the building. At the same moment the siren sounded again, giving an all-clear for a threat that hadn't appeared.

Fischer went firstly to report to the competent authority, but through the door glass he could see Krohne on the telephone, speaking quietly to someone who probably wasn't his wife. He went to the Den instead, nodded in reply to two disinterested glances and sat at the desk of a man who had caused him a deal of trouble from beyond the grave. Eventually, he hoped, he might come to think of it as his own.

Across the room, Freddie Holleman noticed who was on parade, dropped his pencil and clambered upright. Fischer braced himself for an inquisition, but as the object loomed its unlovely face wore a broad smile and only a hint of puzzlement.

'You're back, Otto.'

'I am, Freddie.'

'That Milch fellow was here again.'

'Yes, I saw him outside.'

'I went 'round to your lodgings the other day, hoping for news of you. But I gave the old lady a fit. Tell her I'm sorry, will you?'

'Of course. What's the news in the KdL?'

Holleman looked around the Liars' Den. 'Nothing worth wasting breath on. Have you been in trouble?'

'Not at all. I just had a job to do. It's a bit confidential, so ...'

'That's alright. Friedrich Melancthon Holleman is no longer in the business of other people's business.'.'

'Very wise. What we need is a quiet war, with only the occasional air-raid to clear pigeons from the ledges. Melancthon?'

'My father's family have always been religious. The tradition ends with me, though.'

'I'm glad to hear it. We must put all of our faith in National Socialism.'

'So they say. Ooh, I forgot, there's a sweepstake on whether Karl's going to get a dose from the hairdresser. Are you in?'

'How much?'

'Five marks. Whoever guesses closest to the day he taps Kondom Körner for sulfonamide wins.'

'Ernst will tell you?'

'You're kidding? He's handed me his five marks already.'

'Alright. Put me down for the second Sunday in May.'

'Muttertag? He'll be at home with his wife that day, surely?'

'Not if his ardour doesn't cool in the next three weeks. And even if he leaves it until Monday I may still win.'

'You're in the book. *Silver Birch* later?'

Fischer sighed. He needed to go straight home and apologize to Frau Traugott for any anguish he'd caused, but it was bound to be an ordeal, punctuated by a detailed commentary on her post-fit symptoms. On the other hand, falling into Jonas-Strasse 17 at midnight wouldn't improve her opinion of him. He surrendered the decision to a small, hedonistic voice, which told him he'd earned a modest respite from life's back-handed slaps.

'Alright. But only for the one drink.'

'Good man! You know what the Romans said about seizing the day?'

'No.'

'Well, they did - something, anyway. A drink, a song and civilized conversation about ladies' arses and football – what could be better?'

'Not much.'

'There it is again!'

'What?'

'That feeling I have about you. Since you joined the Liars we've had almost-daily visits from respectful generalfeldmarschalls, almost-good news from the Eastern Front to twist, and even that bad business about our old colleague ...'

'What?'

'Well, you're back, breathing, so I assume it's gone away?'

'I don't know, Freddie. If I'm still here at the end of the week, probably.'

'You'd better be. God knows, we deserve some luck.'

'And I'm it?'

Holleman grinned. 'A hare's foot, at least. Not very lucky for the hare, but everyone who touches it gets the benefit.'

A man stepped off the omnibus at the Kleine Burg halt in Braunschweig, only a short distance from the Dom. He was well-dressed, very well-groomed and received appreciative glances from each of three ladies who passed him in the first hundred metres of his northward trek. He hardly noticed. It was something that had happened all his adult life, and only to be expected.

His journey had taken longer than was strictly necessary, He might have caught a bus directly outside the gates of his worksite, but instead had walked down the lane from Völkenrode to Bortfeld and boarded a different service there. It had been a mild inconvenience in pleasant surroundings, and the day was warm without being oppressive. Even had it not been important that he not be recognized by a fellow passenger, he might have made the detour anyway.

Now that he was here, though, his sense of urgency quickened, and for once he hardly appreciated one of the least-spoiled medieval centres to be found in any German city. He had an assignation, a tryst even, with a very pleasant young lady who worked in the administration building at Völkenrode, and he wasn't going to keep her waiting.

Naturally, she had made her interest clear as soon as he noticed him. Even so, he had been careful to court her, visiting the typists' office almost every day for the past three weeks on a variety of thin pretexts and offering subtle flatteries each time. He was an accomplished flirt, and knew how to make her feel desired without being so crude as to make a bald proposition. She wasn't expecting him today, but he didn't doubt that she would be pleased to see him.

It was Saturday morning, when she assisted on her mother's stall in the city's principal markthalle. He had endured numerous anecdotes regarding the older woman's struggle to keep their bakery business on its feet during her husband's military service, and made polite expressions of understanding and sympathy to each of them. The ordeal had begun to test his desires, but he comforted himself that it had brought at least one concrete result - he knew exactly where the girl would be, and, as this was Germany, that she would be free from 1pm precisely, when virtually all of the nation's family enterprises halted abruptly for the weekend. He would be walking by, not realising that, my goodness!, *this* was where she worked, and on the spur of an unexpected moment offer to buy her lunch. There was a risk that she would ask if her mother might join them, but the looks she had been giving him recently made it a very small one. What she had in mind wouldn't be improved by a parent's presence.

A light meal, with enough wine to remove the last of any hesitation she might be feeling, and then a romantic walk by the river, the museum park. There would be plenty of people around them, making the world seem safer than it was, and he would be on his best form, amusing and impressing her with risqué anecdotes about the top men at Vŏlkenrode. There was nothing like talk of other people's amorous activities to turn a girl's mind to her own prospects.

And after that, a chaste kiss to the cheek and a confession that he couldn't stop thinking about her. Then would come the delicate moment. He had no doubt that she would respond favourably, but it wasn't unusual for the heat of unexpected emotion to incline a woman to pause – to want a little time to consider, or savour, the prospect before her. That would be most unfortunate.

He would seize that moment, therefore, and before she could say anything apologize for his affront, beg her forgiveness and suggest that she no doubt wished to curtail their outing. Of course, she would wish nothing of the sort. Reassured by his old-world gallantry, her own ardour would strain at its stays. She was halfway there already, after all.

Their passionate consummation wouldn't be problematic. He would mention that his home was just across the river, on Moltkestrasse, and no doubt she would make a shy, decorous display of inviting him to invite her there. Recently, a stroke of good fortune had transferred one of his colleague to a semi-permanent posting at Adlershof, and a casual offer to air his house occasionally had been accepted gratefully. The keys were in his pocket, ready to open the final scene of his play.

Strolling down Moltkestrasse, he would entertain her with a few made-up stories about his neighbours, and then they would be home. He had decided already that another plea at the front door – that she mustn't judge a lonely bachelor's domestic arrangements too harshly – would soften her further, exciting the maternal instinct that almost always had the effect of loosening female underwear. Of course, it would take only a few moments for the window shutters and carefully covered furniture to betray his lie, but that hardly mattered. By then, he would have hit her.

He would take his time, posing the unconscious body to expose the lust that filled it – legs slightly apart and tucked beneath the abdomen, rump pushed up lasciviously as if she was a bitch in heat (and she was, of course) to take every centimetre he had. When she was perfect he would undress quickly, sheath himself to prevent infection from her filthy fluids and then give her what she wanted with the roughness that women like her preferred. It wouldn't take long, and while his heart was still racing he would finish the job. This one wouldn't be saying anything to embarrass him, ever.

Afterwards, when he had washed thoroughly and dressed, he would let himself out, lock the door, stroll back across the river and take the direct bus back to Völkenrode. They would be angry, of course, and assume that he had been indulging what he had promised so many times to quell. But where was the proof of it? He would say - would *persist* in saying – that he'd had a pleasant day out in wonderful Braunschweig, enjoying the mediaeval streets, a leisurely lunch and then a stroll beside the river before returning, innocent of any wrongdoing. They wouldn't believe him, but what could they do? He was too valuable to press too hard, too innocent for want of evidence to the contrary. Best of all, the only person who might otherwise have testified to the day's events would be lying naked in a house in Moltkestrasse still, her legs splayed, offering her sex to anyone who might want it. That image would remain with him, clear and strong, ready for whenever he needed release.

Surprised suddenly, he stopped on the edge of the kerb. His pleasant daydream had brought him as far as Bohlweg, just a few metres from the Markthalle's entrance. She was inside, waiting for him, selling loaves and having no idea how close she was to getting what every woman wanted. The thought aroused him further, if that were possible. He paused for a moment, examined his reflection in a shop window to confirm that everything was as it should be, and stepped onto Bohlweg.

It was the only street in this part of old Braunschweig where a vehicle could gain any kind of velocity, and the Kübelwagen, already half-on the pavement, accelerated beyond the speed limit. It took him at mid-thigh level, the radiator bar breaking both legs instantly. Carried upward on the bonnet's low slope and bouncing off the spare wheel mounted there, he executed a neat, half-turn somersault as a trapeze artist might, but, landing less than perfectly on the asphalt, his neck snapped cleanly. He was dead before the vehicle behind (another, much smaller Volkswagen, driven by a wholly innocent civilian gentleman) went over his head, crushing it. By the time that several onlookers had converged upon the body, the Kübelwagen had reached Fallersleberstrasse, braked sharply and veered right.

An hour later, in a clearing in Rieseberg woods, a slightly-built man, dressed in a Luftwaffe uniform that had been stripped of all insignia, soaked a rag in petrol and stuffed it into the Kübelwagen's fuel-intake. Lighting it, he withdrew quickly to a fallen tree nearby, upon which a much larger man with a clean, temple-to-jawline scar was putting himself around two thick slices of bread stuffed with cheese. As the Kübelwagen ignited, he reached into a bag by his side and offered an equally heroic portion to his arsonist companion, who refused it, lit a cigarette instead and watched the display until it had almost burned out.

The two men finished their lunch and smoke, picked up every scrap of evidence that they had ever been there and walked into the tree-line, where a twin of the consumed vehicle sat beside a track. The larger man took the driver's seat; the other climbed into the rear as though he were a fare or senior officer, removed a book from his satchel (a much-thumbed copy of Kierkegaard's *Tractatus*), opened it and began to read. As the engine turned over he looked up.

'How long?'

'To Berlin? Three hours, roughly.'

'We go past Magdeburg?'

'Close, yeah.'

'Well, now I feel awful. We could have offered him a lift instead.'

Though by no means a quick driver (other than when circumstances demanded it) the big man had brought them almost out of the woods and onto the Ententeich road before he managed to stop laughing.

Author's Note

'Five-Five-Five' was Martin Bormann, Hitler's personal secretary and the Third Reich's most accomplished political infighter (555 was the SS number bestowed upon him by Himmler, in recognition of his long service to National Socialism; his original number – he joined SS as late as 1937 – was 278,267).

In February 1943, Bormann had himself appointed (with Hans Lammers and Feldmarschall Wilhelm Keitel) to what became known as the Committee of Three, tasked by Hitler with centralizing control of the war economy. This was an unnecessary duplication of existing responsibilities (a typical device to divide and rule, it usually had the effect of doing the Allies' work for them). The committee immediately came into conflict with its war production counterpart, the Central Planning Board comprising Speer, Milch and Paul Körner. Bormann incited and amplified their disagreements to wound Speer in particular, whose long-term personal relationship with the Führer he regarded as a continuing threat to his own power. For this reason, he strongly backed Fritz Sauckel in his manpower disputes with the Board.

Ostensibly, the latter could count upon the support of Hermann Göring, who was responsible for the delivery of the Four Year Economic Plan. However, by April 1943 Göring was under great pressure, being blamed by Hitler for Luftwaffe's failure to adequately supply von Paulus' Sixth Army in the Stalingrad pocket and for the unsatisfactory progress of the Plan to date. By now, Bormann was virtually the sole key-holder to access to the Führer, and Göring, desperate to regain favour, swallowed his pride and sought to end their old enmity. He also feared that

Bormann – and, possibly, Sauckel - knew of his addiction to cocaine and planned to reveal it to Hitler.

The post-meeting discussion between Speer and Milch, related in chapter 14, is presented largely as recollected by Speer himself in his invaluable semi-autobiography 'Inside the Third Reich'. Göring's *volte face* and support of Sauckel that day came as a complete surprise to the two men, who continued (largely unsuccessfully) to press for more and better-trained labourers without any of the support they had expected. Drily, Speer was later to observe:

> 'Our attempt to mobilize Göring against Bormann was probably doomed to failure from the start for financial reasons ... for as was later revealed by a Nuremberg document, Bormann had made Göring a gift of six million marks from the industrialists' Adolf Hitler Fund.'

In effect, the Reich's major industrialists had been paying to have their war effort sabotaged.

That a schedule of the labour-force discrepancies existed is almost certain, though its entrusting to Bruno Ahle (or anyone else), and subsequent efforts to retrieve it, are a fiction. Ahle himself, his murder and the 'boffins' who commissioned it to save the neck of a depraved but invaluable associate, are similarly figments of the author's over-active imagination.

At the Nuremberg trials, Speer – who, alone among his fellow accused, fully acknowledged his culpability - was sentenced to twenty years' imprisonment for his involvement in the use of forced and slave labour in German industry, and served all of it. Milch, having survived a thrashing from a British Brigadier with his own Feldmarschall's baton (and then, when it broke, a champagne bottle), was sentenced to life imprisonment for his role in the same crimes. In 1951 the tariff was reduced to fifteen years, and three years later he was paroled. During his own trial, Fritz Sauckel argued that he was less culpable than Speer because he had merely supplied the labour force that was subsequently subjected to inhuman conditions. He failed to convince the court, and was was hanged on 16 October 1946, proclaiming from the scaffold: 'I die an innocent man.'

Printed in Great Britain
by Amazon